THE CLER

Books by P. G. Wodehouse

Fiction

Aunts Aren't Gentlemen
The Adventures of Sally
Bachelors Anonymous
Barmy in Wonderland
Big Money
Bill the Conqueror
Blandings Castle and
   Elsewhere
Carry On, Jeeves
The Clicking of Cuthbert
Cocktail Time
The Code of the Woosters
The Coming of Bill
Company for Henry
A Damsel in Distress
Do Butlers Burgle Banks?
Doctor Sally
Eggs, Beans and Crumpets
A Few Quick Ones
French Leave
Frozen Assets
Full Moon
Galahad at Blandings
A Gentleman of Leisure
The Girl in Blue
The Girl on the Boat
The Gold Bat
The Head of Kay's
The Heart of a Goof
Heavy Weather
Hot Water
Ice in the Bedroom
If I Were You
Indiscretions of Archie
The Inimitable Jeeves
Jeeves and the Feudal Spirit
Jeeves in the Offing
Jill the Reckless
Joy in the Morning
Laughing Gas
Leave it to Psmith
The Little Nugget
Lord Emsworth and Others
Louder and Funnier
Love Among the Chickens
The Luck of the Bodkins
The Man Upstairs
The Man with Two Left Feet
The Mating Season
Meet Mr Mulliner
Mike and Psmith
Mike at Wrykyn
Money for Nothing
Money in the Bank
Mr Mulliner Speaking
Much Obliged, Jeeves
Mulliner Nights
Not George Washington
Nothing Serious
The Old Reliable
Pearls, Girls and Monty Bodkin
A Pelican at Blandings

Piccadilly Jim
Pigs Have Wings
Plum Pie
The Pothunters
A Perfect Uncle
The Prince and Betty
Psmith, Journalist
Psmith in the City
Quick Service
Right Ho, Jeeves
Ring for Jeeves
Sam the Sudden
Service with a Smile
The Small Bachelor
Something Fishy
Something Fresh
Spring Fever
Stiff Upper Lip, Jeeves
Summer Lightning
Summer Moonshine
Sunset at Blandings
The Swoop
Tales of St Austin's
Thank You, Jeeves
Ukridge
Uncle Dynamite
Uncle Fred in the Springtime
Uneasy Money
Very Good, Jeeves
The White Feather
William Tell Told Again
Young Men in Spats

Omnibi

The World of Blandings
The World of Jeeves
The World of Mr Mulliner
The World of Psmith
The World of Ukridge
The World of Uncle Fred
Wodehouse Nuggets
   (edited by Richard Usborne)
The Hollywood Omnibus
Weekend Wodehouse

Paperback Omnibi

The Golf Omnibus
The Aunts Omnibus
The Clergy Omnibus
The Drones Omnibus
The Jeeves Omnibus 1
The Jeeves Omnibus 2
The Jeeves Omnibus 3
The Jeeves Omnibus 4

Poems

The Parrot and Other Poems

Autobiographical

Wodehouse on Wodehouse
   (comprising Bring on the Girls,
   Over Seventy, Performing Flea)

Letters

Yours, Plum

THE CLERGY OMNIBUS

P.G. WODEHOUSE

HUTCHINSON
London

First published as *The World of Wodehouse Clergy* 1984

This edition first published in 1992 by
Hutchinson

Reprinted 1992

Random Century Group Ltd
20 Vauxhall Bridge Road, London SW1V 2SA

Random Century Australia (Pty) Ltd
20 Alfred Street, Milsons Point, Sydney, NSW 2061, Australia

Random Century New Zealand Ltd
18 Poland Road, Glenfield, Auckland, New Zealand

Random Century South Africa (Pty) Ltd
PO Box 337, Bergvlei, 2012, South Africa

A CIP catalogue record for this book is available
from the British Library

ISBN 0 09 175335 X

Printed and bound in Great Britain by
Mackays of Chatham PLC, Chatham, Kent

CONTENTS

COMPLETE STORIES

'MULLINER'S BUCK-U-UPPO'

Meet Mr Mulliner

The village Choral Society had been giving a performance of Gilbert and Sullivan's *Sorcerer* in aid of the Church Organ Fund; and, as we sat in the window of the Anglers' Rest, smoking our pipes, the audience came streaming past us down the little street. Snatches of song floated to our ears, and Mr Mulliner began to croon in unison.

'Ah me! I was a pa-ale you-oung curate then!' chanted Mr Mulliner in the rather snuffling voice in which the amateur singer seems to find it necessary to render the old songs.

'Remarkable,' he said, resuming his natural tones, 'how fashions change, even in clergymen. There are very few pale young curates nowadays.'

'True,' I agreed. 'Most of them are beefy young fellows who rowed for their colleges. I don't believe I have ever seen a pale young curate.'

'You never met my nephew Augustine, I think?'

'Never.'

'The description in the song would have fitted him perfectly. You will want to hear all about my nephew Augustine.'

At the time of which I am speaking (said Mr Mulliner) my nephew Augustine was a curate, and very young and extremely pale. As a boy he had completely outgrown his strength, and I rather think at his theological college some of the wilder spirits must have bullied him; for when he went to Lower Briskett-in-the-Midden to assist the vicar, the Rev. Stanley Brandon, in his cure of souls, he was as meek and mild a young man as you could meet in a day's journey. He had flaxen hair, weak blue eyes, and the general demeanour of a saintly but timid cod-fish. Precisely, in short, the sort of young curate who seems to have been so common in the eighties, or whenever it was that Gilbert wrote *The Sorcerer*.

The personality of his immediate superior did little or nothing to help him to overcome his native diffidence. The Rev. Stanley Brandon was a huge and sinewy man of violent temper, whose red face and glittering eyes might well have intimidated the toughest curate. The Rev. Stanley had been a heavyweight boxer at Cambridge, and I gather from Augustine that he seemed to be always on the point of introducing into debates on parish matters the methods which had made him so successful in the roped ring. I remember Augustine telling me that once, on the occasion when he had ventured to oppose the other's views in the matter of decorating the church for the Harvest Festival, he thought for a moment that the vicar was going to drop him with a right hook to the chin. It was some quite trivial point that had come up – a question as to whether the pumpkin would look better in the apse or the clerestory, if I recollect rightly – but for several seconds it seemed as if blood was about to be shed.

Such was the Rev. Stanley Brandon. And yet it was to the daughter of this formidable man that Augustine Mulliner had permitted himself to lose his heart. Truly, Cupid makes heroes of us all.

Jane was a very nice girl, and just as fond of Augustine as he was of her. But, as each lacked the nerve to go to the girl's father and put him abreast of the position of affairs, they were forced to meet surreptitiously. This jarred upon Augustine who, like all the Mulliners, loved the truth and hated any form of deception. And one evening, as they paced beside the laurels at the bottom of the vicarage garden, he rebelled.

'My dearest,' said Augustine, 'I can no longer brook this secrecy. I shall go into the house immediately and ask your father for your hand.'

Jane paled and clung to his arm. She knew so well that it was not her hand but her father's foot which he would receive if he carried out this mad scheme.

'No, no, Augustine! You must not!'

'But, darling, it is the only straightforward course.'

'But not tonight. I beg of you, not tonight.'

'Why not?'

'Because father is in a very bad temper. He has just had a letter from the bishop, rebuking him for wearing too many orphreys on his chasuble, and it has upset him terribly. You see, he and the bishop were at school together, and father can never forget it. He said at dinner that if old Boko Bickerton thought he was going to order him about he would jolly well show him.'

'And the bishop comes here tomorrow for the Confirmation services!' gasped Augustine.

'Yes. And I'm so afraid they will quarrel. It's such a pity father hasn't some other bishop over him. He always remembers that he once hit this one in the eye for pouring ink on his collar, and this lowers his respect for his spiritual authority. So you won't go in and tell him tonight, will you?'

'I will not,' Augustine assured her with a slight shiver.

'And you will be sure to put your feet in hot mustard and water when you get home? The dew has made the grass so wet.'

'I will indeed, dearest.'

'You are not strong, you know.'

'No, I am not strong.'

'You ought to take some really good tonic.'

'Perhaps I ought. Good night, Jane.'

'Good night, Augustine.'

The lovers parted. Jane slipped back into the vicarage, and Augustine made his way to his cosy rooms in the High Street. And the first thing he noticed on entering was a parcel on the table, and beside it a letter.

He opened it listlessly, his thoughts far away.

'*My dear Augustine.*'

He turned to the last page and glanced at the signature. The letter was from his Aunt Angela, the wife of my brother, Wilfred Mulliner. You may remember that I once told you the story of how these two came together. If so, you will recall that my brother Wilfred was the eminent chemical researcher who had invented, among other specifics, such world-famous preparations as Mulliner's Raven Gipsy Face-Cream and the Mulliner Snow of the Mountains Lotion. He and Augustine had never been particularly intimate, but between Augustine and his aunt there had always existed a warm friendship.

My dear Augustine (wrote Angela Mulliner),
    I have been thinking so much about you lately, and I cannot forget that, when I saw you

last, you seemed very fragile and deficient in vitamins. I do hope you take care of yourself.

I have been feeling for some time that you ought to take a tonic, and by a lucky chance Wilfred has just invented one which he tells me is the finest thing he has ever done. It is called Buck-U-Uppo, and acts directly on the red corpuscles. It is not yet on the market, but I have managed to smuggle a sample bottle from Wilfred's laboratory, and I want you to try it at once. I am sure it is just what you need.

Your affectionate aunt,
Angela Mulliner.

P.S. You take a tablespoonful before going to bed, and another just before breakfast.

Augustine was not an unduly superstitious young man, but the coincidence of this tonic arriving so soon after Jane had told him that a tonic was what he needed affected him deeply. It seemed to him that this thing must have been meant. He shook the bottle, uncorked it, and, pouring out a liberal tablespoonful, shut his eyes and swallowed it.

The medicine, he was glad to find, was not unpleasant to the taste. It had a slightly pungent flavour, rather like old boot-soles beaten up in sherry. Having taken the dose, he read for a while in a book of theological essays, and then went to bed.

And as his feet slipped between the sheets, he was annoyed to find that Mrs Wardle, his housekeeper, had once more forgotten his hot-water bottle.

'Oh, dash!' said Augustine.

He was thoroughly upset. He had told the woman over and over again that he suffered from cold feet and could not get to sleep unless the dogs were properly warmed up. He sprang out of bed and went to the head of the stairs.

'Mrs Wardle!' he cried.

There was no reply.

'Mrs Wardle!' bellowed Augustine in a voice that rattled the window-panes like a strong nor'-easter. Until tonight he had always been very much afraid of his housekeeper and had both walked and talked softly in her presence. But now he was conscious of a strange new fortitude. His head was singing a little, and he felt equal to a dozen Mrs Wardles.

Shuffling footsteps made themselves heard.

'Well, what is it now?' asked a querulous voice.

Augustine snorted.

'I'll tell you what it is now,' he roared. 'How many times have I told you always to put a hot-water bottle in my bed? You've forgotten it again, you old cloth-head!'

Mrs Wardle peered up, astounded and militant.

'Mr Mulliner, I am not accustomed – '

'Shut up!' thundered Augustine. 'What I want from you is less back-chat and more hot-water bottles. Bring it up at once, or I leave tomorrow. Let me endeavour to get it into your concrete skull that you aren't the only person letting rooms in this village. Any more lip and I walk straight round the corner, where I'll be appreciated. Hot-water bottle ho! And look slippy about it.'

'Yes, Mr Mulliner. Certainly, Mr Mulliner. In one moment, Mr Mulliner.'

'Action! Action!' boomed Augustine. 'Show some speed. Put a little snap into it.'

'Yes, yes, most decidedly, Mr Mulliner,' replied the chastened voice from below.

An hour later, as he was dropping off to sleep, a thought crept into Augustine's mind.

Had he not been a little brusque with Mrs Wardle? Had there not been in his manner something a shade abrupt – almost rude? Yes, he decided regretfully, there had. He lit a candle and reached for the diary which lay on the table at his bedside.

He made an entry.

The meek shall inherit the earth. Am I sufficiently meek? I wonder. This evening, when reproaching Mrs Wardle, my worthy housekeeper, for omitting to place a hot-water bottle in my bed, I spoke quite crossly. The provocation was severe, but still I was surely to blame for allowing my passions to run riot. Mem: Must guard agst. this.

But when he woke next morning, different feelings prevailed. He took his ante-breakfast dose of Buck-U-Uppo: and looking at the entry in the diary, could scarcely believe that it was he who had written it. 'Quite cross?' Of course he had been quite cross. Wouldn't anybody be quite cross who was for ever being persecuted by beetle-wits who forgot hot-water bottles?

Erasing the words with one strong dash of a thick-leaded pencil, he scribbled in the margin a hasty 'Mashed potatoes! Served the old idiot right!' and went down to breakfast.

He felt amazingly fit. Undoubtedly, in asserting that this tonic of his acted forcefully upon the red corpuscles, his Uncle Wilfred had been right. Until that moment Augustine had never supposed that he had any red corpuscles; but now, as he sat waiting for Mrs Wardle to bring him his fried egg, he could feel them dancing about all over him. They seemed to be forming rowdy parties and sliding down his spine. His eyes sparkled, and from sheer joy of living he sang a few bars from the hymn for those of riper years at sea.

He was still singing when Mrs Wardle entered with a dish.

'What's this?' demanded Augustine, eyeing it dangerously.

'A nice fried egg, sir.'

'And what, pray, do you mean by nice? It may be an amiable egg. It may be a civil, well-meaning egg. But if you think it is fit for human consumption, adjust that impression. Go back to your kitchen, woman; select another; and remember this time that you are a cook, not an incinerating machine. Between an egg that is fried and an egg that is cremated there is a wide and substantial difference. This difference, if you wish to retain me as a lodger in these far too expensive rooms, you will endeavour to appreciate.'

The glowing sense of well-being with which Augustine had begun the day did not diminish with the passage of time. It seemed, indeed, to increase. So full of effervescing energy did the young man feel that, departing from his usual custom of spending the morning crouched over the fire, he picked up his hat, stuck it at a rakish angle on his head, and sallied out for a healthy tramp across the fields.

It was while he was returning, flushed and rosy, that he observed a sight which is rare in the country districts of England – the spectacle of a bishop running. It is not often in a place like Lower Briskett-in-the-Midden that you see a bishop at all; and when you do he is either riding in a stately car or pacing at a dignified walk. This one was sprinting like a Derby winner, and Augustine paused to drink in the sight.

The bishop was a large, burly bishop, built for endurance rather than speed; but he was making excellent going. He flashed past Augustine in a whirl of flying gaiters: and then, proving himself thereby no mere specialist but a versatile all-round athlete, suddenly dived for a tree and climbed rapidly into its branches. His motive, Augustine readily divined, was to elude a rough, hairy dog which was toiling in his wake. The dog reached the tree a moment after his quarry had climbed it, and stood there, barking.

Augustine strolled up.

'Having a little trouble with the dumb friend, Bish?' he asked, genially.

The bishop peered down from his eyrie.

'Young man,' he said, 'save me!'

'Right most indubitably ho!' replied Augustine. 'Leave it to me.'

Until today he had always been terrified of dogs, but now he did not hesitate. Almost quicker than words can tell, he picked up a stone, discharged it at the animal, and whooped cheerily as it got home with a thud. The dog, knowing when he had had enough, removed himself at some forty-five m.p.h.; and the bishop, descending cautiously, clasped Augustine's hand in his.

'My preserver!' said the bishop.

'Don't give it another thought,' said Augustine, cheerily. 'Always glad to do a pal a good turn. We clergymen must stick together.'

'I thought he had me for a minute.'

'Quite a nasty customer. Full of rude energy.'

The bishop nodded.

'His eye was not dim, nor his natural force abated. Deuteronomy xxxiv. 7,' he agreed. 'I wonder if you can direct me to the vicarage? I fear I have come a little out of my way.'

'I'll take you there.'

'Thank you. Perhaps it would be as well if you did not come in. I have a serious matter to discuss with old Pieface – I mean, with the Rev. Stanley Brandon.'

'I have a serious matter to discuss with his daughter. I'll just hang about the garden.'

'You are a very excellent young man,' said the bishop, as they walked along. 'You are a curate, eh?'

'At present. But,' said Augustine, tapping his companion on the chest, 'just watch my smoke. That's all I ask you to do – just watch my smoke.'

'I will. You should rise to great heights – to the very top of the tree.'

'Like you did just now, eh? Ha, ha!'

'Ha, ha!' said the bishop. 'You young rogue!'

He poked Augustine in the ribs.

'Ha, ha, ha!' said Augustine.

He slapped the bishop on the back.

'But all joking aside,' said the bishop as they entered the vicarage grounds, 'I really shall keep my eye on you and see that you receive the swift preferment which your talents and character deserve. I say to you, my dear young friend, speaking seriously and weighing my words, that the way you picked that dog off with that stone was the smoothest thing I ever saw. And I am a man who always tells the strict truth.'

'Great is truth and mighty above all things. Esdras iv. 41,' said Augustine.

He turned away and strolled towards the laurel bushes, which were his customary meeting-place with Jane. The bishop went on to the front door and rang the bell.

Although they had made no definite appointment, Augustine was surprised when the minutes passed and no Jane appeared. He did not know that she had been told off by her father to entertain the bishop's wife that morning, and show her the sights of Lower Briskett-in-the-Midden. He waited some quarter of an hour with growing impatience, and was about to leave when suddenly from the house there came to his ears the sound of voices raised angrily.

He stopped. The voices appeared to proceed from a room on the ground floor facing the garden.

Running lightly over the turf, Augustine paused outside the window and listened. The window was open at the bottom, and he could hear quite distinctly.

The vicar was speaking in a voice that vibrated through the room.

'Is that so?' said the vicar.

'Yes, it is!' said the bishop.

'Ha, ha!'

'Ha, ha! to you, and see how you like it!' rejoined the bishop with spirit.

Augustine drew a step closer. It was plain that Jane's fears had been justified and that there was serious trouble afoot between these two old schoolfellows. He peeped in. The vicar, his hands behind his coat-tails, was striding up and down the carpet, while the bishop, his back to the fireplace, glared defiance at him from the hearth-rug.

'Who ever told you you were an authority on chasubles?' demanded the vicar.

'That's all right who told me,' rejoined the bishop.

'I don't believe you know what a chasuble is.'

'Is that so?'

'Well, what is it, then?'

'It's a circular cloak hanging from the shoulders, elaborately embroidered with a pattern and with orphreys. And you can argue as much as you like, young Pieface, but you can't get away from the fact that there are too many orphreys on yours. And what I'm telling you is that you've jolly well got to switch off a few of these orphreys or you'll get it in the neck.'

The vicar's eyes glittered furiously.

'Is that so?' he said. 'Well, I just won't, so there! And it's like your cheek coming here and trying to high-hat me. You seem to have forgotten that I knew you when you were an inky-faced kid at school, and that, if I liked, I could tell the world one or two things about you which would probably amuse it.'

'My past is an open book.'

'Is it?' The vicar laughed malevolently. 'Who put the white mouse in the French master's desk?'

The bishop started.

'Who put jam in the dormitory prefect's bed?' he retorted.

'Who couldn't keep his collar clean?'

'Who used to wear a dickey?' The bishop's wonderful organ-like voice, whose softest whisper could be heard throughout a vast cathedral, rang out in tones of thunder. 'Who was sick at the house supper?'

The vicar quivered from head to foot. His rubicund face turned to deeper crimson.

'You know jolly well,' he said, in shaking accents, 'that there was something wrong with the turkey. Might have upset anyone.'

'The only thing wrong with the turkey was that you ate too much of it. If you had paid as much attention to developing your soul as you did to developing your tummy, you might by now,' said the bishop, 'have risen to my own eminence.'

'Oh, might I?'

'No, perhaps I am wrong. You never had the brain.'

The vicar uttered another discordant laugh.

'Brain is good! We know all about your eminence, as you call it, and how you rose to that eminence.'

'What do you mean?'

'You are a bishop. How you became one we will not inquire.'

'What do you mean?'

'What I say. We will not inquire.'

'Why don't you inquire?'

'Because,' said the vicar, 'it is better not!'

The bishop's self-control left him. His face contorted with fury, he took a step forward. And simultaneously Augustine sprang lightly into the room.

'Now, now, now!' said Augustine. 'Now, now, now, now, now!'

The two men stood transfixed. They stared at the intruder dumbly.

'Come, come!' said Augustine.

The vicar was the first to recover. He glowered at Augustine.

'What do you mean by jumping through my window?' he thundered. 'Are you a curate or a harlequin?'

Augustine met his gaze with an unfaltering eye.

'I am a curate,' he replied, with a dignity that well became him. 'And, as a curate, I cannot stand by and see two superiors of the cloth, who are moreover old schoolfellows, forgetting themselves. It isn't right. Absolutely not right, my old superiors of the cloth.'

The vicar bit his lip. The bishop bowed his head.

'Listen,' proceeded Augustine, placing a hand on the shoulder of each. 'I hate to see you two dear good chaps quarrelling like this.'

'He started it,' said the vicar, sullenly.

'Never mind who started it.' Augustine silenced the bishop with a curt gesture as he made to speak. 'Be sensible, my dear fellow. Respect the decencies of debate. Exercise a little good-humoured give-and-take. You say,' he went on, turning to the bishop, 'that our good friend here has too many orphreys on his chasuble?'

'I do. And I stick to it.'

'Yes, yes, yes. But what,' said Augustine, soothingly, 'are a few orphreys between friends? Reflect! You and our worthy vicar here were at school together. You are bound by the sacred ties of the old Alma Mater. With him you sported on the green. With him you shared a crib and threw inked darts in the hour supposed to be devoted to the study of French. Do these things mean nothing to you? Do these memories touch no chord?' He turned appealingly from one to the other. 'Vicar! Bish!'

The vicar had moved away and was wiping his eyes. The bishop fumbled for a pocket-handkerchief. There was a silence.

'Sorry, Pieface,' said the bishop, in a choking voice.

'Shouldn't have spoken as I did, Boko,' mumbled the vicar.

'If you want to know what I think,' said the bishop, 'you are right in attributing your indisposition at the house supper to something wrong with the turkey. I recollect saying at the time that the bird should never have been served in such a condition.'

'And when you put that white mouse in the French master's desk,' said the vicar, 'you performed one of the noblest services to humanity of which there is any record. They ought to have made you a bishop on the spot.'

'Pieface!'

'Boko!'

The two men clasped hands.

'Splendid!' said Augustine. 'Everything hotsy-totsy now?'

'Quite, quite,' said the vicar.

'As far as I am concerned, completely hotsy-totsy,' said the bishop. He turned to his old friend solicitously. 'You will continue to wear all the orphreys you want – will you not, Pieface?'

'No, no. I see now that I was wrong. From now on, Boko, I abandon orphreys altogether.'

'But, Pieface – '

'It's all right,' the vicar assured him. 'I can take them or leave them alone.'

'Splendid fellow!' The bishop coughed to hide his emotion, and there was another silence. 'I think, perhaps,' he went on, after a pause, 'I should be leaving you now, my dear chap, and going in search of my wife. She is with your daughter, I believe, somewhere in the village.'

'They are coming up the drive now.'

'Ah, yes, I see them. A charming girl, your daughter.'

Augustine clapped him on the shoulder.

'Bish,' he exclaimed, 'you said a mouthful. She is the dearest, sweetest girl in the whole world. And I should be glad, vicar, if you would give your consent to our immediate union. I love Jane with a good man's fervour, and I am happy to inform you that my sentiments are returned. Assure us, therefore, of your approval, and I will go at once and have the banns put up.'

The vicar leaped as though he had been stung. Like so many vicars, he had a poor opinion of curates, and he had always regarded Augustine as rather below than above the general norm or level of the despised class.

'What!' he cried.

'A most excellent idea,' said the bishop, beaming. 'A very happy notion, I call it.'

'My daughter!' The vicar seemed dazed. 'My daughter marry a curate.'

'You were a curate once yourself, Pieface.'

'Yes, but not a curate like that.'

'No!' said the bishop. 'You were not. Nor was I. Better for us both had we been. This young man, I would have you know, is the most outstandingly excellent young man I have ever encountered. Are you aware that scarcely an hour ago he saved me with the most consummate address from a large shaggy dog with black spots and a kink in his tail? I was sorely pressed, Pieface, when this young man came up and, with a readiness of resource and an accuracy of aim which it would be impossible to over-praise, got that dog in the short ribs with a rock and sent him flying.'

The vicar seemed to be struggling with some powerful emotion. His eyes had widened.

'A dog with black spots?'

'Very black spots. But no blacker, I fear, than the heart they hid.'

'And he really plugged him in the short ribs?'

'As far as I could see, squarely in the short ribs.'

The vicar held out his hand.

'Mulliner,' he said, 'I was not aware of this. In the light of the facts which have just been drawn to my attention, I have no hesitation in saying that my objections are removed. I have had it in for that dog since the second Sunday before Septuagesima, when he pinned me by the ankle as I paced beside the river composing a sermon on Certain Alarming Manifestations of the So-called Modern Spirit. Take Jane. I give my consent freely. And may she be as happy as any girl with such a husband ought to be.'

A few more affecting words were exchanged, and then the bishop and Augustine left the house. The bishop was silent and thoughtful.

'I owe you a great deal, Mulliner,' he said at length.

'Oh, I don't know,' said Augustine. 'Would you say that?'

'A very great deal. You saved me from a terrible disaster. Had you not leaped through that window at that precise juncture and intervened, I really believe I should have pasted my dear old friend Brandon in the eye. I was sorely exasperated.'

'Our good vicar can be trying at times,' agreed Augustine.

'My fist was already clenched, and I was just hauling off for the swing when you checked me. What the result would have been, had you not exhibited a tact and discretion beyond your years, I do not like to think. I might have been unfrocked.' He shivered at the thought, though the weather was mild. 'I could never have shown my face at the Athenæum again. But, tut, tut!' went on the bishop, patting Augustine on the shoulder, 'let us not dwell on what might have been. Speak to me of yourself. The vicar's charming daughter – you really love her?'

'I do, indeed.'

The bishop's face had grown grave.

'Think well, Mulliner,' he said. 'Marriage is a serious affair. Do not plunge into it without due reflection. I myself am a husband and, though singularly blessed in the possession of a devoted helpmeet, cannot but feel sometimes that a man is better off as a bachelor. Women, Mulliner, are odd.'

'True,' said Augustine.

'My own dear wife is the best of women. And, as I never weary of saying, a good woman is a wondrous creature, cleaving to the right and the good under all change; lovely in youthful comeliness, lovely all her life in comeliness of heart. And yet – '

'And yet?' said Augustine.

The bishop mused for a moment. He wriggled a little with an expression of pain, and scratched himself between the shoulder-blades.

'Well, I'll tell you,' said the bishop. 'It is a warm and pleasant day today, is it not?'

'Exceptionally clement,' said Augustine.

'A fair, sunny day, made gracious by a temperate westerly breeze. And yet, Mulliner, if you will credit my statement, my wife insisted on my putting on my thick winter woollies this morning. Truly,' sighed the bishop, 'as a jewel of gold in a swine's snout, so is a fair woman which is without discretion. Proverbs xi.21.'

'Twenty-two,' corrected Augustine.

'I should have said twenty-two. They are made of thick flannel, and I have an exceptionally sensitive skin. Oblige me, my dear fellow, by rubbing me in the small of the back with the ferrule of your stick. I think it will ease the irritation.'

'But, my poor dear old Bish,' said Augustine, sympathetically, 'this must not be.'

The bishop shook his head ruefully.

'You would not speak so hardily, Mulliner, if you knew my wife. There is no appeal from her decrees.'

'Nonsense,' cried Augustine, cheerily. He looked through the trees to where the lady bishopess, escorted by Jane, was examining a lobelia through her lorgnette with just the right blend of cordiality and condescension. 'I'll fix that for you in a second.'

The bishop clutched at his arm.

'My boy! What are you going to do?'

'I'm just going to have a word with your wife and put the matter up to her as a reasonable woman. Thick winter woollies on a day like this! Absurd!' said Augustine. 'Preposterous! I never heard such rot.'

The bishop gazed after him with a laden heart. Already he had come to love this young man like a son, and to see him charging so light-heartedly into the very jaws of destruction afflicted him with a deep and poignant sadness. He knew what his wife was like when even the highest in the land attempted to thwart her; and this brave lad was but a curate. In another moment she would be looking at him through her lorgnette: and England was littered with the shrivelled remains of curates at whom the lady bishopess had looked through her lorgnette. He had seen them wilt like salted slugs at the episcopal breakfast-table.

He held his breath. Augustine had reached the lady bishopess, and the lady bishopess was even now raising her lorgnette.

The bishop shut his eyes and turned away. And then – years afterwards, it seemed to him – a cheery voice hailed him: and, turning, he perceived Augustine bounding back through the trees.

'It's all right, Bish,' said Augustine.

'All – all right?' faltered the bishop.

'Yes. She says you can go and change into the thin cashmere.'

The bishop reeled.

'But – but – but what did you say to her? What arguments did you employ?'

'Oh, I just pointed out what a warm day it was and jollied her along a bit – '

'Jollied her along a bit!'

'And she agreed in the most friendly and cordial manner. She has asked me to call at the Palace one of these days.'

The bishop seized Augustine's hand.

'My boy,' he said in a broken voice, 'you shall do more than call at the Palace. You shall come and live at the Palace. Become my secretary, Mulliner, and name your own salary. If you intend to marry, you will require an increased stipend. Become my secretary, boy, and never leave my side. I have needed somebody like you for years.'

It was late in the afternoon when Augustine returned to his rooms, for he had been invited to lunch at the vicarage and had been the life and soul of the cheery little party.

'A letter for you, sir,' said Mrs Wardle, obsequiously.

Augustine took the letter.

'I am sorry to say I shall be leaving you shortly, Mrs Wardle.'

'Oh sir! If there's anything I can do – '

'Oh, it's not that. The fact is, the bishop has made me his secretary, and I shall have to shift my toothbrush and spats to the Palace, you see.'

'Well, fancy that, sir! Why, you'll be a bishop yourself one of these days.'

'Possibly,' said Augustine. 'Possibly. And now let me read this.'

He opened the letter. A thoughtful frown appeared on his face as he read.

My dear Augustine,

I am writing in some haste to tell you that the impulsiveness of your aunt has led to a rather serious mistake.

She tells me that she dispatched to you yesterday by parcels post a sample bottle of my new Buck-U-Uppo, which she obtained without my knowledge from my laboratory. Had she mentioned what she was intending to do, I could have prevented a very unfortunate occurrence.

Mulliner's Buck-U-Uppo is of two grades or qualities – the A and the B. The A is a mild, but strengthening, tonic designed for human invalids. The B, on the other hand, is purely for circulation in the animal kingdom, and was invented to fill a long-felt want throughout our Indian possessions.

As you are doubtless aware, the favourite pastime of the Indian Maharajahs is the hunting of the tiger of the jungle from the backs of elephants; and it has happened frequently in the past that hunts have been spoiled by the failure of the elephant to see eye to eye with its owner in the matter of what constitutes sport.

Too often elephants, on sighting the tiger, have turned and galloped home: and it was to correct this tendency on their part that I invented Mulliner's Buck-U-Uppo 'B'. One teaspoonful of the Buck-U-Uppo 'B' administered in its morning bran-mash will cause the most timid elephant to trumpet loudly and charge the fiercest tiger without a qualm.

Abstain, therefore, from taking any of the contents of the bottle you now possess,

And believe me,

> *Your affectionate uncle,*
> *Wilfred Mulliner.*

Augustine remained for some time in deep thought after perusing this communication. Then, rising, he whistled a few bars of the psalm appointed for the twenty-sixth of June and left the room.

Half an hour later a telegraphic message was speeding over the wires.

It ran as follows:

Wilfred Mulliner,
  The Gables,
    Lesser Lossingham,
      Salop.

Letter received. Send immediately, C.O.D., three cases of the 'B'. 'Blessed shall be thy basket and thy store'. Deuteronomy xxviii. 5.

> *Augustine.*

'THE BISHOP'S MOVE'

Meet Mr Mulliner

Another Sunday was drawing to a close, and Mr Mulliner had come into the bar-parlour of the Anglers' Rest wearing on his head, in place of the seedy old wideawake which usually adorned it, a glistening top hat. From this, combined with the sober black of his costume and the rather devout voice in which he ordered hot Scotch and lemon, I deduced that he had been attending Evensong.

'Good sermon?' I asked.

'Quite good. The new curate preached. He seems a nice young fellow.'

'Speaking of curates,' I said, 'I have often wondered what became of your nephew – the one you were telling me about the other day.'

'Augustine?'

'That fellow who took the Buck-U-Uppo.'

'That was Augustine. And I am pleased and not a little touched,' said Mr Mulliner, beaming, 'that you should have remembered the trivial anecdote which I related. In this self-centred world one does not always find such a sympathetic listener to one's stories. Let me see, where did we leave Augustine?'

'He had just become the bishop's secretary and gone to live at the Palace.'

'Ah, yes. We will take up his career, then, some six months after the date which you have indicated.'

It was the custom of the good Bishop of Stortford – for, like all the prelates of our Church, he loved his labours – to embark upon the duties of the day (said Mr Mulliner) in a cheerful and jocund spirit. Usually, as he entered his study to dispatch such business as might have arisen from the correspondence which had reached the Palace by the first post, there was a smile upon his face and possibly upon his lips a snatch of some gay psalm. But on the morning on which this story begins an observer would have noted that he wore a preoccupied, even a sombre, look. Reaching the study door, he hesitated as if reluctant to enter; then, pulling himself together with a visible effort, he turned the handle.

'Good morning, Mulliner, my boy,' he said. His manner was noticeably embarrassed.

Augustine glanced brightly up from the pile of letters which he was opening.

'Cheerio, Bish. How's the lumbago today?'

'I find the pain sensibly diminished, thank you, Mulliner – in fact, almost non-existent. This pleasant weather seems to do me good. For lo! the winter is past, the rain is over and gone; the flowers appear on the earth; the time of the singing birds is come, and the voice of the turtle is heard in the land. Song of Solomon ii. 11,12.'

'Good work,' said Augustine. 'Well, there's nothing much of interest in these letters so far. The vicar of St Beowulf's in the West wants to know, How about incense?'

'Tell him he mustn't.'

'Right ho.'

The bishop stroked his chin uneasily. He seemed to be nerving himself for some unpleasant task.

'Mulliner,' he said.

'Hullo?'

'Your mention of the word "vicar" provides a cue, which I must not ignore, for alluding to a matter which you and I had under advisement yesterday – the matter of the vacant living of Steeple Mummery.'

'Yes?' said Augustine eagerly. 'Do I click?'

A spasm of pain passed across the bishop's face. He shook his head sadly.

'Mulliner, my boy,' he said. 'You know that I look upon you as a son and that, left to my own initiative, I would bestow this vacant living on you without a moment's hesitation. But an unforeseen complication has arisen. Unhappy lad, my wife has instructed me to give the post to a cousin of hers. A fellow,' said the bishop bitterly, 'who bleats like a sheep and doesn't know an alb from a reredos.'

Augustine, as was only natural, was conscious of a momentary pang of disappointment. But he was a Mulliner and a sportsman.

'Don't give it another thought, Bish,' he said cordially. 'I quite understand. I don't say I hadn't hopes, but no doubt there will be another along in a minute.'

'You know how it is,' said the bishop, looking cautiously round to see that the door was closed. 'It is better to dwell in a corner of the housetop than with a brawling woman in a wide house. Proverbs xxi. 9.'

'A continual dropping in a very rainy day and a contentious woman are alike. Proverbs xxvii. 15,' agreed Augustine.

'Exactly. How well you understand me, Mulliner.'

'Meanwhile,' said Augustine, holding up a letter, 'here's something that calls for attention. It's from a bird of the name of Trevor Entwhistle.'

'Indeed? An old schoolfellow of mine. He is now Headmaster of Harchester, the foundation at which we both received our early education. What does he say?'

'He wants to know if you will run down for a few days and unveil a statue which they have just put up to Lord Hemel of Hempstead.'

'Another old schoolfellow. We called him Fatty.'

'There's a postscript over the page. He says he still has a dozen of the '87 port.'

The bishop pursed his lips.

'These earthly considerations do not weigh with me so much as old Catsmeat – as the Reverend Trevor Entwhistle seems to suppose. However, one must not neglect the call of the dear old school. We will certainly go.'

'We?'

'I shall require your company. I think you will like Harchester, Mulliner. A noble pile, founded by the seventh Henry.'

'I know it well. A young brother of mine is there.'

'Indeed? Dear me,' mused the bishop, 'it must be twenty years and more since I last visited Harchester. I shall enjoy seeing the old, familiar scenes once again. After all, Mulliner, to whatever eminence we may soar, howsoever great may be the prizes which life has bestowed upon us, we never wholly lose our sentiment for the dear old school. It is our Alma Mater, Mulliner, the gentle mother that has set our hesitating footsteps on the – '

'Absolutely,' said Augustine.

'And, as we grow older, we see that never can we recapture the old, careless gaiety of our school days. Life was not complex then, Mulliner. Life in that halcyon period was free from problems. We were not faced with the necessity of disappointing our friends.'

'Now listen, Bish,' said Augustine cheerily, 'if you're still worrying about that living, forget it. Look at me. I'm quite chirpy, aren't I?'

The bishop sighed.

'I wish I had your sunny resilience, Mulliner. How do you manage it?'

'Oh, I keep smiling, and take the Buck-U-Uppo daily.'

'The Buck-U-Uppo?'

'It's a tonic my Uncle Wilfred invented. Works like magic.'

'I must ask you to let me try it one of these days. For somehow, Mulliner, I am finding life a little grey. What on earth,' said the bishop, half to himself and speaking peevishly, 'they wanted to put up a statue to old Fatty for, I can't imagine. A fellow who used to throw inked darts at people. However,' he continued, abruptly abandoning this train of thought, 'that is neither here nor there. If the Board of Governors of Harchester College has decided that Lord Hemel of Hempstead has by his services in the public weal earned a statue, it is not for us to cavil. Write to Mr Entwhistle, Mulliner, and say that I shall be delighted.'

Although, as he had told Augustine, fully twenty years had passed since his last visit to Harchester, the bishop found, somewhat to his surprise, that little or no alteration had taken place in the grounds, buildings and personnel of the school. It seemed to him almost precisely the same as it had been on the day, forty-three years before, when he had first come there as a new boy.

There was the tuck-shop where, a lissom stripling with bony elbows, he had shoved and pushed so often in order to get near the counter and snaffle a jam-sandwich in the eleven o'clock recess. There were the baths, and fives courts, the football fields, the library, the gymnasium, the gravel, the chestnut trees, all just as they had been when the only thing he knew about bishops was that they wore bootlaces in their hats.

The sole change that he could see was that on the triangle of turf in front of the library there had been erected a granite pedestal surmounted by a shapeless something swathed in a large sheet – the statue to Lord Hemel of Hempstead which he had come down to unveil.

And gradually, as his visit proceeded, there began to steal over him an emotion which defied analysis.

At first he supposed it to be a natural sentimentality. But, had it been that, would it not have been a more pleasurable emotion? For his feelings had begun to be far from unmixedly agreeable. Once, when rounding a corner, he came upon the captain of football in all his majesty, and there had swept over him a hideous blend of fear and shame which had made his gaitered legs wobble like jellies. The captain of football doffed his cap respectfully, and the feeling passed as quickly as it had come: but not so soon that the bishop had not recognized it. It was exactly the feeling he had been wont to have forty-odd years ago when, sneaking softly away from football practice, he had encountered one in authority.

The bishop was puzzled. It was as if some fairy had touched him with her wand, sweeping away the years and making him an inky-faced boy again. Day by day this illusion grew, the constant society of the Rev. Trevor Entwhistle doing much to foster it. For young Catsmeat Entwhistle had been the bishop's particular crony at Harchester, and he seemed to have altered his appearance since those days in no way whatsoever. The bishop had had a nasty shock when, entering the headmaster's study on the third morning of his visit, he found him sitting in the headmaster's chair with the headmaster's cap and gown on. It seemed to him that young Catsmeat, in order to indulge his distorted sense of humour, was taking the most frightful risk. Suppose the Old Man were to come in and cop him!

Altogether, it was a relief to the bishop when the day of the unveiling arrived.

The actual ceremony, however, he found both tedious and irritating. Lord Hemel of Hempstead had not been a favourite of his in their school days, and there was something extremely disagreeable to him in being obliged to roll out sonorous periods in his praise.

In addition to this, he had suffered from the very start of the proceedings from a bad attack of stage fright. He could not help thinking that he must look the most awful chump standing up there in front of all those people and spouting. He half expected one of the prefects in the audience to step up and clout his head and tell him not to be a funny young swine.

However, no disaster of this nature occurred. Indeed, his speech was notably successful.

'My dear Bishop,' said old General Bloodenough, the Chairman of the College Board of Governors, shaking his hand at the conclusion of the unveiling, 'your magnificent oration put my own feeble efforts to shame, put them to shame, to shame. You were astounding!'

'Thanks awfully,' mumbled the bishop, blushing and shuffling his feet.

The weariness which had come upon the bishop as the result of the prolonged ceremony seemed to grow as the day wore on. By the time he was seated in the headmaster's study after dinner he was in the grip of a severe headache.

The Rev. Trevor Entwhistle also appeared jaded.

'These affairs are somewhat fatiguing, Bishop,' he said, stifling a yawn.

'They are, indeed, Headmaster.'

'Even the '87 port seems an inefficient restorative.'

'Markedly inefficient. I wonder,' said the bishop, struck with an idea, 'if a little Buck-U-Uppo might not alleviate our exhaustion. It is a tonic of some kind which my secretary is in the habit of taking. It certainly appears to do him good. A livelier, more vigorous young fellow I have never seen. Suppose we ask your butler to go to his room and borrow the bottle? I am sure he will be delighted to give it to us.'

'By all means.'

The butler, dispatched to Augustine's room, returned with a bottle half full of a thick, dark coloured liquid. The bishop examined it thoughtfully.

'I see there are no directions given as to the requisite dose,' he said. 'However, I do not like to keep disturbing your butler, who has now doubtless returned to his pantry and is once more settling down to the enjoyment of a well-earned rest after a day more than ordinarily fraught with toil and anxiety. Suppose we use our own judgement?'

'Certainly. Is it nasty?'

The bishop licked the cork warily.

'No. I should not call it nasty. The taste, while individual and distinctive and even striking, is by no means disagreeable.'

'Then let us take a glassful apiece.'

The bishop filled two portly wine-glasses with the fluid, and they sat sipping gravely.

'It's rather good,' said the bishop.

'Distinctly good,' said the headmaster.

'It sort of sends a kind of glow over you.'

'A noticeable glow.'

'A little more, Headmaster?'

'No, I thank you.'

'Oh, come.'

'Well, just a spot, Bishop, if you insist.'

'It's rather good,' said the bishop.

'Distinctly good,' said the headmaster.

Now you, who have listened to the story of Augustine's previous adventures with the Buck-U-Uppo, are aware that my brother Wilfred invented it primarily with the object of providing Indian Rajahs with a specific which would encourage their elephants to face the tiger of the jungle with a jaunty sang-froid: and he had advocated as a medium dose for an adult elephant a teaspoonful stirred up with its morning bran-mash. It is not surprising, therefore, that after they had drunk two wine-glassfuls apiece of the mixture the outlook on life of both the bishop and the headmaster began to undergo a marked change.

Their fatigue had left them, and with it the depression which a few moments before had been weighing on them so heavily. Both were conscious of an extraordinary feeling of good cheer, and the odd illusion of extreme youth which had been upon the bishop since his arrival at Harchester was now more pronounced than ever. He felt a youngish and rather rowdy fifteen.

'Where does your butler sleep, Catsmeat?' he asked, after a thoughtful pause.

'I don't know. Why?'

'I was only thinking that it would be a lark to go and put a booby-trap on his door.'

The headmaster's eyes glistened.

'Yes, wouldn't it!' he said.

They mused for a while. Then the headmaster uttered a deep chuckle.

'What are you giggling about?' asked the bishop.

'I was only thinking what a priceless ass you looked this afternoon, talking all that rot about old Fatty.'

In spite of his cheerfulness, a frown passed over the bishop's fine forehead.

'It went very much against the grain to speak in terms of eulogy – yes, fulsome eulogy – of one whom we both know to have been a blighter of the worst description. Where does Fatty get off, having statues put up to him?'

'Oh well, he's an Empire builder, I suppose,' said the headmaster, who was a fair-minded man.

'Just the sort of thing he would be,' grumbled the bishop. 'Shoving himself forward! If ever there was a chap I barred, it was Fatty.'

'Me, too,' agreed the headmaster. 'Beastly laugh he'd got. Like glue pouring out of a jug.'

'Greedy little beast, if you remember. A fellow in his house told me he once ate three slices of brown boot-polish spread on bread after he had finished the potted meat.'

'Between you and me, I always suspected him of swiping buns at the school shop. I don't wish to make rash charges unsupported by true evidence, but it always seemed to me extremely odd that, whatever time of the term it was, and however hard up every-body else might be, you never saw Fatty without his bun.'

'Catsmeat,' said the bishop, 'I'll tell you something about Fatty that isn't generally known. In a scrum in the final House Match in the year 1888 he deliberately hoofed me on the shin.'

'You don't mean that?'

'I do.'

'Great Scott!'

'An ordinary hack on the shin,' said the bishop coldly, 'no fellow minds. It is part of the give and take of normal social life. But when a bounder deliberately hauls off and lets drive at you with the sole intention of laying you out, it – well, it's a bit thick.'

'And those chumps of Governors have put up a statue to him!'

The bishop leaned forward and lowered his voice.

'Catsmeat.'

'What?'

'Do you know what?'

'No, what?'

'What we ought to do is to wait till twelve o'clock or so, till there's no one about, and then beetle out and paint that statue blue.'

'Why not pink?'

'Pink, if you prefer it.'

'Pink's a nice colour.'

'It is. Very nice.'

'Besides, I know where I can lay my hands on some pink paint.'

'You do?'

'Gobs of it.'

'Peace be on thy walls, Catsmeat, and prosperity within thy palaces,' said the bishop. 'Proverbs cxxxi. 6.'

It seemed to the bishop, as he closed the front door noiselessly behind him two hours later, that providence, always on the side of the just, was extending itself in its efforts to make this little enterprise of his a success. All the conditions were admirable for statue-painting. The rain which had been falling during the evening had stopped; and a moon, which might have proved an embarrassment, was conveniently hidden behind a bank of clouds.

As regarded human interference, they had nothing to alarm them. No place in the world is so deserted as the ground of a school after midnight. Fatty's statue might have been in the middle of the Sahara. They climbed the pedestal and, taking turns fairly with the brush, soon accomplished the task which their sense of duty had indicated to them. It was only when, treading warily lest their steps should be heard on the gravel drive, they again reached the front door that anything occurred to mar the harmony of the proceedings.

'What are you waiting for?' whispered the bishop, as his companion lingered on the top step.

'Half a second,' said the headmaster in a muffled voice. 'It may be in another pocket.'

'What?'

'My key.'

'Have you lost your key?'

'I believe I have.'

'Catsmeat,' said the bishop, with grave censure, 'this is the last time I come out painting statues with you.'

'I must have dropped it somewhere.'

'What shall we do?'

'There's just a chance the scullery window may be open.'

But the scullery window was not open. Careful, vigilant, and faithful to his trust, the butler, on retiring to rest, had fastened it and closed the shutters. They were locked out.

But it has been well said that it is the lessons which we learn in our boyhood days at school that prepare us for the problems of life in the larger world outside. Stealing back from the mists of the past, there came to the bishop a sudden memory.

'Catsmeat!'

'Hullo?'

'If you haven't been mucking the place up with alterations and improvements, there should be a water-pipe round at the back, leading to one of the upstairs windows.'

Memory had not played him false. There, nestling in the ivy, was the pipe up and down which he had been wont to climb when, a piefaced lad in the summer of 1886, he had broken out of this house in order to take nocturnal swims in the river.

'Up you go,' he said briefly.

The headmaster required no further urging. And presently the two were making good time up the side of the house.

It was just as they reached the window and just after the bishop had informed his old friend that, if he kicked him on the head again, he'd hear of it, that the window was suddenly flung open.

'Who's that?' said a clear young voice.

The headmaster was frankly taken aback. Dim though the light was, he could see that the man leaning out of the window was poising in readiness a very nasty-looking golf-club: and his first impulse was to reveal his identity and so clear himself of the suspicion of being the marauder for whom he gathered the other had mistaken him. Then there presented themselves to him certain objections to revealing his identity, and he hung there in silence, unable to think of a suitable next move.

The bishop was a man of readier resource.

'Tell him we're a couple of cats belonging to the cook,' he whispered.

It was painful for one of the headmaster's scrupulous rectitude and honesty to stoop to such a falsehood, but it seemed the only course to pursue.

'It's all right,' he said, forcing a note of easy geniality into his voice. 'We're a couple of cats.'

'Cat-burglars?'

'No. Just ordinary cats.'

'Belonging to the cook,' prompted the bishop from below.

'Belonging to the cook,' added the headmaster.

'I see,' said the man at the window. 'Well, in that case, right ho!'

He stood aside to allow them to enter. The bishop, an artist at heart, mewed gratefully as he passed, to add verisimilitude to the deception: and then made for his bedroom, accompanied by the headmaster. The episode was apparently closed.

Nevertheless, the headmaster was disturbed by a certain uneasiness.

'Do you suppose he thought we really were cats?' he asked anxiously.

'I am not sure,' said the bishop. 'But I think we deceived him by the nonchalance of our demeanour.'

'Yes, I think we did. Who was he?'

'My secretary. The young fellow I was speaking of, who lent us that capital tonic.'

'Oh, then that's all right. He wouldn't give you away.'

'No. And there is nothing else that can possibly lead to our being suspected. We left no clue whatsoever.'

'All the same,' said the headmaster thoughtfully, 'I'm beginning to wonder whether it was in the best sense of the word judicious to have painted that statue.'

'Somebody had to,' said the bishop stoutly.

'Yes, that's true,' said the headmaster, brightening.

The bishop slept late on the following morning, and partook of his frugal breakfast in bed. The day, which so often brings remorse, brought none to him. Something attempted, something done had earned a night's repose, and he had no regrets – except that, now that it was all over, he was not sure that blue paint would not have been more effective. However, his old friend had pleaded so strongly for the pink that it would have been difficult for himself, as a guest, to override the wishes of his host. Still, blue would undoubtedly have been very striking.

There was a knock on the door, and Augustine entered.

'Morning, Bish.'

'Good morning, Mulliner,' said the bishop affably. 'I have lain somewhat late today.'

'I say, Bish,' asked Augustine, a little anxiously. 'Did you take a very big dose of the Buck-U-Uppo last night?'

'Big? No. As I recollect, quite small. Barely two ordinary wine-glasses full.'

'Great Scott!'

'Why do you ask, my dear fellow?'

'Oh, nothing. No particular reason. I just thought your manner seemed a little strange on the water-pipe, that's all.'

The bishop was conscious of a touch of chagrin.

'Then you saw through our – er – innocent deception?'

'Yes.'

'I had been taking a little stroll with the headmaster,' explained the bishop, 'and he had mislaid his key. How beautiful is Nature at night, Mulliner! The dark, fathomless skies, the little winds that seem to whisper secrets in one's ear, the scent of growing things.'

'Yes,' said Augustine. He paused. 'Rather a row on this morning. Somebody appears to have painted Lord Hemel of Hempstead's statue last night.'

'Indeed?'

'Yes.'

'Ah, well,' said the bishop tolerantly, 'boys will be boys.'

'It's a most mysterious business.'

'No doubt, no doubt. But, after all, Mulliner, is not all Life a mystery?'

'And what makes it still more mysterious is that they found your shovel-hat on the statue's head.'

The bishop started up.

'What!'

'Absolutely.'

'Mulliner,' said the bishop, 'leave me. I have one or two matters on which I wish to meditate.'

He dressed hastily, his numbed fingers fumbling with his gaiters. It all came back to him now. Yes, he could remember putting the hat on the statue's head. It had seemed a good thing to do at the time, and he had done it. How little we guess at the moment how far-reaching our most trivial actions may be!

The headmaster was over at the school, instructing the Sixth Form in Greek Composition: and he was obliged to wait, chafing, until twelve-thirty, when the bell rang for the half-way halt in the day's work. He stood at the study window, watching with ill-controlled impatience, and presently the headmaster appeared, walking heavily like one on whose mind there is a weight.

'Well?' cried the bishop, as he entered the study.

The headmaster doffed his cap and gown, and sank limply into a chair.

'I cannot conceive,' he groaned, 'what madness had me in its grip last night.'

The bishop was shaken, but he could not countenance such an attitude as this.

'I do not understand you, Headmaster,' he said stiffly. 'It was our simple duty, as a protest against the undue exaltation of one whom we both know to have been a most unpleasant school-mate, to paint that statue.'

'And I suppose it was your duty to leave your hat on its head?'

'Now there,' said the bishop, 'I may possibly have gone a little too far.' He coughed. 'Has that perhaps somewhat ill-considered action led to the harbouring of suspicions by those in authority?'

'They don't know what to think.'

'What is the view of the Board of Governors?'

'They insist on my finding the culprit. Should I fail to do so they hint at the gravest consequences.'

'You mean they will deprive you of your headmastership?'

'That is what they imply. I shall be asked to hand in my resignation. And, if that happens, bim goes my chance of ever being a bishop.'

'Well, it's not all jam being a bishop. You wouldn't enjoy it, Catsmeat.'

'All very well for you to talk, Boko. You got me into this, you silly ass.'

'I like that! You were just as keen on it as I was.'

'You suggested it.'

'Well, you jumped at the suggestion.'

The two men had faced each other heatedly, and for a moment it seemed as if there was to be a serious falling out. Then the bishop recovered himself.

'Catsmeat,' he said, with that wonderful smile of his, taking the other's hand, 'this is unworthy of us. We must not quarrel. We must put our heads together and see if there is not some avenue of escape from the unfortunate position in which, however creditable our motives, we appear to have placed ourselves. How would it be – ?'

'I thought of that,' said the headmaster. 'It wouldn't do a bit of good. Of course, we might – '

'No, that's no use, either,' said the bishop.

They sat for a while in meditative silence. And, as they sat, the door opened.

'General Bloodenough,' announced the butler.

'Oh, that I had wings like a dove. Psalm xlv. 6,' muttered the bishop.

His desire to be wafted from that spot with all available speed could hardly be considered unreasonable. General Sir Hector Bloodenough, VC, KCIE, MVO, on retiring from the army, had been for many years, until his final return to England, in charge of the Secret Service in Western Africa, where his unerring acumen had won for him from the natives the soubriquet of Wah-nah-B'gosh-B'jingo – which, freely translated, means Big Chief Who Can See Through The Hole In A Doughnut.

A man impossible to deceive. The last man the bishop would have wished to be conducting the present investigations.

The general stalked into the room. He had keen blue eyes, topped by bushy white eyebrows, and the bishop found his gaze far too piercing to be agreeable.

'Bad business, this,' he said. 'Bad business. Bad business.'

'It is, indeed,' faltered the bishop.

'Shocking bad business. Shocking. Shocking. Do you know what we found on the head of that statue, eh? that statue, that statue? Your hat, Bishop. Your hat. Your hat.'

The bishop made an attempt to rally. His mind was in a whirl, for the general's habit of repeating everything three times had the effect on him of making his last night's escapade seem three times as bad. He now saw himself on the verge of standing convicted of having painted three statues with three pots of pink paint, and of having placed on the head of each one a trio of shovel-hats. But he was a strong man, and he did his best.

'You say my hat?' he retorted with spirit. 'How do you know it was my hat? There may have been hundreds of bishops dodging about the school grounds last night.'

'Got your name in it. Your name. Your name.'

The bishop clutched at the arm of the chair in which he sat. The general's eyes were piercing him through and through, and every moment he felt more like a sheep that has had the misfortune to encounter a potted meat manufacturer. He was on the point of protesting that the writing in the hat was probably a forgery when there was a tap at the door.

'Come in,' cried the headmaster, who had been cowering in his seat.

There entered a small boy in an Eton suit, whose face seemed to the bishop vaguely familiar. It was a face that closely resembled a ripe tomato with a nose stuck on it, but that was not what had struck the bishop. It was of something other than tomatoes that this lad reminded him.

'Sir, please, sir,' said the boy.

'Yes, yes, yes,' said General Bloodenough testily. 'Run away, my boy, run away, run away. Can't you see we're busy?'

'But sir, please, sir, it's about the statue.'

'What about the statue? What about it? What about it?'

'Sir, please, sir, it was me.'

'What! What! What! What! What!'

The bishop, the general, and the headmaster had spoken simultaneously: and the 'Whats' had been distributed as follows:

The Bishop	1
The General	3
The Headmaster	1

making five in all. Having uttered these ejaculations, they sat staring at the boy, who turned a brighter vermilion.

'What are you saying?' cried the headmaster. 'You painted that statue?'

'Sir, yes, sir.'

'You?' said the bishop.

'Sir, yes, sir.'

'You? You? You?' said the general.

'Sir, yes, sir.'

There was a quivering pause. The bishop looked at the headmaster. The headmaster looked at the bishop. The general looked at the boy. The boy looked at the floor.

The general was the first to speak.

'Monstrous!' he exclaimed. 'Monstrous. Monstrous. Never heard of such a thing. This boy must be expelled, Headmaster. Expelled. Ex – '

'No!' said the headmaster in a ringing voice.

'Then flogged within an inch of his life. Within an inch. An inch.'

'No!' A strange, new dignity seemed to have descended upon the Rev. Trevor Entwhistle. He was breathing a little quickly through his nose, and his eyes had assumed a somewhat prawnlike aspect. 'In matters of school discipline, General, I must with all deference claim to be paramount. I will deal with this case as I think best. In my opinion this is not an occasion for severity. You agree with me, Bishop?'

The bishop came to himself with a start. He had been thinking of an article which he had just completed for a leading review on the subject of Miracles, and was regretting that the tone he had taken, though in keeping with the trend of Modern Thought, had been tinged with something approaching scepticism.

'Oh, entirely,' he said.

'Then all I can say,' fumed the general, 'is that I wash my hands of the whole business, the whole business, the whole business. And if this is the way our boys are being brought up nowadays, no wonder the country is going to the dogs, the dogs, going to the dogs.'

The door slammed behind him. The headmaster turned to the boy, a kindly winning smile upon his face.

'No doubt,' he said, 'you now regret this rash act?'

'Sir, yes, sir.'

'And you would not do it again?'

'Sir, no, sir.'

'Then I think,' said the headmaster cheerily, 'that we may deal leniently with what, after all, was but a boyish prank, eh, Bishop?'

'Oh, decidedly, Headmaster.'

'Quite the sort of thing – ha, ha! – that you or I might have done – er – at his age?'

'Oh, quite.'

'Then you shall write me twenty lines of Virgil, Mulliner, and we will say no more about it.'

The bishop sprang from his chair.

'Mulliner! Did you say Mulliner?'

'Yes.'

'I have a secretary of that name. Are you, by any chance, a relation of his, my lad?'

'Sir, yes, sir. Brother.'

'Oh!' said the bishop.

The bishop found Augustine in the garden, squirting whale-oil solution on the rose-bushes, for he was an enthusiastic horticulturist. He placed an affectionate hand on his shoulder.

'Mulliner,' he said, 'do not think that I have not detected your hidden hand behind this astonishing occurrence.'

'Eh?' said Augustine. 'What astonishing occurrence?'

'As you are aware, Mulliner, last night, from motives which I can assure you were honourable and in accord with the truest spirit of sound Churchmanship, the Rev.

Trevor Entwhistle and I were compelled to go out and paint old Fatty Hemel's statue pink. Just now, in the headmaster's study, a boy confessed that he had done it. That boy, Mulliner, was your brother.'

'Oh, yes?'

'It was you who, in order to save me, inspired him to that confession. Do not deny it, Mulliner.'

Augustine smiled an embarrassed smile.

'It was nothing, Bish, nothing at all.'

'I trust the matter did not involve you in any too great expense. From what I know of brothers, the lad was scarcely likely to have carried through this benevolent ruse for nothing.'

'Oh, just a couple of quid. He wanted three, but I beat him down. Preposterous, I mean to say,' said Augustine warmly. 'Three quid for a perfectly simple, easy job like that? And so I told him.'

'It shall be returned to you, Mulliner.'

'No, no, Bish.'

'Yes, Mulliner, it shall be returned to you. I have not the sum on my person, but I will forward you a cheque to your new address, The Vicarage, Steeple Mummery, Hants.'

Augustine's eyes filled with sudden tears. He grasped the other's hand.

'Bish,' he said in a choking voice, 'I don't know how to thank you. But – have you considered?'

'Considered?'

'The wife of thy bosom. Deuteronomy xiii. 6. What will she say when you tell her?'

The bishop's eyes gleamed with a resolute light.

'Mulliner,' he said, 'the point you raise had not escaped me. But I have the situation well in hand. A bird of the air shall carry the voice, and that which hath wings shall tell the matter. Ecclesiastes x. 20. I shall inform her of my decision on the long-distance telephone.'

'THE STORY OF WEBSTER'

Mulliner Nights

'Cats are not dogs!'

There is only one place where you can hear good things like that thrown off quite casually in the general run of conversation, and that is the bar-parlour of the Anglers' Rest. It was there, as we sat grouped about the fire, that a thoughtful Pint of Bitter had made the statement just recorded.

Although the talk up to this point had been dealing with Einstein's Theory of Relativity, we readily adjusted our minds to cope with the new topic. Regular attendance at the nightly sessions over which Mr Mulliner presides with such unfailing dignity and geniality tends to produce mental nimbleness. In our little circle I have known an argument on the Final Destination of the South to change inside forty seconds into one concerning the best method of preserving the juiciness of bacon fat.

'Cats,' proceeded the Pint of Bitter, 'are selfish. A man waits on a cat hand and foot for weeks, humouring its slightest whim, and then it goes and leaves him flat because it has found a place down the road where the fish is more frequent.'

'What I've got against cats,' said a Lemon Sour, speaking feelingly, as one brooding on a private grievance, 'is their unreliability. They lack candour and are not square shooters. You get your cat and you call him Thomas or George, as the case may be. So far, so good. Then one morning you wake up and find six kittens in the hat-box and you have to reopen the whole matter, approaching it from an entirely different angle.'

'If you want to know what's the trouble with cats,' said a red-faced man with glassy eyes, who had been rapping on the table for his fourth whisky, 'they've got no tact. That's what's the trouble with them. I remember a friend of mine had a cat. Made quite a pet of that cat, he did. And what occurred? What was the outcome? One night he came home rather late and was feeling for the keyhole with his corkscrew; and, believe me or not, his cat selected that precise moment to jump on the back of his neck out of a tree. No tact.'

Mr Mulliner shook his head.

'I grant you all this,' he said, 'but still, in my opinion, you have not got quite to the root of the matter. The real objection to the great majority of cats is their insufferable air of superiority. Cats, as a class, have never completely got over the snootiness caused by the fact that in Ancient Egypt they were worshipped as gods. This makes them too prone to set themselves up as critics and censors of the frail and erring human beings whose lot they share. They stare rebukingly. They view with concern. And on a sensitive man this often has the worst effects, inducing an inferiority complex of the gravest kind. It is odd that the conversation should have taken this turn,' said Mr Mulliner, sipping his hot Scotch and lemon, 'for I was thinking only this afternoon of the rather strange case of my cousin Edward's son Lancelot.'

'I knew a cat – ' began a Small Bass.

My cousin Edward's son, Lancelot (said Mr Mulliner) was, at the time of which I speak, a comely youth of some twenty-five summers. Orphaned at an early age, he had been brought up in the home of his Uncle Theodore, the saintly Dean of Bolsover; and it was a great shock to that good man when Lancelot, on attaining his majority, wrote from London to inform him that he had taken a studio in Bott Street, Chelsea, and proposed to remain in the metropolis and become an artist.

The dean's opinion of artists was low. As a prominent member of the Bolsover Watch Committee, it had recently been his distasteful duty to be present at a private showing of the super-super-film, *Palettes of Passion*; and he replied to his nephew's communication with a vibrant letter in which he emphasized the grievous pain it gave him to think that one of his flesh and blood should deliberately be embarking on a career which must inevitably lead sooner or later to the painting of Russian princesses lying on divans in the semi-nude with their arms round tame jaguars. He urged Lancelot to return and become a curate while there was yet time.

But Lancelot was firm. He deplored the rift between himself and a relative whom he had always respected; but he was dashed if he meant to go back to an environment where his individuality had been stifled and his soul confined in chains. And for four years there was silence between uncle and nephew.

During these years Lancelot had made progress in his chosen profession. At the time at which this story opens, his prospects seemed bright. He was painting the portrait of Brenda, only daughter of Mr and Mrs B. B. Carberry-Pirbright, of 11 Maxton Square, South Kensington, which meant thirty pounds in his sock on delivery. He had learned to cook eggs and bacon. He had practically mastered the ukulele. And, in addition, he was engaged to be married to a fearless young *vers libre* poetess of the name of Gladys Bingley, better known as The Sweet Singer of Garbidge Mews, Fulham – a charming girl who looked like a pen-wiper.

It seemed to Lancelot that life was very full and beautiful. He lived joyously in the present, giving no thought to the past.

But how true it is that the past is inextricably mixed up with the present and that we can never tell when it may not spring some delayed bomb beneath our feet. One afternoon, as he sat making a few small alterations in the portrait of Brenda Carberry-Pirbright, his fiancée entered.

He had been expecting her to call, for today she was going off for a three weeks' holiday to the South of France, and she had promised to look in on her way to the station. He laid down his brush and gazed at her with a yearning affection, thinking for the thousandth time how he worshipped every spot of ink on her nose. Standing there in the doorway with her bobbed hair sticking out in every direction like a golliwog's, she made a picture that seemed to speak to his very depths.

'Hullo, Reptile!' he said lovingly.

'What ho, Worm!' said Gladys, maidenly devotion shining through the monocle which she wore in her left eye. 'I can stay just half an hour.'

'Oh, well, half an hour soon passes,' said Lancelot. 'What's that you've got there?'

'A letter, ass. What did you think it was?'

'Where did you get it?'

'I found the postman outside.'

Lancelot took the envelope from her and examined it.

'Gosh!' he said.

'What's the matter?'

'It's from my Uncle Theodore.'

'I didn't know you had an Uncle Theodore.'

'Of course I have. I've had him for years.'

'What's he writing to you about?'

'If you'll kindly keep quiet for two seconds, if you know how,' said Lancelot, 'I'll tell you.'

And in a clear voice which, like that of all the Mulliners, however distant from the main branch, was beautifully modulated, he read as follows:

> The Deanery,
> Bolsover,
> Wilts.
>
> *My dear Lancelot,*
>
> *As you have, no doubt, already learned from your* Church Times, *I have been offered and have accepted the vacant Bishopric of Bongo-Bongo in West Africa. I sail immediately to take up my new duties, which I trust will be blessed.*
>
> *In these circumstances, it becomes necessary for me to find a good home for my cat Webster. It is, alas, out of the question that he should accompany me, as the rigours of the climate and the lack of essential comforts might well sap a constitution which has never been robust.*
>
> *I am dispatching him, therefore, to your address, my dear boy, in a straw-lined hamper, in the full confidence that you will prove a kindly and conscientious host.*
>
> *With cordial good wishes,*
> *Your affectionate uncle,*
> *THEODORE BONGO-BONGO.*

For some moments after he had finished reading this communication, a thoughtful silence prevailed in the studio. Finally Gladys spoke.

'Of all the nerve!' she said. 'I wouldn't do it.'

'Why not?'

'What do you want with a cat?'

Lancelot reflected.

'It is true,' he said, 'that, given a free hand, I would prefer not to have my studio turned into a cattery or cat-bin. But consider the special circumstances. Relations between Uncle Theodore and self have for the last few years been a bit strained. In fact, you might say we had definitely parted brass-rags. It looks to me as if he were coming round. I should describe this letter as more or less what you might call an olive-branch. If I lush this cat up satisfactorily, shall I not be in a position later on to make a swift touch?'

'He is rich, this bean?' said Gladys, interested.

'Extremely.'

'Then,' said Gladys, 'consider my objections withdrawn. A good stout cheque from a grateful cat-fancier would undoubtedly come in very handy. We might be able to get married this year.'

'Exactly,' said Lancelot. 'A pretty loathsome prospect, of course, but still, as we've arranged to do it, the sooner we get it over, the better, what?'

'Absolutely.'

'Then that's settled. I accept custody of cat.'

'It's the only thing to do,' said Gladys. 'Meanwhile, can you lend me a comb? Have you such a thing in your bedroom?'

'What do you want with a comb?'

'I got some soup in my hair at lunch. I won't be a minute.'

She hurried out, and Lancelot, taking up the letter again, found that he had omitted to read a continuation of it on the back page.

It was to the following effect:

P.S. In establishing Webster in your home, I am actuated by another motive than the simple desire to see to it that my faithful friend and companion is adequately provided for.

From both a moral and an educative standpoint, I am convinced that Webster's society will prove of inestimable value to you. His advent, indeed, I venture to hope, will be a turning-point in your life. Thrown, as you must be, incessantly among loose and immoral Bohemians, you will find in this cat an example of upright conduct which cannot but act as an antidote to the poison cup of temptation which is, no doubt, hourly pressed to your lips.

P.P.S. Cream only at midday, and fish not more than three times a week.

He was reading these words for the second time, when the front door-bell rang and he found a man on the steps with a hamper. A discreet mew from within revealed its contents, and Lancelot, carrying it into the studio, cut the strings.

'Hi!' he bellowed, going to the door.

'What's up?' shrieked his betrothed from above.

'The cat's come.'

'All right. I'll be down in a jiffy.'

Lancelot returned to the studio.

'What ho, Webster!' he said cheerily. 'How's the boy?'

The cat did not reply. It was sitting with bent head, performing that wash and brush up which a journey by rail renders so necessary.

In order to facilitate these toilet operations, it had raised its left leg and was holding it rigidly in the air. And there flashed into Lancelot's mind an old superstition handed on to him, for what it was worth, by one of the nurses of his infancy. If, this woman had said, you creep up to a cat when its leg is in the air and give it a pull, then you make a wish and your wish comes true in thirty days.

It was a pretty fancy, and it seemed to Lancelot that the theory might as well be put to the test. He advanced warily, therefore, and was in the act of extending his fingers for the pull, when Webster, lowering the leg, turned and raised his eyes.

He looked at Lancelot. And suddenly with sickening force, there came to Lancelot the realization of the unpardonable liberty he had been about to take.

Until this moment, though the postcript to his uncle's letter should have warned him, Lancelot Mulliner had had no suspicion of what manner of cat this was that he had taken into his home. Now, for the first time, he saw him steadily and saw him whole.

Webster was very large and very black and very composed. He conveyed the impression of being a cat of deep reserves. Descendant of a long line of ecclesiastical ancestors who had conducted their decorous courtships beneath the shadow of cathedrals and on the back walls of bishops' palaces, he had that exquisite poise which one sees in high dignitaries of the church. His eyes were clear and steady, and seemed to pierce to the very roots of the young man's soul, filling him with a sense of guilt.

Once, long ago, in his hot childhood, Lancelot, spending his summer holidays at the deanery, had been so far carried away by ginger-beer and original sin as to plug a senior canon in the leg with his air-gun – only to discover, on turning, that a visiting arch-deacon had been a spectator of the entire incident from his immediate rear. As he had felt then, when meeting the archdeacon's eye, so did he feel now as Webster's gaze played silently upon him.

Webster, it is true, had not actually raised his eyebrows. But this, Lancelot felt, was simply because he hadn't any.

He backed, blushing.

'Sorry!' he muttered.

There was a pause. Webster continued his steady scrutiny. Lancelot edged towards the door.

'Er – excuse me – just a moment. . . .' he mumbled. And, sidling from the room, he ran distractedly upstairs.

'I say,' said Lancelot.

'Now what?' asked Gladys.

'Have you finished with the mirror?'

'Why?'

'Well, I – er – I thought,' said Lancelot, 'that I might as well have a shave.'

The girl looked at him, astonished.

'Shave? Why, you shaved only the day before yesterday.'

'I know. But, all the same . . . I mean to say, it seems only respectful. That cat, I mean.'

'What about him?'

'Well, he seems to expect it, somehow. Nothing actually said, don't you know, but you could tell by his manner. I thought a quick shave and perhaps change into my blue serge suit – '

'He's probably thirsty. Why don't you give him some milk?'

'Could one, do you think?' said Lancelot doubtfully. 'I mean, I hardly seem to know him well enough.' He paused. 'I say, old girl,' he went on, with a touch of hesitation.

'Hullo?'

'I know you won't mind my mentioning it, but you've got a few spots of ink on your nose.'

'Of course I have. I always have spots of ink on my nose.'

'Well . . . you don't think . . . a quick scrub with a bit of pumice-stone . . . I mean to say, you know how important first impressions are. . . .'

The girl stared.

'Lancelot Mulliner,' she said, 'if you think I'm going to skin my nose to the bone just to please a mangy cat – '

'Sh!' cried Lancelot, in agony.

'Here, let me go down and look at him,' said Gladys petulantly.

As they re-entered the studio, Webster was gazing with an air of quiet distaste at an illustration from *La Vie Parisienne* which adorned one of the walls. Lancelot tore it down hastily.

Gladys looked at Webster in an unfriendly way.

'So that's the blighter!'

'Sh!'

'If you want to know what I think,' said Gladys, 'that cat's been living too high. Doing himself a dashed sight too well. You'd better cut his rations down a bit.'

In substance, her criticism was not unjustified. Certainly, there was about Webster more than a suspicion of *embonpoint*. He had that air of portly well-being which we associate with those who dwell in cathedral closes. But Lancelot winced uncomfortably. He had so hoped that Gladys would make a good impression, and here she was, starting right off by saying the tactless thing.

He longed to explain to Webster that it was only her way; that in the Bohemian circles of which she was such an ornament genial chaff of a personal order was accepted and, indeed, relished. But it was too late. The mischief had been done. Webster turned in a pointed manner and withdrew silently behind the chesterfield.

Gladys, all unconscious, was making preparations for departure.

'Well, bung-oh,' she said lightly, 'See you in three weeks. I suppose you and that cat'll both be out on the tiles the moment my back's turned.'

'Please! Please!' moaned Lancelot. 'Please!'

He had caught sight of the tip of a black tail protruding from behind the chesterfield. It was twitching slightly, and Lancelot could read it like a book. With a sickening sense of dismay, he knew that Webster had formed a snap judgement of his fiancée and condemned her as frivolous and unworthy.

It was some ten days later that Bernard Worple, the neo-Vorticist sculptor, lunching at the Puce Ptarmigan, ran into Rodney Scollop, the powerful young surrealist. And after talking for a while of their art –

'What's all this I hear about Lancelot Mulliner?' asked Worple. 'There's a wild story going about that he was seen shaved in the middle of the week. Nothing in it, I suppose?'

Scollop looked grave. He had been on the point of mentioning Lancelot himself, for he loved the lad and was deeply exercised about him.

'It is perfectly true,' he said.

'It sounds incredible.'

Scollop leaned forward. His fine face was troubled.

'Shall I tell you something, Worple?'

'What?'

'I know for an absolute fact,' said Scollop, 'that Lancelot Mulliner now shaves every morning.'

Worple pushed aside the spaghetti which he was wreathing about him and through the gap stared at his companion.

'Every morning?'

'Every single morning. I looked in on him myself the other day, and there he was, neatly dressed in blue serge and shaved to the core. And, what is more, I got the distinct impression that he had used talcum powder afterwards.'

'You don't mean that!'

'I do. And shall I tell you something else? There was a book lying open on the table. He tried to hide it, but he wasn't quick enough. It was one of those etiquette books!'

'An etiquette book!'

'*Polite Behaviour*, by Constance, Lady Bodbank.'

Worple unwound a stray tendril of spaghetti from about his left ear. He was deeply agitated. Like Scollop, he loved Lancelot.

'He'll be dressing for dinner next!' he exclaimed.

'I have every reason to believe,' said Scollop gravely, 'that he does dress for dinner. At any rate, a man closely resembling him was seen furtively buying three stiff collars and a black tie at Hope Brothers in the King's Road last Tuesday.'

Worple pushed his chair back, and rose. His manner was determined.

'Scollop,' he said, 'we are friends of Mulliner's, you and I. It is evident from what you tell me that subversive influences are at work and that never has he needed our friendship more. Shall we not go round and see him immediately?'

'It was what I was about to suggest myself,' said Rodney Scollop.

Twenty minutes later they were in Lancelot's studio, and with a significant glance Scollop drew his companion's notice to their host's appearance. Lancelot Mulliner was neatly, even foppishly, dressed in blue serge with creases down the trouser-legs, and his chin, Worple saw with a pang, gleamed smoothly in the afternoon light.

At the sight of his friends' cigars, Lancelot exhibited unmistakable concern.

'You don't mind throwing those away, I'm sure,' he said pleadingly.

Rodney Scollop drew himself up a little haughtily.

'And since when,' he asked, 'have the best fourpenny cigars in Chelsea not been good enough for you?'

Lancelot hastened to soothe him.

'It isn't me,' he exclaimed. 'It's Webster. My cat. I happen to know he objects to tobacco smoke. I had to give up my pipe in deference to his views.'

Bernard Worple snorted.

'Are you trying to tell us,' he sneered, 'that Lancelot Mulliner allows himself to be dictated to by a blasted cat?'

'Hush!' cried Lancelot, trembling. 'If you knew how he disapproves of strong language!'

'Where is this cat?' asked Rodney Scollop. 'Is that the animal?' he said, pointing out of the window to where, in the yard, a tough-looking Tom with tattered ears stood mewing in a hardboiled way out of the corner of its mouth.

'Good heavens, no!' said Lancelot. 'That is an alley-cat which comes round here from time to time to lunch at the dust-bin. Webster is quite different. Webster has a natural dignity and repose of manner. Webster is a cat who prides himself on always being well turned out and whose high principles and lofty ideals shine from his eyes like beacon-fires. . . .' And then suddenly, with an abrupt change of manner, Lancelot broke down and in a low voice added: 'Curse him! Curse him! Curse him! Curse him!'

Worple looked at Scollop. Scollop looked at Worple.

'Come, old man,' said Scollop, laying a gentle hand on Lancelot's bowed shoulder. 'We are your friends. Confide in us.'

'Tell us all,' said Worple. 'What's the matter?'

Lancelot uttered a bitter, mirthless laugh.

'You want to know what's the matter? Listen, then. I'm cat-pecked!'

'Cat-pecked?'

'You've heard of men being hen-pecked, haven't you?' said Lancelot with a touch of irritation. 'Well, I'm cat-pecked.'

And in broken accents he told his story. He sketched the history of his association with Webster from the latter's first entry into the studio. Confident now that the animal was not within earshot, he unbosomed himself without reserve.

'It's something in the beast's eye,' he said in a shaking voice. 'Something hypnotic. He casts a spell upon me. He gazes at me and disapproves. Little by little, bit by bit, I am degenerating under his influence from a wholesome, self-respecting artist into . . . well, I don't know what you would call it. Suffice it to say that I have given up smoking, that I have ceased to wear carpet slippers and go about without a collar, that I never dream of sitting down to my frugal evening meal without dressing, and' – he choked – 'I have sold my ukulele.'

'Not that!' said Worple, paling.

'Yes,' said Lancelot. 'I felt he considered it frivolous.'

There was a long silence.

'Mulliner,' said Scollop, 'this is more serious than I had supposed. We must brood upon your case.'

'It may be possible,' said Worple, 'to find a way out.'

Lancelot shook his head hopelessly.

'There is no way out. I have explored every avenue. The only thing that could possibly free me from this intolerable bondage would be if once – just once – I could catch that cat unbending. If once – merely once – it would lapse in my presence from its austere dignity for but a single instant, I feel that the spell would be broken. But what hope is there of that?' cried Lancelot passionately. 'You were pointing just now to that alley-cat in the yard. There stands one who has strained every nerve and spared no effort to break down Webster's inhuman self-control. I have heard that animal say things to him which you would think no cat with red blood in its veins would suffer for an instant. And Webster merely looks at him like a Suffragan Bishop eyeing an erring choir-boy and turns his head and falls into a refreshing sleep.'

He broke off with a dry sob. Worple, always an optimist, attempted in his kindly way to minimize the tragedy.

'Ah, well,' he said. 'It's bad, of course, but still, I suppose there is no actual harm in shaving and dressing for dinner and so on. Many great artists . . . Whistler, for example –'

'Wait!' cried Lancelot. 'You have not heard the worst.'

He rose feverishly and, going to the easel, disclosed the portrait of Brenda Carberry-Pirbright.

'Take a look at that,' he said, 'and tell me what you think of her.'

His two friends surveyed the face before them in silence. Miss Carberry-Pirbright was a young woman of prim and glacial aspect. One sought in vain for her reasons for wanting to have her portrait painted. It would be a most unpleasant thing to have about any house.

Scollop broke the silence.

'Friend of yours?'

'I can't stand the sight of her,' said Lancelot vehemently.

'Then,' said Scollop, 'I may speak frankly. I think she's a pill.'

'A blister,' said Worple.

'A boil and a disease,' said Scollop, summing up.

Lancelot laughed hackingly.

'You have described her to a nicety. She stands for everything most alien to my artist soul. She gives me a pain in the neck. I'm going to marry her.'

'What!' cried Scollop.

'But you're going to marry Gladys Bingley,' said Worple.

'Webster thinks not,' said Lancelot bitterly. 'At their first meeting he weighed Gladys in the balance and found her wanting. And the moment he saw Brenda Carberry-Pirbright he stuck his tail up at right angles, uttered a cordial gargle, and rubbed his head against her leg. Then, turning, he looked at me. I could read that glance. I knew what was in his mind. From that moment he has been doing everything in his power to arrange the match.'

'But, Mulliner,' said Worple, always eager to point out the bright side, 'why should this girl want to marry a wretched, scrubby, hard-up footler like you? Have courage, Mulliner. It is simply a question of time before you repel and sicken her.'

Lancelot shook his head.

'No,' he said. 'You speak like a true friend, Worple, but you do not understand. Old Ma Carberry-Pirbright, this exhibit's mother, who chaperons her at the sittings, discovered at an early date my relationship to my Uncle Theodore, who, as you know, has got it in gobs. She knows well enough that some day I shall be a rich man. She used to know my Uncle Theodore when he was Vicar of St Botolph's in Knightsbridge, and from the very first she assumed towards me the repellent chumminess of an old family friend. She was always trying to lure me to her At Homes, her Sunday luncheons, her little dinners. Once she actually suggested that I should escort her and her beastly daughter to the Royal Academy.'

He laughed bitterly. The mordant witticisms of Lancelot Mulliner at the expense of the Royal Academy were quoted from Tite Street in the south to Holland Park in the north and eastward as far as Bloomsbury.

'To all these overtures,' resumed Lancelot, 'I remained firmly unresponsive. My attitude was from the start one of frigid aloofness. I did not actually say in so many words that I would rather be dead in a ditch than at one of her At Homes, but my manner indicated it. And I was just beginning to think I had choked her off when in crashed Webster and upset everything. Do you know how many times I have been to that infernal house in the last week? Five. Webster seemed to wish it. I tell you, I am a lost man.'

He buried his face in his hands. Scollop touched Worple on the arm, and together the two men stole silently out.

'Bad!' said Worple.

'Very bad,' said Scollop.

'It seems incredible.'

'Oh, no. Cases of this kind are, alas, by no means uncommon among those who, like Mulliner, possess to a marked degree the highly-strung, ultra-sensitive artistic temperament. A friend of mine, a rhythmical interior decorator, once rashly consented to put his aunt's parrot up at his studio while she was away visiting friends in the north of England. She was a woman of strong evangelical views, which the bird had imbibed from her. It had a way of putting its head on one side, making a noise like someone drawing a cork from a bottle, and asking my friend if he was saved. To cut a long story short, I happened to call on him a month later and he had installed a harmonium in his studio and was singing hymns, ancient and modern, in a rich tenor, while the parrot, standing on one leg on its perch, took the bass. A very sad affair. We were all much upset about it.'

Worple shuddered.

'You appal me, Scollop! Is there nothing we can do?'

Rodney Scollop considered for a moment.

'We might wire Gladys Bingley to come home at once. She might possibly reason with the unhappy man. A woman's gentle influence. . . . Yes, we could do that. Look in at the post office on your way home and send Gladys a telegram. I'll owe you for my half of it.'

In the studio they had left, Lancelot Mulliner was staring dumbly at a black shape which had just entered the room. He had the appearance of a man with his back to the wall.

'No!' he was crying. 'No! I'm dashed if I do!'

Webster continued to look at him.

'Why should I?' demanded Lancelot weakly.

Webster's gaze did not flicker.

'Oh, all right,' said Lancelot sullenly.

He passed from the room with leaden feet and, proceeding upstairs, changed into morning clothes and a top hat. Then, with a gardenia in his buttonhole, he made his way to 11 Maxton Square, where Mrs Carberry-Pirbright was giving one of her intimate little teas ('just a few friends') to meet Clare Throckmorton Stooge, authoress of *A Strong Man's Kiss*.

Gladys Bingley was lunching at her hotel in Antibes when Worple's telegram arrived. It occasioned her the gravest concern.

Exactly what it was all about, she was unable to gather, for emotion had made Bernard Worple rather incoherent. There were moments, reading it, when she fancied that Lancelot had met with a serious accident; others when the solution seemed to be that he had sprained his brain to such an extent that rival lunatic asylums were competing eagerly for his custom; others, again, when Worple appeared to be suggesting that he had gone into partnership with his cat to start a harem. But one fact emerged clearly. Her loved one was in serious trouble of some kind, and his best friends were agreed that only her immediate return could save him.

Gladys did not hesitate. Within half an hour of the receipt of the telegram she had packed her trunk, removed a piece of asparagus from her right eyebrow, and was negotiating for accommodation on the first train going north.

Arriving in London, her first impulse was to go straight to Lancelot. But a natural feminine curiosity urged her, before doing so, to call upon Bernard Worple and have light thrown on some of the more abstruse passages in the telegram.

Worple, in his capacity of author, may have tended towards obscurity, but, when confining himself to the spoken word, he told a plain story well and clearly. Five minutes of his society enabled Gladys to obtain a firm grasp on the salient facts, and there appeared on her face that grim, tight-lipped expression which is seen only on the faces of fiancées who have come back from a short holiday to discover that their dear one has been straying in their absence from the straight and narrow path.

'Brenda Carberry-Pirbright, eh?' said Gladys, with ominous calm. 'I'll give him Brenda Carberry-Pirbright! My gosh, if one can't go off to Antibes for the merest breather without having one's betrothed getting it up his nose and starting to act like a Mormon Elder, it begins to look a pretty tough world for a girl.'

Kind-hearted Bernard Worple did his best.

'I blame the cat,' he said. 'Lancelot, to my mind, is more sinned against than sinning. I consider him to be acting under undue influence or duress.'

'How like a man!' said Gladys. 'Shoving it all off on to an innocent cat!'

'Lancelot says it has a sort of something in its eye.'

'Well, when I meet Lancelot,' said Gladys, 'he'll find that I have a sort of something in my eye.'

She went out, breathing flame quietly through her nostrils. Worple, saddened, heaved a sigh and resumed his neo-Vorticist sculpting.

It was some five minutes later that Gladys, passing through Maxton Square on her way to Bott Street, stopped suddenly in her tracks. The sight she had seen was enough to make any fiancée do so.

Along the pavement leading to Number Eleven two figures were advancing. Or three, if you counted a morose-looking dog of a semi-Dachshund nature which preceded them, attached to a leash. One of the figures was that of Lancelot Mulliner, natty in grey herring-bone tweed and a new Homburg hat. It was he who held the leash. The other Gladys recognized from the portrait which she had seen on Lancelot's easel as that modern Du Barry, that notorious wrecker of homes and breaker-up of love-nests, Brenda Carberry-Pirbright.

The next moment they had mounted the steps of Number Eleven, and had gone in to tea, possibly with a little music.

It was perhaps an hour and a half later that Lancelot, having wrenched himself with difficulty from the lair of the Philistines, sped homeward in a swift taxi. As always after an extended *tête-à-tête* with Miss Carberry-Pirbright, he felt dazed and bewildered, as if he had been swimming in a sea of glue and had swallowed a good deal of it. All he could think of clearly was that he wanted a drink and that the materials for that drink were in the cupboard behind the chesterfield in his studio.

He paid the cab and charged in with his tongue rattling dryly against his front teeth. And there before him was Gladys Bingley, whom he had supposed far, far away.

'You!' exclaimed Lancelot.

'Yes, me!' said Gladys.

Her long vigil had not helped to restore the girl's equanimity. Since arriving at the studio she had had leisure to tap her foot three thousand, one hundred and forty-two times on the carpet, and the number of bitter smiles which had flitted across her face was nine hundred and eleven. She was about ready for the battle of the century.

She rose and faced him, all the woman in her flashing from her eyes.

'Well, you Casanova!' she said.

'You who?' said Lancelot.

'Don't say "Yoo-hoo!" to me!' cried Gladys. 'Keep that for your Brenda Carberry-Pirbright. Yes, I know all about it, Lancelot Don Juan Henry the Eighth Mulliner! I saw you with her just now. I hear that you and she are inseparable. Bernard Worple says you said you were going to marry her.'

'You mustn't believe everything a neo-Vorticist sculptor tells you,' quavered Lancelot.

'I'll bet you're going back to dinner there tonight,' said Gladys.

She had spoken at a venture, basing the charge purely on a possessive cock of the head which she had noticed in Brenda Carberry-Pirbright at their recent encounter. There, she had said to herself at the time, had gone a girl who was about to invite – or had just invited – Lancelot Mulliner to dine quietly and take her to the pictures afterwards. But the shot went home. Lancelot hung his head.

'There was some talk of it,' he admitted.

'Ah!' exclaimed Gladys.

Lancelot's eyes were haggard.

'I don't want to go,' he pleaded. 'Honestly I don't. But Webster insists.'

'Webster!'

'Yes, Webster. If I attempt to evade the appointment, he will sit in front of me and look at me.'

'Tchah!'

'Well, he will. Ask him for yourself.'

Gladys tapped her foot six times in rapid succession on the carpet, bringing the total to three thousand, one hundred and forty-eight. Her manner had changed and was now dangerously calm.

'Lancelot Mulliner,' she said, 'you have your choice. Me, on the one hand, Brenda Carberry-Pirbright on the other. I offer you a home where you will be able to smoke in bed, spill the ashes on the floor, wear pyjamas and carpet slippers all day and shave only on Sunday mornings. From her, what have you to hope? A house in South Kensington – possibly the Brompton Road – probably with her mother living with you. A life that will be one long round of stiff collars and tight shoes, of morning-coats and top hats.'

Lancelot quivered, but she went on remorselessly.

'You will be at home on alternate Thursdays, and will be expected to hand the cucumber sandwiches. Every day you will air the dog, till you become a confirmed dog-airer. You will dine out in Bayswater and go for the summer to Bournemouth or Dinard. Choose well, Lancelot Mulliner! I will leave you to think it over. But one last word. If by seven-thirty on the dot you have not presented yourself at 6A Garbidge Mews ready to take me out to dinner at the Ham and Beef, I shall know what to think and shall act accordingly.'

And brushing the cigarette ashes from her chin, the girl strode haughtily from the room.

'Gladys!' cried Lancelot.

But she had gone.

For some minutes Lancelot Mulliner remained where he was, stunned. Then insistently, there came to him the recollection that he had not had that drink. He rushed to the cupboard and produced the bottle. He uncorked it, and was pouring out a lavish stream, when a movement on the floor below him attracted his attention.

Webster was standing there, looking up at him. And in his eyes was that familiar expression of quiet rebuke.

'Scarcely what I have been accustomed to at the deanery,' he seemed to be saying.

Lancelot stood paralysed. The feeling of being bound hand and foot, of being caught in a snare from which there was no escape, had become more poignant than ever. The bottle fell from his nerveless fingers and rolled across the floor, spilling its contents in an amber river, but he was too heavy in spirit to notice it. With a gesture such as Job might have made on discovering a new boil, he crossed to the window and stood looking moodily out.

Then, turning with a sigh, he looked at Webster again – and, looking, stood spell-bound.

The spectacle which he beheld was of a kind to stun a stronger man than Lancelot Mulliner. At first, he shrank from believing his eyes. Then, slowly, came the realization that what he saw was no mere figment of a disordered imagination. This unbelievable thing was actually happening.

Webster sat crouched upon the floor beside the widening pool of whisky. But it was not horror and disgust that had caused him to crouch. He was crouched because, crouching, he could get nearer to the stuff and obtain crisper action. His tongue was moving in and out like a piston.

And then abruptly, for one fleeting instant, he stopped lapping and glanced up at Lancelot, and across his face there flitted a quick smile – so genial, so intimate, so full of jovial camaraderie, that the young man found himself automatically smiling back, and not only smiling but winking. And in answer to that wink Webster winked, too – a wholehearted, roguish wink that said as plainly as if he had spoken the words:

'How long has this been going on?'

Then with a slight hiccough he turned back to the task of getting his quick before it soaked into the floor.

Into the murky soul of Lancelot Mulliner there poured a sudden flood of sunshine. It was as if a great burden had been lifted from his shoulders. The intolerable obsession of the last two weeks had ceased to oppress him, and he felt a free man. At the eleventh hour the reprieve had come. Webster, that seeming pillar of austere virtue, was one of the boys, after all. Never again would Lancelot quail beneath his eye. He had the goods on him.

Webster, like the stag at eve, had now drunk his fill. He had left the pool of alcohol and was walking round in slow, meditative circles. From time to time he mewed tentatively, as if he were trying to say 'British Constitution'. His failure to articulate the syllables appeared to tickle him, for at the end of each attempt he would utter a slow, amused chuckle. It was at about this moment that he suddenly broke into a rhythmic dance, not unlike the old Saraband.

It was an interesting spectacle, and at any other time Lancelot would have watched it raptly. But now he was busy at his desk, writing a brief note to Mrs Carberry-Pirbright, the burden of which was that if she thought he was coming within a mile of her foul house that night or any other night she had vastly underrated the dodging powers of Lancelot Mulliner.

And what of Webster? The Demon Rum now had him in an iron grip. A lifetime of abstinence had rendered him a ready victim to the fatal fluid. He had now reached the stage when geniality gives way to belligerence. The rather foolish smile had gone from his face, and in its stead there lowered a fighting frown. For a few moments he stood on his hind legs, looking about him for a suitable adversary: then, losing all vestiges of self-control, he ran five times round the room at a high rate of speed and, falling foul of a small footstool, attacked it with the utmost ferocity, sparing neither tooth nor claw.

But Lancelot did not see him. Lancelot was not there. Lancelot was out in Bott Street, hailing a cab.

'6A Garbidge Mews, Fulham,' said Lancelot to the driver.

'CATS WILL BE CATS'

Mulliner Nights

There had fallen upon the bar-parlour of the Anglers' Rest one of those soothing silences which from time to time punctuate the nightly feasts of Reason and flows of Soul in that cosy resort. It was broken by a Whisky and Splash.

'I've been thinking a lot,' said the Whisky and Splash, addressing Mr Mulliner, 'about that cat of yours, that Webster.'

'Has Mr Mulliner got a cat named Webster?' asked a Small Port who had rejoined our little circle after an absence of some days.

The Sage of the bar-parlour shook his head smilingly.

'Webster,' he said, 'did not belong to me. He was the property of the Dean of Bolsover who, on being raised to a bishopric and sailing from England to take up his episcopal duties at his See of Bongo-Bongo in West Africa, left the animal in the care of his nephew, my cousin Edward's son Lancelot, the artist. I was telling these gentlemen the other evening how Webster for a time completely revolutionized Lancelot's life. His early upbringing at the deanery had made him austere and censorious, and he exerted on my cousin's son the full force of a powerful and bigoted personality. It was as if Savonarola or some minor prophet had suddenly been introduced into the carefree, Bohemian atmosphere of the studio.'

'He stared at Lancelot and unnerved him,' explained a Pint of Bitter.

'He made him shave daily and knock off smoking,' added a Lemon Sour.

'He thought Lancelot's fiancée, Gladys Bingley, worldly,' said a Rum and Milk, 'and tried to arrange a match between him and a girl called Brenda Carberry-Pirbright.'

'But one day,' concluded Mr Mulliner. 'Lancelot discovered that the animal, for all its apparent rigid principles, had feet of clay and was no better than the rest of us. He happened to drop a bottle of alcoholic liquid and the cat drank deeply of its contents and made a sorry exhibition of itself, with the result that the spell was, of course, instantly broken. What aspect of the story of Webster,' he asked the Whisky and Splash, 'has been engaging your thoughts?'

'The psychological aspect,' said the Whisky and Splash. 'As I see it, there is a great psychological drama in this cat. I visualize his higher and lower selves warring. He has taken the first false step, and what will be the issue? Is this new, demoralizing atmosphere into which he has been plunged to neutralize the pious teachings of early kittenhood at the deanery? Or will sound churchmanship prevail and keep him the cat he used to be?'

'If,' said Mr Mulliner, 'I am right in supposing that you want to know what happened to Webster at the conclusion of the story I related the other evening, I can tell you. There was nothing that you could really call a war between his higher and lower selves. The lower self won hands down. From the moment when he went on that first majestic toot this once saintly cat became a Bohemian of Bohemians. His days started early and finished late, and were a mere welter of brawling and loose gallantry. As early as the end of the second week his left ear had been reduced through incessant gang-warfare to a mere tattered scenario and his battle-cry had become as familiar to the denizens of Bott Street, Chelsea, as the yodel of the morning milkman.'

The Whisky and Splash said it reminded him of some great Greek tragedy. Mr Mulliner said yes, there were points of resemblance.

'And what,' enquired the Rum and Milk, 'did Lancelot think of all this?'

'Lancelot,' said Mr Mulliner, 'had the easy live-and-let-live creed of the artist. He was indulgent towards the animal's excesses. As he said to Gladys Bingley one evening, when she was bathing Webster's right eye in a boric solution, cats will be cats. In fact, he would scarcely have given a thought to the matter had there not arrived one morning from his uncle a wireless message, dispatched in mid-ocean, announcing that he had resigned his bishopric for reasons of health and would shortly be back in England once more. The communication ended with the words: "All my best to Webster".'

If you recall the position of affairs between Lancelot and the Bishop of Bongo-Bongo, as I described them the other night (said Mr Mulliner), you will not need to be told how deeply this news affected the young man. It was a bomb-shell. Lancelot, though earning enough by his brush to support himself, had been relying on touching his uncle for that extra bit which would enable him to marry Gladys Bingley. And when he had been placed *in loco parentis* to Webster, he had considered this touch a certainty. Surely, he told himself, the most ordinary gratitude would be sufficient to cause his uncle to unbelt.

But now what?

'You saw that wire,' said Lancelot, agitatedly discussing the matter with Gladys. 'You remember the closing words: "All my best to Webster." Uncle Theodore's first act on landing in England will undoubtedly be to hurry here for a sacred reunion with this cat. And what will he find? A feline plugugly. A gangster. The Big Shot of Bott Street. Look at the animal now,' said Lancelot, waving a distracted hand at the cushion where it lay. 'Run your eye over him. I ask you!'

Certainly Webster was not a natty spectacle. Some tough cats from the public-house on the corner had recently been trying to muscle in on his personal dust-bin, and, though he had fought them off, the affair had left its mark upon him. A further section had been removed from his already abbreviated ear, and his once sleek flanks were short of several patches of hair. He looked like the late Legs Diamond after a social evening with a few old friends.

'What,' proceeded Lancelot, writhing visibly, 'will Uncle Theodore say on beholding that wreck? He will put the entire blame on me. He will insist that it was I who dragged that fine spirit down into the mire. And phut will go any chance I ever had of getting into his ribs for a few hundred quid for honeymoon expenses.'

Gladys Bingley struggled with a growing hopelessness.

'You don't think a good wig-maker could do something?'

'A wig-maker might patch on a little extra fur,' admitted Lancelot, 'but how about that ear?'

'A facial surgeon?' suggested Gladys.

Lancelot shook his head.

'It isn't merely his appearance,' he said. 'It's his entire personality. The poorest reader of character, meeting Webster now, would recognize him for what he is – a hard egg and a bad citizen.'

'When do you expect your uncle?' asked Gladys, after a pause.

'At any moment. He must have landed by this time. I can't understand why he has not turned up.'

At this moment there sounded from the passage outside the *plop* of a letter falling into the box attached to the front door. Lancelot went listlessly out. A few moments later Gladys heard him utter a surprised exclamation, and he came hurrying back, a sheet of note-paper in his hand.

'Listen to this,' he said. 'From Uncle Theodore.'

'Is he in London?'

'No. Down in Hampshire, at a place called Widdrington Manor. And the great point is that he does not want to see Webster yet.'

'Why not?'

'I'll read you what he says.'

And Lancelot proceeded to do so, as follows:

> *Widdrington Manor,*
> *Bottleby-in-the-Vale,*
> *Hants.*

My dear Lancelot,

You will doubtless be surprised that I have not hastened to greet you immediately upon my return to these shores. The explanation is that I am being entertained at the above address by Lady Widdrington, widow of the late Sir George Widdrington, CBE and her mother, Mrs Pulteney-Banks, whose acquaintance I made on shipboard during my voyage home.

I find our English countryside charming after the somewhat desolate environment of Bongo-Bongo, and am enjoying a pleasant and restful visit. Both Lady Widdrington and her mother are kindness itself, especially the former, who is my constant companion on every country ramble. We have a strong bond in our mutual love of cats.

And this, my dear boy, brings me to the subject of Webster. As you can readily imagine, I am keenly desirous of seeing him once more and noting all the evidences of the loving care which, I have no doubt, you have lavished upon him in my absence, but I do not wish you to forward him to me here. The fact is, Lady Widdrington, though a charming woman, seems entirely lacking in discrimination in the matter of cats. She owns and is devoted to a quite impossible orange-coloured animal of the name of Percy, whose society could not but prove distasteful to one of Webster's high principles. When I tell you that only last night this Percy was engaging in personal combat – quite obviously from the worst motives – with a large tortoiseshell beneath my very window, you will understand what I mean.

My refusal to allow Webster to join me here is, I fear, puzzling my kind hostess, who knows how greatly I miss him, but I must be firm.

Keep him, therefore, my dear Lancelot, until I call in person, when I shall remove him to the quiet rural retreat where I plan to spend the evening of my life.

> *With every good wish to you both,*
> *Your affectionate uncle,*
> *THEODORE.*

Gladys Bingley had listened intently to this letter, and as Lancelot came to the end of it she breathed a sigh of relief.

'Well, that gives us a bit of time,' she said.

'Yes,' agreed Lancelot. 'Time to see if we can't awake in this animal some faint echo of its old self-respect. From today Webster goes into monastic seclusion. I shall take him round to the vet's with instructions that he be forced to lead the simple life. In those pure surroundings, with no temptations, no late nights, plain food and a strict milk diet, he may become himself again.'

' "The Man Who Came Back",' said Gladys.

'Exactly,' said Lancelot.

And so for perhaps two weeks something approaching tranquillity reigned once more in my cousin Edward's son's studio in Bott Street, Chelsea. The veterinary surgeon issued encouraging reports. He claimed a distinct improvement in Webster's character and appearance, though he added that he would still not care to meet him at night in a lonely alley. And then one morning there arrived from his Uncle Theodore a telegram which caused the young man to knit his brows in bewilderment.

It ran thus:

On receipt of this come immediately Widdrington Manor prepared for indefinite visit period Circumstances comma I regret to say comma necessitate innocent deception semicolon so will you state on arrival that you are my legal representative and have come to discuss important family matters with me period Will explain fully when see you comma but rest assured comma my dear boy comma that would not ask this were it not absolutely essential period Do not fail me period Regards to Webster.

Lancelot finished reading this mysterious communication, and looked at Gladys with raised eyebrows. There is unfortunately in most artists a material streak which leads them to place an unpleasant interpretation on telegrams like this. Lancelot was no exception to the rule.

'The old boy's been having a couple,' was his verdict.

Gladys, a woman and therefore more spiritual, demurred.

'It sounds to me,' she said, 'more as if he had gone off his onion. Why should he want you to pretend to be a lawyer?'

'He says he will explain fully.'

'And how *do* you pretend to be a lawyer?'

Lancelot considered.

'Lawyers cough dryly, I know that,' he said. 'And then I suppose one would put the tips of the fingers together a good deal and talk about Rex *v.* Biggs Ltd and torts and malfeasances and so forth. I think I could give a reasonably realistic impersonation.'

'Well, if you're going, you'd better start practising.'

'Oh, I'm going all right,' said Lancelot. 'Uncle Theodore is evidently in trouble of some kind, and my place is by his side. If all goes well, I might be able to bite his ear before he sees Webster. About how much ought we to have in order to get married comfortably?'

'At least five hundred.'

'I will bear it in mind,' said Lancelot, coughing dryly and putting the tips of his fingers together.

Lancelot had hoped, on arriving at Widdrington Manor, that the first person he met would be his Uncle Theodore, explaining fully. But when the butler ushered him into the drawing-room only Lady Widdrington, her mother Mrs Pulteney-Banks, and her cat Percy were present. Lady Widdrington shook hands, Mrs Pulteney-Banks bowed from the arm-chair in which she sat swathed in shawls, but when Lancelot advanced with the friendly intention of tickling the cat Percy under the right ear, he gave the young man a cold, evil look out of the corner of his eye, and backing a pace, took an inch of skin off his hand with one well-judged swipe of a steel-pronged paw.

Lady Widdrington stiffened.

'I'm afraid Percy does not like you,' she said in a distant voice.

'They know, they know!' said Mrs Pulteney-Banks darkly. She knitted and purled a moment, musing. 'Cats are cleverer than we think,' she added.

Lancelot's agony was too keen to permit him even to cough dryly. He sank into a chair and surveyed the little company with watering eyes.

They looked to him a hard bunch. Of Mrs Pulteney-Banks he could see little but a cocoon of shawls, but Lady Widdrington was right out in the open, and Lancelot did not like her appearance. The chatelaine of Widdrington Manor was one of those agate-eyed, purposeful, tweed-clad women of whom rural England seems to have a monopoly. She was not unlike what he imagined Queen Elizabeth must have been in her day. A determined and vicious specimen. He marvelled that even a mutual affection for cats could have drawn his gentle uncle to such a one.

As for Percy, he was pure poison. Orange of body and inky-black of soul, he lay stretched out on the rug, exuding arrogance and hate. Lancelot, as I have said, was tolerant of toughness in cats, but there was about this animal none of Webster's jolly, wholehearted, swashbuckling rowdiness. Webster was the sort of cat who would charge, roaring and ranting, to dispute with some rival the possession of a decaying sardine, but there was no more vice in him than in the late John L. Sullivan. Percy, on the other hand, for all his sleek exterior, was mean and bitter. He had no music in his soul, and was fit for treasons, stratagems and spoils. One could picture him stealing milk from a sick tabby.

Gradually the pain of Lancelot's wound began to abate, but it was succeeded by a more spiritual discomfort. It was plain to him that the recent episode had made a bad impression on the two women. They obviously regarded him with suspicion and dislike. The atmosphere was frigid, and conversation proceeded jerkily. Lancelot was glad when the dressing-gong sounded and he could escape to his room.

He was completing the tying of his tie when the door opened and the Bishop of Bongo-Bongo entered.

'Lancelot, my boy!' said the bishop.

'Uncle!' cried Lancelot.

They clasped hands. More than four years had passed since these two had met, and Lancelot was shocked at the other's appearance. When last he had seen him, at the dear old deanery, his Uncle Theodore had been a genial, robust man who wore his gaiters with an air. Now, in some subtle way, he seemed to have shrunk. He looked haggard and hunted. He reminded Lancelot of a rabbit with a good deal on its mind.

The bishop had moved to the door. He opened it and glanced along the passage. Then he closed it and, tip-toeing back, spoke in a cautious undertone.

'It was good of you to come, my dear boy,' he said.

'Why, of course I came,' replied Lancelot heartily. 'Are you in trouble of some kind, Uncle Theodore?'

'In the gravest trouble,' said the bishop, his voice a mere whisper. He paused for a moment. 'You have met Lady Widdrington?'

'Yes.'

'Then when I tell you that, unless ceaseless vigilance is exercised, I shall undoubtedly propose marriage to her, you will appreciate my concern.'

Lancelot gaped.

'But why do you want to do a potty thing like that?'

The bishop shivered.

'I do not want to do it, my boy,' he said. 'Nothing is further from my wishes. The salient point, however, is that Lady Widdrington and her mother want me to do it, and you must have seen for yourself that they are strong, determined women. I fear the worst.'

He tottered to a chair and dropped into it, shaking. Lancelot regarded him with affectionate pity.

'When did this start?' he asked.

'On board ship,' said the bishop. 'Have you ever made an ocean voyage, Lancelot?'

'I've been to America a couple of times.'

'That can scarcely be the same thing,' said the bishop, musingly. 'The transatlantic trip is so brief, and you do not get those nights of tropic moon. But even on your voyages to America you must have noticed the peculiar attitude towards the opposite sex induced by the salt air.'

'They all look good to you at sea,' agreed Lancelot.

'Precisely,' said the bishop. 'And during a voyage, especially at night, one finds oneself expressing oneself with a certain warmth which even at the time one tells oneself is injudicious. I fear that on board the liner with Lady Widdrington, my dear boy, I rather let myself go.'

Lancelot began to understand.

'You shouldn't have come to her house,' he said.

'When I accepted the invitation, I was, if I may use a figure of speech, still under the influence. It was only after I had been here some ten days that I awoke to the realization of my peril.'

'Why didn't you leave?'

The bishop groaned softly.

'They would not permit me to leave. They countered every excuse. I am virtually a prisoner in this house, Lancelot. The other day I said that I had urgent business with my legal adviser and that this made it imperative that I should proceed instantly to the metropolis.'

'That should have worked,' said Lancelot.

'It did not. It failed completely. They insisted that I invite my legal adviser down here where my business could be discussed in the calm atmosphere of the Hampshire countryside. I endeavoured to reason with them, but they were firm. You do not know how firm women can be,' said the bishop, shivering, 'till you have placed yourself in my unhappy position. How well I appreciate now that powerful image of Shakespeare's – the one about grappling with hoops of steel. Every time I meet Lady Widdrington, I can feel those hoops drawing me ever closer to her. And the woman repels me even as that cat of hers repels me. Tell me, my boy, to turn for an instant to a pleasanter subject, how is my dear Webster?'

Lancelot hesitated.

'Full of beans,' he said.

'He is on a diet?' asked the bishop anxiously. 'The doctor has ordered vegetarianism?'

'Just an expression,' explained Lancelot, 'to indicate robustness.'

'Ah!' said the bishop, relieved. 'And what disposition have you made of him in your absence? He is in good hands, I trust?'

'The best,' said Lancelot. 'His host is the ablest veterinary in London – Doctor J. G. Robinson of 9 Bott Street, Chelsea, a man not only skilled in his profession but of the highest moral tone.'

'I knew I could rely on you to see that all was well with him,' said the bishop emotionally. 'Otherwise, I should have shrunk from asking you to leave London and come here – strong shield of defence though you will be to me in my peril.'

'But what use can I be to you?' said Lancelot, puzzled.

'The greatest,' the bishop assured him. 'Your presence will be invaluable. You must keep the closest eye upon Lady Widdrington and myself, and whenever you observe us wandering off together – she is assiduous in her efforts to induce me to visit the rose-garden in her company, for example – you must come hurrying up and detach me with the ostensible purpose of discussing legal matters. By these means we may avert what I had come to regard as the inevitable.'

'I understand thoroughly,' said Lancelot. 'A jolly good scheme. Rely on me.'

'The ruse I have outlined,' said the bishop regretfully, 'involves, as I hinted in my telegram, a certain innocent deception, but at times like this one cannot afford to be too nice in one's methods. By the way, under what name did you make your appearance here?'

'I used my own.'

'I would have preferred Polkinghorne or Gooch or Withers,' said the bishop pensively. 'They sound more legal. However, that is a small matter. The essential thing is that I may rely on you to – er – to – ?'

'To stick around?'

'Exactly. To adhere. From now on, my boy, you must be my constant shadow. And if, as I trust, our efforts are rewarded, you will not find me ungrateful. In the course of a lifetime I have contrived to accumulate no small supply of this world's goods, and if there is any little venture or enterprise for which you require a certain amount of capital – '

'I am glad,' said Lancelot, 'that you brought this up, Uncle Theodore. As it so happens, I am badly in need of five hundred pounds – and could, indeed, do with a thousand.'

The bishop grasped his hand.

'See me through this ordeal, my dear boy,' he said, 'and you shall have it. For what purpose do you require this money?'

'I want to get married.'

'Ugh!' said the bishop, shuddering strongly. 'Well, well,' he went on, recovering himself, 'it is no affair of mine. No doubt you know your own mind best. I must confess, however, that the mere mention of the holy state occasions in me an indefinable sinking feeling. But then, of course, you are not proposing to marry Lady Widdrington.'

'And nor,' cried Lancelot heartily, 'are you, Uncle – not while I'm around. Tails up, Uncle Theodore, tails up!'

'Tails up!' repeated the bishop dutifully, but he spoke the words without any real ring of conviction in his voice.

It was fortunate that, in the days which followed, my cousin Edward's son Lancelot was buoyed up not only by the prospect of collecting a thousand pounds, but also by a genuine sympathy and pity for a well-loved uncle. Otherwise, he must have faltered and weakened.

To a sensitive man – and all artists are sensitive – there are few things more painful than the realization that he is an unwelcome guest. And not even if he had had the vanity of a Narcissus could Lancelot have persuaded himself that he was *persona grata* at Widdrington Manor.

The march of civilization has done much to curb the natural ebullience of woman. It has brought to her the power of self-restraint. In emotional crises nowadays women seldom give physical expression to their feelings; and neither Lady Widdrington nor her mother, the aged Mrs Pulteney-Banks, actually struck Lancelot or spiked him with a knitting-needle. But there were moments when they seemed only by a miracle of strong will to check themselves from such manifestations of dislike.

As the days went by, and each day the young man skilfully broke up a promising *tête-à-tête*, the atmosphere grew more tense and electric. Lady Widdrington spoke dreamily of the excellence of the train service between Bottleby-in-the-Vale and London, paying a particularly marked tribute to the 8.45 a.m. express. Mrs Pulteney-Banks mumbled from among her shawls of great gowks – she did not specify more exactly, courteously refraining from naming names – who spent their time idling in the country (where they were not wanted) when their true duty and interest lay in the metropolis. The cat Percy, by word and look, continued to affirm his low opinion of Lancelot.

And, to make matters worse, the young man could see that his principal's *morale* was becoming steadily lowered. Despite the uniform success of their manœuvres, it was evident that the strain was proving too severe for the bishop. He was plainly cracking. A settled hopelessness had crept into his demeanour. More and more had he come to resemble a rabbit who, fleeing from a stoat, draws no cheer from the reflection that he is all right so far, but flings up his front paws in a gesture of despair, as if to ask what profit there can be in attempting to evade the inevitable.

And, at length, one night when Lancelot had switched off his light and composed himself for sleep, it was switched on again and he perceived his uncle standing by the bedside, with a haggard expression on his fine features.

At a glance Lancelot saw that the good old man had reached breaking-point.

'Something the matter, Uncle?' he asked.

'My boy,' said the bishop, 'we are undone.'

'Oh, surely not?' said Lancelot, as cheerily as his sinking heart would permit.

'Undone,' repeated the bishop hollowly. 'Tonight Lady Widdrington specifically informed me that she wishes you to leave the house.'

Lancelot drew in his breath sharply. Natural optimist though he was, he could not minimize the importance of this news.

'She has consented to allow you to remain for another two days, and then the butler has instructions to pack your belongings in time for the eight-forty-five express.'

'H'm!' said Lancelot.

'H'm, indeed,' said the bishop. 'This means that I shall be left alone and defenceless. And even with you sedulously watching over me it has been a very near thing once or twice. That afternoon in the summer-house!'

'And that day in the shrubbery,' said Lancelot. There was a heavy silence for a moment.

'What are you going to do?' asked Lancelot.

'I must think . . . think,' said the bishop. 'Well, good night, my boy.'

He left the room with bowed head, and Lancelot, after a long period of wakeful meditation, fell into a fitful slumber.

From this he was aroused some two hours later by an extraordinary commotion somewhere outside his room. The noise appeared to proceed from the hall and, donning a dressing-gown, he hurried out.

A strange spectacle met his eyes. The entire numerical strength of Widdrington Manor seemed to have assembled in the hall. There was Lady Widdrington in a mauve *négligé*, Mrs Pulteney-Banks in a system of shawls, the butler in pyjamas, a footman or two, several maids, the odd-job man, and the boy who cleaned the shoes. They were gazing in manifest astonishment at the Bishop of Bongo-Bongo, who stood, fully clothed, near the front door, holding in one hand an umbrella, in the other a bulging suitcase.

In a corner sat the cat, Percy, swearing in a quiet undertone.

As Lancelot arrived the bishop blinked and looked dazedly about him.

'Where am I?' he said.

Willing voices informed him that he was at Widdrington Manor, Bottleby-in-the-Vale, Hants, the butler going so far as to add the telephone number.

'I think,' said the bishop, 'I must have been walking in my sleep.'

'Indeed?' said Mrs Pulteney-Banks, and Lancelot could detect the dryness in her tone.

'I am sorry to have been the cause of robbing the household of its well-earned slumber,' said the bishop nervously. 'Perhaps it would be best if I now retired to my room.'

'Quite,' said Mrs Pulteney-Banks, and once again her voice cracked dryly.

'I'll come and tuck you up,' said Lancelot.

'Thank you, my boy,' said the bishop.

Safe from observation in his bedroom, the bishop sank wearily on the bed, and allowed the umbrella to fall hopelessly to the floor.

'It is Fate,' he said. 'Why struggle further?'

'What happened?' asked Lancelot.

'I thought matters over,' said the bishop, 'and decided that my best plan would be to escape quietly under cover of the night. I had intended to wire Lady Widdrington on the morrow that urgent matters of personal importance had necessitated a sudden visit to London. And just as I was getting the front door open I trod on that cat.'

'Percy?'

'Percy,' said the bishop bitterly. 'He was prowling about in the hall, on who knows what dark errand. It is some small satisfaction to me in my distress to recall that I must have flattened out his tail properly. I came down on it with my full weight, and I am not a slender man. Well,' he said, sighing drearily, 'this is the end. I give up. I yield.'

'Oh, don't say that, Uncle.'

'I do say that,' replied the bishop, with some asperity. 'What else is there to say?'

It was a question which Lancelot found himself unable to answer. Silently he pressed the other's hand, and walked out.

In Mrs Pulteney-Banks's room, meanwhile, an earnest conference was taking place.

'Walking in his sleep, indeed!' said Mrs Pulteney-Banks.

Lady Widdrington seemed to take exception to the older woman's tone.

'Why shouldn't he walk in his sleep?' she retorted.

'Why should he?'

'Because he was worrying.'

'Worrying!' sniffed Mrs Pulteney-Banks.

'Yes, worrying,' said Lady Widdrington, with spirit. 'And I know why. You don't understand Theodore as I do.'

'As slippery as an eel,' grumbled Mrs Pulteney-Banks. 'He was trying to sneak off to London.'

'Exactly,' said Lady Widdrington. 'To his cat. You don't understand what it means to Theodore to be separated from his cat. I have noticed for a long time that he was restless and ill at ease. The reason is obvious. He is pining for Webster. I know what it is myself. That time when Percy was lost for two days I nearly went off my head. Directly after breakfast tomorrow I shall wire to Doctor Robinson of Bott Street, Chelsea, in whose charge Webster now is, to send him down here by the first train. Apart from anything else, he will be nice company for Percy.'

'Tchah!' said Mrs Pulteney-Banks.

'What do you mean, Tchah?' demanded Lady Widdrington.

'I mean Tchah,' said Mrs Pulteney-Banks.

An atmosphere of constraint hung over Widdrington Manor throughout the following day. The natural embarrassment of the bishop was increased by the attitude of Mrs Pulteney-Banks, who had contracted a habit of looking at him over her zareba of shawls and sniffing meaningly. It was with relief that towards the middle of the afternoon he accepted Lancelot's suggestion that they should repair to the study and finish up what remained of their legal business.

The study was on the ground floor, looking out on pleasant lawns and shrubberies. Through the open window came the scent of summer flowers. It was a scene which should have soothed the most bruised soul, but the bishop was plainly unable to draw refreshment from it. He sat with his head in his hands, refusing all Lancelot's well-meant attempts at consolation.

'Those sniffs!' he said, shuddering, as if they still rang in his ears. 'What meaning they held! What a sinister significance!'

'She may just have got a cold in the head,' urged Lancelot.

'No. The matter went deeper than that. They meant that that terrible old woman saw through my subterfuge last night. She read me like a book. From now on there will be added vigilance. I shall not be permitted out of their sight, and the end can be only a question of time. Lancelot, my boy,' said the bishop, extending a trembling hand pathetically towards his nephew, 'you are a young man on the threshold of life. If you wish that life to be a happy one, always remember this: when on an ocean voyage, never visit the boat-deck after dinner. You will be tempted. You will say to yourself that the lounge is stuffy and that the cool breezes will correct that replete feeling which so many of us experience after the evening meal . . . you will think how pleasant it must be up there, with the rays of the moon turning the waves to molten silver . . . but don't go, my boy, don't go!'

'Right-ho, Uncle,' said Lancelot soothingly.

The bishop fell into a moody silence.

'It is not merely,' he resumed, evidently having followed some train of thought, 'that, as one of Nature's bachelors, I regard the married state with alarm and concern. It is the peculiar conditions of my tragedy that render me distraught. My lot once linked to that of Lady Widdrington, I shall never see Webster again.'

'Oh, come, Uncle. This is morbid.'

The bishop shook his head.

'No,' he said. 'If this marriage takes place, my path and Webster's must divide. I could not subject that pure cat to life at Widdrington Manor, a life involving, as it would, the constant society of the animal Percy. He would be contaminated. You know Webster, Lancelot. He has been your companion – may I not almost say your mentor? – for months. You know the loftiness of his ideals.'

For an instant, a picture shot through Lancelot's mind – the picture of Webster, as he had seen him only a brief while since – standing in the yard with the backbone of a herring in his mouth, crooning a war-song at the alley-cat from whom he had stolen the *bonne-bouche*. But he replied without hesitation.

'Oh, rather.'

'They are very high.'

'Extremely high.'

'And his dignity,' said the bishop. 'I deprecate a spirit of pride and self-esteem, but Webster's dignity was not tainted with those qualities. It rested on a clear conscience and the knowledge that, even as a kitten, he had never permitted his feet to stray. I wish you could have seen Webster as a kitten, Lancelot.'

'I wish I could, Uncle.'

'He never played with balls of wool, preferring to sit in the shadow of the cathedral wall, listening to the clear singing of the choir as it melted on the sweet stillness of the summer day. Even then you could see that deep thoughts exercised his mind. I remember once . . . .'

But the reminiscence, unless some day it made its appearance in the good old man's memoirs, was destined to be lost to the world. For at this moment the door opened and the butler entered. In his arms he bore a hamper, and from this hamper there proceeded the wrathful ejaculations of a cat who has had a long train-journey under constricted conditions and is beginning to ask what it is all about.

'Bless my soul!' cried the bishop, startled.

A sickening sensation of doom darkened Lancelot's soul. He had recognized that voice. He knew what was in that hamper.

'Stop!' he exclaimed. 'Uncle Theodore, don't open that hamper!'

But it was too late. Already the bishop was cutting the strings with a hand that trembled with eagerness. Chirruping noises proceeded from him. In his eyes was the wild gleam seen only in the eyes of cat-lovers restored to their loved one.

'Webster!' he called in a shaking voice.

And out of the hamper shot Webster, full of strange oaths. For a moment he raced about the room, apparently searching for the man who had shut him up in the thing, for there was flame in his eye. Becoming calmer, he sat down and began to lick himself, and it was then for the first time that the bishop was enabled to get a steady look at him.

Two weeks' residence at the vet's had done something for Webster, but not enough. Not, Lancelot felt agitatedly, nearly enough. A mere fortnight's seclusion cannot bring back fur to lacerated skin; it cannot restore to a chewed ear that extra inch which makes all the difference. Webster had gone to Doctor Robinson looking as if he had just been caught in machinery of some kind, and that was how, though in a very slightly modified degree, he looked now. And at the sight of him the bishop uttered a sharp, anguished cry. Then, turning on Lancelot, he spoke in a voice of thunder.

'So this, Lancelot Mulliner, is how you have fulfilled your sacred trust!'

Lancelot was shaken, but he contrived to reply.

'It wasn't my fault, Uncle. There was no stopping him.'

'Pshaw!'

'Well, there wasn't,' said Lancelot. 'Besides, what harm is there in an occasional healthy scrap with one of the neighbours? Cats will be cats.'

'A sorry piece of reasoning,' said the bishop, breathing heavily.

'Personally,' Lancelot went on, though speaking dully, for he realized how hopeless it all was, 'if I owned Webster, I should be proud of him. Consider his record,' said Lancelot, warming a little as he proceeded. 'He comes to Bott Street without so much as a single fight under his belt and, despite this inexperience, shows himself possessed of such genuine natural talent that in two weeks he has every cat for streets around jumping walls and climbing lamp-posts at the mere sight of him. I wish,' said Lancelot, now carried away by this theme, 'that you could have seen him clean up a puce-coloured Tom from Number Eleven. It was the finest sight I have ever witnessed. He was conceding pounds to this animal, who, in addition, had a reputation extending as far afield as the Fulham Road. The first round was even, with the exchanges perhaps a shade in favour of his opponent. But when the gong went for Round Two . . . .'

The bishop raised his hand. His face was drawn.

'Enough!' he cried. 'I am inexpressibly grieved. I . . . .'

He stopped. Something had leaped upon the window-sill at his side, causing him to start violently. It was the cat Percy who, hearing a strange feline voice, had come to investigate.

There were days when Percy, mellowed by the influence of cream and the sunshine, could become, if not agreeable, at least free from active venom. Lancelot had once seen him actually playing with a ball of paper. But it was evident immediately that this was not one of those days. Percy was plainly in evil mood. His dark soul gleamed from his narrow eyes. He twitched his tail to and fro, and for a moment stood regarding Webster with a hard sneer.

Then, wiggling his whiskers, he said something in a low voice.

Until he spoke, Webster had apparently not observed his arrival. He was still cleaning himself after the journey. But hearing this remark, he started and looked up. And, as he saw Percy, his ears flattened and the battlelight came into his eye.

There was a moment's pause. Cat stared at cat. Then, swishing his tail to and fro, Percy repeated his statement in a louder tone. And from this point, Lancelot tells me, he could follow the conversation word for word as easily as if he had studied cat-language for years.

This, he says, is how the dialogue ran:

WEBSTER: Who, me?

PERCY: Yes, you.

WEBSTER: A what?

PERCY: You heard.

WEBSTER: Is that so?

PERCY: Yeah.

WEBSTER: Yeah?

PERCY: Yeah. Come on up here and I'll bite the rest of your ear off.

WEBSTER: Yeah? You and who else?

PERCY: Come on up here. I dare you.

WEBSTER: *(flushing hotly)* You do, do you? Of all the nerve! Of all the crust! Why, I've eaten better cats than you before breakfast.

(to Lancelot)

Here, hold my coat and stand to one side. Now, then!

And, with this, there was a whizzing sound and Webster had advanced in full battle-order. A moment later, a tangled mass that looked like seventeen cats in close communion fell from the window-sill into the room.

A cat-fight of major importance is always a spectacle worth watching, but Lancelot tells me that, vivid and stimulating though this one promised to be, his attention was riveted not upon it, but upon the Bishop of Bongo-Bongo.

In the first few instants of the encounter the prelate's features had betrayed no emotion beyond a grievous alarm and pain. 'How art thou fallen from Heaven, oh, Lucifer, Son of Morning,' he seemed to be saying as he watched his once blameless pet countering Percy's onslaught with what had the appearance of being about sixteen simultaneous legs. And then, almost abruptly, there seemed to awake in him at the same instant a passionate pride in Webster's prowess and that sporting spirit which lies so near the surface in all of us. Crimson in the face, his eyes gleaming with partisan enthusiasm, he danced round the combatants, encouraging his nominee with word and gesture.

'Capital! Excellent! Ah, stoutly struck, Webster!'

'Hook him with your left, Webster!' cried Lancelot.

'Precisely!' boomed the bishop.

'Soak him, Webster!'

'Indubitably!' agreed the bishop. 'The expression is new to me, but I appreciate its pith and vigour. By all means, soak him, my dear Webster.'

And it was at this moment that Lady Widdrington, attracted by the noise of battle, came hurrying into the room. She was just in time to see Percy run into a right swing and bound for the window-sill, closely pursued by his adversary. Long since, Percy had begun to realize that, in inviting this encounter, he had gone out of his class and come up against something hot. All he wished for now was flight. But Webster's hat was still in the ring, and cries from without told that the battle had been joined once more on the lawn.

Lady Widdrington stood appalled. In the agony of beholding her pet so manifestly getting the loser's end she had forgotten her matrimonial plans. She was no longer the calm, purposeful woman who intended to lead the bishop to the altar if she had to use chloroform; she was an outraged cat-lover, and she faced him with blazing eyes.

'What,' she demanded, 'is the meaning of this?'

The bishop was still labouring under obvious excitement.

'That beastly animal of yours asked for it, and did Webster give it to him!'

'Did he!' said Lancelot. 'That corkscrew punch with the left!'

'That sort of quick upper-cut with the right!' cried the bishop.

'There isn't a cat in London that could beat him.'

'In London?' said the bishop warmly. 'In the whole of England. Oh, admirable Webster!'

Lady Widdrington stamped a furious foot.

'I insist that you destroy that cat!'

'Which cat?'

'That cat,' said Lady Widdrington, pointing.

Webster was standing on the window-sill. He was panting slightly, and his ear was in worse repair than ever, but on his face was the satisfied smile of a victor. He moved his head from side to side, as if looking for the microphone through which his public expected him to speak a modest word or two.

'I demand that that savage animal be destroyed,' said Lady Widdrington.

The bishop met her eye steadily.

'Madam,' he replied, 'I shall sponsor no such scheme.'

'You refuse?'

'Most certainly I refuse. Never have I esteemed Webster so highly as at this moment. I consider him a public benefactor, a selfless altruist. For years every right-thinking person must have yearned to handle that inexpressibly abominable cat of yours as Webster has just handled him, and I have no feelings towards him but those of gratitude and admiration. I intend, indeed, personally and with my own hands to give him a good plate of fish.'

Lady Widdrington drew in her breath sharply.

'You will not do it here,' she said.

She pressed the bell.

'Fotheringay,' she said in a tense, cold voice, as the butler appeared, 'the bishop is leaving us tonight. Please see that his bags are packed for the six-forty-one.'

She swept from the room. The bishop turned to Lancelot with a benevolent smile.

'It will just give me nice time,' he said, 'to write you that cheque, my boy.'

He stooped and gathered Webster into his arms, and Lancelot, after one quick look at them, stole silently out. This sacred moment was not for his eyes.

'THE VOICE FROM THE PAST'

Mulliner Nights

At the ancient and historic public school which stands a mile or two up the river from the Anglers' Rest there had recently been a change of headmasters, and our little group in the bar-parlour, naturally interested, was discussing the new appointment.

A grizzled Tankard of Stout frankly viewed it with concern.

'Benger!' he exclaimed. 'Fancy making Benger a headmaster.'

'He has a fine record.'

'Yes, but, dash it, he was at school with me.'

'One lives these things down in time,' we urged.

The Tankard said we had missed his point, which was that he could remember young Scrubby Benger in an Eton collar with jam on it, getting properly cursed by the Mathematics beak for bringing white mice into the form-room.

'He was a small, fat kid with a pink face,' proceeded the Tankard. 'I met him again only last July, and he looked just the same. I can't see him as a headmaster. I thought they had to be a hundred years old and seven feet high, with eyes of flame, and long white beards. To me, a headmaster has always been a sort of blend of Epstein's Genesis and something out of the Book of Revelations.'

Mr Mulliner smiled tolerantly.

'You left school at an early age, I imagine?'

'Sixteen. I had to go into my uncle's business.'

'Exactly,' said Mr Mulliner, nodding sagely. 'You completed your school career, in other words, before the age at which a boy, coming into personal relationship with the man up top, learns to regard him as a guide, philosopher and friend. The result is that you are suffering from the well-known Headmaster Fixation or Phobia – precisely as my nephew Sacheverell did. A rather delicate youth, he was removed by his parents from Harborough College shortly after his fifteenth birthday and educated at home by a private tutor; and I have frequently heard him assert that the Rev. J. G. Smethurst, the ruling spirit of Harborough, was a man who chewed broken bottles and devoured his young.'

'I strongly suspected my headmaster of conducting human sacrifices behind the fives-courts at the time of the full moon,' said the Tankard.

'Men like yourself and my nephew Sacheverell who leave school early,' said Mr Mulliner, 'never wholly lose these poetic boyish fancies. All their lives, the phobia persists. And sometimes this has curious results – as in the case of my nephew Sacheverell.'

It was to the terror inspired by his old headmaster (said Mr Mulliner) that I always attributed my nephew Sacheverell's extraordinary mildness and timidity. A nervous boy, the years seemed to bring him no store of self-confidence. By the time he arrived at man's estate, he belonged definitely to the class of humanity which never gets a seat on an underground train and is ill at ease in the presence of butlers, traffic policemen, and female assistants in post offices. He was the sort of young fellow at whom people laugh when the waiter speaks to them in French.

And this was particularly unfortunate, as he had recently become secretly affianced to Muriel, only daughter of Lieut.-Colonel Sir Redvers Branksome, one of the old-school type of squire and as tough an egg as ever said 'Yoicks' to a fox-hound. He had met her while she was on a visit to an aunt in London, and had endeared himself to her partly by his modest and diffident demeanour and partly by doing tricks with a bit of string, an art at which he was highly proficient.

Muriel was one of those hearty, breezy girls who abound in the hunting counties of England. Brought up all her life among confident young men who wore gaiters and smacked them with riding-crops, she had always yearned sub-consciously for something different: and Sacheverell's shy, mild, shrinking personality seemed to wake the maternal in her. He was so weak, so helpless, that her heart went out to him. Friendship speedily ripened into love, with the result that one afternoon my nephew found himself definitely engaged and faced with the prospect of breaking the news to the old folks at home.

'And if you think you've got a picnic ahead of you,' said Muriel, 'forget it. Father's a gorilla. I remember when I was engaged to my Cousin Bernard – '

'When you were what to your what?' gasped Sacheverell.

'Oh, yes,' said the girl. 'Didn't I tell you? I was engaged once to my Cousin Bernard, but I broke it off because he tried to boss me. A little too much of the dominant male there was about old B., and I handed him his hat. Though we're still good friends. But what I was saying was that Bernard used to gulp like a seal and stand on one leg when father came along. And he's in the Guards. That just shows you. However, we'll start the thing going. I'll get you down to the Towers for a weekend, and we'll see what happens.'

If Muriel had hoped that mutual esteem would spring up between her father and her betrothed during this weekend visit, she was doomed to disappointment. The thing was a failure from the start. Sacheverell's host did him extremely well, giving him the star guest-room, the Blue Suite, and bringing out the oldest port for his benefit, but it was plain that he thought little of the young man. The colonel's subjects were sheep (in sickness and in health), manure, wheat, mangold-wurzels, huntin', shootin' and fishin': while Sacheverell was at his best on Proust, the Russian Ballet, Japanese prints, and the influence of James Joyce on the younger Bloomsbury novelists. There was no fusion between these men's souls. Colonel Branksome did not actually bite Sacheverell in the leg; but when you had said that you had said everything.

Muriel was deeply concerned.

'I'll tell you what it is, Dogface,' she said, as she was seeing her loved one to his train on the Monday, 'we've got off on the wrong foot. The male parent may have loved you at sight, but, if he did, he took another look and changed his mind.'

'I fear we were not exactly *en rapport*,' sighed Sacheverell. 'Apart from the fact that the mere look of him gave me a strange, sinking feeling, my conversation seemed to bore him.'

'You didn't talk about the right things.'

'I couldn't. I know so little of mangold-wurzels. Manure is a sealed book to me.'

'Just what I'm driving at,' said Muriel. 'And all that must be altered. Before you spring the tidings on father, there will have to be a lot of careful preliminary top-dressing of the soil, if you follow what I mean. By the time the bell goes for the second round and old Dangerous Dan McGrew comes out of his corner at you, breathing fire, you must have acquired a good working knowledge of Scientific Agriculture. That'll tickle him pink.'

'But how?'

'I'll tell you how. I was reading a magazine the other day, and there was an advertisement in it of a Correspondence School which teaches practically everything. You put a cross against the course you want to take and clip out the coupon and bung it in, and they do the rest. I suppose they send you pamphlets and things. So the moment you get back to London, look up this advertisement – it was in the *Piccadilly Magazine* – and write to these people and tell them to shoot the works.'

Sacheverell pondered this advice during the railway journey, and the more he pondered it the more clearly did he see how excellent it was. It offered the solution to all his troubles. There was no doubt whatever that the bad impression he had made on Colonel Branksome was due chiefly to his ignorance of the latter's pet subjects. If he were in a position to throw off a good thing from time to time on Guano or the Influence of Dip on the Younger Leicestershire Sheep, Muriel's father would unquestionably view him with a far kindlier eye.

He lost no time in clipping out the coupon and forwarding it with a covering cheque to the address given in the advertisement. And two days later a bulky package arrived, and he settled down to an intensive course of study.

By the time Sacheverell had mastered the first six lessons, a feeling of perplexity had begun to steal over him. He knew nothing, of course, of the methods of Correspondence Schools and was prepared to put his trust blindly in his unseen tutor; but it did strike him as odd that a course on Scientific Agriculture should have absolutely no mention of Scientific Agriculture in it. Though admittedly a child in these matters, he had supposed that that was one of the first topics on which the thing would have touched.

But such was not the case. The lessons contained a great deal of advice about deep breathing and regular exercise and cold baths and Yogis and the training of the mind, but on the subject of Scientific Agriculture they were vague and elusive. They simply would not come to the point. They said nothing about sheep, nothing about manure, and from the way they avoided mangold-wurzels you might have thought they considered these wholesome vegetables almost improper.

At first, Sacheverell accepted this meekly, as he accepted everything in life. But gradually, as his reading progressed, a strange sensation of annoyance began to grip him. He found himself chafing a good deal, particularly in the mornings. And when the seventh lesson arrived and still there was this absurd coyness on the part of his instructors to come to grips with Scientific Agriculture, he decided to put up with it no longer. He was enraged. These people, he considered, were deliberately hornswoggling him. He resolved to go round and see them and put it to them straight that he was not the sort of man to be trifled with in this fashion.

The headquarters of the Leave-It-To-Us Correspondence School were in a large building off Kingsway. Sacheverell, passing through the front door like an east wind, found himself confronted by a small boy with a cold and supercilious eye.

'Yes?' said the boy, with deep suspicion. He seemed to be a lad who distrusted his fellow men and attributed the worst motives to their actions.

Sacheverell pointed curtly to a door on which was the legend 'Jno. B. Philbrick, Mgr.'

'I wish to see Jno. B. Philbrick, Mgr.,' he said.

The boy's lip curled contemptuously. He appeared to be on the point of treating the application with silent disdain. Then he vouchsafed a single, scornful word.

'Can'tseeMrPhilbrickwithoutanappointment,' he said.

A few weeks before, a rebuff like this would have sent Sacheverell stumbling blushfully out of the place, tripping over his feet. But now he merely brushed the child aside like a feather, and strode to the inner office.

A bald-headed man with a walrus moustache was seated at the desk.

'Jno. Philbrick?' said Sacheverell brusquely.

'That is my name.'

'Then listen to me, Philbrick,' said Sacheverell. 'I paid fifteen guineas in advance for a course on Scientific Agriculture. I have here the seven lessons which you have sent me to date, and if you can find a single word in them that has anything even remotely to do with Scientific Agriculture, I will eat my hat – and yours, too, Philbrick.'

The manager had produced a pair of spectacles and through them was gazing at the mass of literature which Sacheverell had hurled before him. He raised his eyebrows and clicked his tongue.

'Stop clicking!' said Sacheverell. 'I came here to be explained to, not clicked at.'

'Dear me!' said the manager. 'How very curious.'

Sacheverell banged the desk forcefully.

'Philbrick,' he shouted, 'do not evade the issue. It is not curious. It is scandalous, monstrous, disgraceful, and I intend to take very strong steps. I shall give this outrage the widest and most pitiless publicity, and spare no effort to make a complete *exposé*.'

The manager held up a deprecating hand.

'Please!' he begged. 'I appreciate your indignation, Mr . . . Mulliner? Thank you . . . I appreciate your indignation, Mr Mulliner. I sympathize with your concern. But I can assure you that there has been no desire to deceive. Merely an unfortunate blunder on the part of our clerical staff, who shall be severely reprimanded. What has happened is that the wrong course has been sent to you.'

Sacheverell's righteous wrath cooled a little.

'Oh?' he said, somewhat mollified. 'I see. The wrong course, eh?'

'The wrong course,' said Mr Philbrick. 'And,' he went on, with a sly glance at his visitor, 'I think you will agree with me that such immediate results are a striking testimony to the efficacy of our system.'

Sacheverell was puzzled.

'Results?' he said. 'How do you mean, results?'

The manager smiled genially.

'What you have been studying for the past few weeks, Mr Mulliner,' he said, 'is our course on How to Acquire Complete Self-Confidence and an Iron Will.'

A strange elation filled Sacheverell Mulliner's bosom as he left the offices of the Correspondence School. It is always a relief to have a mystery solved which has been vexing one for any considerable time: and what Jno. Philbrick had told him made several puzzling things clear. For quite a little while he had been aware that a change had taken place in his relationship to the world about him. He recalled taxi-cabmen whom he had looked in the eye and made to wilt; intrusive pedestrians to whom he had refused to yield an inch of the pavement, where formerly he would have stepped meekly aside. These episodes had perplexed him at the time, but now everything was explained.

But what principally pleased him was the thought that he was relieved of the tedious necessity of making a study of Scientific Agriculture, a subject from which his artist soul had always revolted. Obviously, a man with a will as iron as his would be merely wasting time boning up a lot of dull facts simply with the aim of pleasing Sir Redvers Branksome. Sir Redvers Branksome, felt Sacheverell, would jolly well take him as he was, and like it.

He anticipated no trouble from that quarter. In his mind's eye he could see himself lolling at the dinner-table at the Towers and informing the colonel over a glass of port that he proposed, at an early date, to marry his daughter. Possibly, purely out of courtesy, he would make the graceful gesture of affecting to seek the old buster's approval of the match: but at the slightest sign of obduracy he would know what to do about it.

Well pleased, Sacheverell was walking to the Carlton Hotel, where he intended to lunch, when, just as he entered the Haymarket, he stopped abruptly, and a dark frown came into his resolute face.

A cab had passed him, and in that cab was sitting his fiancée, Muriel Branksome. And beside her, with a grin on his beastly face, was a young man in a Brigade of Guards tie. They had the air of a couple on their way to enjoy a spot of lunch somewhere.

That Sacheverell should have deduced immediately that the young man was Muriel's cousin, Bernard, was due to the fact that, like all the Mulliners, he was keenly intuitive. That he should have stood, fists clenched and eyes blazing, staring after the cab, we may set down to the circumstance that the spectacle of these two, squashed together in carefree proximity on the seat of a taxi, had occasioned in him the utmost rancour and jealousy.

Muriel, as she had told him, had once been engaged to her cousin, and the thought that they were still on terms of such sickening intimacy acted like acid on Sacheverell's soul.

Hobnobbing in cabs, by Jove! Revelling *tête-à-tête* at luncheon-tables, forsooth! Just the sort of goings-on that got the Cities of the Plain so disliked. He saw clearly that Muriel was a girl who would have to be handled firmly. There was nothing of the possessive Victorian male about him – he flattered himself that he was essentially modern and broadminded in his outlook – but if Muriel supposed that he was going to stand by like a clam while she went on Babylonian orgies all over the place with pop-eyed, smirking, toothbrush-moustached Guardees, she was due for a rude awakening.

And Sacheverell Mulliner did not mean maybe.

For an instant, he toyed with the idea of hailing another cab and following them. Then he thought better of it. He was enraged, but still master of himself. When he ticked Muriel off, as he intended to do, he wished to tick her off alone. If she was in London, she was, no doubt, staying with her aunt in Ennismore Gardens. He would get a bit of food and go on there at his leisure.

The butler at Ennismore Gardens informed Sacheverell, when he arrived, that Muriel was, as he supposed, visiting the house, though for the moment out to lunch. Sacheverell waited, and presently the door of the drawing-room opened and the girl came in.

She seemed delighted to see him.

'Hullo, old streptococcus,' she said. 'Here you are, eh? I rang you up this morning to ask you to give me a bite of lunch, but you were out, so I roped in Bernard instead and we buzzed off to the Savoy in a taximeter.'

'I saw you,' said Sacheverell coldly.

'Did you? You poor chump, why didn't you yell?'

'I had no desire to meet your Cousin Bernard,' said Sacheverell, still speaking in the same frigid voice. 'And, while we are on this distasteful subject, I must request you not to see him again.'

The girl stared.

'You must do how much?'

'I must request you not to see him again,' repeated Sacheverell. 'I do not wish you to continue your Cousin Bernard's acquaintance. I do not like his looks, nor do I approve of my fiancée lunching alone with young men.'

Muriel seemed bewildered.

'You want me to tie a can to poor old Bernàrd?' she gasped.

'I insist upon it.'

'But, you poor goop, we were children together.'

Sacheverell shrugged his shoulders.

'If,' he said, 'you survived knowing Bernard as a child, why not be thankful and let it go at that? Why deliberately come up for more punishment by seeking him out now? Well, there it is,' said Sacheverell crisply. 'I have told you my wishes, and you will respect them.'

Muriel appeared to be experiencing a difficulty in finding words. She was bubbling like a saucepan on the point of coming to the boil. Nor could any unprejudiced critic have blamed her for emotion. The last time she had seen Sacheverell, it must be remembered, he had been the sort of man who made a shrinking violet look like a Chicago gangster. And here he was now, staring her in the eye and shooting off his head for all the world as if he were Mussolini informing the Italian Civil Service of a twelve per cent cut in their weekly salary.

'And now,' said Sacheverell, 'there is another matter of which I wish to speak. I am anxious to see your father as soon as possible, in order to announce our engagement to him. It is quite time that he learned what my plans are. I shall be glad, therefore, if you will make arrangements to put me up at the Towers this coming weekend. Well,' concluded Sacheverell, glancing at his watch, 'I must be going. I have several matters to attend to, and your luncheon with your cousin was so prolonged that the hour is already late. Goodbye. We shall meet on Saturday.'

Sacheverell was feeling at the top of his form when he set out for Branksome Towers on the following Saturday. The eighth lesson of his course on how to develop an iron will had reached him by the morning post, and he studied it on the train. It was a pippin. It showed you exactly how Napoleon had got that way, and there was some technical stuff about narrowing the eyes and fixing them keenly on people which alone was worth the money. He alighted at Market Branksome Station in a glow of self-confidence. The only thing that troubled him was a fear lest Sir Redvers might madly attempt anything in the nature of opposition to his plans. He did not wish to be compelled to scorch the poor old man to a crisp at his own dinner-table.

He was meditating on this and resolving to remember to do his best to let the colonel down as lightly as possible, when a voice spoke his name.

'Mr Mulliner?'

He turned. He supposed he was obliged to believe his eyes. And, if he did believe his eyes, the man standing beside him was none other than Muriel's cousin Bernard.

'They sent me down to meet you,' continued Bernard. 'I'm the old boy's nephew. Shall we totter to the car?'

Sacheverell was beyond speech. The thought that, after what he had said, Muriel should have invited her cousin to the Towers had robbed him of utterance. He followed the other to the car in silence.

In the drawing-room of the Towers they found Muriel, already dressed for dinner, brightly shaking up cocktails.

'So you got here?' said Muriel.

At another time her manner might have struck Sacheverell as odd. There was an unwonted hardness in it. Her eye, though he was too preoccupied to notice it, had a dangerous gleam.

'Yes,' he replied shortly. 'I got here.'

'The Bish arrived yet?' asked Bernard.

'Not yet. Father had a telegram from him. He won't be along till late-ish. The Bishop of Bognor is coming to confirm a bevy of the local yokels,' said Muriel, turning to Sacheverell.

'Oh?' said Sacheverell. He was not interested in bishops. They left him cold. He was interested in nothing but her explanation of how her repellent cousin came to be here tonight in defiance of his own expressed wishes.

'Well,' said Bernard, 'I suppose I'd better be going up and disguising myelf as a waiter.'

'I, too,' said Sacheverell. He turned to Muriel. 'I take it I am in the Blue Suite, as before?'

'No,' said Muriel. 'You're in the Garden Room. You see – '

'I see perfectly,' said Sacheverell curtly.

He turned on his heel and stalked to the door.

The indignation which Sacheverell had felt on seeing Bernard at the station was as nothing compared with that which seethed within him as he dressed for dinner. That Bernard should be at the Towers at all was monstrous. That he should have been given the star bedroom in preference to himself, Sacheverell Mulliner, was one of those things before which the brain reels.

As you are doubtless aware, the distribution of bedrooms in country houses is as much a matter of rigid precedence as the distribution of dressing-rooms at a theatre. The nibs get the best ones, the small fry squash in where they can. If Sacheverell had been a *prima donna* told off to dress with the second character-woman, he could not have been more mortified.

It was not simply that the Blue Suite was the only one in the house with a bathroom of its own: it was the principle of the thing. The fact that he was pigging it in the Garden Room, while Bernard wallowed in luxury in the Blue Suite was tantamount to a declaration on Muriel's part that she intended to get back at him for the attitude which he had taken over her luncheon-party. It was a slight, a deliberate snub, and Sacheverell came down to dinner coldly resolved to nip all this nonsense in the bud without delay.

Wrapped in his thoughts, he paid no attention to the conversation during the early part of dinner. He sipped a moody spoonful or two of soup and toyed with a morsel of salmon, but spiritually he was apart. It was only when the saddle of lamb had been distributed and the servitors had begun to come round with the vegetables that he was roused from his reverie by a sharp, barking noise from the head of the table, not unlike the note of a man-eating tiger catching sight of a Hindu peasant; and, glancing up, he perceived that it proceeded from Sir Redvers Branksome. His host was staring in an unpleasant manner at a dish which had just been placed under his nose by the butler.

It was in itself a commonplace enough occurence – merely the old, old story of the head of the family kicking at the spinach; but for some reason it annoyed Sacheverell intensely. His strained nerves were jangled by the animal cries which had begun to fill the air, and he told himself that Sir Redvers, if he did not switch it off pretty quick, was going to be put through it in no uncertain fashion.

Sir Redvers, meanwhile, unconscious of impending doom, was glaring at the dish.

'What,' he inquired in a hoarse, rasping voice, 'is this dashed, sloppy, disgusting, slithery, gangrened mess?'

The butler did not reply. He had been through all this before. He merely increased in volume the detached expression which good butlers wear on these occasions. He looked like a prominent banker refusing to speak without advice of counsel. It was Muriel who supplied the neccessary information.

'It's spinach, Father.'

'Then take it away and give it to the cat. You know I hate spinach.'

'But it's so good for you.'

'Who says it's good for me?'

'All the doctors. It bucks you up if you haven't enough hæmoglobins.'

'I have plenty of hæmoglobins,' said the colonel testily. 'More than I know what to do with.'

'It's full of iron.'

'Iron!' The colonel's eyebrows had drawn themselves together into a single, formidable zareba of hair. He snorted fiercely. 'Iron! Do you take me for a sword-swallower? Are you under the impression that I am an ostrich, that I should browse on iron? Perhaps you would like me to tuck away a few door-knobs and a couple of pairs of roller-skates? Or a small portion of tin-tacks? Iron, forsooth!'

Just, in short, the ordinary, conventional spinach-row of the better-class English home; but Sacheverell was in no mood for it. This bickering and wrangling irritated him, and he decided that it must stop. He half rose from his chair.

'Branksome,' he said in a quiet, level voice, 'you will eat your spinach.'

'Eh? What? What's that?'

'You will eat your nice spinach immediately, Branksome,' said Sacheverell. And at the same time he narrowed his eyes and fixed them keenly on his host.

And suddenly the rich purple colour began to die out of the man's cheeks. Gradually his eyebrows crept back into their normal position. For a brief while he met Sacheverell's eye; then he dropped his own and a weak smile came into his face.

'Well, well,' he said, with a pathetic attempt at bluffness, as he reached over and grabbed the spoon. 'What have we here? Spinach, eh? Capital, capital! Full of iron, I believe, and highly recommended by the medical profession.'

And he dug in and scooped up a liberal portion.

A short silence followed, broken only by the sloshing sound of the colonel eating spinach. Then Sacheverell spoke.

'I wish to see you in your study immediately after dinner, Branksome,' he said curtly.

                              *   *   *

Muriel was playing the piano when Sacheverell came into the drawing-room some forty minutes after the conclusion of dinner. She was interpreting a work by one of those Russian composers who seem to have been provided by Nature especially with a view to soothing the nervous systems of young girls who are not feeling quite themselves. It was a piece from which the best results are obtained by hauling off and delivering a series of overhand swings which make the instrument wobble like the engine-room of a liner; and Muriel, who was a fine, sturdy girl, was putting a lot of beef into it.

The change in Sacheverell had distressed Muriel Branksome beyond measure. Contemplating him, she felt as she had sometimes felt at a dance when she had told her partner to bring her ice-cream and he had come frisking up with a bowl of mock-turtle soup. Cheated – that is what she felt she had been. She had given her heart to a mild, sweet-natured, lovable lamb; and the moment she had done so he had suddenly flung off his sheep's clothing and said: 'April fool! I'm a wolf!'

Haughty by nature, Muriel Branksome was incapable of bearing anything in the shape of bossiness from the male. Her proud spirit revolted at it. And bossiness had become Sacheverell Mulliner's middle name.

The result was that, when Sacheverell entered the drawing-room, he found his loved one all set for the big explosion.

He suspected nothing. He was pleased with himself, and looked it.

'I put your father in his place all right at dinner, what?' said Sacheverell, buoyantly. 'Put him right where he belonged, I think.'

Muriel gnashed her teeth in a quiet undertone.

'He isn't so hot,' said Sacheverell. 'The way you used to talk about him, one would have thought he was the real ginger. Quite the reverse I found him. As nice a soft-spoken old bird as one could wish to meet. When I told him about our engagement, he just came and rubbed his head against my leg and rolled over with his paws in the air.'

Muriel swallowed softly.

'Our what?' she said.

'Our engagement.'

'Oh?' said Muriel. 'You told him we were engaged, did you?'

'I certainly did.'

'Then you can jolly well go back,' said Muriel, blazing into sudden fury, 'and tell him you were talking through your hat.'

Sacheverell stared.

'That last remark once again, if you don't mind.'

'A hundred times, if you wish it,' said Muriel. 'Get this well into your fat head. Memorize it carefully. If necessary, write it on your cuff. I am not going to marry you. I wouldn't marry you to win a substantial bet or to please an old school-friend. I wouldn't marry you if you offered me all the money in the world. So there!'

Sacheverell blinked. He was taken aback.

'This sounds like the bird,' he said.

'It is the bird.'

'You are really giving me the old raspberry?'

'I am.'

'Don't you love your little Sacheverell?'

'No, I don't. I think my little Sacheverell is a mess.'

There was a silence. Sacheverell regarded her with lowered brows. Then he uttered a short, bitter laugh.

'Oh, very well,' he said.

Sacheverell Mulliner boiled with jealous rage. Of course, he saw what had happened. The girl had fallen once more under the glamorous spell of her Cousin Bernard, and proposed to throw a Mulliner's heart aside like a soiled glove. But if she thought he was going to accept the situation meekly and say no more about it, she would soon discover her error.

Sacheverell loved this girl – not with the tepid preference which passes for love in these degenerate days, but with all the medieval fervour of a rich and passionate soul. And he intended to marry her. Yes, if the whole Brigade of Guards stood between, he was resolved to walk up the aisle with her arm in his and help her cut the cake at the subsequent breakfast.

Bernard . . . ! He would soon settle Bernard.

For all his inner ferment, Sacheverell retained undiminished the clearness of mind which characterizes Mulliners in times of crisis. An hour's walk up and down the terrace had shown him what he must do. There was nothing to be gained by acting hastily. He must confront Bernard alone in the silent night, when they would be free from danger of interruption and he could set the full force of his iron personality playing over the fellow like a hose.

And so it came about that the hour of eleven, striking from the clock above the stables, found Sacheverell Mulliner sitting grimly in the Blue Suite, waiting for his victim to arrive.

His brain was like ice. He had matured his plan of campaign. He did not intend to hurt the man – merely to order him to leave the house instantly and never venture to see or speak to Muriel again.

So mused Sacheverell Mulliner, unaware that no Cousin Bernard would come within ten yards of the Blue Suite that night. Bernard had already retired to rest in the Pink Room on the third floor, which had been his roosting-place from the beginning of his visit. The Blue Suite, being the abode of the most honoured guest had, of course, been earmarked from the start for the Bishop of Bognor.

Carburettor trouble and a series of detours had delayed the bishop in his journey to Branksome Towers. At first, he had hoped to make it in time for dinner. Then he had anticipated an arrival at about nine-thirty. Finally, he was exceedingly relieved to reach his destination shortly after eleven.

A quick sandwich and a small limejuice and soda were all that the prelate asked of his host at that advanced hour. These consumed, he announced himself ready for bed, and Colonel Branksome conducted him to the door of the Blue Suite.

'I hope you will find everything comfortable, my dear Bishop,' he said.

'I am convinced of it, my dear Branksome,' said the bishop. 'And tomorrow, I trust I shall feel less fatigued and in a position to meet the rest of your guests.'

'There is only one beside my nephew Bernard. A young fellow named Mulliner.'

'Mulligan?'

'Mulliner.'

'Ah, yes,' said the bishop. 'Mulliner.'

And simultaneously, inside the room, my nephew Sacheverell sprang from his chair, and stood frozen, like a statue.

In narrating this story, I have touched lightly upon Sacheverell's career at Harborough College. I shall not be digressing now if I relate briefly what had always been to him the high spot in it.

One sunny summer day, when a lad of fourteen and a half, my nephew had sought to relieve the tedium of school routine by taking a golf-ball and flinging it against the side of the building, his intention being to catch it as it rebounded. Unfortunately, when it came to the acid test, the ball did not rebound. Instead of going due north, it went nor'-nor'-east, with the result that it passed through the window of the headmaster's library at the precise moment when that high official was about to lean out for a breath of air. And the next moment, a voice, proceeding apparently from heaven, had spoken one word. The voice was like the deeper notes of a great organ, and the word was the single word:

'MULLINER !!!'

And, just as the word Sacheverell now heard was the same word, so was the voice the same voice.

To appreciate my nephew's concern, you must understand that the episode which I have just related had remained green in his memory right through the years. His pet nightmare, and the one which had had so depressing an effect on his *morale*, had always been the one where he found himself standing, quivering and helpless, while a voice uttered the single word 'Mulliner!'

Little wonder, then, that he now remained for an instant paralysed. His only coherent thought was a bitter reflection that somebody might have had the sense to tell him that the Bishop of Bognor was his old headmaster, the Rev. J. G. Smethurst. Naturally, in that case, he would have been out of the place in two strides. But they had simply said the Bishop of Bognor, and it had meant nothing to him.

Now that it was too late, he seemed to recall having heard somebody somewhere say something about the Rev. J. G. Smethurst becoming a bishop; and even in this moment of collapse he was able to feel a thrill of justifiable indignation at the shabbiness of the act. It wasn't fair for headmasters to change their names like this and take people unawares. The Rev. J. G. Smethurst might argue as much as he liked, but he couldn't get away from the fact that he had played a shady trick on the community. The man was practically going about under an alias.

But this was no time for abstract meditations on the question of right and wrong. He must hide . . . hide.

Yet why, you are asking, should my nephew Sacheverell wish to hide? Had he not in eight easy lessons from the Leave-It-To-Us Correspondence School acquired complete self-confidence and an iron will? He had, but in this awful moment all that he had learned had passed from him like a dream. The years had rolled back, and he was a fifteen-year-old jelly again, in the full grip of his Headmaster Phobia.

To dive under the bed was with Sacheverell Mulliner the work of a moment. And, there, as the door opened, he lay, holding his breath and trying to keep his ears from rustling in the draught.

Smethurst (alias Bognor) was a leisurely undresser. He doffed his gaiters, and then for some little time stood, apparently in a reverie, humming one of the song-hits from the psalms. Eventually, he resumed his disrobing, but even then the ordeal was not over. As far as Sacheverell could see, in the constrained position in which he was lying, the bishop was doing a few setting-up exercises. Then he went into the bathroom and cleaned his teeth. It was only at the end of half an hour that he finally climbed between the sheets and switched off the light.

For a long while after he had done so, Sacheverell remained where he was, motion-less. But presently a faint, rhythmical sound from the neighbourhood of the pillows assured him that the other was asleep, and he crawled cautiously from his lair. Then, stepping with infinite caution, he moved to the door, opened it, and passed through.

The relief which Sacheverell felt as he closed the door behind him would have been less intense, had he realized that through a slight mistake in his bearings he had not, as he supposed, reached the haven of the passage outside but had merely entered the bath-room. This fact was not brought home to him until he had collided with an unexpected chair, upset it, tripped over a bath-mat, clutched for support into the darkness and brushed from off the glass shelf above the basin a series of bottles, containing – in the order given – Scalpo ('It Fertilizes the Follicles'), Soothine – for applying to the face after shaving, and Doctor Wilberforce's Golden Gargle in the large or seven-and-sixpenny size. These, crashing to the floor, would have revealed the truth to a far duller man than Sacheverell Mulliner.

He acted swiftly. From the room beyond, there had come to his ears the unmistakable sound of a bishop sitting up in bed, and he did not delay. Hastily groping for the switch, he turned on the light. He found the bolt and shot it. Only then did he sit down on the edge of the bath and attempt to pass the situation under careful review.

He was not allowed long for quiet thinking. Through the door came the sound of deep breathing. Then a voice spoke.

'Who is they-ah?'

As always in the dear old days of school, it caused Sacheverell to leap six inches. He had just descended again, when another voice spoke in the bedroom. It was that of Colonel Sir Redvers Branksome, who had heard the crashing of glass and had come, in the kindly spirit of a good host, to make inquiries.

'What is the matter, my dear Bishop?' he asked.

'It is a burglar, my dear Colonel,' said the bishop.

'A burglar?'

'A burglar. He has locked himself in the bathroom.'

'Then how extremely fortunate,' said the colonel heartily, 'that I should have brought along this battle-axe and shotgun on the chance.'

Sacheverell felt that it was time to join in the conversation. He went to the door and put his lips against the keyhole.

'It's all right,' he said, quaveringly.

The colonel uttered a surprised exclamation.

'He says it's all right,' he reported.

'Why does he say it is all right?' asked the bishop.

'I didn't ask him,' replied the colonel. 'He just said it was all right.'

The bishop sniffed peevishly.

'It is not all right,' he said, with a certain heat. 'And I am at a loss to understand why the man should affect to assume that it is. I suggest, my dear Colonel, that our best method of procedure is as follows: you take the shotgun and stand in readiness, and I will hew down the door with this admirable battle-axe.'

And it was at this undeniably critical point in the proceedings that something soft and clinging brushed against Sacheverell's right ear, causing him to leap again – this time a matter of eight inches and a quarter. And, spinning round, he discovered that what had touched his ear was the curtain of the bathroom window.

There now came a splintering crash, and the door shook on its hinges. The bishop, with all the blood of a hundred Militant Churchmen ancestors afire within him, had started operations with the axe.

But Sacheverell scarcely heard the noise. The sight of the open window had claimed his entire attention. And now, moving nimbly, he clambered through it, alighting on what seemed to be leads.

For an instant he gazed wildly about him; then, animated, perhaps by some subconscious memory of the boy who bore 'mid snow and ice the banner with the strange device 'Excelsior!', he leaped quickly upwards and started to climb the roof.

Muriel Branksome, on retiring to her room on the floor above the Blue Suite, had not gone to bed. She was sitting at her open window, thinking, thinking.

Her thoughts were bitter ones. It was not that she felt remorseful. In giving Sacheverell the air at their recent interview, her conscience told her that she had acted rightly. He had behaved like a domineering sheik of the desert: and a dislike for domineering shieks of the desert had always been an integral part of her spiritual make-up.

But the consciousness of having justice on her side is not always enough to sustain a girl at such a time: and an aching pain gripped Muriel as she thought of the Sacheverell she had loved – the old, mild, sweet-natured Sacheverell who had asked nothing better than to gaze at her with adoring eyes, removing them only when he found it necessary to give his attention to the bit of string with which he was doing tricks. She mourned for the vanished Sacheverell.

Obviously, after what had happened, he would leave the house early in the morning – probably long before she came down, for she was a late riser. She wondered if she would ever see him again.

At this moment, she did. He was climbing up the slope of the roof towards her on his hands and knees – and, for one who was not a cat, doing it extremely well. She had hardly risen to her feet before he was standing at the window, clutching the sill.

Muriel choked. She stared at him with wide, tragic eyes.

'What do you want?' she asked harshly.

'Well, as a matter of fact,' said Sacheverell, 'I was wondering if you would mind if I hid under your bed for a bit.'

And suddenly, in the dim light, the girl saw that his face was contorted with a strange terror. And, at the spectacle, all her animosity seemed to be swept away as if on a tidal wave, and back came the old love and esteem, piping hot and as fresh as ever. An instant before, she had been wanting to beat him over the head with a brick. Now, she ached to comfort and protect him. For here once more was the Sacheverell she had worshipped – the poor, timid, fluttering, helpless pip-squeak whose hair she had always wanted to stroke and to whom she had felt a strange intermittent urge to offer lumps of sugar.

'Come right in,' she said.

He threw her a hasty word of thanks and shot over the sill. Then abruptly he stiffened, and the wild, hunted look was in his eyes again. From somewhere below there had come the deep baying of a bishop on the scent. He clutched at Muriel, and she held him to her like a mother soothing a nightmare-ridden child.

'Listen!' he whispered.

'Who are they?' asked Muriel.

'Headmasters,' panted Sacheverell. 'Droves of headmasters. And colonels. Coveys of colonels. With battle-axes and shotguns. Save me, Muriel!'

'There, there!' said Muriel. 'There, there, there!'

She directed him to the bed, and he disappeared beneath it like a diving duck.

'You will be quite safe there,' said Muriel. 'And now tell me what it is all about.'

Outside, they could hear the noise of the hue-and-cry. The original strength of the company appeared to have been augmented by the butler and a few sporting footmen. Brokenly, Sacheverell told her all.

'But what were you doing in the Blue Suite?' asked the girl, when he had concluded his tale. 'I don't understand.'

'I went to interview your Cousin Bernard, to tell him that he should marry you only over my dead body.'

'What an unpleasant idea!' said Muriel, shivering a little. 'And I don't see how it could have been done, anyway.' She paused a moment, listening to the uproar. Somewhere downstairs, footmen seemed to be falling over one another: and once there came the shrill cry of a Hunting Bishop stymied by a hat-stand. 'But what on earth,' she asked, resuming her remarks, 'made you think that I was going to marry Bernard?'

'I thought that that was why you gave me the bird.'

'Of course it wasn't. I gave you the bird because you had suddenly turned into a beastly, barking, bullying, overbearing blighter.'

There was a pause before Sacheverell spoke.

'Had I?' he said at length. 'Yes, I suppose I had. Tell me,' he contined, 'is there a good milk-train in the morning?'

'At three-forty, I believe.'

'I'll catch it.'

'Must you really go?'

'I must, indeed.'

'Oh, well,' said Muriel. 'It won't be long before we meet again. I'll run up to London one of these days, and we'll have a bit of lunch together and get married and . . .'

A gasp came from beneath the bed.

'Married! Do you really mean that you will marry me, Muriel?'

'Of course I will. The past is dead. You are my own precious angel pet again, and I love you madly, passionately. What's been the matter with you these last few weeks I can't imagine, but I can see it's all over now, so don't let's talk any more about it. Hark!' she said, holding up a finger as a sonorous booming noise filled the night, accompanied by a flood of rich oaths in what appeared to be some foreign language, possibly Hindustani. 'I think Father has tripped over the dinner-gong.'

Sacheverell did not answer. His heart was too full for words. He was thinking how deeply he loved this girl and how happy those few remarks of hers had made him.

And yet, mingled with his joy, there was something of sorrow. As the old Roman poet has it, *surgit amari aliquid.* He had just remembered that he had paid the Leave-It-To-Us Correspondence School fifteen guineas in advance for a course of twenty lessons. He was abandoning the course after taking eight. And the thought that stabbed him like a knife was that he no longer had enough self-confidence and iron will left to enable him to go to Jno. B. Philbrick, Mgr., and demand a refund.

'GALA NIGHT'

Mulliner Nights

The bar-parlour of the Anglers' Rest was fuller than usual. Our local race meeting had been held during the afternoon, and this always means a rush of custom. In addition to the *habitués*, that faithful little band of listeners which sits nightly at the feet of Mr Mulliner, there were present some half a dozen strangers. One of these, a fair-haired young Stout and Mild, wore the unmistakable air of a man who has not been fortunate in his selections. He sat staring before him with dull eyes and a drooping jaw, and nothing that his companions could do seemed able to cheer him up.

A genial Sherry and Bitters, one of the regular patrons, eyed the sufferer with bluff sympathy.

'What your friend appears to need, gentlemen,' he said, 'is a dose of Mulliner's Buck-U-Uppo.'

'What's Mulliner's Buck-U-Uppo?' asked one of the strangers, a Whisky Sour, interested. 'Never heard of it myself.'

Mr Mulliner smiled indulgently.

'He is referring,' he explained, 'to a tonic invented by my brother Wilfred, the well-known analytical chemist. It is not often administered to human beings, having been designed primarily to encourage elephants in India to conduct themselves with an easy nonchalance during the tiger-hunts which are so popular in that country. But occasionally human beings do partake of it, with impressive results. I was telling the company here not long ago of the remarkable effect it had on my nephew Augustine, the curate.'

'It bucked him up?'

'It bucked him up very considerably. It acted on his bishop, too, when he tried it, in a similar manner. It is undoubtedly a most efficient tonic, strong and invigorating.'

'How is Augustine, by the way?' asked the Sherry and Bitters.

'Extremely well. I received a letter from him only this morning. I am not sure if I told you, but he is a vicar now, at Walsingford-below-Chiveney-on-Thames. A delightful resort, mostly honeysuckle and apple-cheeked villagers.'

'Anything been happening to him lately?'

'It is strange that you should ask that,' said Mr Mulliner, finishing his hot Scotch and lemon and rapping gently on the table. 'In this letter to which I allude he has quite an interesting story to relate. It deals with the love of Ronald Bracy-Gascoigne and Hypatia Wace. Hypatia is a school-friend of my nephew's wife. She has been staying at the vicarage nursing her through a sharp attack of mumps. She is also the niece and ward of Augustine's superior of the Cloth, the Bishop of Stortford.'

'Was that the bishop who took the Buck-U-Uppo?'

'The same,' said Mr Mulliner. 'As for Ronald Bracy-Gascoigne, he is a young man of independent means who resides in the neighbourhood. He is, of course, one of the Berkshire Bracy-Gascoignes.'

'Ronald,' said a Lemonade and Angostura thoughtfully. 'Now, there's a name I never cared for.'

'In that respect,' said Mr Mulliner, 'you differ from Hypatia Wace. She thought it swell. She loved Ronald Bracy-Gascoigne with all the fervour of a young girl's heart, and they were provisionally engaged to be married. Provisionally, I say, because, before the firing-squad could actually be assembled, it was necessary for the young couple to obtain the consent of the Bishop of Stortford. Mark that, gentlemen. Their engagement was subject to the Bishop of Stortford's consent. This was the snag that protruded jaggedly from the middle of the primrose path of their happiness, and for quite a while it seemed as if Cupid must inevitably stub his toe on it.'

I will select as the point at which to begin my tale (said Mr Mulliner) a lovely evening in June, when all Nature seemed to smile and the rays of the setting sun fell like molten gold upon the picturesque garden of the vicarage at Walsingford-below-Chiveney-on-Thames. On a rustic bench beneath a spreading elm, Hypatia Wace and Ronald Bracy-Gascoigne watched the shadows lengthening across the smooth lawn: and to the girl there appeared something symbolical and ominous about this creeping blackness. She shivered. To her, it was as if the sunbathed lawn represented her happiness and the shadows the doom that was creeping upon it.

'Are you doing anything at the moment, Ronnie?' she asked.

'Eh?' said Ronald Bracy-Gascoigne. 'What? Doing anything? Oh, you mean doing anything? No, I'm not doing anything.'

'Then kiss me,' cried Hypatia.

'Right-ho,' said the young man. 'I see what you mean. Rather a scheme. I will.'

He did so: and for some moments they clung together in a close embrace. Then Ronald, releasing her gently, began to slap himself between the shoulder-blades.

'Beetle or something down my back,' he explained. 'Probably fell off the tree.'

'Kiss me again,' whispered Hypatia.

'In one second, old girl,' said Ronald. 'The instant I've dealt with this beetle or something. Would you mind just fetching me a whack on about the fourth knob of the spine, reading from the top downwards. I fancy that would make it think a bit.'

Hypatia uttered a sharp exclamation.

'Is this a time,' she cried passionately, 'to talk of beetles?'

'Well, you know, don't you know,' said Ronald, with a touch of apology in his voice, 'they seem rather to force themselves on your attention when they get down your back. I dare say you've had the same experience yourself. I don't suppose in the ordinary way I mention beetles half a dozen times a year, but . . . I should say the fifth knob would be about the spot now. A good, sharp slosh with plenty of follow-through ought to do the trick.'

Hypatia clenched her hands. She was seething with that febrile exasperation which, since the days of Eve, has come upon women who find themselves linked to a cloth-head.

'You poor sap,' she said tensely. 'You keep babbling about beetles, and you don't appear to realize that, if you want to kiss me, you'd better cram in all the kissing you can now, while the going is good. It doesn't seem to have occurred to you that after tonight you're going to fade out of the picture.'

'Oh, I say, no! Why?'

'My Uncle Percy arrives this evening.'

'The Bishop?'

'Yes. And my Aunt Priscilla.'

'And you think they won't be any too frightfully keen on me?'

'I know they won't. I wrote and told them we were engaged, and I had a letter this afternoon saying you wouldn't do.'

'No, I say, really? Oh, I say, dash it!'

' "Out of the question", my uncle said. And underlined it.'

'Not really? Not absolutely underlined it?'

'Yes. Twice. In very black ink.'

A cloud darkened the young man's face. The beetle had begun to try out a few tentative dancesteps on the small of his back, but he ignored it. A Tiller troupe of beetles could not have engaged his attention now.

'But what's he got against me?'

'Well, for one thing he has heard that you were sent down from Oxford.'

'But all the best men are. Look at What's-his-name. Chap who wrote poems. Shellac, or some such name.'

'And then he knows that you dance a lot.'

'What's wrong with dancing? I'm not very well up in these things, but didn't David dance before Saul? Or am I thinking of a couple of other fellows? Anyway, I know that somebody danced before somebody and was extremely highly thought of in consequence.'

'David . . .'

'I'm not saying it *was* David, mind you. It may quite easily have been Samuel.'

'David . . .'

'Or even Nimshi, the son of Bimshi, or somebody like that.'

'David or Samuel, or Nimshi the son of Bimshi,' said Hypatia, 'did not dance at the Home From Home.'

Her allusion was to the latest of those frivolous night-clubs which spring up from time to time on the reaches of the Thames which are within a comfortable distance from London. This one stood some half a mile from the vicarage gates.

'Is that what the Bish is beefing about?' demanded Ronald, genuinely astonished. 'You don't mean to tell me he really objects to the Home From Home? Why, a cathedral couldn't be more rigidly respectable. Does he realize that the place has only been raided five times in the whole course of its existence? A few simple words of explanation will put all this right. I'll have a talk with the old boy.'

Hypatia shook her head.

'No,' she said. 'It's no use talking. He has made his mind up. One of the things he said in his letter was that, rather than countenance my union to a worthless worldling like you, he would gladly see me turned into a pillar of salt like Lot's wife, Genesis xix. 26. And nothing could be fairer than that, could it? So what I would suggest is that you start in immediately to fold me in your arms and cover my face with kisses. It's the last chance you'll get.'

The young man was about to follow her advice, for he could see that there was much in what she said: but at this moment there came from the direction of the house the sound of a manly voice trolling the Psalm for the Second Sunday after Septuagesima. And an instant later their host, the Rev. Augustine Mulliner, appeared in sight. He saw them and came hurrying across the garden, leaping over the flower-beds with extraordinary lissomness.

'Amazing elasticity that bird has, both physical and mental,' said Ronald Bracy-

Gascoigne, eyeing Augustine, as he approached, with a gloomy envy. 'How does he get that way?'

'He was telling me last night,' said Hypatia. 'He has a tonic which he takes regularly. It is called Mulliner's Buck-U-Uppo, and acts directly upon the red corpuscles.'

'I wish he would give the Bish a swig of it,' said Ronald moodily. A sudden light of hope came into his eyes. 'I say, Hyp, old girl,' he exclaimed. 'That's rather a notion. Don't you think it's rather a notion? It looks to me like something of an idea. If the Bish were to dip his beak into the stuff, it might make him take a brighter view of me.'

Hypatia, like all girls who intend to be good wives, made it a practice to look on any suggestions thrown out by her future lord and master as fatuous and futile.

'I never heard anything so silly,' she said.

'Well, I wish you would try it. No harm in trying it, what?'

'Of course I shall do nothing of the kind.'

'Well, I do think you might try it,' said Ronald. 'I mean, try it, don't you know.'

He could speak no further on the matter, for now they were no longer alone. Augustine had come up. His kindly face looked grave.

'I say, Ronnie, old bloke,' said Augustine, 'I don't want to hurry you, but I think I ought to inform you that the Bishes, male and female, are even now on their way up from the station. I should be popping, if I were you. The prudent man looketh well to his going. Proverbs, xiv. 15.'

'All right,' said Ronald sombrely. 'I suppose,' he added, turning to the girl, 'you wouldn't care to sneak out tonight and come and have one final spot of shoe-slithering at the Home From Home? It's a Gala Night. Might be fun, what? Give us a chance of saying goodbye properly, and all that.'

'I never heard anything so silly,' said Hypatia, mechanically. 'Of course I'll come.'

'Right-ho. Meet you down the road about twelve then,' said Ronald Bracy-Gascoigne.

He walked swiftly away, and presently was lost to sight behind the shrubbery. Hypatia turned with a choking sob, and Augustine took her hand and squeezed it gently.

'Cheer up, old onion,' he urged. 'Don't lose hope. Remember, many waters cannot quench love. Song of Solomon, viii.7.'

'I don't see what quenching love has got to do with it,' said Hypatia peevishly. 'Our trouble is that I've got an uncle complete with gaiters and a hat with bootlaces on it who can't see Ronnie with a telescope.'

'I know.' Augustine nodded sympathetically. 'And my heart bleeds for you. I've been through all this sort of thing myself. When I was trying to marry Jane, I was stymied by a father-in-law-to-be who had to be seen to be believed. A chap, I assure you, who combined chronic shortness of temper with the ability to bend pokers round his biceps. Tact was what won him over, and tact is what I propose to employ in your case. I have an idea at the back of my mind. I won't tell you what it is, but you may take it from me it's the real tabasco.'

'How kind you are, Augustine!' sighed the girl.

'It comes from mixing with Boy Scouts. You may have noticed that the village is stiff with them. But don't you worry, old girl. I owe you a lot for the way you've looked after Jane these last weeks, and I'm going to see you through. If I can't fix up your little affair, I'll eat my Hymns Ancient and Modern. And uncooked at that.'

And with these brave words Augustine Mulliner turned two hand-springs, vaulted over the rustic bench, and went about his duties in the parish.

Augustine was rather relieved, when he came down to dinner that night, to find that Hypatia was not to be among those present. The girl was taking her meal on a tray with Jane, his wife, in the invalid's bedroom, and he was consequently able to embark with freedom on the discussion of her affairs. As soon as the servants had left the room, accordingly he addressed himself to the task.

'Now listen, you two dear good souls,' he said. 'What I want to talk to you about, now that we are alone, is the business of Hypatia and Ronald Bracy-Gascoigne.'

The lady bishopess pursed her lips, displeased. She was a woman of ample and majestic build. A friend of Augustine's, who had been attached to the Tank Corps during the War, had once said that he knew nothing that brought the old days back more vividly than the sight of her. All she needed, he maintained, was a steering-wheel and a couple of machine-guns, and you could have moved her up into any Front Line and no questions asked.

'Please, Mr Mulliner!' she said coldly.

Augustine was not to be deterred. Like all the Mulliners, he was at heart a man of reckless courage.

'They tell me you are thinking of bunging a spanner into the works,' he said. 'Not true, I hope?'

'Quite true, Mr Mulliner. Am I not right, Percy?'

'Quite,' said the bishop.

'We have made careful enquiries about the young man, and are satisfied that he is entirely unsuitable.'

'Would you say that?' said Augustine. 'A pretty good egg, I've always found him. What's your main objection to the poor lizard?'

The lady bishopess shivered.

'We learn that he is frequently to be seen dancing at an advanced hour, not only in gilded London night-clubs but even in what should be the purer atmosphere of Walsingford-below-Chiveney-on-Thames. There is a resort in this neighbourhood known, I believe, as the Home From Home.'

'Yes, just down the road,' said Augustine. 'It's a Gala Night tonight, if you cared to look in. Fancy dress optional.'

'I understand that he is to be seen there almost nightly. Now, against dancing *qua* dancing,' proceeded the lady bishopess, 'I have nothing to say. Properly conducted, it is a pleasing and innocuous pastime. In my own younger days I myself was no mean exponent of the polka, the schottische and the Roger de Coverley. Indeed, it was at a Dance in Aid of the Distressed Daughters of Clergymen of the Church of England Relief Fund that I first met my husband.'

'Really?' said Augustine. 'Well, cheerio!' he said, draining his glass of port.

'But dancing, as the term is understood nowadays, is another matter. I have no doubt that what you call a Gala Night would prove, on inspection, to be little less than one of those orgies where perfect strangers of both sexes unblushingly throw coloured celluloid balls at one another and in other ways behave in a manner more suitable to the Cities of the Plain than to our dear England. No, Mr Mulliner, if this young man Ronald Bracy-Gascoigne is in the habit of frequenting places of the type of the Home From Home, he is not a fit mate for a pure young girl like my niece Hypatia. Am I not correct, Percy?'

'Perfectly correct, my dear.'

'Oh, right-ho, then,' said Augustine philosophically, and turned the conversation to the forthcoming Pan-Anglican synod.

Living in the country had given Augustine Mulliner the excellent habit of going early to bed. He had a sermon to compose on the morrow, and in order to be fresh and at his best in the morning he retired shortly before eleven. And, as he had anticipated an unbroken eight hours of refreshing sleep, it was with no little annoyance that he became aware, towards midnight, of a hand on his shoulder, shaking him. Opening his eyes, he found that the light had been switched on and that the Bishop of Stortford was standing at his bedside.

'Hullo!' said Augustine. 'Anything wrong?'

The bishop smiled genially, and hummed a bar or two of the hymn for those of riper years at sea. He was plainly in excellent spirits.

'Nothing, my dear fellow,' he replied. 'In fact, very much the reverse. How are you, Mulliner?'

'I feel fine, Bish.'

'I'll bet you two chasubles to a hassock you don't feel as fine as I do,' said the bishop. 'It must be something in the air of this place. I haven't felt like this since Boat Race Night of the year 1893. Wow!' he continued. 'Whoopee! How goodly are thy tents, O Jacob, and thy tabernacles, O Israel! Numbers, xliv. 5.' And, gripping the rail of the bed, he endeavoured to balance himself on his hands with his feet in the air.

Augustine looked at him with growing concern. He could not rid himself of a curious feeling that there was something sinister behind this ebullience. Often before, he had seen his guest in a mood of dignified animation, for the robust cheerfulness of the other's outlook was famous in ecclesiastical circles. But here, surely, was something more than dignified animation.

'Yes,' proceeded the bishop, completing his gymnastics and sitting down on the bed, 'I feel like a fighting-cock, Mulliner. I am full of beans. And the idea of wasting the golden hours of the night in bed seemed so silly that I had to get up and look in on you for a chat. Now, this is what I want to speak to you about, my dear fellow. I wonder if you recollect writing to me – round about Epiphany, it would have been – to tell me of the hit you made in the Boy Scouts pantomime here? You played Sindbad the Sailor, if I am not mistaken?'

'That's right.'

'Well, what I came here to ask, my dear Mulliner, was this. Can you, by any chance, lay your hand on that Sindbad costume? I want to borrow it, if I may.'

'What for?'

'Never mind what for, Mulliner. Sufficient for you to know that motives of the soundest churchmanship render it essential for me to have that suit.'

'Very well, Bish. I'll find it for you tomorrow.'

'Tomorrow will not do. This dilatory spirit of putting things off, this sluggish attitude of *laissez-faire* and procrastination,' said the bishop, frowning, 'are scarcely what I expected to find in you, Mulliner. But there,' he added, more kindly, 'let us say no more. Just dig up that Sindbad costume and look slippy about it, and we will forget the whole matter. What does it look like?'

'Just an ordinary sailor-suit, Bish.'

'Excellent. Some species of head-gear goes with it, no doubt?'

'A cap with HMS *Blotto* on the band.'

'Admirable. Then, my dear fellow,' said the bishop, beaming, 'if you will just let me have it, I will trouble you no further tonight. Your day's toil in the vineyard has earned repose. The sleep of the labouring man is sweet. Ecclesiastes, v. 12.'

As the door closed behind his guest, Augustine was conscious of a definite uneasiness. Only once before had he seen his spiritual superior in quite this exalted condition. That had been two years ago, when they had gone down to Harchester College to unveil the statue of Lord Hemel of Hempstead. On that occasion, ·he recollected, the bishop, under the influence of an overdose of Buck-U-Uppo, had not been content with unveiling the statue. He had gone out in the small hours of the night and painted it pink. Augustine could still recall the surge of emotion which had come upon him when, leaning out of the window, he had observed the prelate climbing up the waterspout on his way back to his room. And he still remembered the sorrowful pity with which he had listened to the other's lame explanation that he was a cat belonging to the cook.

Sleep, in the present circumstances, was out of the question. With a pensive sigh, Augustine slipped on a dressing-gown and went downstairs to his study. It would ease his mind, he thought, to do a little work on that sermon of his.

Augustine's study was on the ground floor, looking on to the garden. It was a lovely night, and he opened the french windows, the better to enjoy the soothing scents of the flowers beyond. Then, seating himself at his desk, he began to work.

The task of composing a sermon which should practically make sense and yet not be above the heads of his rustic flock was always one that caused Augustine Mulliner to concentrate intensely. Soon he was lost in his labour and oblivious to everything but the problem of how to find a word of one syllable that meant Supralapsarianism. A glaze of preoccupation had come over his eyes, and the tip of his tongue, protruding from the left corner of his mouth, revolved in slow circles.

From this waking trance he emerged slowly to the realization that somebody was speaking his name and that he was no longer alone in the room.

Seated in his arm-chair, her lithe young body wrapped in a green dressing-gown, was Hypatia Wace.

'Hullo!' said Augustine, staring. 'You here?'

'Hullo,' said Hypatia. 'Yes, I'm here.'

'I thought you had gone to the Home From Home to meet Ronald.'

Hypatia shook her head.

'We never made it,' she said. 'Ronnie rang up to say that he had had a private tip that the place was to be raided tonight. So we thought it wasn't safe to start anything.'

'Quite right,' said Augustine approvingly. 'Prudence first. Whatsoever thou takest in hand, remember the end and thou shalt never do amiss. Ecclesiastes, vii.36.'

Hypatia dabbed at her eyes with her handkerchief.

'I couldn't sleep, and I saw the light, so I came down. I'm so miserable, Augustine.'

'About this Ronnie business?'

'Yes.'

'There, there. Everything's going to be hotsy-totsy.'

'I don't see how you make that out. Have you heard Uncle Percy and Aunt Priscilla talk about Ronnie? They couldn't be more off the poor, unfortunate fish if he were the Scarlet Woman of Babylon.'

'I know. I know. But, as I hinted this afternoon, I have a little plan. I have been giving your case a good deal of thought, and I think you will agree with me that it is your Aunt Priscilla who is the real trouble. Sweeten her, and the Bish will follow her lead. What she thinks today, he always thinks tomorrow. In other words, if we can win her over, he will give his consent in a minute. Am I wrong or am I right?'

Hypatia nodded.

'Yes,' she said. 'That's right, as far as it goes. Uncle Percy always does what Aunt Priscilla tells him to. But how are you going to sweeten her?'

'With Mulliner's Buck-U-Uppo. You remember how often I have spoken to you of the properties of that admirable tonic. It changes the whole mental outlook like magic. We have only to slip a few drops into your Aunt Priscilla's hot milk tomorrow night, and you will be amazed at the results.'

'You really guarantee that?'

'Absolutely.'

'Then that's fine,' said the girl, brightening visibly, 'because that's exactly what I did this evening. Ronnie was suggesting it when you came up this afternoon, and I thought I might as well try it. I found the bottle in the cupboard in here, and I put some in Aunt Priscilla's hot milk and, in order to make a good job of it, some in Uncle Percy's toddy, too.'

An icy hand seemed to clutch at Augustine's heart. He began to understand the inwardness of the recent scene in his bedroom.

'How much?' he gasped.

'Oh, not much,' said Hypatia. 'I didn't want to poison the dear old things. About a tablespoon apiece.'

A shuddering groan came raspingly from Augustine's lips.

'Are you aware,' he said in a low, toneless voice, 'that the medium dose for an adult elephant is one teaspoonful?'

'No!'

'Yes. The most fearful consequences result from anything in the nature of an overdose.' He groaned. 'No wonder the bishop seemed a little strange in his manner just now.'

'Did he seem strange in his manner?'

Augustine nodded dully.

'He came into my room and did hand-springs on the end of the bed and went away in my Sindbad the Sailor suit.'

'What did he want that for?'

Augustine shuddered.

'I scarcely dare to face the thought,' he said, 'but can he have been contemplating a visit to the Home From Home? It is Gala Night, remember.'

'Why, of course,' said Hypatia. 'And that must have been why Aunt Priscilla came to me about an hour ago and asked me if I could lend her my Columbine costume.'

'She did!' cried Augustine.

'Certainly she did. I couldn't think what she wanted it for. But now, of course, I see.'

Augustine uttered a moan that seemed to come from the depths of his soul.

'Run up to her room and see if she is still there,' he said. 'If I'm not very much mistaken, we have sown the wind and we shall reap the whirlwind. Hosea, viii. 7.'

The girl hurried away, and Augustine began to pace the floor feverishly. He had completed five laps and was beginning a sixth, when there was a noise outside the french windows and a sailorly form shot through and fell panting into the arm-chair.

'Bish!' cried Augustine.

The bishop waved a hand, to indicate that he would be with him as soon as he had attended to this matter of taking in a fresh supply of breath, and continued to pant. Augustine watched him, deeply concerned. There was a shop-soiled look about the guest. Part of the Sindbad costume had been torn away as if by some irresistible force, and the hat was missing. His worst fears appeared to have been realized.

'Bish!' he cried. 'What has been happening?'

The bishop sat up. He was breathing more easily now, and a pleased, almost complacent, look had come into his face.

'Woof!' he said. 'Some binge!'

'Tell me what happened,' pleaded Augustine, agitated.

The bishop reflected, arranging his facts in chronological order.

'Well,' he said, 'when I got to the Home From Home, everybody was dancing. Nice orchestra. Nice tune. Nice floor. So I danced, too.'

'You danced?'

'Certainly I danced, Mulliner,' replied the bishop with a dignity that sat well upon him. 'A hornpipe. I consider it the duty of the higher clergy on these occasions to set an example. You didn't suppose I would go to a place like the Home From Home to play solitaire? Harmless relaxation is not forbidden, I believe?'

'But can you dance?'

'*Can* I dance?' said the bishop. 'Can I *dance*, Mulliner? Have you ever heard of Nijinsky?'

'Yes.'

'My stage name,' said the bishop.

Augustine swallowed tensely.

'Who did you dance with?' he asked.

'At first,' said the bishop, 'I danced alone. But then, most fortunately, my dear wife arrived, looking perfectly charming in some sort of filmy material, and we danced together.'

'But wasn't she surprised to see you there?'

'Not in the least. Why should she be?'

'Oh, I don't know.'

'Then why did you put the question?'

'I wasn't thinking.'

'Always think before you speak, Mulliner,' said the bishop reprovingly.

The door opened, and Hypatia hurried in.

'She's not – ' She stopped. 'Uncle!' she cried.

'Ah, my dear,' said the bishop. 'But I was telling you, Mulliner. After we had been dancing for some time, a most annoying thing occurred. Just as we were enjoying ourselves – everybody cutting up and having a good time – who should come in but a lot of interfering policemen. A most brusque and unpleasant body of men. Inquisitive, too. One of them kept asking me my name and address. But I soon put a stop to all that sort of nonsense. I plugged him in the eye.'

'You plugged him in the eye?'

'I plugged him in the eye, Mulliner. That's when I got this suit torn. The fellow was annoying me intensely. He ignored my repeated statement that I gave my name and address only to my oldest and closest friends, and had the audacity to clutch me by what I suppose a costumier would describe as the slack of my garment. Well, naturally I plugged him in the eye. I come of a fighting line, Mulliner. My ancestor, Bishop Odo, was famous in William the Conqueror's day for his work with the battle-axe. So I biffed this bird. And did he take a toss? Ask me!' said the bishop, chuckling contentedly.

Augustine and Hypatia exchanged glances.

'But, uncle – ' began Hypatia.

'Don't interrupt, my child,' said the bishop. 'I cannot marshal my thoughts if you persist in interrupting. Where was I? Ah, yes. Well, then the already existing state of confusion grew intensified. The whole *tempo* of the proceedings became, as it were, quickened. Somebody turned out the lights, and somebody else upset a table and I decided to come away.' A pensive look flitted over his face. 'I trust,' he said, 'that my dear wife also contrived to leave without undue inconvenience. The last I saw of her, she was diving through one of the windows in a manner which, I thought, showed considerable lissomness and resource. Ah, here she is and looking none the worse for her adventures. Come in, my dear, I was just telling Hypatia and our good host here of our little evening from home.'

The lady bishopess stood breathing heavily. She was not in the best of training. She had the appearance of a tank which is missing on one cylinder.

'Save me, Percy,' she gasped.

'Certainly, my dear,' said the bishop cordially. 'From what?'

In silence the lady bishopess pointed at the window. Through it, like some figure of doom, was striding a policeman. He, too, was breathing in a laboured manner, like one touched in the wind.

The bishop drew himself up.

'And what, pray,' he asked coldly, 'is the meaning of this intrusion?'

'Ah!' said the policeman.

He closed the windows and stood with his back against them.

It seemed to Augustine that the moment had arrived for a man of tact to take the situation in hand.

'Good evening, constable,' he said genially. 'You appear to have been taking exercise. I have no doubt that you would enjoy a little refreshment.'

The policeman licked his lips, but did not speak.

'I have an excellent tonic here in my cupboard,' proceeded Augustine, 'and I think you will find it most restorative. I will mix it with a little seltzer.'

The policeman took the glass, but in a preoccupied manner. His attention was still riveted on the bishop and his consort.

'Caught you, have I?' he said.

'I fail to understand you, officer,' said the bishop frigidly.

'I've been chasing her,' said the policeman, pointing to the lady bishopess, 'a good mile it must have been.'

'Then you acted,' said the bishop severely, 'in a most offensive and uncalled-for way. On her physician's recommendation, my dear wife takes a short cross-country run each night before retiring to rest. Things have come to a sorry pass if she cannot follow her doctor's orders without being pursued – I will use a stronger word – chivvied – by the constabulary.'

'And it was by her doctor's orders that she went to the Home From Home, eh?' said the policeman keenly.

'I shall be vastly surprised to learn,' said the bishop, 'that my dear wife has been anywhere near the resort you mention.'

'And you were there, too. I saw you.'

'Absurd!'

'I saw you punch Constable Booker in the eye.'

'Ridiculous!'

'If you weren't there,' said the policeman, 'what are you doing wearing that sailor-suit?'

The bishop raised his eyebrows.

'I cannot permit my choice of costume,' he said, 'arrived at – I need scarcely say – only after much reflection and meditation, to be criticized by a man who habitually goes about in public in a blue uniform and a helmet. What, may I inquire, is it that you object to in this sailor-suit? There is nothing wrong, I venture to believe, nothing degrading in a sailor-suit. Many of England's greatest men have worn sailor-suits. Nelson . . . Admiral Beatty – '

'And Arthur Prince,' said Hypatia.

'And, as you say, Arthur Prince.'

The policeman was scowling darkly. As a dialectician, he seemed to be feeling he was outmatched. And yet, he appeared to be telling himself, there must be some answer even to the apparently unanswerable logic to which he had just been listening. To assist thought, he raised the glass of Buck-U-Uppo and seltzer in his hand, and drained it at a draught.

And, as he did so, suddenly, abruptly, as breath fades from steel, the scowl passed from his face, and in its stead there appeared a smile of infinite kindliness and good-will. He wiped his moustache, and began to chuckle to himself, as at some diverting memory.

'Made me laugh, that did,' he said. 'When old Booker went head over heels that time. Don't know when I've seen a nicer punch. Clean, crisp. . . . Don't suppose it travelled more than six inches, did it? I reckon you've done a bit of boxing in your time, sir.'

At the sight of the constable's smiling face, the bishop had relaxed the austerity of his demeanour. He no longer looked like Savonarola rebuking the sins of the people. He was his old genial self once more.

'Quite true, Officer,' he said, beaming. 'When I was a somewhat younger man than I am at present, I won the Curates' Open Heavyweight Championship two years in succession. Some of the ancient skill still lingers, it would seem.'

The policeman chuckled again.

'I should say it does, sir. But,' he continued, a look of annoyance coming into his face, 'what all the fuss was about is more than I can say. Our fat-headed inspector says, "You go and raid that Home From Home, chaps, see?" he says, and so we went and done it. But my heart wasn't in it, no more was any of the other fellers' hearts in it. What's wrong with a little rational enjoyment? That's what I say. What's wrong with it?'

'Precisely, officer.'

'That's what I say. What's wrong with it? Let people enjoy themselves how they like is what I say. And if the police come interfering – well, punch them in the eye, I say, same as you did Constable Booker. That's what I say.'

'Exactly,' said the bishop. He turned to his wife. 'A fellow of considerable intelligence, this, my dear.'

'I like his face right from the beginning,' said the lady bishopess. 'What is your name, Officer?'

'Smith, lady. But call me Cyril.'

'Certainly,' said the lady bishopess. 'It will be a pleasure to do so. I used to know some Smiths in Lincolnshire years ago, Cyril. I wonder if they were any relation.'

'Maybe, lady. It's a small world.'

'Though, now I come to think of it, their name was Robinson.'

'Well, that's life, lady, isn't it?' said the policeman.

'That's just about what it is, Cyril,' agreed the bishop. 'You never spoke a truer word.'

Into this love-feast, which threatened to become glutinous every moment, there cut the cold voice of Hypatia Wace.

'Well, I must say,' said Hypatia, 'that you're a nice lot!'

'Who's a nice lot, lady?' asked the policeman.

'Those two,' said Hypatia. 'Are you married, officer?'

'No, lady. I'm just a solitary chip drifting on the river of life.'

'Well, anyway, I expect you know what it feels like to be in love.'

'Too true, lady.'

'Well, I'm in love with Mr Bracy-Gascoigne. You've met him, probably. Wouldn't you say he was a person of the highest character?'

'The whitest man I know, lady.'

'Well, I want to marry him, and my uncle and aunt here won't let me, because they say he's worldly. Just because he goes out dancing. And all the while they are dancing the soles of their shoes through. I don't call it fair.'

She buried her face in her hands with a stifled sob. The bishop and his wife looked at each other in blank astonishment.

'I don't understand,' said the bishop.

'Nor I,' said the lady bishopess. 'My dear child, what is all this about our not consenting to your marriage with Mr Bracy-Gascoigne? However did you get that idea into your head? Certainly, as far as I am concerned, you may marry Mr Bracy-Gascoigne. And I think I speak for my dear husband?'

'Quite,' said the bishop. 'Most decidedly.'

Hypatia uttered a cry of joy.

'Good egg! May I really?'

'Certainly you may. You have no objection, Cyril?'

'None whatever, lady.'

Hypatia's face fell.

'Oh, dear!' she said.

'What's the matter?'

'It just struck me that I've got to wait hours and hours before I can tell him. Just think of having to wait hours and hours!'

The bishop laughed his jolly laugh.

'Why wait hours and hours, my dear? No time like the present.'

'But he's gone to bed.'

'Well, rout him out,' said the bishop heartily. 'Here is what I suggest that we should do. You and I and Priscilla – and you, Cyril? – will all go down to his house and stand under his window and shout.'

'Or throw gravel at the window,' suggested the lady bishopess.

'Certainly, my dear, if you prefer it.'

'And when he sticks his head out,' said the policeman, 'how would it be to have the garden hose handy and squirt him? Cause a lot of fun and laughter, that would.'

'My dear Cyril,' said the bishop, 'you think of everything. I shall certainly use any influence I may possess with the authorities to have you promoted to a rank where your remarkable talents will enjoy greater scope. Come, let us be going. You will accompany us, my dear Mulliner?'

Augustine shook his head.

'Sermon to write, Bish.'

'Just as you say, Mulliner. Then if you will be so good as to leave the window open, my dear fellow, we shall be able to return to our beds at the conclusion of our little errand of goodwill without disturbing the domestic staff.'

'Right-ho, Bish.'

'Then, for the present, pip-pip, Mulliner.'

'Toodle-oo, Bish,' said Augustine.

He took up his pen, and resumed his composition. Out in the sweet-scented night he could hear the four voices dying away in the distance. They seemed to be singing an old English part-song. He smiled benevolently.

'A merry heart doeth good like a medicine. Proverbs xvii, 22,' murmured Augustine.

'ANSELM GETS HIS CHANCE'

Eggs, Beans and Crumpets

The Summer Sunday was drawing to a close. Twilight had fallen on the little garden of the Anglers' Rest, and the air was fragrant with the sweet scent of jasmine and tobacco plant. Stars were peeping out. Blackbirds sang drowsily in the shrubberies. Bats wheeled through the shadows, and a gentle breeze played fitfully among the hollyhocks. It was, in short, as a customer who had looked in for a gin and tonic rather happily put it, a nice evening.

Nevertheless, to Mr Mulliner and the group assembled in the bar-parlour of the inn there was a sense of something missing. It was due to the fact that Miss Postlethwaite, the efficient barmaid, was absent. Some forty minutes had elapsed before she arrived and took over from the pot-boy. When she did so, the quiet splendour of her costume and the devout manner in which she pulled the beerhandle told their own story.

'You've been to church,' said a penetrating Sherry and Angostura.

Miss Postlethwaite said Yes, she had, and it had been lovely.

'Beautiful in every sense of the word,' said Miss Postlethwaite, filling an order for a pint of bitter. 'I do adore evening service in the summer. It sort of does something to you, what I mean. All that stilly hush and what not.'

'The vicar preached the sermon, I suppose?' said Mr Mulliner.

'Yes,' said Miss Postlethwaite, adding that it had been extremely moving.

Mr Mulliner took a thoughtful sip of his hot Scotch and lemon.

'The old old story,' he said, a touch of sadness in his voice. 'I do not know if you gentlemen were aware of it, but in the rural districts of England vicars always preach the evening sermon during the summer months, and this causes a great deal of discontent to seethe among curates. It exasperates the young fellows, and one can understand their feelings. As Miss Postlethwaite rightly says, there is something about the atmosphere of evensong in a village church that induces a receptive frame of mind in a congregation, and a preacher, preaching under such conditions, can scarcely fail to grip and stir. The curates, withheld from so preaching, naturally feel that they are being ground beneath the heel of an iron monopoly and chiselled out of their big chance.'

A Whisky and Splash said he had never thought of that.

'In that respect,' said Mr Mulliner, 'you differ from my cousin Rupert's younger son, Anselm. He thought of it a great deal. He was the curate of the parish of Rising Mattock in Hampshire, and when he was not dreaming fondly of Myrtle Jellaby, niece of Sir Leopold Jellaby, OBE, the local squire, you would generally find him chafing at his vicar's high-handed selfishness in always hogging the evening sermon from late in April till well on in September. He told me once that it made him feel like a caged skylark.'

'Why did he dream fondly of Myrtle Jellaby?' asked a Stout and Mild, who was not very quick at the uptake.

'Because he loved her. And she loved him. She had, indeed, consented to become his wife.'

'They were engaged?' said the Stout and Mild, beginning to get it.

'Secretly. Anselm did not dare to inform her uncle of the position of affairs, because all he had to marry on was his meagre stipend. He feared the wrath of that millionaire philatelist.'

'Millionaire what?' asked a Small Bass.

'Sir Leopold,' explained Mr Mulliner, 'collected stamps.'

The Small Bass said that he had always thought that a philatelist was a man who was kind to animals.

'No,' said Mr Mulliner, 'a stamp collector. Though many philatelists are, I believe, also kind to animals. Sir Leopold Jellaby had been devoted to this hobby for many years, ever since he had retired from business as a promoter of companies in the City of London. His collection was famous.'

'And Anselm didn't like to tell him about Myrtle,' said the Stout and Mild.

'No. As I say, he lacked the courage. He pursued instead the cautious policy of lying low and hoping for the best. And one bright summer day the happy ending seemed to have arrived. Myrtle, calling at the vicarage at breakfast-time, found Anselm dancing round the table, in one hand a half-consumed piece of toast, in the other a letter, and learned from him that under the will of his late godfather, the recently deceased Mr J. G. Beenstock, he had benefited by an unexpected legacy – to wit, the stout stamp album which now lay beside the marmalade dish.

The information caused the girl's face to light up (continued Mr Mulliner). A philatelist's niece, she knew how valuable these things could be.

'What's it worth?' she asked eagerly.

'It is insured, I understand, for no less a sum than five thousand pounds.'

'Golly!'

'Golly, indeed,' assented Anselm.

'Nice sugar!' said Myrtle.

'Exceedingly nice,' agreed Anselm.

'You must take care of it. Don't leave it lying about. We don't want somebody pinching it.'

A look of pain passed over Anselm's spiritual face.

'You are not suggesting that the vicar would stoop to such an act?'

'I was thinking more,' said Myrtle, 'of Joe Beamish.'

She was alluding to a member of her loved one's little flock who had at one time been a fairly prosperous burglar. Seeing the light after about sixteen prison sentences, he had given up his life-work and now raised vegetables and sang in the choir.

'Old Joe is supposed to have reformed and got away from it all, but, if you ask me, there's a lot of life in the old dog yet. If he gets to hear that there's a five-thousand-pound stamp collection lying around . . .'

'I think you wrong our worthy Joe, darling. However, I will take precautions. I shall place the album in a drawer in the desk in the vicar's study. It is provided with a stout lock. But before doing so, I thought I might take it round and show it to your uncle. It is possible that he may feel disposed to make an offer for the collection.'

'That's a thought,' agreed Myrtle. 'Soak him good.'

'I will assuredly omit no effort to that end,' said Anselm.

And, kissing Myrtle fondly, he went about his parochial duties.

It was towards evening that he called upon Sir Leopold, and the kindly old squire, learning the nature of his errand and realizing that he had not come to make a touch on behalf of the Church Organ Fund, lost the rather strained look which he had worn when his name was announced and greeted him warmly.

'Stamps?' he said. 'Yes, I am always ready to add to my collection, provided that what I am offered is of value and the price reasonable. Had you any figure in mind for these of yours, my dear Mulliner?'

Anselm said that he had been thinking of something in the neighbourhood of five thousand pounds, and Sir Leopold shook from stem to stern like a cat that had received half a brick in the short ribs. All his life the suggestion that he should part with large sums of money had shocked him.

'Oh?' he said. Then, seeming to master himself with a strong effort. 'Well, let me look at them.'

Ten minutes later, he had closed the volume and was eyeing Anselm compassionately.

'I am afraid you must be prepared for bad news, my boy,' he said.

A sickening feeling of apprehension gripped Anselm.

'You don't mean they are not valuable?'

Sir Leopold put the tips of his fingers together and leaned back in his chair in the rather pontifical manner which he had been accustomed to assume in the old days when addressing meetings of shareholders.

'The term "valuable", my dear fellow, is a relative one. To some people five pounds would be a large sum.'

'Five pounds!'

'That is what I am prepared to offer. Or, seeing that you are a personal friend, shall we say ten?'

'But they are insured for five thousand.'

Sir Leopold shook his head with a half-smile.

'My dear Mulliner, if you knew as much as I do about the vanity of stamp collectors, you would not set great store by that. Well, as I say, I don't mind giving you ten pounds for the lot. Think it over and let me know.'

On leaden feet Anselm left the room. His hopes were shattered. He felt like a man who, chasing rainbows, has had one of them suddenly turn and bite him in the leg.

'Well?' said Myrtle, who had been awaiting the result of the conference in the passage.

Anselm broke the sad news. The girl was astounded.

'But you told me the thing was insured for – '

Anselm sighed.

'Your uncle appeared to attribute little or no importance to that. It seems that stamp collectors are in the habit of insuring their collections for fantastic sums, out of a spirit of vanity. I intend,' said Anselm broodingly, 'to preach a very strong sermon shortly on the subject of Vanity.'

There was a silence.

'Ah, well,' said Anselm, 'these things are no doubt sent to try us. It is by accepting such blows in a meek and chastened spirit . . .'

'Meek and chastened spirit my left eyeball,' cried Myrtle, who, like so many girls today, was apt to be unguarded in her speech. 'We've got to do something about this.'

'But what? I am not denying,' said Anselm, 'that the shock has been a severe one, and I regret to confess that there was a moment when I was sorely tempted to utter one or two of the observations which I once heard the coach of my college boat at Oxford make to Number Five when he persisted on obtruding his abdomen as he swung his oar. It would have been wrong, but it would unquestionably have relieved my . . .'

'I know!' cried Myrtle. 'Joe Beamish!'

Anselm stared at her.

'Joe Beamish? I do not understand you, dear.'

'Use your bean, boy, use your bean. You remember what I told you. All we've got to do is let old Joe know where those stamps are, and he will take over from there. And there we shall be with our nice little claim for five thousand of the best on the insurance company.'

'Myrtle!'

'It would be money for jam,' the enthusiastic girl continued. 'Just so much velvet. Go and see Joe at once.'

'Myrtle! I beg you, desist. You shock me inexpressibly.'

She gazed at him incredulously. 'You mean you won't do it?'

'I could not even contemplate such a course.'

'You won't unleash old Joe and set him acting for the best?'

'Certainly not. Most decidedly not. A thousand times, no.'

'But what's wrong with the idea?'

'The whole project is ethically unsound.'

There was a pause. For a moment it seemed as if the girl was about to express her chagrin in an angry outburst. A frown darkened her brow, and she kicked petulantly at a passing beetle. Then she appeared to get the better of her emotion. Her face cleared, and she smiled at him tenderly, like a mother at her fractious child.

'Oh, all right. Just as you say. Where are you off to now?'

'I have a Mothers' Meeting at six.'

'And I,' said Myrtle, 'have got to take a few pints of soup to the deserving poor. I'd better set about it. Amazing the way these bimbos absorb soup. Like sponges.'

They walked together as far as the Village Hall. Anselm went in to meet the Mothers. Myrtle, as soon as he was out of sight, turned and made her way to Joe Beamish's cosy cottage. The crooning of a hymn from within showing that its owner was at home, she walked through its honeysuckle-covered porch.

'Well, Joe, old top,' she said, 'how's everything?'

Joe Beamish was knitting a sock in the tiny living-room, which smelled in equal proportions of mice, ex-burglars and shag tobacco, and Myrtle, as her gaze fell upon his rugged features, felt her heart leap within her like that of the poet Wordsworth when beholding a rainbow in the sky. His altered circumstances had not changed the erstwhile porch-climber's outward appearance. It remained that of one of those men for whom the police are always spreading drag-nets; and Myrtle, eyeing him, had the feeling that in supposing that in this pre-eminent plugugly there still lurked something of the Old Adam, she had called her shots correctly.

For some minutes after her entry, the conversation was confined to neutral topics – the weather, the sock and the mice behind the wainscoting. It was only when it turned to the decorations of the church for the forthcoming Harvest Festival – to which, she learned, her host would be in a position to contribute two cabbages and a pumpkin – that Myrtle saw her opportunity of approaching a more intimate subject.

'Mr Mulliner will be pleased about that,' she said. 'He's nuts on the Harvest Festival.'

'R,' said Joe Beamish. 'He's a good man, Mr Mulliner.'

'He's a lucky man,' said Myrtle. 'Have you heard what's just happened to him? Some sort of deceased Beenstock has gone and left him five thousand quid.'

'Coo! Is that right?'

'Well, it comes to the same thing. An album of stamps that's worth five thousand. You know how valuable stamps are. Why, my uncle's collection is worth ten times that. That's why we've got all those burglar alarms up at the Hall.'

A rather twisted expression came into Joe Beamish's face.

'I've heard there's a lot of burglar alarms up at the Hall,' he said.

'But there aren't any at the vicarage, and, between you and me, Joe, it's worrying me rather. Because, you see, that's where Mr Mulliner is keeping his stamps.'

'R,' said Joe Beamish, speaking now with a thoughtful intonation.

'I told him he ought to keep them at his bank.'

Joe Beamish started.

'Wot ever did you go and say a silly thing like that for?' he asked.

'It wasn't at all silly,' said Myrtle warmly. 'It was just ordinary common sense. I don't consider those stamps are safe, left lying in a drawer in the desk in the vicar's study, that little room on the ground floor to the right of the front door with its flimsy french windows that could so easily be forced with a chisel or something. They are locked up, of course, but what good are locks? I've seen these, and anybody could open them with a hairpin. I tell you, Joe, I'm worried.'

Joe Beamish bent over his socks, knitting and purling for a while in silence. When he spoke again, it was to talk of pumpkins and cabbages, and after that, for he was a man of limited ideas, of cabbages and pumpkins.

Anselm Mulliner, meanwhile, was passing through a day of no little spiritual anguish. At the moment when it had been made, Myrtle's proposal had shaken him to his foundations. He had not felt so utterly unmanned since the evening when he had been giving young Willie Purvis a boxing lesson at the Lads' Club, and Willie, by a happy accident, had got home squarely on the button.

This revelation of the character of the girl to whom he had given a curate's unspotted heart had stunned him. Myrtle, it seemed to him, appeared to have no notion whatsoever of the distinction between right and wrong. And while this would not have mattered, of course, had he been a gun-man and she his prospective moll, it made a great deal of difference to one who hoped later on to become a vicar and, in such event, would want his wife to look after the parish funds. He wondered what the prophet Isaiah would have had to say about it, had he been informed of her views on strategy and tactics.

All through the afternoon and evening he continued to brood on the thing. At supper that night he was distrait and preoccupied. Busy with his own reflections, he scarcely listened to the conversation of the Rev. Sidney Gooch, his vicar. And this was perhaps fortunate, for it was a Saturday and the vicar, as was his custom at Saturday suppers, harped a good deal on the subject of the sermon which he was proposing to deliver at evensong on the morrow. He said, not once but many times, that he confidently expected, if the fine weather held up, to knock his little flock cockeyed. The Rev. Sidney was a fine, upstanding specimen of the muscular Christian, but somewhat deficient in tact.

Towards nightfall, however, Anselm found a kindlier, mellower note creeping into his meditations. Possibly it was the excellent round of beef of which he had partaken, and the wholesome ale with which he had washed it down, that caused this softer mood. As he smoked his after-supper cigarette, he found himself beginning to relax in his austere attitude towards Myrtle's feminine weakness. He reminded himself that it must be placed to her credit that she had not been obdurate. On the contrary, the moment he had made plain his disapproval of her financial methods, conscience had awakened, her better self had prevailed and she had abandoned her dubious schemes. That was much.

Happy once more, he went to bed and, after dipping into a good book for half an hour, switched off the light and fell into a restful sleep.

But it seemed to him that he had scarcely done so when he was awakened by loud noises. He sat up, listening. Something in the nature of a free-for-all appeared to be in progress in the lower part of the house. His knowledge of the vicarage's topography suggested to him that the noises were proceeding from the study and, hastily donning a dressing-gown, he made his way thither.

The room was in darkness, but he found the switch and, turning on the light, perceived that the odd, groaning sound which had greeted him as he approached the door proceeded from the Rev. Sidney Gooch. The vicar was sitting on the floor, a hand pressed to his left eye.

'A burglar!' he said, rising. 'A beastly bounder of a burglar.'

'He has injured you, I fear,' said Anselm commiseratingly.

'Of course he has injured me,' said the Rev. Sidney, with some testiness. 'Can a man take fire in his bosom and his clothes not be burned? Proverbs vi. 27. I heard a sound and came down and seized the fellow, and he struck me so violently that I was compelled to loosen my grip, and he made his escape through the window. Be so kind, Mulliner, as to look about and see if he has taken anything. There were some manuscript sermons which I should not care to lose.'

Anselm was standing beside the desk. He had to pause for a moment in order to control his voice.

'The only object that appears to have been removed,' he said, 'is an album of stamps belonging to myself.'

'The sermons are there?'

'Still there.'

'Bitter,' said the vicar. 'Bitter.'

'I beg your pardon?' said Anselm.

He turned. His superior of the cloth was standing before the mirror, regarding himself in it with a rueful stare.

'Bitter!' he repeated. 'I was thinking,' he explained, 'of the one I had planned to deliver at evensong tomorrow. A pippin, Mulliner, in the deepest and truest sense a pippin. I am not exaggerating when I say that I would have had them tearing up the pews. And now that dream is ended. I cannot possibly appear in the pulpit with a shiner like this. It would put wrong ideas into the heads of the congregation – always, in these rural communities, so prone to place the worst construction on such disfigurements. Tomorrow, Mulliner, I shall be confined to my bed with a slight chill, and you will conduct both matins and evensong. Bitter!' said the Rev. Sidney Gooch. 'Bitter!'

Anselm did not speak. His heart was too full for words.

In Anselm's deportment and behaviour on the following morning there was nothing to indicate that his soul was a maelstrom of seething emotions. Most curates who find themselves unexpectedly allowed to preach on Sunday evening in the summer time are like dogs let off the chain. They leap. They bound. They sing snatches of the more rollicking psalms. They rush about saying 'Good morning, good morning', to every-body and patting children on the head. Not so Anselm. He knew that only by conserving his nervous energies would he be able to give of his best when the great moment came.

To those of the congregation who were still awake in the later stages of the service his sermon at matins seemed dull and colourless. And so it was. He had no intention of frittering away eloquence on a morning sermon. He deliberately held himself back, concentrating every fibre of his being on the address which he was to deliver in the evening.

He had had it by him for months. Every curate throughout the English countryside keeps tucked away among his effects a special sermon designed to prevent him being caught short, if suddenly called upon to preach at evensong. And all through the afternoon he remained closeted in his room, working upon it. He pruned. He polished. He searched the Thesaurus for the telling adjective. By the time the church bells began to ring out over the fields and spinneys of Rising Mattock in the quiet gloaming, his masterpiece was perfected to the last comma.

Feeling more like a volcano than a curate, Anselm Mulliner pinned together the sheets of manuscript and set forth.

The conditions could not have been happier. By the end of the pre-sermon hymn the twilight was far advanced, and through the door of the little church there poured the scent of trees and flowers. All was still, save for the distant tinkling of sheep bells and the drowsy calling of rooks among the elms. With quiet confidence Anselm mounted the pulpit steps. He had been sucking throat pastilles all day and saying 'Mi-mi' to himself in an undertone throughout the service, and he knew that he would be in good voice.

For an instant he paused and gazed about him. He was rejoiced to see that he was playing to absolute capacity. Every pew was full. There, in the squire's highbacked stall, was Sir Leopold Jellaby, OBE, with Myrtle at his side. There, among the choir, looking indescribably foul in a surplice, sat Joe Beamish. There, in their respective places, were the butcher, the baker, the candlestick-maker and all the others who made up the personnel of the congregation. With a little sigh of rapture, Anselm cleared his throat and gave out the simple text of Brotherly Love.

I have been privileged (said Mr Mulliner) to read the script of this sermon of Anselm's, and it must, I can see, have been extremely powerful. Even in manuscript form, without the added attraction of the young man's beautifully modulated tenor voice, one can clearly sense its magic.

Beginning with a thoughtful excursus on Brotherly Love among the Hivites and Hittites, it came down through the Early Britons, the Middle Ages and the spacious days of Queen Elizabeth to these modern times of ours, and it was here that Anselm Mulliner really let himself go. It was at this point, if one may employ the phrase, that he – in the best and most reverent spirit of the words – reached for the accelerator and stepped on it.

Earnestly, in accents throbbing with emotion, he spoke of our duty to one another; of the task that lies clear before all of us to make this a better and a sweeter world for our fellows; of the joy that waits for those who give no thought to self but strain every nerve to do the square thing by one and all. And with each golden phrase he held his audience in an ever-tightening grip. Tradesmen who had been nodding somnolently woke up and sat with parted lips. Women dabbed at their eyes with handkerchiefs. Choirboys who had been sucking acid drops swallowed them remorsefully and stopped shuffling their feet.

Even at a morning service, such a sermon would have been a smash hit. Delivered in the gloaming, with all its adventitious aids to success, it was a riot.

It was not immediately after the conclusion of the proceedings that Anselm was able to tear himself away from the crowd of admirers that surged round him in the vestry. There were churchwardens who wanted to shake his hand, other churchwardens who insisted on smacking him on the back. One even asked for his autograph. But eventually he laughingly shook himself free and made his way back to the vicarage. And scarcely had he passed through the garden gate when something shot out at him from the scented darkness, and he found Myrtle Jellaby in his arms.

'Anselm!' she cried. 'My wonder-man! However did you do it? I never heard such a sermon in my life!'

'It got across, I think?' said Anselm modestly.

'It was terrific. Golly! When you admonish a congregation, it stays admonished. How you think of all these things beats me.'

'Oh, they come to one.'

'And another thing I can't understand is how you came to be preaching at all in the evening. I thought you told me the vicar always did.'

'The vicar,' began Anselm, 'has met with a slight . . .'

And then it suddenly occurred to him that in the excitement of being allowed to preach at evensong he had quite forgotten to inform Myrtle of that other important happening, the theft of the stamp album.

'A rather extraordinary thing occurred last night, darling,' he said. 'The vicarage was burgled.'

Myrtle was amazed.

'Not really?'

'Yes. A marauder broke in through the study window.'

'Well, fancy that! Did he take anything?'

'He took my collection of stamps.'

Myrtle uttered a cry of ecstasy.

'Then we collect!'

Anselm did not speak for a moment.

'I wonder.'

'What do you mean, you wonder? Of course we collect. Shoot the claim in to the insurance people without a moment's delay.'

'But have you reflected, dearest? Am I justified in doing as you suggest?'

'Of course. Why ever not?'

'It seems to me a moot point. The collection, we know, is worthless. Can I justly demand of this firm – The London and Midland Counties Aid and Benefit Association is its name – that they pay me five thousand pounds for an album of stamps that is without value?'

'Of course you can. Old Beenstock paid the premiums, didn't he?'

'That is true. Yes. I had forgotten that.'

'It doesn't matter whether a thing's valuable or not. The point is what you insure it for. And it isn't as if it's going to hurt these Mutual Aid and Benefit birds to brass up. It's sinful the amount of money those insurance companies have. Must be jolly bad for them, if you ask me.'

Anselm had not thought of that. Examining the point now, it seemed to him that Myrtle, with her woman's intuition, had rather gone to the root of the matter and touched the spot.

Was there not, he asked himself, a great deal to be said for this theory of hers that insurance companies had much too much money and would be better, finer, more spiritual insurance companies if somebody came along occasionally and took a bit of the stuff off them? Unquestionably there was. His doubts were removed. He saw now that it was not only a pleasure, but a duty, to nick the London and Midland Counties Mutual Aid and Benefit Association for five thousand. It might prove the turning-point in the lives of its Board of Directors.

'Very well,' he said. 'I will send in the claim.'

'At-a-boy! And the instant we touch, we'll get married.'

'Myrtle!'

'Anselm!'

'Guv'nor,' said the voice of Joe Beamish at their side, 'could I 'ave a word with you?' They drew apart with a start, and stared dumbly at the man.

'Guv'nor,' said Joe Beamish, and it was plain from the thickness of his utterance that he was in the grip of some strong emotion, 'I want to thank you, guv'nor, for that there sermon of yours. That there wonderful sermon.'

Anselm smiled. He had recovered from the shock of hearing this sudden voice in the night. It was a nuisance, of course, to be interrupted like this at such a moment, but one must, he felt, be courteous to the fans. No doubt he would have to expect a lot of this sort of thing from now on.

'I am rejoiced that my poor effort should have elicited so striking an encomium.'

'Wot say?'

'He says he's glad you liked it,' said Myrtle, a little irritably, for she was not feeling her most amiable. A young girl who is nestling in the arms of the man she loves resents having cracksmen popping up through traps at her elbow.

'R,' said Joe Beamish, enlightened. 'Yes, guv'nor, that was a sermon, that was. That was what I call a blinking sermon.'

'Thank you, Joe, thank you. It is nice to feel that you were pleased.'

'You're right, I was pleased, guv'nor. I've 'eard sermons in Pentonville, and I've 'eard sermons in Wormwood Scrubs, and I've 'eard sermons in Dartmoor, and very good sermons they were, but of all the sermons I've 'eard I never 'eard a sermon that could touch this 'ere sermon for class and pep and . . .'

'Joe,' said Myrtle.

'Yes, lady?'

'Scram!'

'Pardon, lady?'

'Get out. Pop off. Buzz along. Can't you see you're not wanted? We're busy.'

'My dear,' said Anselm, with gentle reproach, 'is not your manner a little peremptory? I would not have the honest fellow feel . . .'

'R,' interrupted Joe Beamish, and there was a suggestion of unshed tears in his voice, 'but I'm not an honest feller, guv'nor. There, if you don't mind me saying so, no offence meant and none, I 'ope, taken, is where you make your bloomin' error. I'm a pore sinner and backslider and evildoer and . . .'

'Joe,' said Myrtle, with a certain menacing calm, 'if you get a thick ear, always remember that you asked for it. The same applies to a lump the size of an egg on top of your ugly head through coming into violent contact with the knob of my parasol. Will you or will you not,' she said, taking a firmer grip of the handle of the weapon to which she had alluded, 'push off?'

'Lady,' said Joe Beamish, not without a rough dignity, 'as soon as I've done what I come to do, I will withdraw. But first I got to do what I come to do. And what I come to do is 'and back in a meek and contrite spirit this 'ere album of stamps what I snitched last night, never thinking that I was to 'ear that there wonderful sermon and see the light. But 'avin' 'eard that there wonderful sermon and seen the light, I now 'ave great pleasure in doing what I come to do, namely,' said Joe Beamish, thrusting the late J. G. Beenstock's stamp collection into Anselm's hand, 'this 'ere. Lady. . . . Guv'nor. . . . With these few words, 'opin' that you are in the pink as it leaves me at present, I will now withdraw.'

'Stop!' cried Anselm.

'R?'

Anselm's face was strangely contorted. He spoke with difficulty.

'Joe. . . .'

'Yes, guv'nor?'

'Joe . . . I would like . . . I would prefer . . . In a very real sense I do so feel . . . In short, I would like you to keep this stamp album, Joe.'

The burglar shook his head.

'No, guv'nor. It can't be done. When I think of that there wonderful sermon and all those beautiful things you said in that there wonderful sermon about the 'Ivites and the 'Ittites and doing the right thing by the neighbours and 'elping so far as in you lies to spread sweetness and light throughout the world, I can't keep no albums which 'ave come into my possession through gettin' in at other folks' french winders on account of not 'avin' seen the light. It don't belong to me, not that album don't, and I now take much pleasure in 'anding' it back with these few words. Goo' night, guv'nor. Goo' night, lady. Goo' night all. I will now withdraw.'

His footsteps died away, and there was silence in the quiet garden. Both Anselm and Myrtle were busy with their thoughts. Once more through Anselm's mind there was racing that pithy address which the coach of his college boat had delivered when trying to do justice to the spectacle of Number Five's obtrusive stomach: while Myrtle, on her side, was endeavouring not to give utterance to a rough translation of something she had once heard a French taxi-driver say to a gendarme during her finishing-school days in Paris.

Anselm was the first to speak.

'This, dearest,' he said, 'calls for discussion. One does so feel that little or nothing can be accomplished without earnest thought and a frank round-table conference. Let us go indoors and thresh the whole matter out in as calm a spirit as we can achieve.'

He led the way to the study and seated himself moodily, his chin in his hands, his brow furrowed. A deep sigh escaped him.

'I understand now,' he said, 'why it is that curates are not permitted to preach on Sunday evenings during the summer months. It is not safe. It is like exploding a bomb in a public place. It upsets existing conditions too violently. When I reflect that, had our good vicar but been able to take evensong tonight, this distressing thing would not have occurred, I find myself saying in the words of the prophet Hosea to the children of Adullam . . .'

'Putting the prophet Hosea to one side for the moment and temporarily pigeon-holing the children of Adullam,' interrupted Myrtle, 'what are we going to do about this?'

Anselm sighed again.

'Alas, dearest, there you have me. I assume that it is no longer feasible to submit a claim to the London and Midland Counties Mutual Aid and Benefit Association.'

'So we lose five thousand of the best and brightest?'

Anselm winced. The lines deepened on his careworn face.

'It is not an agreeable thing to contemplate, I agree. One had been looking on the sum as one's little nest-egg. One did so want to see it safely in the bank, to be invested later in sound, income-bearing securities. I confess to feeling a little vexed with Joe Beamish.'

'I hope he chokes.'

'I would not go so far as that, darling,' said Anselm, with loving rebuke. 'But I must admit that if I heard that he had tripped over a loose shoelace and sprained his ankle, it would – in the deepest and truest sense – be all right with me. I deplore the man's tactless impulsiveness. "Officious" is the word that springs to the lips.'

Myrtle was musing.

'Listen,' she said. 'Why not play a little joke on these London and Midland bozos? Why tell them you've got the stamps back? Why not just sit tight and send in the claim and pouch their cheque? That would be a lot of fun.'

Again, for the second time in two days, Anselm found himself looking a little askance at his loved one. Then he reminded himself that she was scarcely to be blamed for her somewhat unconventional outlook. The niece of a prominent financier, she was per-haps entitled to be somewhat eccentric in her views. No doubt, her earliest childhood memories were of coming down to dessert and hearing her elders discuss over the nuts and wine some burgeoning scheme for trimming the investors.

He shook his head.

'I could hardly countenance such a policy, I fear. To me there seems something – I do not wish to hurt your feelings, dearest – something almost dishonest about what you suggest. Besides,' he added meditatively, 'when Joe Beamish handed back that album, he did it in the presence of witnesses.'

'Witnesses?'

'Yes, dearest. As we came into the house, I observed a shadowy figure. Whose it was, I cannot say, but of this I feel convinced – that this person, whoever he may have been, heard all.'

'You're sure?'

'Quite sure. He was standing beneath the cedar-tree, within easy earshot. And, as you know, our worthy Beamish's voice is of a robust and carrying timbre.'

He broke off. Unable to restrain her pent-up feelings any longer, Myrtle Jellaby had uttered the words which the taxi-driver had said to the gendarme, and there was that about them which might well have rendered a tougher curate than Anselm temporarily incapable of speech. A throbbing silence followed the ejaculation. And during this silence there came to their ears from the garden without a curious sound.

'Hark,' said Myrtle.

They listened. What they heard was unmistakably a human being sobbing.

'Some fellow creature in trouble,' said Anselm.

'Thank goodness,' said Myrtle.

'Should we go and ascertain the sufferer's identity?'

'Let's,' said Myrtle. 'I have an idea it may be Joe Beamish. In which case, what I am going to do to him with my parasol will be nobody's business.'

But the mourner was not Joe Beamish, who had long since gone off to the Goose and Grasshopper. To Anselm, who was short-sighted, the figure leaning against the cedar-tree, shaking with uncontrollable sobs, was indistinct and unrecognizable, but Myrtle, keener-eyed, uttered a cry of surprise.

'Uncle!'

'Uncle?' said Anselm, astonished.

'It is Uncle Leopold.'

'Yes,' said the OBE, choking down a groan and moving away from the tree, 'it is I. Is that Mulliner standing beside you, Myrtle?'

'Yes.'

'Mulliner,' said Sir Leopold Jellaby, 'you find me in tears. And why am I in tears? Because, my dear Mulliner, I am still overwhelmed by that wonderful sermon of yours on Brotherly Love and our duty to our neighbours.'

Anselm began to wonder if ever a curate had had notices like these.

'Oh, thanks,' he said, shuffling a foot. 'Awfully glad you liked it.'

' "Liked it", Mulliner, is a weak term. That sermon has revolutinized my entire outlook. It has made me a different man. I wonder, Mulliner, if you can find me pen and ink inside the house?'

'Pen and ink?'

'Precisely. I wish to write you a cheque for ten thousand pounds for that stamp collection of yours.'

'Ten thousand!'

'Come inside,' said Myrtle. 'Come right in.'

'You see,' said Sir Leopold, as they led him to the study and plied him with many an eager query as to whether he preferred a thick nib or a thin, 'when you showed me those stamps yesterday, I recognized their value immediately – they would fetch five thousand pounds anywhere – so I naturally told you they were worthless. It was one of those ordinary, routine business precautions which a man is bound to take. One of the first things I remember my dear father saying to me, when he sent me out to battle with the world, was "Never give a sucker an even break", and until now I have always striven not to do so. But your sermon tonight has made me see that there is something higher and nobler than a code of business ethics. Shall I cross the cheque?'

'If you please.'

'No,' said Myrtle. 'Make it open.'

'Just as you say, my dear. You appear,' said the kind old squire, smiling archly through his tears, 'to be showing considerable interest in the matter. Am I to infer – ?'

'I love Anselm. We are engaged.'

'Mulliner! Is this so?'

'Er – yes,' said Anselm. 'I was meaning to tell you about that.'

Sir Leopold patted him on the shoulder.

'I could wish her no better husband. There. There is your cheque, Mulliner. The collection, as I say, is worth five thousand pounds, but after that sermon, I give ten freely – freely!'

Anselm, like one in a dream, took the oblong slip of paper and put it in his pocket.

Silently, he handed the album to Sir Leopold.

'Thank you,' said the latter. 'And now, my dear fellow, I think I shall have to ask you for the loan of a clean pocket-handkerchief. My own, as you see, is completely saturated.'

It was while Anselm was in his room, rummaging in the chest of drawers, that a light footstep caused him to turn. Myrtle was standing in the doorway, a finger on her lip.

'Anselm,' she whispered, 'have you a fountain pen?'

'Certainly, dearest. There should be one in this drawer. Yes, here it is. You wish to write something?'

'I wish you to write something. Endorse that cheque here and now, and give it to me, and I will motor to London tonight in my two-seater, so as to be at the bank the moment it opens and deposit it. You see, I know Uncle Leopold. He might take it into his head, after he had slept on it and that sermon had worn off a bit, to 'phone and stop payment. You know how he feels about business precautions. This way we shall avoid all rannygazoo.'

Anselm kissed her fondly.

'You think of everything, dearest,' he said. 'How right you are. One does so wish, does one not, to avoid rannygazoo.'

'AUNT AGATHA TAKES THE COUNT'

The Inimitable Jeeves

'Jeeves,' I said, 'we've backed a winner.'

'Sir?'

'Coming to this place, I mean. Here we are in a topping hotel, with fine weather, good cooking, golf, bathing, gambling of every variety, and my Aunt Agatha miles away on the other side of the English Channel. I ask you, what could be sweeter?'

I had had to leg it, if you remember, with considerable speed from London because my Aunt Agatha was on my track with a hatchet as the result of the breaking-off of my engagement to Honoria Glossop. The thing hadn't been my fault, but I couldn't have convinced Aunt Agatha of that if I'd argued for a week: so it had seemed to me that the judicious course to pursue was to buzz briskly off while the buzzing was good. I was standing now at the window of the extremely decent suite which I'd taken at the Hotel Splendide at Roville on the French coast, and, as I looked down at the people popping to and fro in the sunshine, and reflected that in about a quarter of an hour I was due to lunch with a girl who was the exact opposite of Honoria Glossop in every way, I felt dashed uplifted. Gay, genial, happy-go-lucky and devil-may-care, if you know what I mean.

I had met this girl – Aline Hemmingway her name was – for the first time on the train coming from Paris. She was going to Roville to wait there for a brother who was due to arrive from England. I had helped her with her baggage, got into conversation, had a bite of dinner with her in the restaurant-car, and the result was we had become remarkably chummy. I'm a bit apt, as a rule, to give the modern girl a miss, but there was something different about Aline Hemmingway.

I turned round, humming a blithe melody, and Jeeves shied like a startled mustang.

I had rather been expecting some such display of emotion on the man's part, for I was trying out a fairly fruity cummerbund that morning – one of those silk contrivances, you know, which you tie round your waist, something of the order of a sash, only more substantial. I had seen it in a shop the day before and hadn't been able to resist it, but I'd known all along that there might be trouble with Jeeves. It was a pretty brightish scarlet.

'I beg your pardon, sir,' he said, in a sort of hushed voice. 'You are surely not proposing to appear in public in that thing?'

'What, Cuthbert the Cummerbund?' I said in a careless, debonair way, passing it off. 'Rather!'

'I should not advise it, sir, really I shouldn't.'

'Why not?'

'The effect, sir, is loud in the extreme.'

I tackled the blighter squarely. I mean to say, nobody knows better than I do that Jeeves is a master-mind and all that, but, dash it, a fellow must call his soul his own. You can't be a serf to your valet.

'You know, the trouble with you, Jeeves,' I said, 'is that you're too – what's the word I want? – too bally insular. You can't realize that you aren't in Piccadilly all the time. In a place like this, simply dripping with the gaiety and *joie-de-vivre* of France, a bit of colour and a touch of the poetic is expected of you. Why, last night at the Casino I saw a fellow in a full evening suit of yellow velvet.'

'Nevertheless, sir – '

'Jeeves,' I said, firmly, 'my mind is made up. I'm in a foreign country; it's a corking day; God's in his heaven and all's right with the world and this cummerbund seems to me to be called for.'

'Very good, sir,' said Jeeves, coldly.

Dashed upsetting, this sort of thing. If there's one thing that gives me the pip, it's unpleasantness in the home; and I could see that relations were going to be pretty fairly strained for a while. I suppose the old brow must have been a bit furrowed or something, for Aline Hemmingway spotted that things were wrong directly we sat down to lunch.

'You seem depressed, Mr Wooster,' she said. 'Have you been losing money at the Casino?'

'No,' I said. 'As a matter of fact, I won quite a goodish sum last night.'

'But something is the matter. What is it?'

'Well, to tell you the truth,' I said, 'I've just had rather a painful scene with my man, and it's shaken me a bit. He doesn't like this cummerbund.'

'Why, I've just been admiring it. I think it's very becoming.'

'No, really?'

'It has rather a Spanish effect.'

'Exactly what I thought myself. Extraordinary you should have said that. A touch of the hidalgo, what? Sort of Vincente y Blasco What's-his-name stuff. The jolly old hidalgo off to the bull-fight, what?'

'Yes. Or a corsair of the Spanish Main.'

'Absolutely! I say, you know, you have bucked me up. It's a rummy thing about you – how sympathetic you are, I mean. The ordinary girl you meet today is all bobbed hair and gaspers, but you – '

I was about to continue in this strain, when somebody halted at our table, and the girl jumped up.

'Sidney!' she cried.

The chappie who had anchored in our midst was a small, round cove with a face rather like a sheep. He wore pince-nez, his expression was benevolent, and he had on one of those collars which button at the back. A parson, in fact.

'Well, my dear,' he said, beaming pretty freely, 'here I am at last.'

'Are you very tired?'

'Not at all. A most enjoyable journey, in which tedium was rendered impossible by the beauty of the scenery through which we passed and the entertaining conversation of my fellow-travellers. But may I be presented to this gentleman?' he said, peering at me through the pince-nez.

'This is Mr Wooster,' said the girl, 'who was very kind to me coming from Paris. Mr Wooster, this is my brother.'

We shook hands, and the brother went off to get a wash.

'Sidney's such a dear,' said the girl. 'I know you'll like him.'

'Seems a topper.'

'I do hope he will enjoy his stay here. It's so seldom he gets a holiday. His vicar overworks him dreadfully.'

'Vicars are the devil, what?'

'I wonder if you will be able to spare any time to show him round the place? I can see he's taken such a fancy to you. But, of course, it would be a bother, I suppose, so – '

'Rather not. Only too delighted.' For half a second I thought of patting her hand, then I felt I'd better wait a bit. 'I'll do anything, absolutely anything.'

'It's awfully kind of you.'

'For you,' I said, 'I would – '

At this point the brother returned, and the conversation became what you might call general.

After lunch I fairly curvetted back to my suite, with a most extraordinary braced sensation going all over me like a rash.

'Jeeves,' I said, 'you were all wrong about that cummerbund. It went like a breeze from the start.'

'Indeed, sir?'

'Made an absolutely outstanding hit. The lady I was lunching with admired it. Her brother admired it. The waiter looked as if he admired it. Well, anything happened since I left?'

'Yes, sir. Mrs Gregson has arrived at the hotel.'

A fellow I know who went shooting, and was potted by one of his brother-sportsmen in mistake for a rabbit, once told me that it was several seconds before he realized that he had contributed to the day's bag. For about a tenth of a minute everything seemed quite OK, and then suddenly he got it. It was just the same with me. It took about five seconds for this fearful bit of news to sink in.

'What!' I yelled. 'Aunt Agatha here?'

'Yes, sir.'

'She can't be.'

'I have seen her, sir.'

'But how did she get here?'

'The Express from Paris has just arrived, sir.'

'But, I mean, how the dickens did she know I was here?'

'You left a forwarding-address at the flat for your correspondence, sir. No doubt Mrs Gregson obtained it from the hall-porter.'

'But I told the chump not to give it away to a soul.'

'That would hardly baffle a lady of Mrs Gregson's forceful personality, sir.'

'Jeeves, I'm in the soup.'

'Yes, sir.'

'Right up to the hocks!'

'Yes, sir.'

'What shall I do?'

'I fear I have nothing to suggest, sir.'

I eyed the man narrowly. Dashed aloof his manner was. I saw what was the matter, of course. He was still brooding over that cummerbund.

'I shall go for a walk, Jeeves,' I said.

'Yes, sir?'

'A good long walk.'

'Very good, sir.'

'And if – er – if anybody asks for me, tell 'em you don't know when I'll be back.'

To people who don't know my Aunt Agatha I find it extraordinarily difficult to explain why it is that she has always put the wind up me to such a frightful extent. I mean, I'm not dependent on her financially, or anything like that. It's simply personality, I've come to the conclusion. You see, all through my childhood and when I was a kid at school she was always able to turn me inside out with a single glance, and I haven't come out from under the 'fluence yet. We run to height a bit in our family, and there's about five-foot-nine of Aunt Agatha, topped off with a beaky nose, an eagle eye, and a lot of grey hair, and the general effect is pretty formidable.

Her arrival in Roville at this juncture had made things more than a bit complicated for me. What to do? Leg it quick before she could get hold of me, would no doubt have been the advice most fellows would have given me. But the situation wasn't as simple as that. I was in much the same position as the cat on the garden wall who, when on the point of becoming matey with the cat next door, observes the boot-jack sailing through the air. If he stays where he is, he gets it in the neck; if he biffs, he has to start all over again where he left off. I didn't like the prospect of being collared by Aunt Agatha, but on the other hand I simply barred the notion of leaving Roville by the night-train and parting from Aline Hemmingway. Absolutely a man's cross-roads, if you know what I mean.

I prowled about the neighbourhood all the afternoon and evening, then I had a bit of dinner at a quiet restaurant in the town and trickled cautiously back to the hotel. Jeeves was popping about in the suite.

'There is a note for you, sir,' he said, 'on the mantelpiece.'

The blighter's manner was still so cold and unchummy that I bit the bullet and had a dash at being airy.

'A note, eh?'

'Yes, sir. Mrs Gregson's maid brought it shortly after you had left.'

'Tra-la-la!' I said.

'Precisely, sir.'

I opened the note.

'She wants me to look in on her after dinner some time.'

'Yes, sir?'

'Jeeves,' I said, 'mix me a stiffish brandy-and-soda.'

'Yes, sir.'

'Stiffish, Jeeves. Not too much soda, but splash the brandy about a bit.'

'Very good, sir.'

He shimmered off into the background to collect the materials, and just at that moment there was a knock at the door.

I'm bound to say it was a shock. My heart stood still, and I bit my tongue.

'Come in,' I bleated.

But it wasn't Aunt Agatha after all. It was Aline Hemmingway, looking rather rattled, and her brother, looking like a sheep with a secret sorrow.

'Oh, Mr Wooster!' said the girl, in a sort of gasping way.

'Oh, what ho!' I said. 'Won't you come in? Take a seat or two.'

'I don't know how to begin.'

'Eh?' I said. 'Is anything up?'

'Poor Sidney – it was my fault – I ought never to have let him go there alone.'

At this point the brother, who had been standing by wrapped in the silence, gave a little cough, like a sheep caught in the mist on a mountain-top.

'The fact is, Mr Wooster,' he said. 'I have been gambling at the Casino.'

'Oh!' I said. 'Did you click?'

He sighed heavily.

'If you mean, was I successful, I must answer in the negative. I rashly persisted in the view that the colour red, having appeared no fewer than seven times in succession, must inevitably at no distant date give place to black. I was in error. I lost my little all, Mr Wooster.'

'Tough luck,' I said.

'I left the Casino, and returned to the hotel. There I encountered one of my parishioners, a Colonel Musgrave, who chanced to be holiday-making over here. I – er – induced him to cash me a cheque for one hundred pounds on my bank in London.'

'Well, that was all to the good, what?' I said, hoping to induce the poor egg to look on the bright side. 'I mean bit of luck finding someone to slip it into, first crack out of the box.'

'On the contrary, Mr Wooster, it did but make matter worse. I burn with shame as I make the confession, but I went back to the Casino and lost the entire sum.'

'I say!' I said. 'You *are* having a night out!'

'And,' concluded the chappie, 'the most lamentable feature of the whole affair is that I have no funds in the bank to meet the cheque, when presented.'

I'm free to confess that I gazed at him with no little interest and admiration. Never in my life before had I encountered a curate so genuinely all to the mustard. Little as he might look like one of the lads of the village, he certainly appeared to be the real tabasco.

'Colonel Musgrave,' he went on, gulping somewhat, 'is not a man who would be likely to overlook the matter. He is a hard man. He will expose me to my vic-ah. My vic-ah is a hard man. I shall be ruined if Colonel Musgrave presents that cheque, and he leaves for England tonight.'

'Mr Wooster,' the girl burst out, 'won't you, won't you help us? Oh, do say you will. We must have the money to get back that cheque from Colonel Musgrave before nine o'clock – he leaves on the nine-twenty. I was at my wits' end what to do, when I remembered how kind you had always been and how you had told me at lunch that you had won some money at the Casino last night. Mr Wooster, will you lend it to us, and take these as security?' And, before I knew what she was doing, she had dived into her bag, produced a case, and opened it. 'My pearls,' she said. 'I don't know what they are worth – they were a present from my poor father – but I know they must be worth ever so much more than the amount we want.'

Dashed embarrassing. Made me feel like a pawn-broker. More than a touch of popping the watch about the whole business.

'No, I say, really,' I protested, the haughty old spirit of the Woosters kicking like a mule at the idea. 'There's no need for any security, you know, or any rot of that kind. I mean to say, among pals, you know, what? Only too glad the money'll come in useful.'

And I fished it out and pushed it across. The brother shook his head.

'Mr Wooster,' he said, 'we appreciate your generosity, your beautiful, heartening confidence in us, but we cannot permit this.'

'What Sidney means,' said the girl, 'is that you really don't know anything about us, when you come to think of it. You mustn't risk lending all this money without any security at all to two people who, after all, are almost strangers.'

'Oh, don't say that!'

'I do say it. If I hadn't thought that you would be quite businesslike about this, I would never have dared to come to you. If you will just give me a receipt, as a matter of form – '

'Oh, well.'

I wrote out the receipt and handed it over feeling more or less of an ass.

'Here you are.' I said.

The girl took the piece of paper, shoved it in her bag, grabbed the money and slipped it to brother Sidney, and then, before I knew what was happening, she had darted at me, kissed me, and legged it from the room.

I don't know when I've been so rattled. The whole thing was so dashed sudden and unexpected. Through a sort of mist I could see that Jeeves had appeared from the background and was helping the brother on with his coat; and then the brother came up to me and grasped my hand.

'I can't thank you sufficiently, Mr Wooster!'

'Oh, right-ho!'

'You have saved my good name. "Good name in man or woman, dear my lord",' he said, massaging the fin with some fervour, ' "is the immediate jewel of their souls. Who steals my purse steals trash. 'Twas mine, 'tis his, and has been slave to thousands. But he that filches from me my good name robs me of that which not enriches him and makes me poor indeed". I thank you from the bottom of my heart. Good night, Mr Wooster.'

'Good night, old thing,' I said.

'Your brandy-and-soda, sir,' said Jeeves, as the door shut.

I blinked at him.

'Oh, there you are!'

'Yes, sir.'

'Rather a sad affair, Jeeves.'

'Yes, sir.'

'Lucky I happened to have all that money handy.'

'Well – er – yes, sir.'

'You speak as though you didn't think much of it.'

'It is not my place to criticize your actions, sir, but I will venture to say that I think you behaved a little rashly.'

'What, lending that money?'

'Yes, sir. These fashionable French watering-places are notoriously infested by dishonest characters.'

This was a bit too thick.

'Now, look here, Jeeves,' I said, 'I can stand a lot, but when it comes to your casting asp-whatever-the-word-is on the sweetest girl in the world and a bird in Holy Orders – '

'Perhaps I am over-suspicious, sir. But I have seen a great deal of these resorts. When I was in the employment of Lord Frederick Ranelagh, shortly before I entered your service, his lordship was very neatly swindled by a criminal known, I believe, by the sobriquet of Soapy Sid, who scraped acquaintance with us in Monte Carlo with the assistance of a female accomplice. I have never forgotten the circumstance.'

'I don't want to butt in on your reminiscences, Jeeves,' I said coldly, 'but you're talking through your hat. How can there have been anything fishy about this business?

They've left me the pearls, haven't they? Very well, then, think before you speak. You had better be tooling down to the desk now and having these things shoved in the hotel safe.' I picked up the case and opened it. 'Oh, Great Scott!'

The bally thing was empty!

'Oh, my Lord!' I said, staring, 'don't tell me there's been dirty work at the cross-roads, after all!'

'Precisely, sir. It was in exactly the same manner that Lord Frederick was swindled on the occasion to which I have alluded. While his female accomplice was gratefully embracing his lordship, Soapy Sid substituted a duplicate case for the one containing the pearls, and went off with the jewels, the money, and the receipt. On the strength of the receipt he subsequently demanded from his lordship the return of the pearls, and his lordship, not being able to produce them, was obliged to pay a heavy sum in compensation. It is a simple but effective ruse.'

I felt as if the bottom had dropped out of things with a jerk. I mean to say, Aline Hemmingway, you know. What I mean is, if Love hadn't actually awakened in my heart, there's no doubt it was having a jolly good stab at it, and the thing was only a question of days. And all the time – well, I mean, dash it, you know.

'Soapy Sid? Sid! *Sidney*! Brother Sidney! Why, by Jove, Jeeves, do you think that parson was Soapy Sid?'

'Yes, sir.'

'But it seems so extraordinary. Why, his collar buttoned at the back – I mean, he would have deceived a bishop. Do you really think he was Soapy Sid?'

'Yes, sir. I recognized him directly he came into the room.'

I stared at the blighter.

'You recognized him?'

'Yes, sir.'

'Then, dash it all,' I said, deeply moved, 'I think you might have told me.'

'I thought it would save disturbance and unpleasantness if I merely abstracted the case from the man's pocket as I assisted him with his coat, sir. Here it is.'

He laid another case on the table beside the dud one, and, by Jove, you couldn't tell them apart. I opened it, and there were the good old pearls, as merry and bright as dammit, smiling up at me. I gazed feebly at the man. I was feeling a bit overwrought.

'Jeeves,' I said, 'you're an absolute genius!'

'Yes, sir.'

Relief was surging over me in great chunks by now. I'd almost forgotten that a woman had toyed with my heart and thrown it away like a worn-out tube of tooth-paste and all that sort of thing. What seemed to me the important item was the fact that, thanks to Jeeves, I was not going to be called on to cough up several thousand quid.

'It looks to me as though you had saved the old home. I mean, even a chappie endowed with the immortal rind of dear old Sid is hardly likely to have the nerve to come back and retrieve these little chaps.'

'I should imagine not, sir.'

'Well, then – Oh, I say, you don't think they are just paste or anything like that?'

'No, sir. These are genuine pearls, and extremely valuable.'

'Well, then dash it, I'm on velvet. Absolutely reclining on the good old plush! I may be down a hundred quid, but I'm up a jolly good string of pearls. Am I right or wrong?'

'Hardly that, sir. I think that you will have to restore the pearls.'

'What! To Sid? Not while I have my physique!'

'No, sir. To their rightful owner.'

'But who is their rightful owner?'

'Mrs Gregson, sir.'

'What! How do you know?'

'It was all over the hotel an hour ago that Mrs Gregson's pearls had been abstracted. The man Sid travelled from Paris in the same train as Mrs Gregson, and no doubt marked them down. I was speaking to Mrs Gregson's maid shortly before you came in, and she informed me that the manager of the hotel is now in Mrs Gregson's suite.'

'And having a devil of a time, what?'

'So I should be disposed to imagine, sir.'

The situation was beginning to unfold before me.

'I'll go and give them back to her, eh? It'll put me one up, what?'

'If I might make the suggestion, sir, I think it would strengthen your position if you were to affect to discover the pearls in Mrs Gregson's suite – say, in a bureau drawer.'

'I don't see why.'

'I think I am right, sir.'

'Well, I stand on you. If you say so. I'll be popping, what?'

'The sooner the better, sir.'

Long before I reached Aunt Agatha's lair I could tell that the hunt was up. Divers chappies in hotel uniform and not a few chambermaids of sorts were hanging about in the corridor, and through the panels I could hear a mixed assortment of voices, with Aunt Agatha's topping the lot. I knocked, but no one took any notice, so I trickled in. Among those present I noticed a chambermaid in hysterics, Aunt Agatha with her hair bristling, and a whiskered cove who looked like a bandit, as no doubt he was, being the proprietor of the hotel.

'Oh, hullo,' I said. 'I got your note, Aunt Agatha.'

She waved me away. No welcoming smile for Bertram.

'Oh don't bother me now,' she snapped, looking at me as if I were more or less the last straw.

'Something up?'

'Yes, yes, yes! I've lost my pearls.'

'Pearls? Pearls? Pearls?' I said. 'No, really? Dashed annoying. Where did you see them last?'

'What *does* it matter where I saw them last? They have been stolen.'

Here Wilfred the Whisker-King, who seemed to have been taking a rest between rounds, stepped into the ring again and began to talk rapidly in French. Cut to the quick he seemed. The chambermaid whooped in the corner.

'Sure you've looked everywhere?' I asked.

'Of course I've looked everywhere.'

'Well, you know, I've often lost a collar-stud and – '

'Do try not to be so maddening, Bertie! I have enough to bear without your imbecilities. Oh, be quiet! Be quiet!' she shouted. And such was the magnetism of what Jeeves called her forceful personality that Wilfred subsided as though he had run into a wall. The chambermaid continued to go strong.

'I say,' I said, 'I think there's something the matter with this girl. Isn't she crying or something?'

'She stole my pearls! I am convinced of it.'

This started the whisker-specialist off again, and I left them at it and wandered off on a tour round the room. I slipped the pearls out of the case and decanted them into a drawer. By the time I'd done this and had leisure to observe the free-for-all once more, Aunt Agatha had reached the frozen grande-dame stage and was putting the Last of the Bandits through it in the voice she usually reserves for snubbing waiters in restaurants.

'I tell you, my good man, for the hundredth time, that I have searched thoroughly – everywhere. Why you should imagine that I have overlooked so elementary – '

'I say,' I said, 'don't want to interrupt you and all that sort of thing, but aren't these the little chaps?'

I pulled them out of the drawer and held them up.

'These look like pearls, what?'

I don't know when I've had a more juicy moment. It was one of those occasions about which I shall prattle to my grand-children – if I ever have any, which at the moment of going to press seems more or less of a hundred-to-one shot. Aunt Agatha simply deflated before my eyes. It reminded me of when I once saw some intrepid aeronauts letting the gas out of a balloon.

'Where – where – where?' she gurgled.

'In this drawer. They'd slid under some paper.'

'Oh!' said Aunt Agatha, and there was a bit of silence.

I dug out my entire stock of manly courage, breathed a short prayer, and let her have it right in the thorax.

'I must say, Aunt Agatha, dash it,' I said, crisply, 'I think you have been a little hasty, what? I mean to say, giving this poor man here so much anxiety and worry and generally biting him in the gizzard. You've been very, very unjust to this poor man!'

'Yes, yes,' chipped in the poor man.

'And this unfortunate girl, what about her? Where does she get off? You've accused her of pinching the things on absolutely no evidence. I think she would be jolly well advised to bring an action for – for whatever it is, and soak you for substantial damages.'

'*Mais oui, mais oui, c'est trop fort!*' shouted the Bandit Chief, backing me up like a good 'un. And the chambermaid looked up inquiringly, as if the sun was breaking the clouds.

'I shall recompense her,' said Aunt Agatha, feebly.

'If you take my tip, you jolly well will, and that eftsoones or right speedily. She's got a cast-iron case, and if I were her I wouldn't take a cent under twenty quid. But what gives me the pip most is the way you've abused this poor man and tried to give his hotel a bad name – '

'Yes, by damn! It's too bad!' cried the whiskered marvel. 'You careless old woman! You give my hotel bad names, would you or wasn't it? Tomorrow you leave my hotel.'

And more to the same effect, all good, ripe stuff. And presently, having said his say, he withdrew, taking the chambermaid with him, the latter with a crisp tenner clutched in a vicelike grip. I suppose she and the bandit split it outside. A French hotel-manager wouldn't be likely to let real money wander away from him without counting himself in on the division.

I turned to Aunt Agatha, whose demeanour was now rather like that of one who, picking daisies on the railway, has just caught the down-express in the small of the back.

'There was something you wished to speak to me about?' I said.

'No no. Go away, go away.'

'You said in your note – '

'Yes, yes, never mind. Please go away, Bertie. I wish to be alone.'

'Oh, right-ho!' I said. 'Right-ho! right-ho!' And back to the good old suite.

'Ten o'clock, a clear night, and all's well, Jeeves,' I said, breezing in.

'I am gratified to hear it, sir.'

'If twenty quid would be any use to you, Jeeves – ?'

'I am much obliged, sir.'

There was a pause. And then – well, it was a wrench, but I did it. I unstripped the cummerbund and handed it over.

'Do you wish me to press this, sir?'

I gave the thing one last longing look. It had been very dear to me.

'No,' I said, 'take it away; give it to the deserving poor. I shall never wear it again.'

'Thank you very much, sir,' said Jeeves.

'THE GREAT SERMON HANDICAP'

The Inimitable Jeeves

You can always rely on Jeeves. Just as I was wiping the brow and gasping like a stranded goldfish, in he drifted, merry and bright, with the good old tissue-restorers on a tray.

'Jeeves,' I said, 'it's beastly hot.'

'The weather *is* oppressive, sir.'

'Not all the soda, Jeeves.'

'No, sir.'

'London in August,' I said, quaffing deeply of the flowing b., 'rather tends to give me the pip. All my pals are away, most of the theatres are shut, and they're taking up Piccadilly in large spadefuls. The world is empty and smells of burning asphalt. Shift-ho, I think, Jeeves, what?'

'Just as you say, sir. There is a letter on the tray, sir.'

'By Jove, Jeeves, that was practically poetry. Rhymed, did you notice?' I opened the letter. 'I say, this is rather extraordinary.'

'Sir?'

'You know Twing Hall?'

'Yes, sir.'

'Well, Mr Little is there.'

'Indeed, sir?'

'Absolutely in the flesh. He's had to take another of those tutoring jobs.'

I don't know if you remember, but immediately after that fearful mix-up at Goodwood, young Bingo Little, a broken man, had touched me for a tenner and whizzed silently off into the unknown. I had been all over the place ever since, asking mutual friends if they had heard anything of him, but nobody had. And all the time he had been at Twing Hall. Rummy. And I'll tell you why it was rummy. Twing Hall belongs to old Lord Wickhammersley, a great pal of my guv'nor's when he was alive, and I have a standing invitation to pop down there when I like. I generally put in a week or two some time in the summer, and I was thinking of going there before I read the letter.

'And, what's more, Jeeves, my cousin Claude and my cousin Eustace – you remember them?'

'Very vividly, sir.'

'Well, they're down there, too, reading for some exam or other with the vicar. I used to read with him myself at one time. He's known far and wide as a pretty hot coach for those of fairly feeble intellect. Well, when I tell you he got *me* through Smalls, you'll gather that he's a bit of a hummer. I call this most extraordinary.'

I read the letter again. It was from Eustace. Claude and Eustace are twins, and more or less generally admitted to be the curse of the human race.

* * *

> The Vicarage,
> Twing,
> Glos.

Dear Bertie,

Do you want to make a bit of money? I hear you had a bad Goodwood, so you probably do. Well, come down here quick and get in on the biggest sporting event of the season. I'll explain when I see you, but you can take it from me it's all right.

Claude and I are with a reading-party at old Heppenstall's. There are nine of us, not counting your pal Bingo Little, who is tutoring the kid up at the Hall.

Don't miss this golden opportunity, which may never occur again. Come and join us.

> Yours,
> Eustace.

I handed this to Jeeves. He studied it thoughtfully.

'What do you make of it? A rummy communication, what?'

'Very high-spirited young gentlemen, sir, Mr Claude and Mr Eustace. Up to some game, I should be disposed to imagine.'

'Yes. But what game, do you think?'

'It is impossible to say, sir. Did you observe that the letter continues over the page?'

'Eh, what?' I grabbed the thing. This was what was on the other side of the last page:

SERMON HANDICAP
RUNNERS AND BETTING
PROBABLE STARTERS.

Rev. Joseph Tucker (Badgwick), scratch.
Rev. Leonard Starkie (Stapleton), scratch.
Rev. Alexander Jones (Upper Bingley), receives three minutes.
Rev. W. Dix (Little Clickton-in-the-Wold), receives five minutes.
Rev. Francis Heppenstall (Twing), receives eight minutes.
Rev. Cuthbert Dibble (Boustead Parva), receives nine minutes.
Rev. Orlo Hough (Boustead Magna), receives nine minutes.
Rev. J.J. Roberts (Fale-by-the-Water), receives ten minutes.
Rev. G. Hayward (Lower Bingley), receives twelve minutes.
Rev. James Bates (Gandle-by-the-Hill), receives fifteen minutes.

The above have arrived.

Prices: 5-2, Tucker, Starkie; 3-1, Jones; 9-2, Dix; 6-1, Heppenstall, Dibble, Hough; 100-8 any other.

It baffled me.

'Do you understand it, Jeeves?'

'No sir.'

'Well, I think we ought to have a look into it, anyway, what?'

'Undoubtedly, sir.'

'Right-o, then. Pack our spare dickey and a toothbrush in a neat brown-paper parcel, send a wire to Lord Wickhammersley to say we're coming, and buy two tickets on the five-ten at Paddington tomorrow.'

The five-ten was late as usual, and everybody was dressing for dinner when I arrived at the Hall. It was only by getting into my evening things in record time and taking the stairs to the dining-room in a couple of bounds that I managed to dead-heat with the soup. I slid into the vacant chair, and found that I was sitting next to old Wickhammersley's youngest daughter, Cynthia.

'Oh, hullo, old thing,' I said.

Great pals we've always been. In fact there was a time when I had an idea I was in love with Cynthia. However, it blew over. A dashed pretty and lively and attractive girl, mind you, but full of ideals and all that. I may be wronging her, but I have an idea that she's the sort of girl who would want a fellow to carve out a career and what not. I know I've heard her speak favourably of Napoleon. So what with one thing and another the jolly old frenzy sort of petered out, and now we're just pals. I think she's a topper, and she thinks me next door to a looney, so everything's nice and matey.

'Well, Bertie, so you've arrived?'

'Oh, yes, I've arrived. Yes, here I am. I say, I seem to have plunged into the middle of quite a young dinner party. Who are all these coves?'

'Oh, just people from round about. You know most of them. You remember Colonel Willis, and the Spencers – '

'Of course, yes. And there's old Heppenstall. Who's the other clergyman next to Mrs Spencer?'

'Mr Hayward, from Lower Bingley.'

'What an amazing lot of clergymen there are round here. Why, there's another, next to Mrs Willis.'

'That's Mr Bates, Mr Heppenstall's nephew. He's an assistant-master at Eton. He's down here during the summer holidays, acting as locum tenens for Mr Spettigue, the rector of Gandle-by-the-Hill.'

'I thought I knew his face. He was in his fourth year at Oxford when I was a fresher. Rather a blood. Got his rowing blue and all that.'

I took another look round the table, and spotted young Bingo.

'Ah, there he is,' I said. 'There's the old egg.'

'There's who?'

'Young Bingo Little. Great pal of mine. He's tutoring your brother, you know.'

'Good gracious! Is he a friend of yours?'

'Rather! Known him all my life.'

'Then tell me, Bertie, is he at all weak in the head?'

'Weak in the head?'

'I don't mean simply because he's a friend of yours. But he's so strange in his manner.'

'How do you mean?'

'Well, he keeps looking at me so oddly.'

'Oddly. How? Give an imitation.'

'I can't in front of all these people.'

'Yes, you can. I'll hold my napkin up.'

'All right, then. Quick. There!'

Considering that she had only about a second and half to do it in, I must say it was a jolly fine exhibition. She opened her mouth and eyes pretty wide and let her jaw drop sideways, and managed to look so like a dyspeptic calf that I recognized the symptoms immediately.

'Oh, that's all right,' I said. 'No need to be alarmed. He's simply in love with you.'

'In love with me? Don't be absurd.'

'My dear old thing, you don't know young Bingo. He can fall in love with *anybody*.'

'Thank you!'

'Oh, I didn't mean it that way, you know. I don't wonder at his taking to you. Why, I was in love with you myself once.'

'Once? Ah! And all that remains now are the cold ashes? This isn't one of your tactful evenings, Bertie.'

'Well, my dear sweet thing, dash it all, considering that you gave me the bird and nearly laughed yourself into a permanent state of hiccoughs when I asked you – '

'Oh, I'm not reproaching you. No doubt there were faults on both sides. He's very good-looking, isn't he?'

'Good-looking? Bingo? Bingo good-looking? No, I say, come now, really!'

'I mean, compared with some people,' said Cynthia.

Some time after this, Lady Wickhammersley gave the signal for the females of the species to leg it, and they duly stampeded. I didn't get a chance of talking to young Bingo when they'd gone, and later, in the drawing-room, he didn't show up. I found him eventually in his room, lying on the bed with his feet on the rail, smoking a toofah. There was a notebook on the counterpane beside him.

'Hallo, old scream,' I said.

'Hallo, Bertie,' he replied, in what seemed to me rather a moody, distrait sort of manner.

'Rummy finding you down here. I take it your uncle cut off your allowance after that Goodwood binge and you had to take this tutoring job to keep the wolf from the door?'

'Correct,' said young Bingo, tersely.

'Well, you might have let your pals know where you were.'

He frowned darkly.

'I didn't want them to know where I was. I wanted to creep away and hide myself. I've been through a bad time, Bertie, these last weeks. The sun ceased to shine – '

'That's curious. We've had gorgeous weather in London.'

'The birds ceased to sing – '

'What birds?'

'What the devil does it matter what birds?' said young Bingo, with some asperity. 'Any birds. The birds round about here. You don't expect me to specify them by their pet names, do you? I tell you, Bertie, it hit me hard at first, very hard.'

'What hit you?' I simply couldn't follow the blighter.

'Charlotte's calculated callousness.'

'Oh, ah!' I've seen poor old Bingo through so many unsuccessful love-affairs that I'd almost forgotten there was a girl mixed up with that Goodwood business. Of course! Charlotte Corday Rowbotham. And she had given him the raspberry, I remembered now, and gone off with Comrade Butt.

'I went through torments. Recently, however, I've – er – bucked up a bit. Tell me, Bertie, what are you doing down here? I didn't know you knew these people.'

'Me? Why, I've known them since I was a kid.'

Young Bingo put his feet down with a thud.

'Do you mean to say you've known Lady Cynthia all that time?'

'Rather! She can't have been seven when I met her first.'

'Good Lord!' said young Bingo. He looked at me for the first time as though I amounted to something, and swallowed a mouthful of smoke the wrong way. 'I love that girl, Bertie,' he went on, when he'd finished coughing.

'Yes? Nice girl, of course.'

He eyed me with pretty deep loathing.

'Don't speak of her in that horrible casual way. She's an angel. An angel! Was she talking about me at all at dinner, Bertie?'

'Oh, yes.'

'What did she say?'

'I remember one thing. She said she thought you good-looking.'

Young Bingo closed his eyes in a sort of ecstasy. Then he picked up the notebook.

'Pop off now, old man, there's a good chap,' he said, in a hushed, far-away voice. 'I've got a bit of writing to do.'

'Writing?'

'Poetry, if you must know. I wish the dickens,' said young Bingo, not without some bitterness, 'she had been christened something except Cynthia. There isn't a damn word in the language it rhymes with. Ye gods, how I could have spread myself if she had only been called Jane!'

Bright and early next morning, as I lay in bed blinking at the sunlight on the dressing-table and wondering when Jeeves was going to show up with the cup of tea, a heavy weight descended on my toes, and the voice of young Bingo polluted the air. The blighter had apparently risen with the lark.

'Leave me,' I said, 'I would be alone. I can't see anybody till I've had my tea.'

'When Cynthia smiles,' said young Bingo, 'the skies are blue; the world takes on a roseate hue; birds in the garden trill and sing, and Joy is king of everything, when Cynthia smiles.' He coughed, changing gears. 'When Cynthia frowns – '

'What the devil are you talking about?'

'I'm reading you my poem. The one I wrote to Cynthia last night. I'll go on, shall I?'

'No!'

'No?'

'No. I haven't had my tea.'

At this moment Jeeves came in with the good old beverage, and I sprang on it with a glad cry. After a couple of sips things looked a bit brighter. Even young Bingo didn't offend the eye to quite such an extent. By the time I'd finished the first cup I was a new man, so much so that I not only permitted but encouraged the poor fish to read the rest of the bally thing, and even went so far as to criticize the scansion of the fourth line of the fifth verse. We were still arguing the point when the door burst open and in blew Claude and Eustace. One of the things which discourage me about rural life is the frightful earliness with which events begin to break loose. I've stayed at places in the country where they've jerked me out of the dreamless at about six-thirty to go for a jolly swim in the lake. At Twing, thank heaven, they know me, and let me breakfast in bed.

The twins seemed pleased to see me.

'Good old Bertie!' said Claude.

'Stout fellow!' said Eustace. 'The Rev. told us you had arrived. I thought that letter of mine would fetch you.'

'You can always bank on Bertie,' said Claude. 'A sportsman to the finger-tips. Well, has Bingo told you about it?'

'Not a word. He's been – '

'We've been talking,' said Bingo, hastily, 'of other matters.'

Claude pinched the last slice of thin bread-and-butter, and Eustace poured himself out a cup of tea.

'It's like this, Bertie,' said Eustace, settling down cosily. 'As I told you in my letter, there are nine of us marooned in this desert spot, reading with old Heppenstall. Well, of course, nothing is jollier than sweating up the Classics when it's a hundred in the shade, but there does come a time when you begin to feel the need of a little relaxation; and, by Jove, there are absolutely no facilities for relaxation in this place whatever. And then Steggles got this idea. Steggles is one of our reading-party, and, between ourselves, rather a worm as a general thing. Still, you have to give him credit for getting this idea.'

'What idea?'

'Well, you know how many parsons there are round about here. There are about a dozen hamlets within a radius of six miles, and each hamlet has a church and each church has a parson and each parson preaches a sermon every Sunday. Tomorrow week – Sunday the twenty-third – we're running off the great Sermon Handicap. Steggles is making the book. Each parson is to be clocked by a reliable steward of the course, and the one that preaches the longest sermon wins. Did you study the race-card I sent you?'

'I couldn't understand what it was all about.'

'Why, you chump, it gives the handicaps and the current odds on each starter. I've got another one here, in case you've lost yours. Take a careful look at it. It gives you the thing in a nutshell. Jeeves, old son, do you want a sporting flutter?'

'Sir?' said Jeeves, who had just meandered in with my breakfast.

Claude explained the scheme. Amazing the way Jeeves grasped it right off. But he merely smiled in a paternal sort of way.

'Thank you, sir, I think not.'

'Well, you're with us, Bertie, aren't you?' said Claude, sneaking a roll and a slice of bacon. 'Have you studied that card? Well, tell me, does anything strike you about it?'

Of course it did. It had struck me the moment I looked at it.

'Why, it's a sitter for old Heppenstall,' I said. 'He's got the event sewed up in a parcel. There isn't a parson in the land who could give him eight minutes. Your pal Steggles must be an ass, giving him a handicap like that. Why, in the days when I was with him, old Heppenstall never used to preach under half an hour, and there was one sermon of his on Brotherly Love which lasted forty-five minutes if it lasted a second. Has he lost his vim lately, or what is it?'

'Not a bit of it,' said Eustace. 'Tell him what happened, Claude.'

'Why,' said Claude, 'the first Sunday we were here, we all went to Twing church, and old Heppenstall preached a sermon that was well under twenty minutes. This is what happened. Steggles didn't notice it, and the Rev. didn't notice it himself, but Eustace and I both spotted that he had dropped a chunk of at least half-a-dozen pages out of his sermon-case as he was walking up to the pulpit. He sort of flickered when he got to the gap in the manuscript, but carried on all right, and Steggles went away with the impression that twenty minutes or a bit under was his usual form. The next Sunday we heard Tucker and Starkie, and they both went well over the thirty-five minutes, so Steggles arranged the handicapping as you see on the card. You must come into this, Bertie. You see, the trouble is that I haven't a bean, and Eustace hasn't a bean, and Bingo Little hasn't a bean, so you'll have to finance the syndicate. Don't weaken! It's just putting money in all our pockets. Well, we'll have to be getting back now. Think the thing over, and 'phone me later in the day. And, if you let us down, Bertie, may a cousin's curse – Come on, Claude, old thing.'

The more I studied the scheme, the better it looked.

'How about it, Jeeves?' I said.

Jeeves smiled gently, and drifted out.

'Jeeves has no sporting blood,' said Bingo.

'Well, I have. I'm coming into this. Claude's quite right. It's like finding money by the wayside.'

'Good man!' said Bingo. 'Now I can see daylight. Say I have a tenner on Heppenstall, and cop; that'll give me a bit in hand to back Pink Pill with in the two o'clock at Gatwick the week after next: cop on that, put the pile on Musk-Rat for the one-thirty at Lewes, and there I am with a nice little sum to take to Alexandra Park on September the tenth, when I've got a tip straight from the stable.'

It sounded like a bit out of 'Smiles's Self-Help.'

'And then,' said young Bingo, 'I'll be in a position to go to my uncle and beard him in his lair somewhat. He's quite a bit of a snob, you know, and when he hears that I'm going to marry the daughter of an earl – '

'I say, old man,' I couldn't help saying, 'aren't you looking ahead rather far?'

'Oh, that's all right. It's true nothing's actually settled yet, but she practically told me the other day she was fond of me.'

'What!'

'Well she said that the sort of man she liked was the self-reliant, manly man with strength, good looks, character, ambition, and initiative.'

'Leave me, laddie,' I said. 'Leave me to my fried egg.'

Directly I'd got up I went to the 'phone, snatched Eustace away from his morning's work, and instructed him to put a tenner on the Twing flier at current odds for each of the syndicate; and after lunch Eustace rang me up to say that he had done business at a snappy seven-to-one, the odds having lengthened owing to a rumour in knowledgeable circles that the Rev. was subject to hay-fever and was taking big chances strolling in the paddock behind the vicarage in the early mornings. And it was dashed lucky, I thought next day, that we had managed to get the money on in time, for on the Sunday morning old Heppenstall fairly took the bit between his teeth, and gave us thirty-six solid minutes on Certain Popular Superstitions. I was sitting next to Steggles in the pew, and I saw him blench visibly. He was a little, rat-faced fellow, with shifty eyes and a suspicious nature. The first thing he did when we emerged into the open air was to announce, formally, that anyone who fancied the Rev. could now be accommodated at fifteen-to-eight on, and he added, in a rather nasty manner, that if he had his way, this sort of in-and-out running would be brought to the attention of the Jockey Club, but that he supposed that there was nothing to be done about it. This ruinous price checked the punters at once, and there was little money in sight. And so matters stood till just after lunch on Tuesday afternoon, when, as I was strolling up and down in front of the house with a cigarette, Claude and Eustace came bursting up the drive on bicycles, dripping with momentous news.

'Bertie,' said Claude, deeply agitated, 'unless we take immediate action and do a bit of quick thinking, we're in the cart.'

'What's the matter?'

'G. Hayward's the matter,' said Eustace, morosely. 'The Lower Bingley starter.'

'We never even considered him,' said Claude. 'Somehow or other, he got overlooked. It's always the way. Steggles overlooked him. We all overlooked him. But Eustace and I happened by the merest fluke to be riding through Lower Bingley this morning, and there was a wedding on at the church, and it suddenly struck us that it wouldn't be a bad move to get a line on G. Hayward's form, in case he might be a dark horse.'

'And it was jolly lucky we did,' said Eustace. 'He delivered an address of twenty-six minutes by Claude's stop-watch. At a village wedding, mark you! What'll he do when he really extends himself!'

'There's only one thing to be done, Bertie,' said Claude. 'You must spring some more funds, so that we can hedge on Hayward and save ourselves.'

'But – '

'Well, it's the only way out.'

'But I say, you know, I hate the idea of all that money we put on Heppenstall being chucked away.'

'What else can you suggest? You don't suppose the Rev. can give this absolute marvel a handicap and win, do you?'

'I've got it!' I said.

'What?'

'I see a way by which we can make it safe for our nominee. I'll pop over this afternoon, and ask him as a personal favour to preach that sermon of his on Brotherly Love on Sunday.'

Claude and Eustace looked at each other, like those chappies in the poem, with a wild surmise.

'It's a scheme,' said Claude.

'A jolly brainy scheme,' said Eustace. 'I didn't think you had it in you, Bertie.'

'But even so,' said Claude, 'fizzer as that sermon no doubt is, will it be good enough in the face of a four-minute handicap?'

'Rather!' I said. 'When I told you it lasted forty-five minutes, I was probably understating it. I should call it – from my recollection of the thing – nearer fifty.'

'Then carry on,' said Claude.

I toddled over in the evening and fixed the thing up. Old Heppenstall was most decent about the whole affair. He seemed pleased and touched that I should have remembered the sermon all these years, and said he had once or twice had an idea of preaching it again, only it had seemed to him, on reflection, that it was perhaps a trifle long for a rustic congregation.

'And in these restless times, my dear Wooster,' he said, 'I fear that brevity in the pulpit is becoming more and more desiderated by even the bucolic churchgoer, who one might have supposed would be less afflicted with the spirit of hurry and impatience than his metropolitan brother. I have had many arguments on the subject with my nephew, young Bates, who is taking my old friend Spettigue's cure over at Gandle-by-the-Hill. His view is that a sermon nowadays should be a bright, brisk, straight-from-the-shoulder address, never lasting more than ten or twelve minutes.'

'Long?' I said. 'Why, my goodness! you don't call that Brotherly Love sermon of yours *long*, do you?'

'It takes fully fifty minutes to deliver.'

'Surely not?'

'Your incredulity, my dear Wooster, is extremely flattering – far more flattering, of course, than I deserve. Nevertheless, the facts are as I have stated. You are sure that I would not be well advised to make certain excisions and eliminations? You do not think it would be a good thing to cut, to prune? I might, for example, delete the rather exhaustive excursus into the family life of the early Assyrians?'

'Don't touch a word of it, or you'll spoil the whole thing,' I said earnestly.

'I am delighted to hear you say so, and I shall preach the sermon without fail next Sunday morning.'

What I have always said, and what I always shall say, is that this ante-post betting is a mistake, an error, and a mug's game. You never can tell what's going to happen. If fellows would only stick to the good old S P there would be fewer young men go wrong. I'd hardly finished my breakfast on the Saturday morning, when Jeeves came to my bedside to say that Eustace wanted me on the telephone.

'Good Lord, Jeeves, what's the matter, do you think?'

I'm bound to say I was beginning to get a bit jumpy by this time.

'Mr Eustace did not confide in me, sir.'

'Has he got the wind up?'

'Somewhat vertically, sir, to judge by his voice.'

'Do you know what I think, Jeeves? Something's gone wrong with the favourite.'

'Which is the favourite, sir?'

'Mr Heppenstall. He's gone to odds on. He was intending to preach a sermon on Brotherly Love which would have brought him home by lengths. I wonder if anything's happened to him.'

'You could ascertain, sir, by speaking to Mr Eustace on the telephone. He is holding the wire.'

'By Jove, yes!'

I shoved on a dressing-gown, and flew downstairs like a mighty, rushing wind. The moment I heard Eustace's voice I knew we were for it. It had a croak of agony in it.

'Bertie?'

'Here I am.'

'Deuce of a time you've been. Bertie, we're sunk. The favourite's blown up.'

'No!'

'Yes. Coughing in his stable all last night.'

'What!'

'Absolutely! Hay-fever.'

'Oh, my sainted aunt!'

'The doctor is with him now, and it's only a question of minutes before he's officially scratched. That means the curate will show up at the post instead, and he's no good at all. He is being offered at a hundred-to-six, but no takers. What shall we do?'

I had to grapple with the thing for a moment in silence.

'Eustace.'

'Hullo?'

'What can you get on G. Hayward?'

'Only four-to-one now. I think there's been a leak, and Steggles has heard something. The odds shortened late last night in a significant manner.'

'Well, four-to-one will clear us. Put another fiver all round on G. Hayward for the syndicate. That'll bring us out on the right side of the ledger.'

'If he wins.'

'What do you mean? I thought you considered him a cert., bar Heppenstall.'

'I'm beginning to wonder,' said Eustace, gloomily, 'if there's such a thing as a cert. in this world. I'm told the Rev. Joseph Tucker did an extraordinarily fine trial gallop at a mothers' meeting over at Badgwick yesterday. However, it seems our only chance. So long.'

Not being one of the official stewards, I had my choice of churches next morning, and naturally I didn't hesitate. The only drawback to going to Lower Bingley was that it was ten miles away, which meant an early start, but I borrowed a bicycle from one of the grooms and tooled off. I had only Eustace's word for it that G. Hayward was such a stayer, and it might have been that he had showed too flattering form at that wedding where the twins had heard him preach; but any misgivings I may have had disappeared the moment he got into the pulpit. Eustace had been right. The man was a trier. He was a tall, rangy-looking greybeard, and he went off from the start with a nice, easy action, pausing and clearing his throat at the end of each sentence, and it wasn't five minutes before I realized that here was the winner. His habit of stopping dead and looking round the church at intervals was worth minutes to us, and in the home stretch we gained no little advantage owing to his dropping his pince-nez and having to grope for them. At the twenty-minute mark he had merely settled down. Twenty-five minutes saw him going strong. And when he finally finished with a good burst, the clock showed thirty-five minutes fourteen seconds. With the handicap which he had been given, this seemed to me to make the event easy for him, and it was with much *bonhomie* and goodwill to all men that I hopped on to the old bike and started back to the Hall for lunch.

Bingo was talking on the 'phone when I arrived.

'Fine! Splendid! Topping!' he was saying. 'Eh? Oh, we needn't worry about him. Right-o, I'll tell Bertie.' He hung up the receiver and caught sight of me. 'Oh, hullo, Bertie; I was just talking to Eustace. It's all right, old man. The report from Lower Bingley has just got in. G. Hayward romps home.'

'I knew he would. I've just come from there.'

'Oh, were you there? I went to Badgwick. Tucker ran a splendid race, but the handicap was too much for him. Starkie had a sore throat and was nowhere. Roberts, of Fale-by-the-Water, ran third. Good old G. Hayward!' said Bingo, affectionately, and we strolled out on to the terrace.

'Are all the returns in, then?' I asked.

'All except Gandle-by-the-Hill. But we needn't worry about Bates. He never had a chance. By the way, poor old Jeeves loses his tenner. Silly ass!'

'Jeeves? How do you mean?'

'He came to me this morning, just after you had left, and asked me to put a tenner on Bates for him. I told him he was a chump and begged him not to throw his money away, but he would do it.'

'I beg your pardon, sir. This note arrived for you just after you had left the house this morning.'

Jeeves had materialized from nowhere, and was standing at my elbow.

'Eh? What? Note?'

'The Reverend Mr Heppenstall's butler brought it over from the vicarage, sir. It came too late to be delivered to you at the moment.'

Young Bingo was talking to Jeeves like a father on the subject of betting against the form-book. The yell I gave made him bite his tongue in the middle of a sentence.

'What the dickens is the matter?' he asked, not a little peeved.

'We're dished! Listen to this!'

I read him the note:

> 'The Vicarage,
> 'Twing, Glos.
>
> 'My dear Wooster,
>
> 'As you may have heard, circumstances over which I have no control will prevent my preaching the sermon on Brotherly Love for which you made such a flattering request. I am unwilling, however, that you shall be disappointed, so, if you will attend divine service at Gandle-by-the-Hill this morning, you will hear my sermon preached by young Bates, my nephew. I have lent him the manuscript at his urgent desire, for, between ourselves, there are wheels within wheels. My nephew is one of the candidates for the headmastership of a well-known public school, and the choice has narrowed down between him and one rival.
>
> 'Late yesterday evening James received private information that the head of the Board of Governors of the school proposed to sit under him this Sunday in order to judge of the merits of his preaching, a most important item in swaying the Board's choice. I accceded to his plea that I lend him my sermon on Brotherly Love, of which, like you, he apparently retains a vivid recollection. It would have been too late for him to compose a sermon of suitable length in place of the brief address which – mistakenly, in my opinion – he had designed to deliver to his rustic flock, and I wished to help the boy.
>
> 'Trusting that his preaching of the sermon will supply you with as pleasant memories as you say you have of mine, I remain,
>
> 'Cordially yours,
> 'F. Heppenstall.
>
> 'PS The hay-fever has rendered my eyes unpleasantly weak for the time being, so I am dictating this letter to my butler, Brookfield, who will convey it to you.'

I don't know when I've experienced a more massive silence than the one that followed my reading of this cheery epistle. Young Bingo gulped once or twice, and practically every known emotion came and went on his face. Jeeves coughed one soft, low, gentle cough like a sheep with a blade of grass stuck in its throat, and then stood gazing serenely at the landscape. Finally young Bingo spoke.

'Great Scott!' he whispered, hoarsely. 'An S P job!'

'I believe that is the technical term, sir,' said Jeeves.

'So you had inside information, dash it!' said young Bingo.

'Why, yes, sir,' said Jeeves. 'Brookfield happened to mention the contents of the note to me when he brought it. We are old friends.'

Bingo registered grief, anguish, rage, despair, and resentment.

'Well, all I can say,' he cried, 'is that it's a bit thick! Preaching another man's sermon! Do you call that honest? Do you call that playing the game?'

'Well, my dear old thing,' I said, 'be fair. It's quite within the rules. Clergymen do it all the time. They aren't expected always to make up the sermons they preach.'

Jeeves coughed again, and fixed me with an expressionless eye.

'And in the present case, sir, if I may be permitted to take the liberty of making the observation, I think we should make allowances. We should remember that the securing of this headmastership means everything to the young couple.'

'Young couple! What young couple?'

'The Reverend James Bates, sir, and Lady Cynthia. I am informed by her ladyship's maid that they have been engaged to be married for some weeks – provisionally, so to speak; and his lordship made his consent conditional on Mr Bates securing a really important and remunerative position.'

Young Bingo turned a light green.

'Engaged to be married!'

'Yes, sir.'

There was a silence.

'I think I'll go for a walk,' said Bingo.

'But, my dear old thing,' I said, 'it's just lunchtime. The gong will be going any minute now.'

'I don't want any lunch!' said Bingo.

'THE PURITY OF THE TURF'

The Inimitable Jeeves

When the thing was over, I made my mind up.

'Jeeves,' I said.

'Sir?'

'Never again! The strain is too great. I don't say I shall chuck betting altogether: if I get hold of a good thing for one of the big races no doubt I shall have my bit on as aforetime: but you won't catch me mixing myself up with one of these minor country meetings again. They're too hot.'

'I think perhaps you are right, sir,' said Jeeves.

It was young Bingo Little who lured me into the thing. About the third week of my visit at Twing Hall he blew into my bedroom one morning while I was toying with a bit of breakfast and thinking of this and that.

'Bertie!' he said, in an earnest kind of voice.

I decided to take a firm line from the start. Young Bingo, if you remember, was at a pretty low ebb at about this juncture. He had not only failed to put his finances on a sound basis over the recent Sermon Handicap, but had also discovered that Lady Cynthia Wickhammersley loved another. These things had jarred the unfortunate mutt, and he had developed a habit of dropping in on me at all hours and decanting his anguished soul on me. I could stand this all right after dinner, and even after lunch; but before breakfast, no. We Woosters are amiability itself, but there is a limit.

'Now look here, old friend,' I said. 'I know your bally heart is broken and all that, and at some future time I shall be delighted to hear all about it, but – '

'I didn't come to talk about that.'

'No? Good egg!'

'The past,' said young Bingo, 'is dead. Let us say no more about it.'

'Right-o!'

'I have been wounded to the very depths of my soul, but don't speak about it.'

'I won't.'

'Ignore it. Forget it.'

'Absolutely!'

I hadn't seen him so dashed reasonable for weeks.

'What I came to see you about this morning, Bertie,' he said, fishing a sheet of paper out of his pocket, 'was to ask if you would care to come in on another little flutter.'

If there is one thing we Woosters are simply dripping with, it is sporting blood. I bolted the rest of my sausage, and sat up and took notice.

'Proceed,' I said. 'You interest me strangely, old bird.'

Bingo laid the paper on the bed.

'On Monday week,' he said, 'you may or may not know, the annual village School Treat takes place. Lord Wickhammersley lends the Hall grounds for the purpose. There will be games, and a conjuror, and coconut shies, and tea in a tent. And also sports.'

'I know. Cynthia was telling me.'

Young Bingo winced.

'Would you mind not mentioning that name? I am not made of marble.'

'Sorry!'

'Well, as I was saying, this jamboree is slated for Monday week. The question is, Are we on?'

'How do you mean, "Are we on"?'

'I am referring to the sports. Steggles did so well out of the Sermon Handicap that he has decided to make a book on these sports. Punters can be accommodated at ante-post odds or starting price, according to their preference.'

Steggles, I don't know if you remember, was one of the gang of youths who were reading for some examination or other with old Heppenstall down at the vicarage. He was the fellow who had promoted the Sermon Handicap. A bird of considerable enterprise and vast riches, being the only son of one of the biggest bookies in London, but no pal of mine. I never liked the chap. He was a ferret-faced egg with a shifty eye and not a few pimples. On the whole, a nasty growth.

'I think we ought to look into it,' said young Bingo.

I pressed the bell.

'I'll consult Jeeves. I don't touch any sporting proposition without his advice. Jeeves,' I said, as he drifted in, 'rally round.'

'Sir?'

'Stand by. We want your advice.'

'Very good, sir.'

'State your case, Bingo.'

Bingo stated his case.

'What about it, Jeeves?' I said. 'Do we go in?'

Jeeves pondered to some extent.

'I am inclined to favour the idea, sir.'

That was good enough for me. 'Right,' I said. 'Then we will form a syndicate and bust the Ring. I supply the money, you supply the brains, and Bingo – what do you supply, Bingo?'

'If you will carry me, and let me settle up later,' said young Bingo, 'I think I can put you in the way of winning a parcel on the Mothers' Sack Race.'

'All right. We will put you down as Inside Information. Now, what are the events?'

Bingo reached for his paper and consulted it.

'Girls' Under Fourteen Fifty-Yard Dash seems to open the proceedings.'

'Anything to say about that, Jeeves?'

'No, sir. I have no information.'

'What's the next?'

'Boys' and Girls' Mixed Animal Potato Race, All Ages.'

This was a new one to me. I had never heard of it at any of the big meetings.

'What's that?'

'Rather sporting,' said young Bingo. 'The competitors enter in couples, each couple being assigned an animal cry and a potato. For instance, let's suppose that you and Jeeves entered. Jeeves would stand at a fixed point holding a potato. You would have your head in a sack, and you would grope about trying to find Jeeves and making a noise like a cat; Jeeves also making a noise like a cat. Other competitors would be making noises like cows and pigs and dogs, and so on, and groping about for *their* potato-holders, who would also be making noises like cows and pigs and dogs and so on – '

I stopped the poor fish.

'Jolly if you're fond of animals,' I said, 'but on the whole – '

'Precisely, sir,' said Jeeves. 'I wouldn't touch it.'

'Too open, what?'

'Exactly, sir. Very hard to estimate form.'

'Carry on, Bingo. Where do we go from there?'

'Mothers' Sack Race.'

'Ah! that's better. This is where you know something.'

'A gift for Mrs Penworthy, the tobacconist's wife,' said Bingo, confidently. 'I was in at her shop yesterday, buying cigarettes, and she told me she had won three times at fairs in Worcestershire. She only moved to these parts a short time ago, so nobody knows about her. She promised me she would keep herself dark, and I think we could get a good price.'

'Risk a tenner each way, Jeeves, what?'

'I think so, sir.'

'Girls' Open Egg and Spoon Race,' read Bingo.

'How about that?'

'I doubt if it would be worth while to invest, sir,' said Jeeves. 'I am told it is a certainty for last year's winner, Sarah Mills, who will doubtless start an odds-on favourite.'

'Good, is she?'

'They tell me in the village that she carries a beautiful egg, sir.'

'Then there's the Obstacle Race,' said Bingo. 'Risky, in my opinion. Like betting on the Grand National. Fathers' Hat-Trimming Contest – another speculative event. That's all, except the Choir Boys' Hundred Yards Handicap, for a pewter mug presented by the vicar – open to all whose voices have not broken before the second Sunday in Epiphany. Willie Chambers won last year, in a canter, receiving fifteen yards. This time he will probably be handicapped out of the race. I don't know what to advise.'

'If I might make a suggestion, sir.'

I eyed Jeeves with interest. I don't know that I'd ever seen him look so nearly excited.

'You've got something up your sleeve?'

'I have, sir.'

'Red-hot?'

'That precisely describes it, sir. I think I may confidently assert that we have the winner of the Choir Boys' Handicap under this very roof, sir. Harold, the page-boy.'

'Page-boy? Do you mean the tubby little chap in buttons one sees bobbing about here and there? Why, dash it, Jeeves, nobody has a greater respect for your knowledge of form than I have, but I'm hanged if I can see Harold catching the judge's eye. He's practically circular, and every time I've seen him he's been leaning up against something half-asleep.'

'He receives thirty yards, sir, and could win from scratch. The boy is a flier.'

'How do you know?'

Jeeves coughed, and there was a dreamy look in his eye.

'I was as much astonished as yourself, sir, when I first became aware of the lad's capabilities. I happened to pursue him one morning with the intention of fetching him a clip on the side of the head – '

'Great Scott, Jeeves! You!'

'Yes, sir. The boy is of an outspoken disposition, and had made an opprobrious remark respecting my personal appearance.'

'What did he say about your appearance?'

'I have forgotten, sir,' said Jeeves, with a touch of austerity. 'But it was opprobrious. I endeavoured to correct him, but he out-distanced me by yards, and made good his escape.'

'But, I say, Jeeves, this is sensational. And yet – if he's such a sprinter, why hasn't anybody in the village found it out? Surely he plays with the other boys?'

'No, sir. As his lordship's page-boy, Harold does not mix with the village lads.'

'Bit of a snob, what?'

'He is somewhat acutely alive to the existence of class distinctions, sir.'

'You're absolutely certain he's such a wonder?' said Bingo. 'I mean, it wouldn't do to plunge unless you're sure.'

'If you desire to ascertain the boy's form by personal inspection, sir, it will be a simple matter to arrange a secret trial.'

'I'm bound to say I should feel easier in my mind,' I said.

'Then if I may take a shilling from the money on your dressing-table – '

'What for?'

'I propose to bribe the lad to speak slightingly of the second footman's squint, sir. Charles is somewhat sensitive on the point, and should undoubtedly make the lad extend himself. If you will be at the first-floor passage-window, overlooking the back-door, in half an hour's time – '

I don't know when I've dressed in such a hurry. As a rule, I'm what you might call a slow and careful dresser: I like to linger over the tie and see that the trousers are just so; but this morning I was all worked up. I just shoved on my things anyhow, and joined Bingo at the window with a quarter of an hour to spare.

The passage-window looked down on to a broad sort of paved courtyard, which ended after about twenty yards in an archway through a high wall. Beyond this archway you got on to a strip of the drive, which curved round for another thirty yards or so till it was lost behind a thick shrubbery. I put myself in the stripling's place and thought what steps I would take with a second footman after me. There was only one thing to do – leg it for the shrubbery and take cover; which meant that at least fifty yards would have to be covered – an excellent test. If good old Harold could fight off the second footman's challenge long enough to allow him to reach the bushes, there wasn't a choir-boy in England who could give him thirty yards in the hundred. I waited, all of a twitter, for what seemed hours, and then suddenly there was a confused noise without and something round and blue and buttony shot through the back-door and buzzed for the archway like a mustang. And about two seconds later out came the second footman, going his hardest.

There was nothing to it. Absolutely nothing. The field never had a chance. Long before the footman reached the half-way mark, Harold was in the bushes, throwing stones. I came away from the window thrilled to the marrow; and when I met Jeeves on the stairs I was so moved that I nearly grasped his hand.

'Jeeves,' I said, 'no discussion! The Wooster shirt goes on this boy!'

'Very good, sir,' said Jeeves.

The worst of these country meetings is that you can't plunge as heavily as you would like when you get a good thing, because it alarms the Ring. Steggles, though pimpled, was, as I have indicated, no chump, and if I had invested all I wanted to he would have put two and two together. I managed to get a good solid bet down for the syndicate, however, though it did make him look thoughtful. I heard in the next few days that he had been making searching inquiries in the village concerning Harold; but nobody could tell him anything, and eventually he came to the conclusion, I suppose, that I must be having a long shot on the strength of that thirty yards start. Public opinion wavered between Jimmy Goode, receiving ten yards, at seven-to-two, and Alexander Bartlett, with six yards' start, at eleven-to-four. Willie Chambers, scratch, was offered to the public at two-to-one, but found no takers.

We were taking no chances on the big event, and directly we had got our money on at a nice hundred-to-twelve Harold was put into strict training. It was a wearing business, and I can understand now why most of the big trainers are grim, silent men, who look as though they had suffered. The kid wanted constant watching. It was no good talking to him about honour and glory and how proud his mother would be when he wrote and told her he had won a real cup – the moment blighted Harold discovered that training meant knocking off pastry, taking exercise, and keeping away from the cigarettes, he was all against it, and it was only by unceasing vigilance that we managed to keep him in any shape at all. It was the diet that was the stumbling block. As far as exercise went, we could generally arrange for a sharp dash every morning with the assistance of the second footman. It ran into money, of course, but that couldn't be helped. Still, when a kid has simply to wait till the butler's back is turned to have the run of the pantry and has only to nip into the smoking-room to collect a handful of the best Turkish, training becomes a rocky job. We could only hope that on the day his natural stamina would pull him through.

And then one evening young Bingo came back from the links with a disturbing story. He had been in the habit of giving Harold mild exercise in the afternoons by taking him out as a caddie.

At first he seemed to think it humorous, the poor chump! He bubbled over with merry mirth as he began his tale.

'I say, rather funny this afternoon,' he said. 'You ought to have seen Steggles's face!'

'Seen Steggles's face? What for?'

'When he saw young Harold sprint, I mean.'

I was filled with a grim foreboding of an awful doom.

'Good heavens! You didn't let Harold sprint in front of Steggles?'

Young Bingo's jaw dropped.

'I never thought of that,' he said gloomily. 'It wasn't my fault. I was playing a round with Steggles, and after we'd finished we went into the club-house for a drink, leaving Harold with the clubs outside. In about five minutes we came out, and there was the kid on the gravel practising swings with Steggles's driver and a stone. When he saw us coming, the kid dropped the club and was over the horizon like a streak. Steggles was absolutely dumb-founded. And I must say it was a revelation even to me. The kid certainly gave of his best. Of course, it's a nuisance in a way; but I don't see, on second thoughts,' said Bingo, brightening up, 'that it matters. We're on at a good price. We've nothing to lose by the kid's form becoming known. I take it he will start odds on, but that doesn't affect us.'

I looked at Jeeves. Jeeves looked at me.

'It affects us all right if he doesn't start at all.'

'Precisely, sir.'

'What do you mean?' asked Bingo.

'If you ask me,' I said, 'I think Steggles will try to nobble him before the race.'

'Good Lord! I never thought of that.' Bingo blenched. 'You don't think he would really do it?'

'I think he would have a jolly good try. Steggles is a bad man. From now on, Jeeves, we must watch Harold like hawks.'

'Undoubtedly, sir.'

'Ceaseless vigilance, what?'

'Precisely, sir.'

'You wouldn't care to sleep in his room, Jeeves?'

'No, sir, I should not.'

'No, nor would I, if it comes to that. But dash it all,' I said, 'we're letting ourselves get rattled! We're losing our nerve. This won't do. How can Steggles possibly get at Harold, even if he wants to?'

There was no cheering young Bingo up. He's one of those birds who simply leap at the morbid view, if you give them half a chance.

'There are all sorts of ways of nobbling favourites,' he said, in a sort of death-bed voice. 'You ought to read some of these racing novels. In *Pipped on the Post*, Lord Jasper Mauleverer as near as a toucher outed Bonny Betsy by bribing the head-lad to slip a cobra into her stable the night before the Derby!'

'What are the chances of a cobra biting Harold, Jeeves?'

'Slight, I should imagine, sir. And in such an event, knowing the boy as intimately as I do, my anxiety would be entirely for the snake.'

'Still, unceasing vigilance, Jeeves.'

'Most certainly, sir.'

I must say I got a bit fed up with young Bingo in the next few days. It's all very well for a fellow with a big winner in his stable to exercise proper care, but in my opinion Bingo overdid it. The blighter's mind appeared to be absolutely saturated with racing fiction; and in stories of that kind, as far as I could make out, no horse is ever allowed to start in a race without at least a dozen attempts to put it out of action. He stuck to Harold like a plaster. Never let the unfortunate kid out of his sight. Of course, it meant a lot to the poor old egg if he could collect on this race, because it would give him enough money to chuck his tutoring job and get back to London; but all the same, he needn't have woken me up at three in the morning twice running – once to tell me we ought to cook Harold's food ourselves to prevent doping: the other time to say that he had heard mysterious noises in the shrubbery. But he reached the limit, in my opinion, when he insisted on my going to evening service on Sunday, the day before the sports.

'Why on earth?' I said, never being much of a lad for evensong.

'Well, I can't go myself. I shan't be here. I've got to go to London today with young Egbert.' Egbert was Lord Wickhammersley's son, the one Bingo was tutoring. 'He's going for a visit down in Kent, and I've got to see him off at Charing Cross. It's an infernal nuisance. I shan't be back till Monday afternoon. In fact, I shall miss most of the sports, I expect. Everything, therefore, depends on you, Bertie.'

'But why should either of us go to evening service?'

'Ass! Harold sings in the choir, doesn't he?'

'What about it? I can't stop him dislocating his neck over a high note, if that's what you're afraid of.'

'Fool! Steggles sings in the choir, too. There may be dirty work after the service.'

'What absolute rot!'

'Is it?' said young Bingo. 'Well, let me tell you that in *Jenny, the Girl Jockey*, the villain kidnapped the boy who was to ride the favourite the night before the big race, and he was the only one who understood and could control the horse, and if the heroine hadn't dressed up in riding things and – '

'Oh, all right, all right. But, if there's any danger, it seems to me the simplest thing would be for Harold not to turn out on Sunday evening.'

'He must turn out. You seem to think the infernal kid is a monument of rectitude, beloved by all. He's got the shakiest reputation of any kid in the village. His name is as near being mud as it can jolly well stick. He's played hookey from the choir so often that the vicar told him, if one more thing happened, he would fire him out. Nice chumps we should look if he was scratched the night before the race!'

Well, of course, that being so, there was nothing for it but to toddle along.

There's something about evening service in a country church that makes a fellow feel drowsy and peaceful. Sort of end-of-a-perfect-day feeling. Old Heppenstall, the vicar, was up in the pulpit, and he has a kind of regular, bleating delivery that assists thought. They had left the door open, and the air was full of a mixed scent of trees and honeysuckle and mildew and villagers' Sunday clothes. As far as the eye could reach, you could see farmers propped up in restful attitudes, breathing heavily; and the children in the congregation who had fidgeted during the earlier part of the proceedings were now lying back in a surfeited sort of coma. The last rays of the setting sun shone through the stained-glass windows, birds were twittering in the trees, the women's dresses crackled gently in the stillness. Peaceful. That's what I'm driving at. I felt peaceful. Everybody felt peaceful. And that is why the explosion, when it came, sounded like the end of all things.

I call it an explosion, because that was what it seemed like when it broke loose. One moment a dreamy hush was all over the place, broken only by old Heppenstall talking about our duty to our neighbours; and then, suddenly, a sort of piercing, shrieking squeal that got you right between the eyes and ran all the way down your spine and out at the soles of the feet.

'Ee-ee-ee-ee-ee! Oo-ee! Ee-ee-ee-ee!'

It sounded like about six hundred pigs having their tails twisted simultaneously, but it was simply the kid Harold, who appeared to be having some species of fit. He was jumping up and down and slapping at the back of his neck. And about every other second he would take a deep breath and give out another of the squeals.

Well, I mean, you can't do that sort of thing in the middle of the sermon during evening service without exciting remark. The congregation came out of its trance with a jerk, and climbed on the pews to get a better view. Old Heppenstall stopped in the middle of a sentence and spun round. And a couple of vergers with great presence of mind bounded up the aisle like leopards, collected Harold, still squealing, and marched him out. They disappeared into the vestry, and I grabbed my hat and legged it round to the stage-door, full of apprehension and what not. I couldn't think what the deuce could have happened, but somewhere dimly behind the proceedings there seemed to me to lurk the hand of the blighter Steggles.

By the time I got there and managed to get someone to open the door, which was locked, the service seemed to be over. Old Heppenstall was standing in the middle of a crowd of choirboys and vergers and sextons and what not, putting the wretched Harold through it with no little vim. I had come in at the tail-end of what must have been a fairly fruity oration.

'Wretched boy! How dare you – '

'I got a sensitive skin!'

'This is no time to talk about your – skin.'

'Somebody put a beetle down my back!'

'Absurd!'

'I felt it wriggling – '

'Nonsense!'

'Sounds pretty thin, doesn't it?' said someone at my side.

It was Steggles, dash him. Clad in a snowy surplice or cassock, or whatever they call it, and wearing an expression of grave concern, the blighter had the cold, cynical crust to look me in the eyeball without a blink.

'Did you put a beetle down his neck?' I cried.

'Me!' said Steggles. 'Me!'

Old Heppenstall was putting on the black cap.

'I do not credit a word of your story, wretched boy! I have warned you before, and now the time has come to act. You cease from this moment to be a member of my choir. Go, miserable child!'

Steggles plucked at my sleeve.

'In that case,' he said, 'those bets, you know – I'm afraid you lose your money, dear old boy. It's a pity you didn't put it on SP. I always think SP's the only safe way.'

I gave him one look. Not a bit of good, of course.

'And they talk about the Purity of the Turf!' I said. And I meant it to sting, by Jove!

Jeeves received the news bravely, but I think the man was a bit rattled beneath the surface.

'An ingenious young gentleman, Mr Steggles, sir.'

'A bally swindler, you mean.'

'Perhaps that would be a more exact description. However, these things will happen on the Turf, and it is useless to complain.'

'I wish I had your sunny disposition, Jeeves!'

Jeeves bowed.

'We now rely, then, it would seem, sir, almost entirely on Mrs Penworthy. Should she justify Mr Little's encomiums and show real class in the Mothers' Sack Race, our gains will just balance our losses.'

'Yes; but that's not much consolation when you've been looking forward to a big win.'

'It is just possible that we may still find ourselves on the right side of the ledger after all, sir. Before Mr Little left, I persuaded him to invest a small sum for the syndicate of which you were kind enough to make me a member, sir, on the Girls' Egg and Spoon Race.'

'On Sarah Mills?'

'No, sir. On a long-priced outsider. Little Prudence Baxter, sir, the child of his lordship's head gardener. Her father assures me she has a very steady hand. She is accustomed to bring him his mug of beer from the cottage each afternoon, and he informs me she has never spilled a drop.'

Well, that sounded as though young Prudence's control was good. But how about speed? With seasoned performers like Sarah Mills entered, the thing practically amounted to a classic race, and in these big events you must have speed.

'I am aware that it is what is termed a long shot, sir. Still, I thought it judicious.'

'You backed her for a place, too, of course?'

'Yes, sir. Each way.'

'Well, I suppose it's all right. I've never known you make a bloomer yet.'

'Thank you very much, sir.'

I'm bound to say that, as a general rule, my idea of a large afternoon would be to keep as far away from a village school treat as possible. A sticky business. But with such grave issues toward, if you know what I mean, I sank my prejudices on this occasion and rolled up. I found the proceedings about as scaly as I had expected. It was a warm day, and the Hall grounds were a dense, practically liquid mass of peasantry. Kids seethed to and fro. One of them, a small girl of sorts, grabbed my hand and hung on to it as I clove my way through the jam to where the Mothers' Sack Race was to finish. We hadn't been introduced, but she seemed to think I would do as well as anyone else to talk to about the rag-doll she had won in the Lucky Dip, and she rather spread herself on the topic.

'I'm going to call it Gertrude,' she said. 'And I shall undress it every night and put it to bed, and wake it up in the morning and dress it, and put it to bed at night, and wake it up next morning and dress it – '

'I say, old thing,' I said. 'I don't want to hurry you and all that, but you couldn't condense it a bit, could you? I'm rather anxious to see the finish of this race. The Wooster fortunes are by way of hanging on it.'

'I'm going to run in a race soon,' she said, shelving the doll for the nonce and descending to ordinary chit-chat.

'Yes?' I said. Distrait, if you know what I mean, and trying to peer through the chinks in the crowd.

'What race is that?'

'Egg'n Spoon.'

'No, really? Are you Sarah Mills?'

'Na-ow!' Registering scorn. 'I'm Prudence Baxter.'

Naturally this put our relations on a different footing. I gazed at her with considerable interest. One of the stable. I must say she didn't look much of a flier. She was short and round. Bit out of condition, I thought.

'I say,' I said, 'that being so, you mustn't dash about in the hot sun and take the edge off yourself. You must conserve your energies, old friend. Sit down here in the shade.'

'Don't want to sit down.'

'Well, take it easy, anyhow.'

The kid flitted to another topic like a butterfly hovering from flower to flower.

'I'm a good girl,' she said.

'I bet you are. I hope you're a good egg-and-spoon racer, too.'

'Harold's a bad boy. Harold squealed in church and isn't allowed to come to the treat. I'm glad,' continued this ornament of her sex, wrinkling her nose virtuously, 'because he's a bad boy. He pulled my hair Friday. Harold isn't coming to the treat! Harold isn't coming to the treat! Harold isn't coming to the treat!' she chanted, making a regular song of it.

'Don't rub it in, my dear old gardener's daughter,' I pleaded. 'You don't know it, but you've hit on rather a painful subject.'

'Ah, Wooster, my dear fellow! So you have made friends with this little lady?'

It was old Heppenstall, beaming pretty profusely. Life and soul of the party.

'I am delighted, my dear Wooster,' he went on, 'quite delighted at the way you young men are throwing yourselves into the spirit of this little festivity of ours.'

'Oh, yes?' I said.

'Oh, yes! Even Rupert Steggles. I must confess that my opinion of Rupert Steggles has materially altered for the better this afternoon.'

Mine hadn't. But I didn't say so.

'I had always considered Rupert Steggles, between ourselves, a rather self-centred youth, by no means the kind who would put himself out to further the enjoyment of his fellows. And yet twice within the last half-hour I have observed him escorting Mrs Penworthy, our worthy tobacconist's wife, to the refreshment tent.'

I left him standing. I shook off the clutching hand of the Baxter kid and hared it rapidly to the spot where the Mothers' Sack Race was just finishing. I had a horrid pre-sentiment that there had been more dirty work at the cross-roads. The first person I ran into was young Bingo. I grabbed him by the arm.

'Who won?'

'I don't know. I didn't notice.' There was bitterness in the chappie's voice. 'It wasn't Mrs Penworthy, dash her! Bertie, that hound Steggles is nothing more nor less than one of our leading snakes. I don't know how he heard about her, but he must have got on to it that she was dangerous. Do you know what he did? He lured that miserable woman into the refreshment-tent five minutes before the race, and brought her out so weighed down with cake and tea that she blew up in the first twenty yards. Just rolled over and lay there! Well, thank goodness we still have Harold!'

I gaped at the poor chump.

'Harold! Haven't you heard?'

'Heard?' Bingo turned a delicate green. 'Heard what? I haven't heard anything. I only arrived five minutes ago. Came here straight from the station. What has happened? Tell me!'

I slipped him the information. He stared at me for a moment in a ghastly sort of way, then with a hollow groan tottered away and was lost in the crowd. A nasty knock, poor chap. I didn't blame him for being upset.

They were clearing the decks now for the Egg and Spoon Race, and I thought I might as well stay where I was and watch the finish. Not that I had much hope. Young Prudence was a good conversationalist, but she didn't seem to me to be the build for a winner.

As far as I could see through the mob, they got off to a good start. A short, red-haired child was making the running, with a freckled blonde second and Sarah Mills lying up an easy third. Our nominee was straggling along with the field, well behind the leaders. It was not hard even as early as this to spot the winner. There was a grace, a practised precision, in the way Sarah Mills held her spoon that told its own story. She was cutting out a good pace, but her egg didn't even wobble, a natural egg-and-spooner, if ever there was one.

Class will tell. Thirty yards from the tape, the red-haired kid tripped over her feet and shot her egg on to the turf. The freckled blonde fought gamely, but she had run herself out half-way down the straight, and Sarah Mills came past home on a tight rein by several lengths, a popular winner. The blonde was second. A sniffing female in blue gingham beat a piefaced kid in pink for the place-money, and Prudence Baxter, Jeeves's long shot, was either fifth or sixth, I couldn't see which.

And then I was carried along with the crowd to where old Heppenstall was going to present the prizes. I found myself standing next to the man Steggles.

'Hallo, old chap!' he said, very bright and cheery. 'You've had a bad day, I'm afraid.'

I looked at him with silent scorn. Lost on the blighter, of course.

'It's not been a good meeting for any of the big punters,' he went on. 'Poor old Bingo Little went down badly over that Egg and Spoon Race.'

I hadn't been meaning to chat with the fellow, but I was startled.

'How do you mean badly?' I said. 'We – he only had a small bet on.'

'I don't know what you call small. He had thirty quid each way on the Baxter kid.'

The landscape reeled before me.

'What!'

'Thirty quid at ten to one. I thought he must have heard something, but apparently not. The race went by the form-book all right.'

I was trying to do sums in my head. I was just in the middle of working out the syndicate's losses, when old Heppenstall's voice came sort of faintly to me out of the distance. He had been pretty fatherly and debonair when ladling out the prizes for the other events, but now he had suddenly grown all pained and grieved. He peered sorrowfully at the multitude.

'With regard to the Girls' Egg and Spoon Race, which has just concluded,' he said, 'I have a painful duty to perform. Circumstances have arisen which it is impossible to ignore. It is not too much to say that I am stunned.'

He gave the populace about five seconds to wonder why he was stunned, then went on.

'Three years ago, as you are aware, I was compelled to expunge from the list of events at this annual festival the Fathers' Quarter-Mile, owing to reports coming to my ears of wagers taken and given on the result at the village inn and a strong suspicion that on at least one occasion the race had actually been sold by the speediest runner. That unfortunate occurrence shook my faith in human nature, I admit – but still there was one event at least which I confidently expected to remain untainted by the miasma of Professionalism. I allude to the Girls' Egg and Spoon Race. It seems, alas, that I was too sanguine.'

He stopped again, and wrestled with his feelings.

'I will not weary you with the unpleasant details. I will merely say that before the race was run a stranger in our midst, the manservant of one of the guests at the Hall – I will not specify with more particularity – approached several of the competitors and presented each of them with five shillings on condition that they – er – finished. A belated sense of remorse has led him to confess to me what he did, but it is too late. The evil is accomplished, and retribution must take its course. It is no time for half-measures. I must be firm. I rule that Sarah Mills, Jane Parker, Bessie Clay, and Rosie Jukes, the first four to pass the winning-post, have forfeited their amateur status and are disqualified, and this handsome work-bag, presented by Lord Wickhammersley, goes, in consequence, to Prudence Baxter. Prudence, step forward!'

'THE METROPOLITAN TOUCH'

The Inimitable Jeeves

Nobody is more alive than I am to the fact that young Bingo Little is in many respects a sound old egg; but I must say there are things about him that could be improved. The man's too expansive altogether. When it comes to letting the world in on the secrets of his heart, he has about as much shrinking reticence as a steam calliope. Well, for instance, here's the telegram I got from him one evening in November:

> *'I say Bertie old man I am in love at last. She is the most wonderful girl Bertie old man. This is the real thing at last Bertie. Come here at once and bring Jeeves. Oh I say you know that tobacco shop in Bond Street on the left side as you go up. Will you get me a hundred of their special cigarettes and send them to me here. I have run out. I know when you see her you will think she is the most wonderful girl. Mind you bring Jeeves. Don't forget the cigarettes. – BINGO.'*

It had been handed in at Twing Post Office. In other words, he had submitted that frightful rot to the goggling eye of a village post-mistress who was probably the mainspring of local gossip and would have the place ringing with the news before nightfall. He couldn't have given himself away more completely if he had hired the town-crier. When I was a kid, I used to read stories about Knights and Vikings and that species of chappie who would get up without a blush in the middle of a crowded banquet and loose off a song about how perfectly priceless they thought their best girl. I've often felt that those days would have suited young Bingo down to the ground.

Jeeves had brought the thing in with the evening drink, and I slung it to him.

'It's about due, of course,' I said. 'Young Bingo hasn't been in love for at least a couple of months. I wonder who it is this time?'

'Miss Mary Burgess, sir,' said Jeeves, 'the niece of the Reverend Mr Heppenstall. She is staying at Twing Vicarage.'

'Great Scott!' I knew that Jeeves knew practically everything in the world, but this sounded like second-sight. 'How do you know that?'

'When we were visiting Twing Hall in the summer, sir, I formed a somewhat close friendship with Mr Heppenstall's butler. He is good enough to keep me abreast of the local news from time to time. From this account, sir, the young lady appears to be a very estimable young lady. Of a somewhat serious nature, I understand. Mr Little is very *épris*, sir. Brookfield, my correspondent, wrote that last week he observed him in the moonlight at an advanced hour staring up at his window.'

'Whose window? Brookfield's?'

'Yes, sir. Presumably under the impression that it was the young lady's.'

'But what the deuce is he doing at Twing at all?'

'Mr Little was compelled to resume his old position as tutor to Lord Wickhammersley's son at Twing Hall, sir. Owing to having been unsuccessful in some speculations at Hurst Park at the end of October.'

'Good Lord, Jeeves! Is there anything you don't know?'

'I could not say, sir.'

I picked up the telegram.

'I suppose he wants us to go down and help him out a bit?'

'That would appear to be his motive in dispatching the message, sir.'

'Well, what shall we do? Go?'

'I would advocate it, sir. If I may say so, I think that Mr Little should be encouraged in this particular matter.'

'You think he's picked a winner this time?'

'I hear nothing but excellent reports of the young lady, sir. I think it is beyond question that she would be an admirable influence for Mr Little, should the affair come to a happy conclusion. Such a union would also, I fancy, go far to restore Mr Little to the good graces of his uncle, the young lady being well connected and possessing private means. In short, sir, I think that if there is anything that we can do we should do it.'

'Well, with you behind him,' I said, 'I don't see how he can fail to click.'

'You are very good, sir,' said Jeeves. 'The tribute is much appreciated.'

Bingo met us at Twing Station next day, and insisted on my sending Jeeves on in the car with the bags while he and I walked. He started in about the female the moment we had begun to hoof it.

'She is very wonderful, Bertie. She is not one of these flippant, shallow-minded modern girls. She is sweetly grave and beautifully earnest. She reminds me of – what is the name I want?'

'Clara Bow?'

'Saint Cecilia,' said young Bingo, eyeing me with a great deal of loathing. 'She reminds me of Saint Cecilia. She makes me yearn to be a better, nobler, deeper, broader man.'

'What beats me,' I said, following up a train of thought, 'is what principle you pick them on. The girls you fall in love with, I mean. I mean to say, what's your system? As far as I can see, no two of them are alike. First it was Mabel the waitress, then Honoria Glossop, then that fearful blister Charlotte Corday Rowbotham – '

I own that Bingo had the decency to shudder. Thinking of Charlotte always made me shudder, too.

'You don't seriously mean, Bertie, that you are intending to compare the feeling I have for Mary Burgess, the holy devotion, the spiritual – '

'Oh, all right, let it go,' I said. 'I say, old lad, aren't we going rather a long way round?'

Considering that we were supposed to be heading for Twing Hall, it seemed to me that we were making a longish job of it. The Hall is about two miles from the station by the main road, and we had cut off down a lane, gone across country for a bit, climbed a stile or two, and were now working our way across a field that ended in another lane.

'She sometimes takes her little brother for a walk round this way,' explained Bingo. 'I thought we would meet her and bow, and you could see her, you know, and then we would walk on.'

'Of course,' I said, 'that's enough excitement for anyone, and undoubtedly a corking reward for tramping three miles out of one's way over ploughed fields with tight boots, but don't we do anything else? Don't we tack on to the girl and buzz along with her?'

'Good Lord!' said Bingo, honestly amazed. 'You don't suppose I've got nerve enough for that, do you? I just look at her from afar and all that sort of thing. Quick! Here she comes! No, I'm wrong!'

It was like that song of Harry Lauder's where he's waiting for the girl and says: 'This is her-r-r. No, it's a rabbut.' Young Bingo made me stand there in the teeth of a nor'-east half-gale for ten minutes, keeping me on my toes with a series of false alarms, and I was thinking of suggesting that we should lay off and give the rest of the proceedings a miss, when round the corner there came a fox-terrier, and Bingo quivered like an aspen. Then there hove in sight a small boy, and he shook like a jelly. Finally, like a star whose entrance has been worked up by the personnel of the *ensemble*, a girl appeared, and his emotion was painful to witness. His face got so red that, what with his white collar and the fact that the wind had turned his nose blue, he looked more like a French flag than anything else. He sagged from the waist upwards, as if he had been filleted.

He was just raising his fingers limply to his cap when he saw that the girl wasn't alone. A bloke in clerical costume was also among those present, and the sight of him didn't seem to do Bingo a bit of good. His face got redder and his nose bluer, and it wasn't till they had nearly passed that he managed to get hold of his cap.

The girl bowed, the curate said: 'Ah, Little. Rough weather,' the dog barked, and then they toddled on and the entertainment was over.

The curate was a new factor in the situation to me. I reported his movements to Jeeves when I got to the Hall. Of course, Jeeves knew all about it already.

'That is the Reverend Mr Wingham, Mr Heppenstall's new curate, sir. I gather from Brookfield that he is Mr Little's rival, and that at the moment the young lady appears to favour him. Mr Wingham has the advantage of being on the premises. He and the young lady play duets after dinner, which acts as a bond. Mr Little on these occasions, I understand, prowls about in the road, chafing visibly.'

'That seems to be all the poor fish is able to do, dash it. He can chafe all right, but there he stops. He's lost his pep. He's got no dash. Why, when we met her just now, he hadn't even the common manly courage to say "Good evening"!'

'I gather that Mr Little's affection is not unmingled with awe, sir.'

'Well, how are we to help a man when he's such a rabbit as that? Have you anything to suggest? I shall be seeing him after dinner, and he's sure to ask first thing what you advise.'

'In my opinion, sir, the most judicious course for Mr Little to pursue would be to concentrate on the young gentleman.'

'The small brother? How do you mean?'

'Make a friend of him, sir – take him for walks and so forth.'

'It doesn't sound one of your red-hottest ideas. I must say I expected something fruitier than that.'

'It would be a beginning, sir, and might lead to better things.'

'Well, I'll tell him. I liked the look of her, Jeeves.'

'A thoroughly estimable young lady, sir.'

I slipped Bingo the tip from the stable that night, and was glad to observe that it seemed to cheer him up.

'Jeeves is always right,' he said. 'I ought to have thought of it myself. I'll start in tomorrow.'

It was amazing how the chappie bucked up. Long before I left for town it had become a mere commonplace for him to speak to the girl. I mean, he didn't simply look stuffed when they met. The brother was forming a bond that was a dashed sight stronger than the curate's duets. She and Bingo used to take him for walks together. I asked Bingo what they talked about on these occasions, and he said Wilfred's future. The girl hoped that Wilfred would one day become a curate, but Bingo said no, there was something about curates he didn't quite like.

The day we left, Bingo came to see us off with Wilfred frisking about him like an old college chum. The last I saw of them, Bingo was standing him chocolates out of the slot-machine. A scene of peace and cheery goodwill. Dashed promising, I thought.

Which made it all the more of a jar, about a fortnight later, when his telegram arrived. As follows:

'Bertie old man I say Bertie could you possibly come down here at once. Everything gone wrong hang it all. Dash it Bertie you simply must come. I am in a state of absolute despair and heart-broken. Would you mind sending another hundred of those cigarettes. Bring Jeeves when you come Bertie. You simply must come Bertie. I rely on you. Don't forget to bring Jeeves. – BINGO.'

For a chap who's perpetually hard-up, I must say that young Bingo is the most wasteful telegraphist I ever struck. He's got no notion of condensing. The silly ass simply pours out his wounded soul at twopence a word, or whatever it is, without a thought.

'How about it, Jeeves?' I said. 'I'm getting a bit fed. I can't go chucking all my engagements every second week in order to biff down to Twing and rally round young Bingo. Send him a wire telling him to end it all in the village pond.'

'If you could spare me for the night, sir, I should be glad to run down and investigate.'

'Oh, dash it! Well, I suppose there's nothing else to be done. After all, you're the fellow he wants. All right, carry on.'

Jeeves got back late the next day.

'Well?' I said.

Jeeves appeared perturbed. He allowed his left eyebrow to flicker upwards in a concerned sort of manner.

'I have done what I could, sir,' he said, 'but I fear Mr Little's chances do not appear bright. Since our last visit, sir, there has been a decidedly sinister and disquieting development.'

'Oh, what's that?'

'You may remember Mr Steggles, sir – the young gentleman who was studying for an examination with Mr Heppenstall at the vicarage?'

Of course I remembered Steggles. You'll place him if you throw your mind back. Recollect the rat-faced chappie of sporting tastes who made the book on the Sermon Handicap and then made another on the Choir Boys' Sports? That's the fellow. A blighter of infinite guile and up to every shady scheme on the list. Though, thanks to Jeeves, we had let him in pretty badly on the Girls' Egg and Spoon Race and collected a parcel off him in spite of his villainies.

'What's Steggles got to do with it?' I asked.

'I gather from Brookfield, sir, who chanced to overhear a conversation, that Mr Steggles is interesting himself in the affair.'

'Good Lord! What, making a book on it?'

'I understand that he is accepting wagers from those in his immediate circle, sir. Against Mr Little, whose chances he does not seem to fancy.'

'I don't like that, Jeeves.'

'No, sir. It is sinister.'

'From what I know of Steggles there will be dirty work.'

'It has already occurred, sir.'

'Already?'

'Yes, sir. It seems that, in pursuance of the policy which he had been good enough to allow me to suggest to him, Mr Little escorted Master Burgess to the church bazaar, and there met Mr Steggles, who was in the company of young Master Heppenstall, the Reverend Mr Heppenstall's second son, who is home from Rugby just now, having recently recovered from an attack of mumps. The encounter took place in the refreshment-room, where Mr Steggles was at that moment entertaining Master Heppenstall. To cut a long story short, sir, the two gentlemen became extremely interested in the hearty manner in which the lads were fortifying themselves; and Mr Steggles offered to back his nominee in a weight-for-age eating contest against Master Burgess for a pound a side. Mr Little admitted to me that he was conscious of a certain hesitation as to what the upshot might be, should Miss Burgess get to hear of the matter, but his sporting blood was too much for him and he agreed to the contest. This was duly carried out, both lads exhibiting the utmost willingness and enthusiasm, and eventually Master Burgess justified Mr Little's confidence by winning, but only after a bitter struggle. Next day both contestants were in considerable pain; inquiries were made and confessions extorted, and Mr Little – I learn from Brookfield, who happened to be near the door of the drawing-room at that moment – had an extremely unpleasant interview with the young lady, which ended in her desiring him never to speak to her again.'

There's no getting away from the fact that, if ever a man required watching, it's Steggles. Machiavelli could have taken his correspondence course.

'It was a put-up job, Jeeves!' I said. 'I mean, Steggles worked the whole thing on purpose. It's his old nobbling game.'

'There would seem to be no doubt about that, sir.'

'Well, he seems to have dished poor old Bingo all right.'

'That is the prevalent opinion, sir. Brookfield tells me that down in the village at the Cow and Horses seven-to-one is being freely offered on Mr Wingham and finding no takers.'

'Good Lord! Are they betting about it down in the village, too?'

'Yes, sir. And in adjoining hamlets also. The affair has caused widespread interest. I am told that there is a certain sporting reaction in even so distant a spot as Lower Bingley.'

'Well, I don't see what there is to do. If Bingo is such a chump – '

'One is fighting a losing battle, I fear, sir, but I did venture to indicate to Mr Little a course of action which might prove of advantage. I recommended him to busy himself with good works.'

'Good works?'

'About the village, sir. Reading to the bed-ridden – chatting with the sick – that sort of thing, sir. We can but trust that good results will ensue.'

'Yes, I suppose so,' I said, doubtfully. 'But, by gosh, if I was a sick man I'd hate to have a loony like young Bingo coming and gibbering at my bedside.'

'There *is* that aspect of the matter, sir,' said Jeeves.

I didn't hear a word from Bingo for a couple of weeks, and I took it after a while that he had found the going too hard and had chucked in the towel. And then, one night not long before Christmas, I came back to the flat pretty latish, having been out dancing at the Embassy. I was fairly tired, having swung a practically non-stop shoe from shortly after dinner till two a.m., and bed seemed to be indicated. Judge of my chagrin and all that sort of thing, therefore, when, tottering to my room and switching on the light, I observed the foul features of young Bingo all over the pillow. The blighter had appeared from nowhere and was in my bed, sleeping like an infant with a sort of happy dreamy smile on his map.

A bit thick, I mean to say! We Woosters are all for the good old medieval hosp. and all that, but when it comes to finding chappies collaring your bed, the thing becomes a trifle too mouldy. I hove a shoe, and Bingo sat up, gurgling.

''S matter? 's matter?' said young Bingo.

'What the deuce are you doing in my bed?' I said.

'Oh, hallo, Bertie! So there you are!'

'Yes, here I am. What are you doing in my bed?'

'I came up to town for the night on business.'

'Yes, but what are you doing in my bed?'

'Dash it all, Bertie,' said young Bingo, querulously, 'don't keep harping on your beastly bed. There's another made up in the spare room. I saw Jeeves make it with my own eyes. I believe he meant it for me, but I knew what a perfect host you were, so I just turned in here. I say, Bertie, old man,' said Bingo, apparently fed up with the discussion about sleeping-quarters, 'I see daylight.'

'Well, it's getting on for three in the morning.'

'I was speaking figuratively, you ass. I meant that hope has begun to dawn. About Mary Burgess, you know. Sit down and I'll tell you all about it.'

'I won't. I'm going to sleep.'

'To begin with,' said young Bingo, settling himself comfortably against the pillows and helping himself to a cigarette from my special private box, 'I must once again pay a marked tribute to good old Jeeves. A modern Solomon. I was badly up against it when I came to him for advice, but he rolled up with a tip which has put me – I use the term advisedly and in a conservative spirit – on velvet. He may have told you that he recommended me to win back the lost ground by busying myself with good works? Bertie, old man,' said young Bingo, earnestly, 'for the last two weeks I've been comforting the sick to such an extent that, if I had a brother and you brought him to me on a sickbed at this moment, by Jove, old man, I'd heave a brick at him. However, though it took it out of me like the deuce, the scheme worked splendidly. She softened visibly before I'd been at it a week. Started to bow again when we met in the street, and so forth. About a couple of days ago she distinctly smiled – in a sort of faint, saint-like kind of way, you know – when I ran into her outside the vicarage. And yesterday – I say, you remember that curate chap, Wingham? Fellow with a long nose and a sort of goofy expression?'

'Of course I remember him. Your rival.'

'Rival?' Bingo raised his eyebrows. 'Oh, well, I suppose you could have called him that at one time. Though it sounds a little far-fetched.'

'Does it?' I said, stung by the sickening complacency of the chump's manner. 'Well, let me tell you that the last I heard was that at the Cow and Horses in Twing village and all over the place as far as Lower Bingley they were offering seven-to-one on the curate and finding no takers.'

Bingo started violently, and sprayed cigarette-ash all over my bed.

'Betting!' he gargled. 'Betting! You don't mean that they're betting on this holy, sacred – Oh, I say, dash it all! Haven't people any sense of decency and reverence? Is nothing safe from their beastly, sordid graspingness? I wonder,' said young Bingo, thoughtfully, 'if there's a chance of my getting any of that seven-to-one money? Seven-to-one! What a price! Who's offering it, do you know? Oh, well, I suppose it wouldn't do. No, I suppose it wouldn't be quite the thing.'

'You seem dashed confident,' I said. 'I'd always thought that Wingham – '

'Oh, I'm not worried about him,' said Bingo. 'I was just going to tell you. Wingham's got the mumps, and won't be out and about for weeks. And, jolly as that is in itself, it's not all. You see, he was producing the Village School Christmas Entertainment, and now I've taken over the job. I went to old Heppenstall last night and clinched the contract. Well, you see what that means. It means that I shall be absolutely the centre of the village life and thought for three solid weeks, with a terrific triumph to wind up with. Everybody looking up to me and fawning on me, don't you see, and all that. It's bound to have a powerful effect on Mary's mind. It will show her that I am capable of serious effort; that there is a solid foundation of worth in me; that, mere butterfly as she may once have thought me, I am in reality – '

'Oh, all right, let it go!'

'It's a big thing, you know, this Christmas Entertainment. Old Heppenstall's very much wrapped up in it. Nibs from all over the countryside rolling up. The Squire present, with family. A big chance for me, Bertie, my boy, and I mean to make the most of it. Of course, I'm handicapped a bit by not having been in on the thing from the start. Will you credit it that that uninspired doughnut of a curate wanted to give the public some rotten little fairy play out of a book for children published about fifty years ago, without one good laugh or the semblance of a gag in it? It's too late to alter the thing entirely, but at least I can jazz it up. I'm going to write them in something zippy to brighten the thing up a bit.'

'You can't write.'

'Well, when I say write, I mean pinch. That's why I've popped up to town. I've been to see that revue, *Cuddle Up!* at the Palladium, tonight. Full of good stuff. Of course, it's rather hard to get anything in the nature of a big spectacular effect in the Twing Village Hall, with no scenery to speak of and a chorus of practically imbecile kids of ages ranging from nine to fourteen, but I think I see my way. Have you seen *Cuddle Up!*?'

'Yes. Twice.'

'Well, there's some good stuff in the first act, and I can lift practically all the numbers. Then there's that show at the Palace. I can see the matinée of that tomorrow before I leave. There's sure to be some decent bits in that. Don't you worry about my not being able to write a hit. Leave it to me, laddie, leave it to me. And now, my dear old chap,' said young Bingo, snuggling down cosily, 'you mustn't keep me up talking all night. It's all right for you fellows who have nothing to do, but I'm a busy man. Good night, old thing. Close the door quietly after you and switch out the light. Breakfast about ten tomorrow, I suppose, what? Right-ho. Good night.'

For the next three weeks I didn't see Bingo. He became a sort of Voice Heard Off, developing a habit of ringing me up on long-distance and consulting me on various points arising at rehearsal, until the day when he got me out of bed at eight in the morning to ask whether I thought 'Merry Christmas!' was a good title. I told him then that this nuisance must now cease, and after that he cheesed it, and practically passed out of my life till one afternoon when I got back to the flat to dress for dinner and found Jeeves inspecting a whacking big poster sort of thing which he had draped over the back of an arm-chair.

'Good Lord, Jeeves!' I said. I was feeling rather weak that day, and the thing shook me. 'What on earth's that?'

'Mr Little sent it to me, sir, and desired me to bring it to your notice.'

'Well, you've certainly done it!'

I took another look at the object. There was no doubt about it, it caught the eye. It was about seven feet long, and most of the lettering in about as bright red as I ever struck.

This was how it ran:

TWING VILLAGE HALL
Friday, December 23rd
RICHARD LITTLE
presents
A New and Original Revue
Entitled
WHAT HO, TWING!!
Book by
RICHARD LITTLE
Lyrics by
RICHARD LITTLE
Music by
RICHARD LITTLE
With the Full Twing Juvenile
Company and Chorus
Scenic effects by
RICHARD LITTLE
Produced by
RICHARD LITTLE

A RICHARD LITTLE PRODUCTION

'What do you make of it, Jeeves?' I said.

'I confess I am a little doubtful, sir. I think Mr Little would have done better to follow my advice and confine himself to good works about the village.'

'You think the thing will be a frost?'

'I could not hazard a conjecture, sir. But my experience has been that what pleases the London public is not always so acceptable to the rural mind. The metropolitan touch sometimes proves a trifle too exotic for the provinces.'

'I suppose I ought to go down and see the dashed thing?'

'I think Mr Little would be wounded were you not present, sir.'

The Village Hall at Twing is a smallish building, smelling of apples. It was full when I turned up on the evening of the twenty-third, for I had purposely timed myself to arrive not long before the kick-off. I had had experience of one or two of these binges, and didn't want to run any risk of coming early and finding myself shoved into a seat in one of the front rows where I wouldn't be able to execute a quiet sneak into the open air half-way through the proceedings, if the occasion seemed to demand it. I secured a nice strategic position near the door at the back of the Hall.

From where I stood I had a good view of the audience. As always on these occasions, the first few rows were occupied by the Nibs – consisting of the Squire, a fairly mauve old sportsman with white whiskers, his family, a platoon of local parsons, and perhaps a couple of dozen of prominent pew-holders. Then came a dense squash of what you might call the Lower Middle Classes. And at the back, where I was, we came down with a jerk in the social scale, this end of the hall being given up almost entirely to a collection of frankly Tough Eggs, who had rolled up not so much for any love of the drama as because there was a free tea after the show. Take it for all in all, a representative gathering of Twing life and thought. The Nibs were whispering in a pleased manner to each other, the Lower Middles were sitting up very straight as if they'd been bleached, and the Tough Eggs whiled away the time by cracking nuts and exchanging low rustic wheezes. The girl, Mary Burgess, was at the piano, playing a waltz. Beside her stood the curate, Wingham, apparently recovered. The temperature, I should think, was about a hundred and twenty-seven.

Somebody jabbed me heartily in the lower ribs, and I perceived the man Steggles.

'Hullo!' he said. 'I didn't know you were coming down.'

I didn't like the chap, but we Woosters can wear the mask. I beamed a bit.

'Oh, yes,' I said. 'Bingo wanted me to roll up and see his show.'

'I hear he's giving us something pretty ambitious,' said the man Steggles. 'Big effects and all that sort of thing.'

'I believe so.'

'Of course, it means a lot to him, doesn't it? He's told you about the girl, of course?'

'Yes. And I hear you're laying seven-to-one against him,' I said, eyeing the blighter a trifle austerely.

He didn't even quiver.

'Just a little flutter to relieve the monotony of country life,' he said. 'But you've got the facts a bit wrong. It's down in the village that they're laying seven-to-one. I can do you better than that, if you feel in a speculative mood. How about a tenner at a hundred-to-eight?'

'Good Lord! Are you giving that?'

'Yes. Somehow,' said Steggles, meditatively, 'I have a sort of feeling, a kind of pre-monition, that something's going to go wrong tonight. You know what Little is. A bungler if ever there was one. Something tells me that this show of his is going to be a frost. And if it is, of course I should think it would prejudice the girl against him pretty badly. His standing always was rather shaky.'

'Are you going to try and smash up the show?' I said sternly.

'Me!' said Steggles. 'Why, what could I do? Half a minute, I want to go and speak to a man.'

He buzzed off, leaving me distinctly disturbed. I could see from the fellow's eye that he was meditating some of his customary rough stuff, and I thought Bingo ought to be warned. But there wasn't time and I couldn't get at him. Almost immediately after Steggles had left me the curtain went up.

Except as a prompter, Bingo wasn't much in evidence in the early part of the performance. The thing at the outset was merely one of those weird dramas which you dig out of books published around Christmas time and entitled 'Twelve Little Plays for the Tots', or something like that. The kids drooled on in the usual manner, the booming voice of Bingo ringing out from time to time behind the scenes when the fat-heads forgot their lines; and the audience was settling down into the sort of torpor usual on these occasions, when the first of Bingo's interpolated bits occurred. It was that number which What's-her-name sings in the revue at the Palace – you would recognize the tune if I hummed it, but I never can get hold of the dashed thing. It always got three encores at the Palace, and it went well now, even with a squeaky-voiced child jumping on and off the key like a chamois of the Alps leaping from crag to crag. Even the Tough Eggs liked it. At the end of the second refrain the entire house was shouting for an encore, and the kid with the voice like a slate-pencil took a deep breath and started to let it go once more.

At this point all the lights went out.

I don't know when I've had anything so sudden and devastating happen to me before. They didn't flicker. They just went out. The hall was in complete darkness.

Well, of course, that sort of broke the spell, as you might put it. People started to shout directions, and the Tough Eggs stamped their feet and settled down for a pleasant time. And of course, young Bingo had to make an ass of himself. His voice suddenly shot at us out of the darkness.

'Ladies and gentlemen, something has gone wrong with the lights – '

The Tough Eggs were tickled by this bit of information straight from the stable. They took it up as a sort of battlecry. Then, after about five minutes, the lights went up again, and the show was resumed.

It took ten minutes after that to get the audience back into its state of coma, but eventually they began to settle down, and everything was going nicely when a small boy with a face like a turbot edged out in front of the curtain, which had been lowered after a pretty painful scene about a wishing ring or a fairy's curse or something of that sort, and started to sing that song of George Thingummy's out of *Cuddle Up!* You know the one I mean. 'Always Listen to Mother, Girls!' it's called, and he gets the audience to join in and sing the refrain. Quite a ripeish ballad, and one which I myself have frequently sung in my bath with not a little vim; but by no means – as anyone but a perfect sap-headed prune like young Bingo would have known – by no means the sort of thing for a children's Christmas entertainment in the old Village Hall. Right from the start of the first refrain the bulk of the audience had begun to stiffen in their seats and fan them-selves, and the Burgess girl at the piano was accompanying in a stunned, mechanical sort of way, while the curate at her side averted his gaze in a pained manner. The Tough Eggs, however, were all for it.

At the end of the second refrain the kid stopped and began to sidle towards the wings. Upon which the following brief duologue took place:

YOUNG BINGO (*Voice heard off, ringing against the rafters*): 'Go on!'
THE KID (*Coyly*): 'I don't like to.'
YOUNG BINGO (*Still louder*): 'Go on, you little blighter, or I'll slay you!'

I suppose the kid thought it over swiftly and realized that Bingo, being in a position to get at him, had better be conciliated whatever the harvest might be; for he shuffled down to the front and, having shut his eyes and giggled hysterically, said: 'Ladies and gentlemen, I will now call upon Squire Tressidder to oblige by singing the refrain!'

You know, with the most charitable feelings towards him, there are moments when you can't help thinking that young Bingo ought to be in some sort of a home. I suppose, poor fish, he had pictured this as the big punch of the evening. He had imagined, I take it, that the Squire would spring jovially to his feet, rip the song off his chest, and all would be gaiety and mirth. Well, what happened was simply that old Tressidder – and, mark you, I'm not blaming him – just sat where he was, swelling and turning a brighter purple every second. The lower middle classes remained in frozen silence, waiting for the roof to fall. The only section of the audience that really seemed to enjoy the idea was the Tough Eggs, who yelled with enthusiasm. It was jam for the Tough Eggs.

And then the lights went out again.

When they went up, some minutes later, they disclosed the Squire marching stiffly out at the head of his family, fed up to the eyebrows; the Burgess girl at the piano with a pale, set look; and the curate gazing at her with something in his expression that seemed to suggest that, though all this was no doubt deplorable, he had spotted the silver lining.

The show went on once more. There were great chunks of Plays-for-the-Tots dialogue, and then the girl at the piano struck up the prelude to that Orange-Girl number that's the big hit of the Palace revue. I took it that this was to be Bingo's smashing act one finale. The entire company was on the stage, and a clutching hand had appeared round the edge of the curtain, ready to pull at the right moment. It looked like the finale all right. It wasn't long before I realized that it was something more. It was the finish.

I take it you know that Orange number at the Palace? It goes –

> Oh, won't you something something oranges,
>   My something oranges,
>   My something oranges;
> Oh, won't you something something something I forget,
> Something something something tumty tumty yet:
>
>   Oh –

or words to that effect. It's a dashed clever lyric, and the tune's good, too; but the thing that made the number was the business where the girls take oranges out of their baskets, you know, and toss them lightly to the audience. I don't know if you've ever noticed it, but it always seems to tickle an audience to bits when they get things thrown at them from the stage. Every time I've been to the Palace the customers have simply gone wild over this number.

But at the Palace, of course, the oranges are made of yellow wool and the girls don't so much chuck them as drop them limply into the first and second rows. I began to gather that the business was going to be treated rather differently tonight, when a dashed great chunk of pips and mildew sailed past my ear and burst on the wall behind me. Another landed with a squelch on the neck of one of the Nibs in the third row. And then a third took me right on the tip of the nose, and I kind of lost interest in the proceedings for a while.

When I had scrubbed my face and got my eyes to stop watering for a moment, I saw that the evening's entertainment had begun to resemble one of Belfast's livelier nights. The air was thick with shrieks and fruit. The kids on the stage, with Bingo buzzing distractedly to and fro in their midst, were having the time of their lives. I suppose they realized that this couldn't go on for ever, and were making the most of their chances. The Tough Eggs had begun to pick up all the oranges that hadn't burst and were shooting them back, so that the audience got it both coming and going. In fact, take it all round, there was a certain amount of confusion; and, just as things had begun really to hot up, out went the lights again.

It seemed to me about my time for leaving, so I slid for the door. I was hardly outside when the audience began to stream out. They surged about me in twos and threes, and I've never seen a public body so dashed unanimous on any point. To a man – and to a woman – they were cursing poor old Bingo; and there was a large and rapidly growing school of thought which held that the best thing to do would be to waylay him as he emerged and splash him about in the village pond a bit.

There were such a dickens of a lot of these enthusiasts and they looked so jolly determined that it seemed to me that the only matey thing to do was to go behind and warn young Bingo to turn his coat-collar up and breeze off shakily by some side-exit. I went behind, and found him sitting on a box in the wings, perspiring pretty freely and looking more or less like the spot marked with a cross where the accident happened. His hair was standing up and his ears were hanging down, and one harsh word would undoubtedly have made him burst into tears.

'Bertie,' he said hollowly, as he saw me, 'it was that blighter Steggles! I caught one of the kids before he could get away and got it all out of him. Steggles substituted real oranges for the balls of wool which with infinite sweat and at a cost of nearly a quid I had specially prepared. Well, I will now proceed to tear him limb from limb. It'll be something to do.'

I hated to spoil his day-dreams, but it had to be. 'Good heavens, man,' I said, 'you haven't time for frivolous amusements now. You've got to get out. And quick!'

'Bertie,' said Bingo in a dull voice, 'she was here just now. She said it was all my fault and that she would never speak to me again. She said she had always suspected me of being a heartless practical joker, and now she knew. She said – Oh, well, she ticked me off properly.'

'That's the least of your troubles,' I said. It seemed impossible to rouse the poor zib to a sense of his position. 'Do you realize that about two hundred of Twing's heftiest are waiting for you outside to chuck you into the pond?'

'No!'

'Absolutely!'

For a moment the poor chap seemed crushed. But only for a moment. There has always been something of the good old English bulldog breed about Bingo. A strange, sweet smile flickered for an instant over his face.

'It's all right,' he said. 'I can sneak out through the cellar and climb over the wall at the back. They can't intimidate *me*!'

It couldn't have been more than a week later when Jeeves, after he had brought me my tea, gently steered me away from the sporting page of the *Morning Post* and directed my attention to an announcement in the engagements and marriages column.

It was a brief statement that a marriage had been arranged and would shortly take place between the Hon. and Rev. Hubert Wingham third son of the Right Hon. the Earl of Sturridge, and Mary, only daughter of the late Matthew Burgess, of Weatherly Court, Hants.

'Of course,' I said, after I had given it the east-to-west, 'I expected this, Jeeves.'

'Yes, sir.'

'She would never forgive him what happened that night.'

'No, sir.'

'Well,' I said, as I took a sip of the fragrant and steaming, 'I don't suppose it will take old Bingo long to get over it. It's about the hundred and eleventh time this sort of thing has happened to him. You're the man I'm sorry for.'

'Me, sir?'

'Well, dash it all, you can't have forgotten what a deuce of a lot of trouble you took to bring the thing off for Bingo. It's too bad that all your work should have been wasted.'

'Not entirely wasted, sir.'

'Eh?'

'It is true that my efforts to bring about the match between Mr Little and the young lady were not successful, but still I look back upon the matter with a certain satisfaction.'

'Because you did your best, you mean?'

'Not entirely, sir, though of course that thought also gives me pleasure. I was alluding more particularly to the fact that I found the affair financially remunerative.'

'Financially remunerative? What do you mean?'

'When I learned that Mr Steggles had interested himself in the contest, sir, I went shares with my friend Brookfield and bought the book which had been made on the issue by the landlord of the Cow and Horses. It has proved a highly profitable investment. Your breakfast will be ready almost immediately, sir. Kidneys on toast and mushrooms. I will bring it when you ring.'

'TRIED IN THE FURNACE'

Young Men in Spats

The annual smoking-concert of the Drones Club had just come to an end, and it was the unanimous verdict of the little group assembled in the bar for a last quick one that the gem of the evening had been item number six on the programme, the knockabout cross-talk act of Cyril ('Barmy') Fotheringay-Phipps and Reginald ('Pongo') Twistleton-Twistleton. Both Cyril, in the red beard, and Reginald, in the more effective green whiskers, had shown themselves, it was agreed, at the very peak of their form. With sparkling repartee and vigorous by-play they had gripped the audience from the start.

'In fact,' said an Egg, 'it struck me that they were even better than last year. Their art seemed to have deepened somehow.'

A thoughtful Crumpet nodded.

'I noticed the same thing. The fact is, they passed through a soul-testing experience not long ago and it has left its mark upon them. It also dashed nearly wrecked the act. I don't know if any of you fellows are aware of it, but at one time they had definitely decided to scratch the fixture and not give a performance at all.'

'What!'

'Absolutely. They were within a toucher of failing to keep faith with their public. Bad blood had sprung up between them. Also pique and strained relations. They were not on speaking terms.'

His hearers were frankly incredulous. They pointed out that the friendship between the two artistes had always been a by-word or whatever you called it. A well-read Egg summed it up by saying that they were like Thingummy and What's-his-name.

'Nevertheless,' insisted the Crumpet, 'what I am telling you is straight, official stuff. Two weeks ago, if Barmy had said to Pongo: "Who was that lady I saw you coming down the street with?" Pongo would not have replied: "That was no lady, that was my wife," – he would simply have raised his eyebrows coldly and turned away in a marked manner.'

It was a woman, of course (proceeded the Crumpet) who came between them. Angelica Briscoe was her name, and she was the daughter of the Rev. P. P. Briscoe, who vetted the souls of the local peasantry at a place called Maiden Eggesford down in Somersetshire. This hamlet is about half a dozen miles from the well-known resort, Bridmouth-on-Sea, and it was in the establishment of the Messrs. Thorpe and Widgery, the popular grocers of that town, that Barmy and Pongo first set eyes on the girl.

They had gone to Bridmouth partly for a splash of golf, but principally to be alone and away from distractions, so that they would be able to concentrate on the rehearsing and building-up of this cross-talk act which we had just witnessed. And on the morning of which I speak they had strolled into the Thorpe and Widgery emporium to lay in a few little odds and ends, and there, putting in a bid for five pounds of streaky bacon, was a girl so lovely that they congealed in their tracks. And, as they stood staring, she said to the bloke behind the counter:

'That's the lot. Send them to Miss Angelica Briscoe, The Vicarage, Maiden Eggesford.'

She then pushed off, and Barmy and Pongo, feeling rather as if they had been struck by lightning, bought some sardines and a segment of certified butter in an overwrought sort of way and went out.

They were both pretty quiet for the rest of the day, and after dinner that night Pongo said to Barmy:

'I say, Barmy.'

And Barmy said:

'Hullo?'

And Pongo said:

'I say, Barmy, it's a bally nuisance, but I'll have to buzz up to London for a day or two. I've suddenly remembered some spots of business that call for my personal attention. You won't mind my leaving you?'

Barmy could scarcely conceal his bracedness. Within two minutes of seeing that girl, he had made up his mind that somehow or other he must repair to Maiden Eggesford and get to know her, and the problem which had been vexing him all day had been what to do with the body – viz. Pongo's.

'Not a bit,' he said.

'I'll be back as soon as I can.'

'Don't hurry,' said Barmy heartily. 'As a matter of fact, a few days' lay-off will do the act all the good in the world. Any pro. will tell you that the worst thing possible is to over-rehearse. Stay away as long as you like.'

So next morning – it was a Saturday – Pongo climbed on to a train, and in the afternoon Barmy collected his baggage and pushed off to the Goose and Grasshopper at Maiden Eggesford. And, having booked a room there and toddled into the saloon bar for a refresher with the love-light in his eyes, the first thing he saw was Pongo chatting across the counter with the barmaid.

Neither was much bucked. A touch of constraint about sums it up.

'Hullo!' said Barmy.

'Hullo!' said Pongo.

'You here?'

'Yes. You here?'

'Yes.'

'Oh.'

There was a bit of a silence.

'So you didn't go to London?' said Barmy.

'No,' said Pongo.

'Oh,' said Barmy.

'And you didn't stick on at Bridmouth?' said Pongo.

'No,' said Barmy.

'Oh,' said Pongo.

There was some more silence.

'You came here, I see,' said Pongo.

'Yes,' said Barmy. 'I see *you* came here.'

'Yes,' said Pongo. 'An odd coincidence.'

'Very odd.'

'Well, skin off your nose,' said Pongo.

'Fluff in your latchkey,' said Barmy.

He drained his glass and tried to exhibit a light-hearted nonchalance, but his mood was sombre. He was a chap who could put two and two together and sift and weigh the evidence and all that sort of thing, and it was plain to him that love had brought Pongo also to this hamlet, and he resented the fact. Indeed, it was at this instant, he tells me, that there came to him the first nebulous idea of oiling out of that cross-talk act of theirs. The thought of having to ask a beastly, butting-in blighter like Reginald Twistleton-Twistleton if he was fond of mutton-broth and being compelled to hit him over the head with a rolled-up umbrella when he replied 'No, Mutt and Jeff', somehow seemed to revolt his finest feelings.

Conversation rather languished after this, and presently Pongo excused himself in a somewhat stiff manner and went upstairs to his room. And it was while Barmy was at the counter listening in a distrait kind of way to the barmaid telling him what cucumber did to her digestive organs that a fellow in plus fours entered the bar and Barmy saw that he was wearing the tie of his old school.

Well, you know how it is when you're in some public spot and a stranger comes in wearing the old school tie. You shove a hasty hand over your own and start to sidle out before the chap can spot it and grab you and start gassing. And Barmy was just doing this when the barmaid uttered these sensational words:

'Good evening, Mr Briscoe.'

Barmy stood spellbound. He turned to the barmaid and spoke in a hushed whisper.

'Did you say "Briscoe"?'

'Yes, sir.'

'From the vicarage?'

'Yes, sir.'

Barmy quivered like a jelly. The thought that he had had the amazing luck to find in the brother of the girl he loved an old school-mate made him feel boneless. After all, he felt, as he took his hand away from his tie, there is no bond like that of the old school. If you meet one of the dear old school in a public spot, he meant to say, why, you go straight up to him and start fraternizing.

He made a bee-line for the chap's table.

'I say,' he said, 'I see you're wearing a . . .'

The chap's hand had shot up to his tie with a sort of nervous gesture, but he evidently realized that the time had gone by for protective measures. He smiled a bit wryly.

'Have a drink,' he said.

'I've got one, thanks,' said Barmy. 'I'll bring it along to your table, shall I? Such a treat meeting someone from the dear old place, what?'

'Oh, rather.'

'I think I'd have been a bit after your time, wouldn't I?' said Barmy, for the fellow was well stricken in years – twenty-eight, if a day. 'Fotheringay-Phipps is more or less my name. Yours is Briscoe, what?'

'Yes.'

Barmy swallowed a couple of times.

'Er . . . Ah . . . Um . . . I think I saw your sister yesterday in Bridmouth,' he said, blushing prettily.

So scarlet, indeed, did his countenance become that the other regarded him narrowly, and Barmy knew that he had guessed his secret.

'You saw her in Bridmouth yesterday, eh?'

'Yes.'

'And now you're here.'

'Er – yes.'

'Well, well,' said the chap, drawing his breath in rather thoughtfully.

There was a pause, during which Barmy's vascular motors continued to do their bit.

'You must meet her,' said the chap.

'I should like to,' said Barmy. 'I only saw her for a moment buying streaky bacon, but she seemed a charming girl.'

'Oh, she is.'

'I scarcely noticed her, of course, but rather attractive she struck me as.'

'Quite.'

'I gave her the merest glance, you understand, but I should say at a venture that she has a great white soul. In fact,' said Barmy, losing his grip altogether, 'you wouldn't be far out in describing her as divine.'

'You must certainly meet her,' said the chap. Then he shook his head. 'No, it wouldn't be any good.'

'Why not?' bleated Barmy.

'Well, I'll tell you,' said the chap. 'You know what girls are. They have their little enthusiasms and it hurts them when people scoff at them. Being a parson's daughter, Angelica is wrapped up at present in the annual village School Treat. I can see at a glance the sort of fellow you are – witty, mordant, ironical. You would get off one of your devastating epigrams at the expense of the School Treat, and, while she might laugh at the wit, she would be deeply wounded by the satire.'

'But I wouldn't dream . . .'

'Ah, but if you didn't, if you spoke approvingly of the School Treat, what then? The next thing that would happen would be that she would be asking you to help her run it. And that would bore you stiff.'

Barmy shook from stem to stern. This was better even that he had hoped.

'You don't mean she would let me help her with the School Treat?'

'Why, you wouldn't do it, would you?'

'I should enjoy it above all things.'

'Well, if that's the way you feel, the matter can easily be arranged. She will be here any moment now to pick me up in her car.'

And, sure enough, not two minutes later there floated through the open window a silvery voice, urging the fellow, who seemed to answer to the name of 'Fathead', to come out quick, because the voice did not intend to remain there all night.

So the fellow took Barmy out, and there was the girl, sitting in a two-seater. He introduced Barmy. The girl beamed. Barmy beamed. The fellow said that Barmy was anxious to come and help with the School Treat. The girl beamed again. Barmy beamed again. And presently the car drove off, the girl's last words being a reminder that the binge started at two sharp on the Monday.

That night, as they dined together, Barmy and Pongo put in their usual spot of rehearsing. It was their practice to mould and shape the act during meals, as they found that mastication seemed to sharpen their intellect. But tonight it would have been plain to an observant spectator that their hearts were not in it. There was an unmistakable coolness between them. Pongo said he had an aunt who complained of rheumatism, and Barmy said, Well, who wouldn't? And Barmy said his father could not meet his creditors, and Pongo said, Did he want to? But the old fire and sparkle were absent. And they had relapsed into a moody silence when the door opened and the barmaid pushed her head in.

'Miss Briscoe has just sent over a message, Mr Phipps,' said the barmaid. 'She says she would like you to be there a little earlier than two, if you can manage it. One-fifteen, if possible, because there's always so much to do.'

'Oh, right,' said Barmy, a bit rattled, for he had heard the sharp hiss of his companion's indrawn breath.

'I'll tell her,' said the barmaid.

She withdrew, and Barmy found Pongo's eyes resting on him like a couple of blobs of vitriol.

'What's all this?' asked Pongo.

Barmy tried to be airy.

'Oh, it's nothing. Just the local School Treat. The vicar's daughter here – a Miss Briscoe – seems anxious that I should drop round on Monday and help her run it.'

Pongo started to grind his teeth, but he had a chunk of potato in his mouth at the moment and was hampered. But he gripped the table till his knuckles stood out white under the strain.

'Have you been sneaking round behind my back and inflicting your beastly society on Miss Briscoe?' he demanded.

'I do not like your tone, Reginald.'

'Never mind about my tone. I'll attend to my tone. Of all the bally low hounds that ever stepped you are the lowest. So this is what the friendship of years amounts to, is it? You crawl in here and try to cut me out with the girl I love.'

'Well, dash it . . .'

'That is quite enough.'

'But, dash it . . .'

'I wish to hear no more.'

'But, dash it, I love her, too. It's not my fault if you happen to love her, too, is it? I mean to say, if a fellow loves a girl and another fellow loves her, too, you can't expect the fellow who loves the girl to edge out because he happens to be acquainted with the fellow who loves her, too. When it comes to Love, a chap has got to look out for his own interests, hasn't he? You didn't find Romeo or any of those chaps easing away from the girl just to oblige a pal, did you? Certainly not. So I don't see . . .'

'Please!' said Pongo.

A silence fell.

'Might I trouble you to pass the mustard, Fotheringay-Phipps,' said Pongo coldly.

'Certainly, Twistleton-Twistleton,' replied Barmy, with equal hauteur.

It is always unpleasant not to be on speaking terms with an old friend. To be cooped up alone in a mouldy village pub with an old friend with whom one has ceased to converse is simply rotten. And this is especially so if the day happens to be a Sunday.

Maiden Eggesford, like so many of our rural hamlets, is not at its best and brightest on a Sunday. When you have walked down the main street and looked at the Jubilee Watering-Trough, there is nothing much to do except go home and then come out again and walk down the main street once more and take another look at the Jubilee Watering-Trough. It will give you some rough idea of the state to which Barmy Fotheringay-Phipps had been reduced by the end of the next day when I tell you that the sound of the church bells ringing for evensong brought him out of the Goose and Grasshopper as if he had heard a fire-engine. The thought that at last something was going to happen in Maiden Eggesford in which the Jubilee Watering-Trough *motif* was not stressed, stirred him strangely. He was in his pew in three jumps. And as the service got under way he began to feel curious emotions going on in his bosom.

There is something about evening church in a village in the summer time that affects the most hard-boiled. They had left the door open, and through it came the scent of lime trees and wall-flowers and the distant hum of bees fooling about. And gradually there poured over Barmy a wave of sentiment. As he sat and listened to the First Lesson he became a changed man.

The Lesson was one of those chapters of the Old Testament all about how Abimelech begat Jazzbo and Jazzbo begat Zachariah. And, what with the beauty of the words and the peace of his surroundings, Barmy suddenly began to become conscious of a great remorse.

He had not done the square thing, he told himself, by dear old Pongo. Here was a chap, notoriously one of the best, as sound an egg as ever donned a heliotrope sock, and he was deliberately chiselling him out of the girl he loved. He was doing the dirty on a fellow whom he had been pally with since their Eton jacket days – a bloke who time and again had shared with him his last bar of almond-rock. Was this right? Was this just? Would Abimelech have behaved like that to Jazzbo or – for the matter of that – Jazzbo to Zachariah? The answer, he could not disguise it from himself, was in the negative.

It was a different, stronger Barmy, a changed, chastened Cyril Fotheringay-Phipps, who left the sacred edifice at the conclusion of the vicar's fifty-minute sermon. He had made the great decision. It would play the dickens with his heart and probably render the rest of his life a blank, but nevertheless he would retire from the unseemly struggle and give the girl up to Pongo.

That night, as they cold-suppered together, Barmy cleared his throat and looked across at Pongo with a sad, sweet smile.

'Pongo,' he said.

The other glanced distantly up from his baked potato.

'There is something you wish to say to me, Fotheringay-Phipps?'

'Yes,' said Barmy. 'A short while ago I sent a note to Miss Briscoe, informing her that I shall not be attending the School Treat and mentioning that you will be there in my stead. Take her, Pongo, old man. She is yours. I scratch my nomination.'

Pongo stared. His whole manner changed. It was as if he had been a Trappist monk who had suddenly decided to give Trappism a miss and become one of the boys again.

'But, dash it, this is noble!'

'No, no.'

'But it is! It's . . . well, dash it, I hardly know what to say.'

'I hope you will be very, very happy.'

'Thanks, old man.'

'Very, very, very happy.'

'Rather! I should say so. And I'll tell you one thing. In the years to come there will always be a knife and fork for you at our little home. The children shall be taught to call you Uncle Barmy.'

'Thanks,' said Barmy. 'Thanks.'

'Not at all,' said Pongo. 'Not at all.'

At this moment, the barmaid entered with a note for Barmy. He read it and crumpled it up.

'From Her?' asked Pongo.

'Yes.'

'Saying she quite understands, and so forth?'

'Yes.'

Pongo ate a piece of cheese in a meditative manner. He seemed to be pursuing some train of thought.

'I should think,' he said, 'that a fellow who married a clergyman's daughter would get the ceremony performed at cut rates, wouldn't he?'

'Probably.'

'If not absolutely on the nod?'

'I shouldn't wonder.'

'Not,' said Pongo, 'that I am influenced by any consideration like that, of course. My love is pure and flamelike, with no taint of dross. Still, in times like these, every little helps.'

'Quite,' said Barmy. 'Quite.'

He found it hard to control his voice. He had lied to his friend about that note. What Angelica Briscoe had really said in it was that it was quite all right if he wanted to edge out of the School Treat, but that she would require him to take the Village Mothers for their Annual Outing on the same day. There had to be some responsible person with them, and the curate had sprained his ankle tripping over a footstool in the vestry.

Barmy could read between the lines. He saw what this meant. His fatal fascination had done its deadly work, and the girl had become infatuated with him. No other explanation would fit the facts. It was absurd to suppose that she would lightly have selected him for this extraordinarily important assignment. Obviously it was the big event of the village year. Anyone would do to mess about at the School Treat, but Angelica Briscoe would place in charge of the Mothers' Annual Outing only a man she trusted . . . respected . . . loved.

He sighed. What must be, he felt, must be. He had done his conscientious best to retire in favour of his friend, but Fate had been too strong.

I found it a little difficult (said the Crumpet) to elicit from Barmy exactly what occurred at the annual outing of the Village Mothers of Maiden Eggesford. When telling me the story, he had the air of a man whose old wound is troubling him. It was not, indeed, till the fourth cocktail that he became really communicative. And then, speaking with a kind of stony look in his eye, he gave me a fairly comprehensive account. But even then each word seemed to hurt him in some tender spot.

The proceedings would appear to have opened in a quiet and orderly manner. Sixteen females of advanced years assembled in a motor coach, and the expedition was seen off from the vicarage door by the Rev. P. P. Briscoe in person. Under his eye, Barmy tells me, the Beauty Chorus was demure and docile. It was a treat to listen to their murmured responses. As nice and respectable a bunch of mothers, Barmy says, as he had ever struck. His only apprehension at this point, he tells me, was lest the afternoon's proceedings might possibly be a trifle stodgy. He feared a touch of ennui.

He needn't have worried. There was no ennui.

The human cargo, as I say, had started out in a spirit of demureness and docility. But it was amazing what a difference a mere fifty yards of the high road made to these Mothers. No sooner were they out of sight of the vicarage than they began to effervesce to an almost unbelievable extent. The first intimation Barmy had that the binge was going to be run on lines other than those which he had anticipated was when a very stout Mother in a pink bonnet and a dress covered with bugles suddenly picked off a passing cyclist with a well-directed tomato, causing him to skid into a ditch. Upon which, all sixteen mothers laughed like fiends in hell, and it was plain that they considered that the proceedings had now been formally opened.

Of course, looking back at it now in a calmer spirit, Barmy tells me that he can realize that there is much to be said in palliation of the exuberance of these ghastly female pimples. When you are shut up all the year round in a place like Maiden Eggesford, with nothing to do but wash underclothing and attend Divine Service, you naturally incline to let yourself go a bit at times of festival and holiday. But at the moment he did not think of this, and his spiritual agony was pretty pronounced.

If there's one thing Barmy hates it's being conspicuous, and conspicuous is precisely what a fellow cannot fail to be when he's in a motor coach with sixteen women of mature ages who alternate between singing ribald songs and hurling volleys of homely chaff at passers-by. In this connection, he tells me, he is thinking particularly of a Mother in spectacles and a Homburg hat, which she had pinched from the driver of the vehicle, whose prose style appeared to have been modelled on that of Rabelais.

It was a more than usually penetrating sally on the part of this female which at length led him to venture a protest.

'I say! I mean, I say. I say, dash it, you know. I mean, dash it,' said Barmy, feeling, even as he spoke, that the rebuke had not been phrased as neatly as he could have wished.

Still, lame though it had been, it caused a sensation which can only be described as profound. Mother looked at Mother. Eyebrows were raised, breath drawn in censoriously.

'Young man,' said the Mother in the pink bonnet, who seemed to have elected herself forewoman, 'kindly keep your remarks to yourself.'

Another Mother said: 'The idea!' and a third described him as a kill-joy.

'We don't want none of *your* impudence,' said the one in the pink bonnet.

'Ah!' agreed the others.

'A slip of a boy like that!' said the Mother in the Homburg hat, and there was a general laugh, as if the meeting considered that the point had been well taken.

Barmy subsided. He was wishing that he had yielded to the advice of his family and become a curate after coming down from the University. Curates are specially trained to handle this sort of situation. A tough, hard-boiled curate, spitting out of the corner of his mouth, would soon have subdued these Mothers, he reflected. He would have played on them as on a stringed instrument – or, rather, as on sixteen stringed instruments. But Barmy, never having taken Orders, was helpless.

So helpless, indeed, that when he suddenly discovered that they were heading for Bridmouth-on-Sea he felt that there was nothing he could do about it. From the vicar's own lips he had had it officially that the programme was that the expedition should drive to the neighbouring village of Bottsford Mortimer, where there were the ruins of an old abbey, replete with interest; lunch among these ruins; visit the local museum (founded and pre-sented to the village by the late Sir Wandesbury Pott, JP); and, after filling in with a bit of knitting, return home. And now the whole trend of the party appeared to be towards the Amusement Park on the Bridmouth pier. And, though Barmy's whole soul shuddered at the thought of these sixteen Bacchantes let loose in an Amusement Park, he hadn't the nerve to say a word.

It was at about this point, he tells me, that a vision rose before him of Pongo happily loafing through the summer afternoon amidst the placid joys of the School Treat.

Of what happened at the Amusement Park Barmy asked me to be content with the sketch-iest of outlines. He said that even now he could not bear to let his memory dwell upon it. He confessed himself perplexed by the psychology of the thing. These mothers, he said, must have had mothers of their own and at those mothers' knees must have learned years ago the difference between right and wrong, and yet . . . Well, what he was thinking of particularly, he said, was what occurred on the Bump the Bumps apparatus. He refused to specify exactly, but he said that there was one woman in a puce mantle who definitely seemed to be living for pleasure alone.

It was a little unpleasantness with the proprietor of this concern that eventually led to the expedition leaving the Amusement Park and going down to the beach. Some purely technical point of finance, I understand – he claiming that a Mother in bombazine had had eleven rides and only paid once. It resulted in Barmy getting lugged into the brawl and rather roughly handled – which was particularly unfortunate, because the bombazined Mother explained on their way down to the beach that the whole thing had been due to a misunderstanding. In actual fact, what had really happened was that she had had twelve rides and paid twice.

However, he was so glad to get his little troupe out of the place that he counted an eye well blacked as the price of deliverance, and his spirits, he tells me, had definitely risen when suddenly the sixteen Mothers gave a simultaneous whoop and made for a sailing-boat which was waiting to be hired, sweeping him along with them. And the next moment they were off across the bay, bowling along before a nippy breeze which, naturally, cheesed it abruptly as soon as it had landed them far enough away from shore to make things interesting for the unfortunate blighter who had to take to the oars.

This, of course, was poor old Barmy. There was a man in charge of the boat, but he, though but a rough, untutored salt, had enough sense not to let himself in for a job like rowing this Noah's Ark home. Barmy did put it up to him tentatively, but the fellow said that he had to attend to the steering, and when Barmy said that he, Barmy, knew how to steer, the fellow said that he, the fellow, could not entrust a valuable boat to an amateur. After which, he lit his pipe and lolled back in the stern sheets with rather the air of an ancient Roman banqueter making himself cosy among the cushions. And Barmy, attaching himself to a couple of oars of about the size of those served out to galley-slaves in the old trireme days, started to put his back into it.

For a chap who hadn't rowed anything except a light canoe since he was up at Oxford, he considers he did dashed well, especially when you take into account the fact that he was much hampered by the Mothers. They would insist on singing that thing about 'Give yourself a pat on the back', and, apart from the fact that Barmy considered that something on the lines of the Volga Boat-Song would have been far more fitting, it was a tune it was pretty hard to keep time to. Seven times he caught crabs, and seven times those sixteen Mothers stopped singing and guffawed like one Mother. All in all, a most painful experience. Add the fact that the first thing the females did on hitting the old Homeland again was to get up an informal dance on the sands and that the ride home in the quiet evenfall was more or less a repetition of the journey out, and you will agree with me that Barmy, as he eventually tottered into the saloon bar of the Goose and Grasshopper, had earned the frothing tankard which he now proceeded to order.

He had just sucked it down and was signalling for another, when the door of the saloon bar opened and in came Pongo.

If Barmy had been less preoccupied with his own troubles he would have seen that Pongo was in poorish shape. His collar was torn, his hair dishevelled. There were streaks of chocolate down his face and half a jam sandwich attached to the back of his coat. And so moved was he at seeing Barmy that he started ticking him off before he had so much as ordered a gin and ginger.

'A nice thing you let me in for!' said Pongo. 'A jolly job you shoved off on me!'

Barmy was feeling a little better after his ingurgitations, and he was able to speak.

'What are you talking about?'

'I am talking about School Treats,' replied Pongo, with an intense bitterness. 'I am talking about seas of children, all with sticky hands, who rubbed those hands on me. I am talking . . . Oh, it's no good your gaping like a diseased fish, Fotheringay-Phipps. You know dashed well that you planned the whole thing. Your cunning fiend's brain formulated the entire devilish scheme. You engineered the bally outrage for your own foul purposes, to queer me with Angelica. You thought that when a girl sees a man blind-folded and smacked with rolled-up newspapers by smelly children she can never feel the same to him again. Ha!' said Pongo, at last ordering his gin and ginger.

Barmy was stunned, of course, by this violent attack, but he retained enough of the nice sense of propriety of the Fotheringay-Phippses to realize that this discussion could not be continued in public. Already the barmaid's ears had begun to work loose at the roots as she pricked them up.

'I don't know what the dickens you're talking about,' he said, 'but bring your drink up to my room and we'll go into the matter there. We cannot bandy a woman's name in a saloon bar.'

'Who's bandying a woman's name?'

'You are. You bandied it only half a second ago. If you don't call what you said bandying, there are finer-minded men who do.'

So they went upstairs, and Barmy shut the door.

'Now, then,' he said. 'What's all this drivel?'

'I've told you.'

'Tell me again.'

'I will.'

'Right ho. One moment.'

Barmy went to the door and opened it sharply. There came the unmistakable sound of a barmaid falling downstairs. He closed the door again.

'Now, then,' he said.

Pongo drained his gin and ginger.

'Of all the dirty tricks one man ever played on another,' he began, 'your sneaking out of that School Treat and letting me in for it is one which the verdict of history will undoubtedly rank the dirtiest. I can read you now like a book, Fotheringay-Phipps. Your motive is crystal-clear to me. You knew at what a disadvantage a man appears at a School Treat, and you saw to it that I and not you should be the poor mutt to get smeared with chocolate and sloshed with newspapers before the eyes of Angelica Briscoe. And I believed you when you handed me all that drip about yielding your claim and what not. My gosh!'

For an instant, as he heard these words, stupefaction rendered Barmy speechless. Then he found his tongue. His generous soul was seething with indignation at the thought of how his altruism, his great sacrifice, had been misinterpreted.

'What absolute rot!' he cried. 'I never heard such bilge in my life. My motives in sending you to that School Treat instead of me were unmixedly chivalrous. I did it simply and solely to enable you to ingratiate yourself with the girl, not reflecting that it was out of the question that she should ever love a pop-eyed, pimply-faced poop like you.'

Pongo started.

'Pop-eyed?'

'Pop-eyed was what I said.'

'Pimply-faced?'

'Pimply-faced was the term I employed.'

'Poop?'

'Poop was the expression with which I concluded. If you want to know the real obstacle in the way of any wooing you may do now or in the years to come, Twistleton-Twistleton, it is this – that you entirely lack sex-appeal and look like nothing on earth. A girl of the sweet, sensitive nature of Angelica Briscoe does not have to see you smeared with chocolate to recoil from you with loathing. She does it automatically, and she does it on her head.'

'Is that so?'

'That is so.'

'Oh? Well, let me inform you that in spite of what had happened, in spite of the fact that she has seen me at my worst, there is something within me that tells me that Angelica Briscoe loves me and will one day be mine.'

'Mine, you mean. I can read the message in a girl's shy, drooping eyes, Twistleton-Twistleton, and I am prepared to give you odds of eleven-to-four that before the year is out I shall be walking down the aisle with Angelica Fotheringay-Phipps on my arm. I will go further. Thirty-three-to-eight.'

'What in?'

'Tenners.'

'Done.'

It was at this moment that the door opened.

'Excuse me, gentlemen,' said the barmaid.

The two rivals glared at the intruder. She was a well-nourished girl with a kind face. She was rubbing her left leg, which appeared to be paining her. The staircases are steep at the Goose and Grasshopper.

'You'll excuse me muscling in like this, gentlemen,' said the barmaid, or words to that effect, 'but I happened inadvertently to overhear your conversation, and I feel it my duty to put you straight on an important point of fact. Gentlemen, all bets are off. Miss Angelica Briscoe is already engaged to be married.'

You can readily conceive the effect of this announcement. Pongo biffed down into the only chair, and Barmy staggered against the wash-hand stand.

'What!' said Pongo.

'What!' said Barmy.

The barmaid turned to Barmy.

'Yes, sir. To the gentleman you were talking to in my bar the afternoon you arrived.'

Her initial observation had made Barmy feel as if he had been punched in the wind by sixteen Mothers, but at this addendum he was able to pull himself together a bit.

'Don't be an ass, my dear old barmaid,' he said. 'That was Miss Briscoe's brother.'

'No, sir.'

'But his name was Briscoe, and you told me he was at the vicarage.'

'Yes, sir. He spends a good deal of his time at the vicarage, being the young lady's second cousin, and engaged to her since last Christmas!'

Barmy eyed her sternly. He was deeply moved.

'Why did you not inform me of this earlier, you chump of a barmaid? With your gift for listening at doors you must long since have become aware that this gentlemen here and myself were deeply enamoured of Miss Briscoe. And yet you kept these facts under your hat, causing us to waste our time and experience the utmost alarm and despondency. Do you realize, barmaid, that, had you spoken sooner, my friend here would not have been subjected to nameless indignities at the School Treat . . .'

'Yes, sir. It was the School Treat that Mr Briscoe was so bent on not having to go to, which he would have had to have done, Miss Angelica insisting. He had a terrible time there last year, poor gentleman. He was telling me about it. And that was why he asked me as a particular favour not to mention that he was engaged to Miss Briscoe, because he said that, if he played his cards properly and a little secrecy and silence were observed in the proper quarters, there was a mug staying at the inn that he thought he could get to go instead of him. It would have done you good, sir, to have seen the way his face lit up as he said it. He's a very nice gentleman, Mr Briscoe, and we're all very fond of him. Well, I mustn't stay talking here, sir. I've got my bar to see to.'

She withdrew, and for some minutes there was silence in the room. It was Barmy who was the first to break it.

'After all, we still have our Art,' said Barmy.

He crossed the room and patted Pongo on the shoulder.

'Of course, it's a nasty knock, old man. . . .'

Pongo had raised his face from his hands and was fumbling for his cigarette-case. There was a look in his eyes as if he had just wakened from a dream.

'Well, *is* it?' he said. 'You've got to look at these things from every angle. Is a girl who can deliberately allow a man to go through the horrors of a School Treat worth bothering about?'

Barmy started.

'I never thought of that. Or a girl, for that matter, who could callously throw a fellow to the Village Mothers.'

'Remind me some time to tell you about a game called "Is Mr Smith At Home?" where you put your head in a sack and the younger generation jab you with sticks.'

'And don't let me forget to tell you about that Mother in the puce mantle on the Bump the Bumps.'

'There was a kid called Horace . . .'

'There was a Mother in a Homburg hat . . .'

'The fact is,' said Pongo, 'we have allowed ourselves to lose our sober judgement over a girl whose idea of a mate is a mere "Hey, you", to be ordered hither and thither at her will, and who will unleash the juvenile population of her native village upon him without so much as a pang of pity – in a word, a parson's daughter. If you want to know the secret of a happy and successful life, Barmy, old man, it is this: Keep away from parsons' daughters.'

'Right away,' agreed Barmy. 'How do you react to hiring a car and pushing off to the metropolis at once?'

'I am all for it. And if we're to give of our best on the evening of the eleventh *prox.* we ought to start rehearsing again immediately.'

'We certainly ought.'

'We haven't any too much time, as it is.'

'We certainly haven't. I've got an aunt who complains of rheumatism.'

'Well, who wouldn't? My father can't meet his creditors.'

'Does he want to? My uncle Joe's in very low water just now.'

'Too bad. What's he doing?'

'Teaching swimming. Listen, Pongo,' said Barmy. 'I've been thinking. You take the green whiskers this year.'

'No, no.'

'Yes, really. I mean it. If I've said it to myself once, I've said it a hundred times – good old Pongo simply must have the green whiskers this year.'

'Barmy!'

'Pongo!'

They clasped hands. Tried in the furnace, their friendship had emerged strong and true. Cyril Fotheringay-Phipps and Reginald Twistleton-Twistleton were themselves again.

'BUTTERCUP DAY'

Eggs, Beans and Crumpets

'Laddie,' said Ukridge, 'I need capital, old horse – need it sorely.'

He removed his glistening silk hat, looked at it in a puzzled way, and replaced it on his head. We had met by chance near the eastern end of Piccadilly, and that breath-taking gorgeousness of his costume told me that, since I had seen him last, there must have occurred between him and his Aunt Julia one of those periodical reconciliations which were wont to punctuate his hectic and disreputable career. For those who know Stanley Featherstonehaugh Ukridge, that much-enduring man, are aware that he is the nephew of Miss Julia Ukridge, the wealthy and popular novelist, and that from time to time, when she can bring herself to forgive and let bygones be bygones, he goes to dwell for a while in gilded servitude at her house in Wimbledon.

'Yes, Corky, my boy, I want a bit of capital.'

'Oh?'

'And want it quick. The truest saying in this world is that you can't accumulate if you don't speculate. But how the deuce are you to start speculating unless you accumulate a few quid to begin with?'

'Ah,' I said non-committally.

'Take my case,' proceeded Ukridge, running a·large, beautifully gloved finger round the inside of a spotless collar which appeared to fit a trifle too snugly to the neck. 'I have an absolutely safe double for Kempton Park on the fifteenth, and even a modest investment would bring me in several hundred pounds. But bookies, blast them, require cash down in advance, so where am I? Without capital, enterprise is strangled at birth.'

'Can't you get some from your aunt?'

'Not a cent. She is one of those women who simply do not disgorge. All her surplus cash is devoted to adding to her collection of mouldy snuff-boxes. When I look at those snuff-boxes and reflect that any single one of them, judiciously put up the spout, would set my feet on the road to Fortune, only my innate sense of honesty keeps me from pinching them.'

'You mean they're locked up?'

'It's hard, laddie. Very hard and bitter and ironical. She buys me suits. She buys me hats. She buys me boots. She buys me spats. And, what is more, insists on my wearing the damned things. With what result? Not only am I infernally uncomfortable but my exterior creates a totally false impression in the minds of any blokes I meet to whom I may happen to owe a bit of money. When I go about looking as if I owned the Mint, it becomes difficult to convince them that I am not in a position to pay them their beastly one pound fourteen and eleven, or whatever it is. I tell you, laddie, the strain has begun to weigh upon me to such an extent that the breaking-point may arrive at any moment. Every day it is becoming more imperative that I clear out and start life again upon my own. But this cannot be done without cash. And that is why I look around me and say to myself: "How am I to acquire a bit of capital?" '

I thought it best to observe at this point that my own circumstances were extremely straitened. Ukridge received the information with a sad, indulgent smile.

'I was not dreaming of biting your ear, old horse,' he said. 'What I require is something far beyond your power to supply. Five pounds at least. Or three, anyway. Of course, if, before we part, you think fit to hand over a couple of bob or half-a-crown as a small temporary – '

He broke off with a start, and there came into his face the look of one who has perceived snakes in his path. He gazed along the street; then, wheeling round, hurried abruptly down Church Place.

'One of your creditors?' I asked.

'Girl with flags,' said Ukridge briefly. A peevish note crept into his voice. 'This modern practice, laddie, of allowing females with trays of flags and collecting-boxes to flood the metropolis is developing into a scourge. If it isn't Rose Day it's Daisy Day and if it isn't Daisy Day it's Pansy Day. And though now, thanks to a bit of quick thinking, we have managed to escape without – '

At this moment a second flag-girl, emerging from Jermyn Street, held us up with a brilliant smile, and we gave till it hurt – which, in Ukridge's case, was almost immediately.

'And so it goes on,' he said bitterly. 'Sixpence here, a shilling there. Only last Friday I was touched for twopence at my very door. How can a man amass a huge fortune if there is this constant drain on his resources? What was that girl collecting for?'

'I didn't notice.'

'Nor did I. One never does. For all we know, we may have contributed to some cause of which we heartily disapprove. And that reminds me, Corky, my aunt is lending her grounds on Tuesday for a bazaar in aid of the local Temperance League. I particularly wish you to put aside all other engagements and roll up.'

'No, thanks. I don't want to meet your aunt again.'

'You won't meet her. She will be away. She's going north on a lecturing tour.'

'Well, I don't want to come to any bazaar. I can't afford it.'

'Have no fear, laddie. There will be no expense involved. You will pass the entire afternoon in the house with me. My aunt, though she couldn't get out of lending these people her grounds, is scared that, with so many strangers prowling about, somebody might edge in and sneak her snuff-boxes. So I am left on guard, with instructions not to stir out till they've all gone. And a very wise precaution too. There is absolutely nothing which blokes whose passions have been inflamed by constant ginger-beer will stick at. You will share my vigil. We will smoke a pipe or two in the study, talk of this and that, and it may be that, if we put our heads together, we shall be able to think up a scheme for collecting a bit of capital.'

'Oh, well, in that case – '

'I shall rely on you. And now, if I don't want to be late, I'd better be getting along. I'm lunching with my aunt at Prince's.'

He gazed malevolently at the flag-girl, who had just stopped another pedestrian, and strode off.

Heath House, Wimbledon, the residence of Miss Julia Ukridge, was one of that row of large mansions which face the Common, standing back from the road in the seclusion of spacious grounds. On any normal day, the prevailing note of the place would have been a dignified calm; but when I arrived on the Tuesday afternoon a vast and unusual activity was in progress. Over the gates there hung large banners advertising the bazaar, and through these gates crowds of people were passing. From somewhere in the interior of the garden came the brassy music of a merry-go-round. I added myself to the throng, and was making for the front door when a silvery voice spoke in my ear, and I was aware of a very pretty girl at my elbow.

'Buy a buttercup?'

'I beg your pardon?'

'Buy a buttercup?'

I then perceived that, attached to her person with a strap, she carried a tray containing a mass of yellow paper objects.

'What's all this?' I inquired, automatically feeling in my pocket.

She beamed upon me like a high priestess initiating some favourite novice into a rite.

'Buttercup Day,' she said winningly.

A man of greater strength of mind would, no doubt, have asked what Buttercup Day was, but I have a spine of wax. I produced the first decent-sized coin on which my fumbling fingers rested, and slipped it into her box. She thanked me with a good deal of fervour and pinned one of the yellow objects in my buttonhole.

The interview then terminated. The girl flitted off like a sunbeam in the direction of a prosperous-looking man who had just gone by, and I went on to the house, where I found Ukridge in the study gazing earnestly through the french windows which commanded a view of the grounds. He turned as I entered; and, as his eye fell upon the saffron ornament in my coat, a soft smile of pleasure played about his mouth.

'I see you've got one,' he said.

'Got what?'

'One of those thingummies.'

'Oh, these? Yes. There was a girl with a tray of them in the front garden. It's Buttercup Day. In aid of something or other, I suppose.'

'It's in aid of me,' said Ukridge, the soft smile developing into a face-splitting grin.

'What do you mean?'

'Corky, old horse,' said Ukridge, motioning me to a chair, 'the great thing in this world is to have a good, level business head. Many men in my position wanting capital and not seeing where they were going to get it, would have given up the struggle as a bad job. Why? Because they lacked Vision and the big, broad, flexible outlook. But what did I do? I sat down and thought. And after many hours of concentrated meditation I was rewarded with an idea. You remember that painful affair in Jermyn Street the other day – when that female bandit got into our ribs? You recall that neither of us knew what we had coughed up our good money for?'

'Well?'

'Well, laddie, it suddenly flashed upon me like an inspiration from above that nobody ever does know what they are coughing up for when they meet a girl with a tray of flags. I hit upon the great truth, old horse – one of the profoundest truths in this modern civilization of ours – that any given man, confronted by a pretty girl with a tray of flags, will automatically and without inquiry shove a coin in her box. So I got hold of a girl I know – a dear little soul, full of beans – and arranged for her to come here this afternoon. I confidently anticipate a clean-up on an impressive scale. The outlay on the pins and bits of paper was practically nil, so there is no overhead and all that comes in will be pure velvet.'

A strong pang shot through me.

'Do you mean to say,' I demanded with feeling, 'that that half-crown of mine goes into your beastly pocket?'

'Half of it. Naturally my colleague and partner is in on the division. Did you really give half-a-crown?' said Ukridge, pleased. 'It was like you, laddie. Generous to a fault. If everyone had your lavish disposition, this world would be a better, sweeter place.'

'I suppose you realize,' I said, 'that in about ten minutes at the outside your colleague and partner, as you call her, will be arrested for obtaining money under false pretences?'

'Not a chance.'

'After which, they will – thank God! – proceed to pinch you.'

'Quite impossible, laddie. I rely on my knowledge of human psychology. What did she say when she stung you?'

'I forget. "Buy a buttercup" or something.'

'And then?'

'Then I asked what it was all about, and she said, "Buttercup Day".'

'Exactly. And that's all she will need to say to anyone. Is it likely, is it reasonable to suppose, that even in these materialistic days Chivalry has sunk so low that any man will require to be told more, by a girl as pretty as that, than that it is Buttercup Day?' He walked to the window and looked out. 'Ah! She's come round into the back garden,' he said, with satisfaction. 'She seems to be doing a roaring trade. Every second man is wearing a buttercup. She is now putting it across a curate, bless her heart.'

'And in a couple of minutes she will probably try to put it across a plain-clothes detective, and that will be the end.'

Ukridge eyed me reproachfully.

'You persist in looking on the gloomy side, Corky. A little more of the congratulatory attitude is what I could wish to see in you, laddie. You do not appear to realize that your old friend's foot is at last on the ladder that leads to wealth. Suppose – putting it at the lowest figure – I net four pounds out of this buttercup business. It goes on Caterpillar in the two o'clock selling race at Kempton. Caterpillar wins, the odds being – let us say – ten-to-one. Stake and winnings go on Bismuth for the Jubilee Cup, again at ten-to-one. There you have a nice, clean four hundred pounds of capital, ample for a man of keen business sense to build a fortune on. For, between ourselves, Corky, I have my eye on what looks like the investment of a lifetime.'

'Yes?'

'Yes. I was reading about it the other day. A cat ranch out in America.'

'A cat ranch?'

'That's it. You collect a hundred thousand cats. Each cat has twelve kittens a year. The skins range from ten cents each for the white ones to seventy-five for the pure black. That gives you twelve million skins per year to sell at an average price of thirty cents per skin, making your annual revenue at a conservative estimate three hundred and sixty thousand dollars. But, you will say, what about overhead expenses?'

'Will I?'

'That has all been allowed for. To feed the cats you start a rat ranch next door. The rats multiply four times as fast as cats, so if you begin with a million rats it gives you four rats per day per cat, which is plenty. You feed the rats on what is left over of the cats after removing the skins, allowing one-fourth of a cat per rat, the business thus becoming automatically self-supporting. The cats will eat the rats, the rats will eat the cats – '

There was a knock upon the door.

'Come in,' bellowed Ukridge irritably. These captains of industry hate to be interrupted when in conference.

It was the butler who had broken in upon his statistics.

'A gentleman to see you, sir,' said he.

'Who is he?'

'He did not give his name, sir. He is a gentleman in Holy Orders.'

'Not the vicar?' cried Ukridge in alarm.

'No, sir. The gentleman is a curate. He inquired for Miss Ukridge. I informed him that Miss Ukridge was absent, but that you were on the premises, and he then desired to see you, sir.'

'Oh, all right,' said Ukridge resignedly. 'Show him in. Though we are running grave risks, Corky,' he added, as the door closed. 'These curates frequently have subscription lists up their sleeves and are extremely apt, unless you are very firm, to soak you for a donation to the Church Organ Fund or something. Still, let us hope – '

The door opened, and our visitor entered. He was a rather small size in curates, with an engaging, ingenuous face, adorned with a pair of pince-nez. He wore a paper buttercup in his coat; and, directly he began to speak, revealed himself as the possessor of a peculiar stammer.

'Pup-pup-pup – ' he said.

'Eh?' said Ukridge.

'Mr pup-pup-pup Ukridge?'

'Yes. This is my friend, Mr Corcoran.'

I bowed. The curate bowed.

'Take a seat,' urged Ukridge hospitably. 'You'll have a drink?'

The visitor raised a deprecatory hand.

'No, thank you,' he replied. 'I find it more beneficial to my health to abstain entirely from alcoholic liquids. At the University I was a moderate drinker, but since I came down I have found it better to pup-pup-pup completely. But pray do not let me stop you. I am no bigot.'

He beamed for an instant in friendly fashion; then there came into his face a look of gravity. Here was a man, one perceived, who had something on his mind.

'I came here, Mr Ukridge,' he said, 'on a pup-pup-pup-pup-pup – '

'Parish matter?' I hazarded, to help him out.

He shook his head.

'No, a pup-pup-pup – '

'Pleasure-trip?' suggested Ukridge.

He shook his head again.

'No, a pup-pup-pup uncongenial errand. I understand that Miss Ukridge is absent and that you, as her nephew, are therefore the presiding genius, if I may use the expression, of these pup-pup-pup festivities.'

'Eh?' said Ukridge, fogged.

'I mean that it is to you that complaints should be made.'

'Complaints?'

'Of what is going on in Miss Ukridge's garden – one might say under the imprimatur.'

Ukridge's classical education had been cut short by the fact that at an early age he had unfortunately been expelled from the school of which in boyhood's days we had been fellow-members, and Latin small-talk was not his forte. This one passed well over his head. He looked at me plaintively, and I translated.

'He means,' I said, 'that your aunt lent her grounds for this binge and so has a right to early information about any rough stuff that is being pulled on the premises.'

'Exactly,' said the curate.

'But, dash it, laddie,' protested Ukridge, now abreast of the situation. 'it's no good complaining of anything that happens at a charity bazaar. You know as well as I do that, when the members of a Temperance League get together and start selling things at stalls, anything goes except gouging and biting. The only thing to do is to be light on your feet and keep away.'

The curate shook his head sadly.

'I have no complaint to make concerning the manner in which the stalls are being conducted, Mr pup-pup-pup. It is only to be expected that at a bazaar in aid of a deserving cause the prices of the various articles on sale will be in excess of those charged in the ordinary marts of trade. But deliberate and calculated swindling is another matter.'

'Swindling?'

'There is a young woman in the grounds extorting money from the public on the plea that it is Buttercup Day. And here is the point, Mr Ukridge. Buttercup Day is the flag-day of the National Orthopaedic Institute, and is not to take place for some weeks. This young person is deliberately cheating the public.'

Ukridge licked his lips, with a hunted expression.

'Probably a local institution of the same name,' I suggested.

'That's it,' said Ukridge gratefully. 'Just what I was going to say myself. Probably a local institution. Fresh Air Fund for the poor of the neighbourhood, I shouldn't wonder. I believe I've heard them talk about it, now I come to think.'

The curate refused to consider the theory.

'No,' he said. 'If that had been so the young woman would have informed me. In answer to my questions, her manner was evasive and I could elicit no satisfactory reply. She merely smiled and repeated the words "Buttercup Day". I feel that the police should be called in.'

'The police!' gurgled Ukridge pallidly.

'It is our pup-pup duty,' said the curate, looking like a man who writes letters to the Press signed 'Pro Bono Publico'.

Ukridge shot out of his chair with a convulsive bound. He grasped my arm and led me to the door.

'Excuse me,' he said. 'Corky,' he whispered tensely, dragging me out into the passage, 'go and tell her to leg it – quick!'

'Right!' I said.

'You will no doubt find a constable in the road,' said Ukridge.

'I bet I will,' I replied in a clear, carrying voice.

'We can't have this sort of thing going on here,' bellowed Ukridge.

'Certainly not,' I shouted with enthusiasm.

He returned to the study, and I went forth upon my errand of mercy. I had reached the front door and was about to open it, when it suddenly opened itself, and the next moment I was gazing into the clear blue eyes of Ukridge's Aunt Julia.

'Oh – ah – er!' I said.

There are certain people in this world in whose presence certain other people can never feel completely at their ease. Notable among the people beneath whose gaze I myself experience a sensation of extreme discomfort and guilt is Miss Julia Ukridge, author of so many widely-read novels, and popular after-dinner speaker at the better class of literary reunion. This was the fourth time we had met, and on each of the previous occasions, I had felt the same curious illusion of having just committed some particularly unsavoury crime and – what is more – of having done it with swollen hands, enlarged feet, and trousers bagging at the knee on a morning when I had omitted to shave.

I stood and gaped. Although she had no doubt made her entry by the simple process of inserting a latchkey in the front door and turning it, her abrupt appearance had on me the effect of a miracle.

'Mr Corcoran!' she observed, without pleasure.

'Er – '

'What are you doing here?'

An inhospitable remark; but justified, perhaps, by the circumstances of our previous relations – which had not been of the most agreeable.

'I came to see – er – Stanley.'

'Oh?'

'He wanted me with him this afternoon.'

'Indeed?' she said; and her manner suggested surprise at what she evidently considered a strange and even morbid taste on her nephew's part.

'We thought – we thought – we both thought you were lecturing up north.'

'When I arrived at the club for luncheon I found a telegram postponing my visit,' she condescended to explain. 'Where is Stanley?'

'In your study.'

'I will go there. I wish to see him.'

I began to feel like Horatius at the Bridge. It seemed to me that, foe of the human race though Ukridge was in so many respects, it was my duty as a life-long friend to prevent this woman winning through to him until the curate was well out of the way. I have a great belief in woman's intuition, and I was convinced that, should Miss Julia Ukridge learn that there was a girl in her grounds selling paper buttercups for a non-existent charity, her keen intelligence would leap without the slightest hesitation to the fact of her nephew's complicity in the disgraceful affair. She had had previous experience of Ukridge's financial methods.

In this crisis I thought rapidly.

'Oh, by the way,' I said. 'It nearly slipped my mind. The – er – the man in charge of all this business told me he particularly wanted to see you directly you came back.'

'What do you mean by the man in charge of all this business?'

'The fellow who got up the bazaar, you know.'

'Do you mean Mr Sims, the president of the Temperance League?'

'That's right. He told me he wanted to see you.'

'How could he possibly know that I should be coming back?'

'Oh, in case you did, I mean.' I had what Ukridge would have called an inspiration from above. 'I think he wants you to say a few words.'

I doubt if anything else would have shifted her. There came into her eyes, softening their steely glitter for a moment, that strange light which is seen only in the eyes of confirmed public speakers who are asked to say a few words.

'Well, I will go and see him.'

She turned away, and I bounded back to the study. The advent of the mistress of the house had materially altered my plans for the afternoon. What I proposed to do now was to inform Ukridge of her arrival, advise him to eject the curate with all possible speed, give him my blessing, and then slide quickly and unostentatiously away, without any further formalities of farewell. I am not unduly sensitive, but there had been that in Miss Ukridge's manner at our recent meeting which told me that I was not her ideal guest.

I entered the study. The curate was gone, and Ukridge, breathing heavily, was fast asleep in an arm-chair.

The disappearance of the curate puzzled me for a moment. He was rather an insignificant little man, but not so insignificant that I would not have noticed him if he had passed me while I was standing at the front door. And then I saw that the french windows were open.

It seemed to me that there was nothing to keep me. The strong distaste for this house which I had never lost since my first entry into it had been growing, and now the great open spaces called to me with an imperious voice. I turned softly, and found my hostess standing in the doorway.

'Oh, ah!' I said; and once more was afflicted by that curious sensation of having swelled in a very loathsome manner about the hands and feet. I have observed my hands from time to time during my life and have never been struck by anything particularly hideous about them: but whenever I encounter Miss Julia Ukridge they invariably take on the appearance and proportions of uncooked hams.

'Did you tell me, Mr Corcoran,' said the woman in that quiet, purring voice which must lose her so many friends, not only in Wimbledon but in the larger world outside, 'that you saw Mr Sims and he said that he wished to speak to me?'

'That's right.'

'Curious,' said Miss Ukridge. 'I find that Mr Sims is confined to his bed with a chill and has not been here today.'

I could sympathize with Mr Sims's chills. I felt as if I had caught one myself. I would – possibly – have made some reply, but at this moment an enormous snore proceeded from the arm-chair behind me, and such was my overwrought condition that I leapt like a young ram.

'Stanley!' cried Miss Ukridge, sighting the chair.

Another snore rumbled through the air, competing with the music of the merry-go-round. Miss Ukridge advanced and shook her nephew's arm.

'I think,' I said, being in the frame of mind when one does say silly things of that sort, 'I think he's asleep.'

'Asleep!' said Miss Ukridge briefly. Her eye fell on the half-empty glass on the table, and she shuddered austerely.

The interpretation which she obviously placed on the matter seemed incredible to me. On the stage and in motion-pictures one frequently sees victims of drink keel over in a state of complete unconsciousness after a single glass, but Ukridge was surely of sterner stuff.

'I can't understand it,' I said.

'Indeed!' said Miss Ukridge.

'Why, I have only been out of the room half a minute, and when I left him he was talking to a curate.'

'A curate?'

'Absolutely a curate. It's hardly likely, is it, that when he was talking to a curate he would – '

My speech for the defence was cut short by a sudden, sharp noise which, proceeding from immediately behind me, caused me once more to quiver convulsively.

'Well, sir?' said Miss Ukridge.

She was looking past me; and, turning, I perceived that a stranger had joined us. He was standing in the french windows, and the noise which had startled me had apparently been caused by him rapping on the glass with the knob of a stick.

'Miss Ukridge?' said the newcomer.

He was one of those hard-faced, keen-eyed men. There clung about him, as he advanced into the room, a subtle air of authority. That he was a man of character and resolution was proved by the fact that he met Miss Ukridge's eye without a tremor.

'I am Miss Ukridge. Might I inquire – '

The visitor looked harder-faced and more keen-eyed than ever.

'My name is Dawson. From the Yard.'

'What yard?' asked the lady of the house, who, it seemed, did not read detective stories.

'Scotland Yard!'

'Oh!'

'I have come to warn you, Miss Ukridge,' said Mr Dawson, looking at me as if I was a bloodstain, 'to be on your guard. One of the greatest rascals in the profession is hanging about your grounds.'

'Then why don't you arrest him?' demanded Miss Ukridge.

The visitor smiled faintly.

'Because I want to get him good,' he said.

'Get him good? Do you mean reform him?'

'I do not mean reform him,' said Mr Dawson, grimly. 'I mean that I want to catch him trying on something worth pulling him in for. There's no sense in taking a man like Stuttering Sam for being a suspected person.'

'Stuttering Sam!' I cried, and Mr Dawson eyed me keenly once more, this time almost as intently as if I had been the blunt instrument with which the murder was committed.

'Eh?' he said.

'Oh, nothing. Only it's curious – '

'What's curious?'

'Oh, no, it couldn't be. This fellow was a curate. A most respectable man.'

'Have you seen a curate who stuttered?' exclaimed Mr Dawson.

'Why, yes. He – '

'Hullo!' said Mr Dawson. 'Who's this?'

'That,' replied Miss Ukridge, eyeing the arm-chair with loathing, 'is my nephew Stanley.'

'Sound sleeper.'

'I prefer not to talk about him.'

'Tell me about this curate,' said Mr Dawson brusquely.

'Well, he came in – '

'Came in? In here?'

'Yes.'

'Why?'

'Well – '

'He must have had some story. What was it?'

I thought it judicious, in the interests of my sleeping friend, to depart somewhat from the precise truth.

'He – er – I think he said something about being interested in Miss Ukridge's collection of snuff-boxes.'

'Have you a collection of snuff-boxes, Miss Ukridge?'

'Yes.'

'Where do you keep them?'

'In the drawing-room.'

'Take me there, if you please.'

'But I don't understand.'

Mr Dawson clicked his tongue in an annoyed manner. He seemed to be an irritable sleuth-hound.

'I should have thought the thing was clear enough by this time. This man worms his way into your house with a plausible story, gets rid of this gentleman here – How did he get rid of you?'

'Oh, I just went, you know. I thought I would like a stroll.'

'Oh? Well, having contrived to be alone with your nephew, Miss Ukridge, he slips knock-out drops in his drink – '

'Knock-out drops?'

'A drug of some kind,' explained Mr Dawson, chafing at her slowness of intelligence.

'But the man was a curate!'

Mr Dawson barked shortly.

'Posing as a curate is the thing Stuttering Sam does best. He works the races in that character. Is this the drawing-room?'

It was. And it did not need the sharp, agonized cry which proceeded from the owner's lips to tell us that the worst had happened. The floor was covered with splintered wood and broken glass.

'They've gone!' cried Miss Ukridge.

It is curious how differently the same phenomenon can strike different people. Miss Ukridge was a frozen statue of grief. Mr Dawson, on the other hand, seemed pleased. He stroked his short moustache with an air of indulgent complacency, and spoke of neat jobs. He described Stuttering Sam as a Tough Baby, and gave it as his opinion that the absent one might justly be considered one of the lads and not the worst of them.

'What shall I do?' wailed Miss Ukridge. I was sorry for the woman. I did not like her, but she was suffering.

'The first thing to do,' said Mr Dawson briskly, 'is to find how much the fellow has got away with. Have you any other valuables in the house?'

'My jewels are in my bedroom.'

'Where?'

'I keep them in a box in the dress-cupboard.'

'Well, it's hardly likely that he would find them there, but I'd better go and see. You be taking a look round in here and make a complete list of what has been stolen.'

'All my snuff-boxes are gone.'

'Well, see if there is anything else missing. Where is your bedroom?'

'On the first floor, facing the front.'

'Right.'

Mr Dawson, all briskness and efficiency, left us. I was sorry to see him go. I had an idea that it would not be pleasant being left alone with this bereaved woman. Nor was it.

'Why on earth,' said Miss Ukridge, rounding on me as if I had been a relation, 'did you not suspect this man when he came in?'

'Why, I – he – '

'A child ought to have been able to tell that he was not a real curate.'

'He seemed – '

'Seemed!' She wandered restlessly about the room, and suddenly a sharp cry proceeded from her. 'My jade Buddha!'

'I beg your pardon?'

'That scoundrel has stolen my jade Buddha. Go and tell the detective.'

'Certainly.'

'Go on! What are you waiting for?'

I fumbled at the handle.

'I don't seem able to get the door open,' I explained meekly.

'Tchah!' said Miss Ukridge, swooping down. One of the rooted convictions of each member of the human race is that he or she is able without difficulty to open a door which has baffled their fellows. She took the handle and gave it a vigorous tug. The door creaked but remained unresponsive.

'What's the matter with the thing?' exclaimed Miss Ukridge petulantly.

'It's stuck.'

'I know it has stuck. Please do something at once. Good gracious, Mr Corcoran, surely you are at least able to open a drawing-room door?'

It seemed, put in that tone of voice, a feat sufficiently modest for a man of good physique and fair general education; but I was reluctantly compelled to confess, after a few more experiments, that it was beyond my powers. This appeared to confirm my hostess in the opinion, long held by her, that I was about the most miserable worm that an inscrutable Providence had ever permitted to enter the world.

She did not actually say as much, but she sniffed, and I interpreted her meaning exactly.

'Ring the bell!'

I rang the bell.

'Ring it again!'

I rang it again.

'Shout!'

I shouted.

'Go on shouting!'

I went on shouting. I was in good voice that day. I shouted 'Hi!'; I shouted 'Here!'; I shouted 'Help!'; I also shouted in a broad, general way. It was a performance which should have received more than a word of grateful thanks. But all Miss Ukridge said, when I paused for breath, was:

'Don't whisper!'

I nursed my aching vocal cords in a wounded silence.

'Help!' cried Miss Ukridge.

Considered as a shout, it was not in the same class as mine. It lacked body, vim, and even timbre. But, by that curious irony which governs human affairs, it produced results. Outside the door a thick voice spoke in answer.

'What's up?'

'Open this door!'

The handle rattled.

'It's stuck,' said a voice, which I now recognized as that of my old friend, Stanley Featherstonehaugh Ukridge.

'I know it has stuck. Is that you, Stanley? See what is causing it to stick.'

A moment of silence followed. Investigations were apparently in progress without.

'There's a wedge jammed under it.'

'Well, take it out at once.'

'I'll have to get a knife or something.'

Another interval for rest and meditation succeeded. Miss Ukridge paced the floor with knit brows; while I sidled into a corner and stood there feeling a little like an inexperienced young animal-trainer who has managed to get himself locked into the lions' den and is trying to remember what Lesson Three of his correspondence course said he ought to do in such circumstances.

Footsteps sounded outside, and then a wrenching and scratching. The door opened and we beheld on the mat Ukridge, with a carving-knife in his hand, looking headachy and dishevelled, and the butler, his professional poise rudely disturbed and his face stained with coal-dust.

It was characteristic of Miss Ukridge that it was to the erring domestic rather than the rescuing nephew that she turned first.

'Barter,' she hissed, as far as a woman, even of her intellectual gifts, is capable of hissing the word 'Barter', 'why didn't you come when I rang?'

'I did not hear the bell, madam. I was – '

'You must have heard the bell.'

'No, madam.'

'Why not?'

'Because I was in the coal-cellar, madam.'

'What on earth were you doing in the coal-cellar?'

'I was induced to go there, madam, by a man. He intimidated me with a pistol. He then locked me in.'

'What! What man?'

'A person with a short moustache and penetrating eyes. He – '

A raconteur with a story as interesting as his to tell might reasonably have expected to be allowed to finish it, but butler Barter at this point ceased to grip his audience. With a gasping moan his employer leaped past him, and we heard her running up the stairs.

Ukridge turned to me plaintively.

'What is all this, laddie? Gosh. I've got a headache. What has been happening?'

'The curate put knock-out drops in your drink, and then – '

I have seldom seen anyone display such poignant emotion as Ukridge did at that moment.

'The curate! It's a little hard. Upon my Sam, it's a trifle thick. Corky, old horse, I have travelled all over the world in tramp-steamers and what not. I have drunk in waterfront saloons from Montevideo to Cardiff. And the only time anyone has ever succeeded in doctoring the stuff on me it was done in Wimbledon – and by a curate. Tell me, laddie, are all curates like that? Because, if so – '

'He has also pinched your aunt's collection of snuff-boxes.'

'The curate?'

'Yes.'

'Golly!' said Ukridge in a low, reverent voice, and I could see a new respect for the Cloth dawning within him.

'And then this other fellow came along – his accomplice, pretending to be a detective – and locked us in and shut the butler in the coal-cellar. And I rather fancy he has got away with your aunt's jewels.'

A piercing scream from above rent the air.

'He has,' I said briefly. 'Well, old man, I think I'll be going.'

'Corky,' said Ukridge, 'stand by me!'

I shook my head.

'In any reasonable circumstances, yes. But I will not meet your aunt again just now. In a year or so, perhaps, but not now.'

Hurrying footsteps sounded on the staircase.

'Goodbye,' I said, pushing past and heading for the open. 'I must be off. Thanks for a very pleasant afternoon.'

Money was tight in those days, but it seemed to me next morning that an outlay of twopence on a telephone call to Heath House could not be considered an unjustifiable extravagance. I was conscious of a certain curiosity to learn at long range what had happened after I had removed myself on the previous afternoon.

'Are you there?' said a grave voice in answer to my ring.

'Is that Barter?'

'Yes, sir.'

'This is Mr Corcoran. I want to speak to Mr Ukridge.'

'Mr Ukridge is no longer here, sir. He left perhaps an hour ago.'

'Oh? Do you mean left – er – for ever?'

'Yes, sir.'

'Oh! Thanks.'

I rang off and, pondering deeply, returned to my rooms. I was not surprised to be informed by Bowles, my landlord, that Ukridge was in my sitting-room. It was this storm-tossed man's practice in times of stress to seek refuge with me.

'Hullo, laddie,' said Ukridge in a graveyard voice.

'So here you are.'

'Here I am.'

'She kicked you out?'

Ukridge winced slightly, as at some painful recollection.

'Words passed, old horse, and in the end we decided that we were better apart.'

'I don't see why she should blame you for what happened.'

'A woman like my aunt, Corky, is capable of blaming anybody for anything. And so I start life again, laddie, a penniless man, with no weapons against the great world but my vision and my brain.'

I endeavoured to attract his attention to the silver lining.

'You're all right,' I said. 'You're just where you wanted to be. You have the money which your buttercup girl collected.'

A strong spasm shook my poor friend, causing, as always happened with him in moments of mental agony, his collar to shoot off its stud and his glasses to fall from his nose.

'The money the girl collected,' he replied, 'is not available. It has passed away. I saw her this morning and she told me.'

'Told you what?'

'That a curate came up to her in the garden while she was selling those buttercups and – in spite of a strong stammer – put it to her so eloquently that she was obtaining money under false pretences that she gave him the entire takings for his Church Expenses Fund and went home, resolved to lead a better life. Women are an unstable, emotional sex, laddie. Have as little to do with them as possible. And, for the moment, give me a drink, old horse, and mix it fairly strong. These are the times that try men's souls.'

'COMPANY FOR GERTRUDE'

Blandings Castle and Elsewhere

The Hon. Freddie Threepwood, married to the charming daughter of Donaldson's Dog-Biscuits of Long Island City, NY, and sent home by his father-in-law to stimulate the sale of the firm's products in England, naturally thought right away of his Aunt Georgiana. There, he reasoned, was a woman who positively ate dog-biscuits. She had owned, when he was last in the country, a matter of four Pekes, two Poms, a Yorkshire terrier, five Sealyhams, a Borzoi and an Airedale: and if that didn't constitute a promising market for Donaldson's Dog-Joy ('get your dog thinking the Donaldson way'), he would like to know what did. The Alcester connection ought, he considered, to be good for at least ten of the half-crown cellophane-sealed packets a week.

A day or so after his arrival, accordingly, he hastened round to Upper Brook Street to make a sales-talk: and it was as he was coming rather pensively out of the house at the conclusion of the interview that he ran into Beefy Bingham, who had been up at Oxford with him. Several years had passed since the other, then a third year Blood and Trial Eights man, had bicycled along tow-paths saying rude things through a megaphone about Freddie's stomach, but he recognized him instantly. And this in spite of the fact that the passage of time appeared to have turned old Beefers into a clergyman. For the colossal frame of this Bingham was now clad in sober black, and he was wearing one of those collars which are kept in position without studs, purely by the exercise of will-power.

'Beefers!' cried Freddie, his slight gloom vanishing in the pleasure of this happy reunion.

The Rev. Rupert Bingham, though he returned his greeting with cordiality, was far from exuberant. He seemed subdued, gloomy, as if he had discovered schism among his flock. His voice, when he spoke, was the voice of a man with a secret sorrow.

'Oh, hullo, Freddie. I haven't seen you for years. Keeping pretty fit?'

'As a fiddle, Beefers, old man, as a fiddle. And you?'

'Oh, I'm all right,' said the Rev. Rupert, still with that same strange gloom. 'What were you doing in that house?'

'Trying to sell dog-biscuits.'

'Do you sell dog-biscuits?'

'I do when people have sense enough to see that Donaldson's Dog-Joy stands alone. But could I make my fatheaded aunt see that? No, Beefers, not though I talked for an hour and sprayed her with printed matter like a – '

'Your aunt? I didn't know Lady Alcester was your aunt.'

'Didn't you, Beefers? I thought it was all over London.'

'Did she tell you about me?'

'What about you? Great Scott! Are you the impoverished bloke who wants to marry Gertrude?'

'Yes.'

'Well, I'm dashed.'

'I love her, Freddie,' said the Rev. Rupert Bingham. 'I love her as no man . . .'

'Rather. Quite. Absolutely. I know. All the usual stuff. And she loves you, what?'

'Yes. And now they've gone and sent her off to Blandings, to be out of my way.'

'Low. Very low. But why are you impoverished? What about tithes? I always understood you birds made a pot out of tithes.'

'There aren't any tithes where I am.'

'No tithes?'

'None.'

'H'm. Not so hot. Well, what are you going to do about it, Beefers?'

'I thought of calling on your aunt and trying to reason with her.'

Freddie took his friend's arm sympathetically and drew him away.

'No earthly good, old man. If a woman won't buy Donaldson's Dog-Joy, it means she has some sort of mental kink and it's no use trying to reason with her. We must think of some other procedure. So Gertrude is at Blandings, is she? She would be. The family seem to look on the place as a sort of Bastille. Whenever the young of the species make a floater like falling in love with the wrong man, they are always shot off to Blandings to recover. The guv'nor has often complained about it bitterly. Now, let me think.'

They passed into Park Street. Some workmen were busy tearing up the paving with pneumatic drills, but the whirring of Freddie's brain made the sound almost inaudible.

'I've got it,' he said at length, his features relaxing from the terrific strain. 'And it's a dashed lucky thing for you, my lad, that I went last night to see that super-film, *Young Hearts Adrift*, featuring Rosalie Norton and Otto Byng. Beefers, old man, you're legging it straight down to Blandings this very afternoon.'

'What!'

'By the first train after lunch. I've got the whole thing planned out. In this super-film, *Young Hearts Adrift*, a poor but deserving young man was in love with the daughter of rich and haughty parents, and they took her away to the country so that she could forget, and a few days later a mysterious stranger turned up at the place and ingratiated himself with the parents and said he wanted to marry their daughter, and they gave their consent, and the wedding took place, then he tore off his whiskers and it was Jim!'

'Yes, but . . .'

'Don't argue. The thing's settled. My aunt needs a sharp lesson. You would think a woman would be only too glad to put business in the way of her nearest and dearest, especially when shown samples and offered a fortnight's free trial. But no! She insists on sticking to Peterson's Pup-Food, a wholly inferior product – lacking, I happen to know, in many of the essential vitamins – and from now on, old boy, I am heart and soul in your cause.'

'Whiskers?' said the Rev. Rupert doubtfully.

'You won't have to wear any whiskers. My guv'nor's never seen you. Or has he?'

'No, I've not met Lord Emsworth.'

'Very well, then.'

'But what good will it do me, ingratiating myself, as you call it, with your father? He's only Gertrude's uncle.'

'What good? My dear chap, are you aware that the guv'nor owns the countryside for miles around? He has all sorts of livings up his sleeve – livings simply dripping with tithes – and can distribute them to whoever he likes. I know, because at one time there was an idea of making me a parson. But I would have none of it.'

The Rev. Rupert's face cleared.

'Freddie, there's something in this.'

'You bet there's something in it.'

'But how can I ingratiate myself with your father?'

'Perfectly easy. Cluster round him. Hang on his every word. Interest yourself in his pursuits. Do him little services. Help him out of chairs. . . . Why, great Scott, I'd undertake to ingratiate myself with Stalin if I gave my mind to it. Pop off and pack the old toothbrush, and I'll go and get the guv'nor on the 'phone.'

At about the time when this pregnant conversation was taking place in London, W.1, far away in distant Shropshire, Clarence, ninth Earl of Emsworth, sat brooding in the library of Blandings Castle. Fate, usually indulgent to this dreamy peer, had suddenly turned nasty and smitten him a grievous blow beneath the belt.

They say Great Britain is still a first-class power, doing well and winning respect from the nations: and, if so, it is, of course, extremely gratifying. But what of the future? That was what Lord Emsworth was asking himself. Could this happy state of things last? He thought not. Without wishing to be pessimistic, he was dashed if he saw how a country containing men like Sir Gregory Parsloe-Parsloe of Matchingham Hall could hope to survive.

Strong? No doubt. Bitter? Granted. But not, we think, too strong, not – in the circumstances – unduly bitter. Consider the facts.

When, shortly after the triumph of Lord Emsworth's pre-eminent sow, Empress of Blandings, in the Fat Pigs Class at the eighty-seventh annual Shropshire Agricultural Show, George Cyril Wellbeloved, his lordship's pig-man, had expressed a desire to hand in his portfolio and seek employment elsewhere, the amiable peer, though naturally grieved, felt no sense of outrage. He put the thing down to the old roving spirit of the Wellbeloveds. George Cyril, he assumed, wearying of Shropshire, wished to try a change of air in some southern or eastern county. A nuisance, undoubtedly, for the man, when sober, was beyond question a force in the piggery. He had charm and personality. Pigs liked him. Still, if he wanted to resign office, there was nothing to be done about it.

But when, not a week later, word was brought to Lord Emsworth that, so far from having migrated to Sussex or Norfolk or Kent or somewhere, the fellow was actually just round the corner in the neighbouring village of Much Matchingham, serving under the banner of Sir Gregory Parsloe-Parsloe of Matchingham Hall, the scales fell from his eyes. He realized that black treachery had been at work. George Cyril Wellbeloved had sold himself for gold, and Sir Gregory Parsloe-Parsloe, hitherto looked upon as a high-minded friend and fellow Justice of the Peace, stood revealed as that lowest of created things, a lurer-away of other people's pig-men.

And there was nothing one could do about it.

Monstrous!

But true.

So deeply was Lord Emsworth occupied with the consideration of this appalling state of affairs that it was only when the knock upon the door was repeated that it reached his consciousness.

'Come in,' he said hollowly.

He hoped it was not his niece Gertrude. A gloomy young woman. He could hardly stand Gertrude's society just now.

It was not Gertrude. It was Beach, the butler.

'Mr Frederick wishes to speak to your lordship on the telephone.'

An additional layer of greyness fell over Lord Emsworth's spirit as he toddled down the great staircase to the telephone closet in the hall. It was his experience that almost any communication from Freddie indicated trouble.

But there was nothing in his son's voice as it floated over the wire to suggest that all was not well.

'Hullo, guv'nor.'

'Well, Frederick?'

'How's everything at Blandings?'

Lord Emsworth was not the man to exhibit the vultures gnawing at his heart to a babbler like the Hon. Freddie. He replied, though it hurt him to do so, that everything at Blandings was excellent.

'Good-oh!' said Freddie. 'Is the old dosshouse very full up at the moment?'

'If,' replied his lordship, 'you are alluding to Blandings Castle, there is nobody at present staying here except myself and your cousin Gertrude. Why?' he added in quick alarm. 'Were you thinking of coming down?'

'Good God, no!' cried his son with equal horror. 'I mean to say, I'd love it, of course, but just now I'm too busy with Dog-Joy.'

'Who is Popjoy?'

'Popjoy? Popjoy? Oh, ah, yes. He's a pal of mine and, as you've plenty of room, I want you to put him up for a bit. Nice chap, You'll like him. Right-ho, then, I'll ship him on the three-fifteen.'

Lord Emsworth's face had assumed an expression which made it fortunate for his son that television was not yet in operation on the telephone systems of England: and he had just recovered enough breath for the delivery of a blistering refusal to have any friend of Freddie's within fifty miles of the place when the other spoke again.

'He'll be company for Gertrude.'

And at these words a remarkable change came over Lord Emsworth. His face untwisted itself. The basilisk glare died out of his eyes.

'God bless my soul! That's true!' he exclaimed. 'That's certainly true. So he will. The three-fifteen, did you say? I will send the car to Market Blandings to meet it.'

Company for Gertrude? A pleasing thought. A fragrant, refreshing, stimulating thought. Somebody to take Gertrude off his hands occasionally was what he had been praying for ever since his sister Georgiana had dumped her down on him.

One of the chief drawbacks to entertaining in your home a girl who has been crossed in love is that she is extremely apt to go about the place doing good. All that life holds for her now is the opportunity of being kind to others, and she intends to be kind if it chokes them. For two weeks Lord Emsworth's beautiful young niece had been moving to and fro through the castle with a drawn face, doing good right and left: and his lordship, being handiest, had had to bear the brunt of it. It was with the first real smile he had smiled that day that he came out of the telephone-cupboard and found the object of his thoughts entering the hall in front of him.

'Well, well, well, my dear,' he said cheerily. 'And what have you been doing?'

There was no answering smile on his niece's face. Indeed, looking at her, you could see that this was a girl who had forgotten how to smile. She suggested something symbolic out of Maeterlinck.

'I have been tidying your study, Uncle Clarence,' she replied listlessly. 'It was in a dreadful mess.'

Lord Emsworth winced as a man of set habits will who has been remiss enough to let a Little Mother get at his study while his back is turned, but he continued bravely on the cheerful note.

'I have been talking to Frederick on the telephone.'

'Yes?' Gertrude sighed, and a bleak wind seemed to blow through the hall. 'Your tie's crooked, Uncle Clarence.'

'I like it crooked,' said his lordship, backing. 'I have a piece of news for you. A friend of Frederick's is coming down here tonight for a visit. His name, I understand, is Popjoy. So you will have some young society at last.'

'I don't want young society.'

'Oh, come, my dear.'

She looked at him thoughtfully with large, sombre eyes. Another sigh escaped her.

'It must be wonderful to be as old as you are, Uncle Clarence.'

'Eh?' said his lordship, starting.

'To feel that there is such a short, short step to the quiet tomb, to the ineffable peace of the grave. To me, life seems to stretch out endlessly, like a long, dusty desert. Twenty-three! That's all I am. Only twenty-three. And all our family live to sixty.'

'What do you mean, sixty?' demanded his lordship, with the warmth of a man who would be that next birthday. 'My poor father was seventy-seven when he was killed in the hunting-field. My uncle Robert lived till nearly ninety. My cousin Claude was eighty-four when he broke his neck trying to jump a five-barred gate. My mother's brother, Alistair . . .'

'Don't!' said the girl with a little shudder. 'Don't! It makes it all seem so awful and hopeless.'

Yes, that was Gertrude: and in Lord Emsworth's opinion she needed company.

The reactions of Lord Emsworth to the young man Popjoy, when he encountered him for the first time in the drawing-room shortly before dinner, were in the beginning wholly favourable. His son's friend was an extraordinarily large and powerful person with a frank, open, ingenuous face about the colour of the inside of a salmon, and he seemed a little nervous. That, however, was in his favour. It was, his lordship felt, a pleasant surprise to find in one of the younger generation so novel an emotion as diffidence.

He condoned, therefore, the other's trick of laughing hysterically even when the subject under discussion was the not irresistibly ludicrous one of green-fly in the rose-garden. He excused him for appearing to find something outstandingly comic in the statement that the glass was going up. And when, springing to his feet at the entrance of Gertrude, the young man performed some complicated steps in conjunction with a table covered with china and photograph-frames, he joined in the mirth which the feat provoked not only from the visitor but actually from Gertrude herself.

Yes, amazing though it might seem, his niece Gertrude, on seeing this young Popjoy, had suddenly burst into a peal of happy laughter. The gloom of the last two weeks appeared to be gone. She laughed. The young man laughed. They proceeded down to dinner in a perfect gale of merriment, rather like a chorus of revellers exiting after a concerted number in an old-fashioned comic opera.

And at dinner the young man had spilt his soup, broken a wine-glass, and almost taken another spectacular toss when leaping up at the end of the meal to open the door. At which Gertrude had laughed, and the young man had laughed, and his lordship had laughed – though not, perhaps, quite so heartily as the young folks, for that wine-glass had been one of a set which he valued.

However, weighing profit and loss as he sipped his port, Lord Emsworth considered that the ledger worked out on the right side. True, he had taken into his home what appeared to be a half-witted acrobat: but then any friend of his son Frederick was bound to be weak in the head, and, after all, the great thing was that Gertrude seemed to appreciate the newcomer's society. He looked forward contentedly to a succession of sunshine days of peace, perfect peace with loved ones far away; days when he would be able to work in his garden without the fear, which had been haunting him for the last two weeks, of finding his niece drooping wanly at his side and asking him if he was wise to stand about in the hot sun. She had company now that would occupy her elsewhere.

His lordship's opinion of his guest's mental deficiencies was strengthened late that night when, hearing footsteps on the terrace, he poked his head out and found him standing beneath his window, blowing kisses at it.

At the sight of his host he appeared somewhat confused.

'Lovely evening,' he said, with his usual hyenaesque laugh. 'I – er – thought . . . or, rather . . . that is to say . . . Ha, ha, ha!'

'Is anything the matter?'

'No, no! No! No, thanks, no! No! No, no! I – er – ho, ho, ho! – just came out for a stroll, ha, ha!'

Lord Emsworth returned to his bed a little thoughtfully. Perhaps some premonition of what was to come afflicted his subconscious mind, for, as he slipped between the sheets, he shivered. But gradually, as he dozed off, his equanimity became restored.

Looking at the thing in the right spirit, it might have been worse. After all, he felt, the mists of sleep beginning to exert their usual beneficent influence, he might have been entertaining at Blandings Castle one of his nephews, or one of his sisters, or even – though this was morbid – his younger son Frederick.

In matters where shades of feeling are involved, it is not always easy for the historian to be as definite as he could wish. He wants to keep the record straight, and yet he cannot take any one particular moment of time, pin it down for the scrutiny of Posterity and say 'This was the moment when Lord Emsworth for the first time found himself wishing that his guest would tumble out of an upper window and break his neck.' To his lordship it seemed that this had been from the beginning his constant day-dream, but such was not the case. When, on the second morning of the other's visit, the luncheon-gong had found them chatting in the library and the young man, bounding up, had extended a hand like a ham and, placing it beneath his host's arm, gently helped him to rise, Lord Emsworth had been quite pleased by the courteous attention.

But when the fellow did the same thing day after day, night after night, every time he caught him sitting; when he offered him an arm to help him across floors; when he assisted him up stairs, along corridors, down paths, out of rooms and into raincoats; when he snatched objects from his hands to carry them himself; when he came galloping out of the house on dewy evenings laden down with rugs, mufflers, hats and, on one occasion, positively a blasted respirator . . . why, then Lord Emsworth's proud spirit rebelled. He was a tough old gentleman and, like most tough old gentlemen, did not enjoy having his juniors look on him as something pathetically helpless that crawled the earth waiting for the end.

It had been bad enough when Gertrude was being the Little Mother. This was infinitely worse. Apparently having conceived for him one of those unreasoning, over-whelming devotions, this young Popjoy stuck closer than a brother; and for the first time Lord Emsworth began to appreciate what must have been the feelings of that Mary who aroused a similar attachment in the bosom of her lamb. It was as if he had been an Oldest Inhabitant fallen into the midst of a troop of Boy Scouts, all doing Good Deeds simultaneously, and he resented it with an indescribable bitterness. One can best illustrate his frame of mind by saying that, during the last phase, if he had been called upon to choose between his guest and Sir Gregory Parsloe-Parsloe as a companion for a summer ramble through the woods, he would have chosen Sir Gregory.

And then, on top of all this, there occurred the episode of the step-ladder.

The Hon. Freddie Threepwood, who had decided to run down and see how matters were developing, learned the details of this rather unfortunate occurrence from his cousin Gertrude. She met him at Market Blandings Station, and he could see there was something on her mind. She had not become positively Maeterlinckian again, but there was sorrow in her beautiful eyes: and Freddie, rightly holding that with a brainy egg like himself directing her destinies they should have contained only joy and sunshine, was disturbed by this.

'Don't tell me the binge has sprung a leak,' he said anxiously.

Gertrude sighed.

'Well, yes and no.'

'What do you mean, yes and no? Properly worked, the thing can't fail. This points to negligence somewhere. Has old Beefers been ingratiating himself?'

'Yes.'

'Hanging on the guv'nor's every word? Interesting himself in his pursuits? Doing him little services? And been at it two weeks? Good heavens! By now the guv'nor should be looking on him as a prize pig. Why isn't he?'

'I don't say he wasn't. Till this afternoon I rather think he was. At any rate, Rupert often says he found Uncle Clarence staring at him in a sort of lingering, rather yearning way. But when that thing happened this afternoon, I'm afraid he wasn't very pleased.'

'What thing?'

'That step-ladder business. It was like this. Rupert and I sort of went for a walk after lunch, and by the time I had persuaded him that he ought to go and find Uncle Clarence and ingratiate himself with him, Uncle Clarence had disappeared. So Rupert hunted about for a long time and at last heard a snipping noise and found him miles away standing on a step-ladder, sort of pruning some kind of tree with a pair of shears. So Rupert said, "Oh, there you are!" And Uncle Clarence said, Yes, there he was, and Rupert said, "Ought you to tire yourself? Won't you let me do that for you?" '

'The right note,' said Freddie approvingly. 'Assiduity. Zeal. Well?'

'Well, Uncle Clarence said, "No, thank you!" – Rupert thinks it was "Thank you" – and Rupert stood there for a bit, sort of talking, and then he suddenly remembered and told Uncle Clarence that you had just 'phoned that you were coming down this evening, and I think Uncle Clarence must have got a touch of cramp or something, because he gave a kind of sudden sharp groan, Rupert says, and sort of quivered all over. This made the steps wobble, of course, so Rupert dashed forward to steady them, and he doesn't know how it happened, but they suddenly seemed to sort of shut up like a pair of scissors, and the next thing he knew Uncle Clarence was sitting on the grass, not seeming to like it much, Rupert says. He had ricked his ankle a bit and shaken himself up a bit, and altogether, Rupert says, he wasn't fearfully sunny. Rupert says he thinks he may have lost ground a little.'

Freddie pondered with knit brows. He was feeling something of the chagrin of a general who, after sweating himself to a shadow planning a campaign, finds his troops unequal to carrying it out.

'It's such a pity it should have happened. One of the vicars near here has just been told by the doctor that he's got to go off to the south of France, and the living is in Uncle Clarence's gift. If only Rupert could have had that, we could have got married. However, he's bought Uncle Clarence some lotion.'

Freddie started. A more cheerful expression came into his sternly careworn face.

'Lotion?'

'For his ankle.'

'He couldn't have done better,' said Freddie warmly. 'Apart from showing the contrite heart, he has given the guv'nor medicine, and medicine to the guv'nor is what catnip is to the cat. Above all things he dearly loves a little bit of amateur doctoring. As a rule he tries it on somebody else – two years ago he gave one of the housemaids some patent ointment for chilblains and she went screaming about the house – but, no doubt, now that the emergency has occurred, he will be equally agreeable to treating himself. Old Beefers has made the right move.'

In predicting that Lord Emsworth would appreciate the gift of lotion, Freddie had spoken with an unerring knowledge of his father's character. The master of Blandings was one of those fluffy-minded old gentlemen who are happiest when experimenting with strange drugs. In a less censorious age he would have been a Borgia. It was not until he had retired to bed that he discovered the paper-wrapped bottle on the table by his side. Then he remembered that the pest Popjoy had mumbled something at dinner about buying him something or other for his injured ankle. He tore off the paper and examined the contents of the bottle with a lively satisfaction. The liquid was a dingy grey and sloshed pleasantly when you shook it. The name on the label – Blake's Balsam – was new to him, and that in itself was a recommendation.

His ankle had long since ceased to pain him, and to some men this might have seemed an argument against smearing it with balsam; but not to Lord Emsworth. He decanted a liberal dose into the palm of his hand. He sniffed it. It had a strong, robust, bracing sort of smell. He spent the next five minutes thoughtfully rubbing it in. Then he put the light out and went to sleep.

It is a truism to say that in the world as it is at present constituted few things have more far-reaching consequences than the accident of birth. Lord Emsworth had probably suspected this. He was now to receive direct proof. If he had been born a horse instead of the heir to an earldom, that lotion would have been just right for him. It was for horses, though the Rev. Rupert Bingham had omitted to note the fact, that Blake had planned his balsam; and anyone enjoying even a superficial acquaintance with horses and earls knows that an important difference between them is that the latter have the more sensitive skins. Waking at a quarter to two from dreams of being burned at the stake by Red Indians, Lord Emsworth found himself suffering acute pain in the right leg.

He was a little surprised. He had not supposed that that fall from the ladder had injured him so badly. However, being a good amateur doctor, he bore up bravely and took immediate steps to cope with the trouble. Having shaken the bottle till it foamed at the mouth, he rubbed in some more lotion. It occurred to him that the previous application might have been too sketchy, so this time he did it thoroughly. He rubbed and kneaded for some twenty minutes. Then he tried to go to sleep.

Nature has made some men quicker thinkers than others. Lord Emsworth's was one of those leisurely brains. It was not till nearly four o'clock that the truth came home to him. When it did, he was just on the point of applying a fifth coating of the balsam to his leg. He stopped abruptly, replaced the cork, and, jumping out of bed, hobbled to the cold-water tap and put as much of himself under it as he could manage.

The relief was perceptible, but transitory. At five he was out again, and once more at half-past. At a quarter to six, succeeding in falling asleep, he enjoyed a slumber, somewhat disturbed by the intermittent biting of sharks, which lasted till a few minutes past eight. Then he woke as if an alarm clock had rung, and realized that further sleep was out of the question.

He rose from his bed and peered out of the window. It was a beautiful morning. There had been rain in the night and a world that looked as if it had just come back from the cleaner's sparkled under a beaming sun. Cedars cast long shadows over the smooth green lawns. Rooks cawed soothingly: thrushes bubbled in their liquid and musical way: and the air was full of a summer humming. Among those present of the insect world, Lord Emsworth noticed several prominent gnats.

Beyond the terrace, glittering through the trees, gleamed the waters of the lake. They seemed to call to him like a bugle. Although he had neglected the practice of late, there was nothing Lord Emsworth enjoyed more than a before-breakfast dip: and today anything in the nature of water had a particularly powerful appeal for him. The pain in his ankle had subsided by now to a dull throbbing, and it seemed to him that a swim might remove it altogether. Putting on a dressing-gown and slippers, he took his bathing-suit from its drawer and went downstairs.

The beauties of a really fine English summer day are so numerous that it is excusable in a man if he fails immediately to notice them all. Only when the sharp agony of the first plunge had passed and he was floating out in mid-water did Lord Emsworth realize that in some extraordinary way he had overlooked what was beyond dispute the best thing that this perfect morning had to offer him. Gazing from his bedroom window, he had observed the sun, the shadows, the birds, the trees, and the insects, but he had omitted to appreciate the fact that nowhere in this magic world that stretched before him was there a trace of his young guest, Popjoy. For the first time in two weeks he appeared to be utterly alone and free from him.

Floating on his back and gazing up into the turquoise sky, Lord Emsworth thrilled at the thought. He kicked sportively in a spasm of pure happiness. But this, he felt, was not enough. It failed to express his full happiness. To the ecstasy of this golden moment only music – that mystic language of the soul – could really do justice. The next instant there had cut quiveringly into the summer stillness that hung over the gardens of Blandings Castle a sudden sharp wail that seemed to tell of a human being in mortal distress. It was the voice of Lord Emsworth, raised in song.

It was a gruesome sound, calculated to startle the stoutest: and two bees, buzzing among the lavender, stopped as one and looked at each other with raised eyebrows. Nor were they alone affected. Snails withdrew into their shells: a squirrel doing calisthenics on the cedar nearly fell off its branch: and – moving a step up in the animal kingdom – the Rev. Rupert Bingham, standing behind the rhododendron bushes, wondering how long it would be before the girl he loved came to keep her tryst, started violently, dropped his cigarette and, tearing off his coat, rushed to the water's edge.

Out in the middle of the lake, Lord Emsworth's transports continued undiminished. His dancing feet kicked up a flurry to foam. His short-sighted, but sparkling, eyes stared into the blue. His voice rose to a pulsing scream.

'Love me,' sang Lord Emsworth, 'and the wo-o-o-o-rld is – ah – mi-yun!'

'It's all right,' said a voice in his ear. 'Keep cool. Keep quite cool.'

The effect of a voice speaking suddenly, as it were out of the void, is always, even in these days of wireless, disconcerting to a man. Had he been on dry land Lord Emsworth would have jumped. Being in ten feet of water, he went under as if a hand had pushed him. He experienced a momentary feeling of suffocation, and then a hand gripped him painfully by the fleshy part of the arm and he was on the surface again, spluttering.

'Keep quite cool,' murmured the voice. 'There's no danger.'

And now he recognized whose voice it was.

There is a point beyond which the human brain loses its kinship with the Infinite and becomes a mere seething mass of deleterious passions. Malays, when pushed past this point, take down the old *kris* from its hook and go out and start carving up the neighbours. Women have hysterics. Earls, if Lord Emsworth may be taken as a sample, haul back their right fists and swing them as violently as their age and physique will permit. For two long weeks Lord Emsworth had been enduring this pestilential young man with outward nonchalance, but the strain had told. Suppressed emotions are always the most dangerous. Little by little, day by day, he had been slowly turning into a human volcano, and this final outrage blew the lid off him.

He raged with a sense of intolerable injury. Was it not enough that this porous plaster of a young man should adhere to him on shore? Must he even pursue him out into the waste of waters and come fooling about and pawing at him when he was enjoying the best swim he had had that summer? In all their long and honourable history no member of his ancient family had ever so far forgotten the sacred obligations of hospitality as to plug a guest in the eye. But then they had never had guests like this. With a sharp, passionate snort, Lord Emsworth extracted his right hand from the foam, clenched it, drew it back and let it go.

He could have made no more imprudent move. If there was one thing the Rev. Rupert Bingham, who in his time had swum for Oxford, knew, it was what to do when drowning men struggled. Something that might have been a very hard and knobbly leg of mutton smote Lord Emsworth violently behind the ear: the sun was turned off at the main: the stars came out, many of them of a singular brightness: there was a sound of rushing waters: and he knew no more.

When Lord Emsworth came to himself, he was lying in bed. And, as it seemed a very good place to be, he remained there. His head ached abominably, but he scarcely noticed this, so occupied was he with the thoughts which surged inside it. He mused on the young man Popjoy: he meditated on Sir Gregory Parsloe-Parsloe: and wondered from time to time which he disliked the more. It was a problem almost too nice for human solution. Here, on the one hand, you had a man who pestered you for two weeks and wound up by nearly murdering you as you bathed, but who did not steal pig-men: there, on the other, one who stole pig-men but stopped short of actual assault on the person. Who could hope to hold the scales between such a pair?

He had just remembered the lotion and was wondering if this might not be considered the deciding factor in this contest for the position of the world's premier blot, when the door opened and the Hon. Freddie Threepwood insinuated himself into the room.

'Hullo, guv'nor.'

'Well, Frederick?'

'How are you feeling?'

'Extremely ill.'

'Might have been worse, you know.'

'Bah!'

'Watery grave and all that.'

'Tchah!' said Lord Emsworth.

There was a pause. Freddie, wandering about the room, picked up and fidgeted with a chair, a vase, a hair-brush, a comb, and a box of matches: then, retracing his steps, fidgeted with them all over again in the reverse order. Finally, he came to the foot of his father's bed and drooped over it like, it seemed to that sufferer's prejudiced eye, some hideous animal gaping over a fence.

'I say, guv'nor.'

'Well, Frederick?'

'Narrow squeak, that, you know.'

'Pah!'

'Do you wish to thank your brave preserver?'

Lord Emsworth plucked at the coverlet.

'If that young man comes near me,' he said, 'I will not be answerable for the consequences.'

'Eh?' Freddie stared. 'Don't you like him?'

'Like him! He is the most appalling young man I ever met.'

It is customary when making statements of this kind to except present company, but so deeply did Lord Emsworth feel on the subject that he omitted to do so. Freddie, having announced that he was dashed, removed himself from the bed-rail and, wandering once more about the room, fidgeted with a toothbrush, a soap-dish, a shoe, a volume on spring bulbs, and a collar-stud.

'I say, guv'nor.'

'Well, Frederick?'

'That's all very well, you know, guv'nor,' said the Hon. Freddie, returning to his post and seeming to draw moral support from the feel of the bed-rail, 'but after what's happened it looks to me as if you were jolly well bound to lend your countenance to the union, if you know what I mean.'

'Union? What are you talking about? What union?'

'Gertrude and old Beefers.'

'Who the devil is old Beefers?'

'Oh, I forgot to tell you about that. This bird Popjoy's name isn't Popjoy. It's Bingham. Old Beefy Bingham. You know, the fellow Aunt Georgie doesn't want to marry Gertrude.'

'Eh?'

'Throw your mind back. They pushed her off to Blandings to keep her out of his way. And I had the idea of sending him down here *incog.* to ingratiate himself with you. The scheme being that, when you had learned to love him, you would slip him a vacant vicarage, thus enabling them to get married. Beefers is a parson, you know.'

Lord Emsworth did not speak. It was not so much the shock of this revelation that kept him dumb as the astounding discovery that any man could really want to marry Gertrude, and any girl this Popjoy. Like many a thinker before him, he was feeling that there is really no limit to the eccentricity of human tastes. The thing made his head swim.

But when it had ceased swimming he perceived that this was but one aspect of the affair. Before him stood the man who had inflicted Popjoy on him, and with something of King Lear in his demeanour Lord Emsworth rose slowly from the pillows. Words trembled on his lips, but he rejected them as not strong enough and sought in his mind for others.

'You know, guv'nor,' proceeded Freddie, 'there's nothing to prevent you doing the square thing and linking two young hearts in the bonds of the Love God, if you want to. I mean to say, old Braithwaite at Much Matchingham has been ordered to the south of France by his doctor, so there's a living going that you've got to slip to somebody.'

Lord Emsworth sank back on the pillows.

'Much Matchingham!'

'Oh, dash it, you must know Much Matchingham, guv'nor. It's just round the corner. Where old Parsloe lives.'

'Much Matchingham!'

Lord Emsworth was blinking, as if his eyes had seen a dazzling light. How wrong, he felt, how wickedly mistaken and lacking in faith he had been when he had said to himself in his folly that Providence offers no method of retaliation to the just whose pig-men have been persuaded by Humanity's dregs to leave their employment and seek advanced wages elsewhere. Conscience could not bring remorse to Sir Gregory Parsloe-Parsloe, and the law, in its present imperfect state, was powerless to punish. But there was still a way. With this young man Popjoy – or Bingham – or whatever his name was, permanently established not a hundred yards from his park gates, would Sir Gregory Parsloe-Parsloe ever draw another really carefree breath? From his brief, but sufficient, acquaintance with the young man Bingham – or Popjoy – Lord Emsworth thought not.

The punishment was severe, but who could say that Sir Gregory had not earned it?

'A most admirable idea,' said Lord Emsworth. 'Certainly I will give your friend the living of Much Matchingham.'

'You will?'

'Most decidedly.'

'At-a-boy, guv'nor!' said Freddie. 'Came the Dawn!'

'BRAMLEY IS SO BRACING'

Nothing Serious

A general meeting had been called at the Drones to decide on the venue for the club's annual golf rally, and the school of thought that favoured Bramley-on-Sea was beginning to make headway when Freddie Widgeon took the floor. In a speech of impassioned eloquence he warned his hearers not to go within fifty miles of the beastly place. And so vivid was the impression he conveyed of Bramley-on-Sea as a spot where the law of the jungle prevailed and anything could happen to anybody that the voters were swayed like reeds and the counter proposal of Cooden Beach was accepted almost unanimously.

His warmth excited comment at the bar.

'Freddie doesn't like Bramley,' said an acute Egg, who had been thinking it over with the assistance of a pink gin.

'Possibly,' suggested a Bean, 'because he was at school there when he was a kid.'

The Crumpet who had joined the group shook his head.

'No, it wasn't that,' he said. 'Poor old Freddie had a very painful experience at Bramley recently, culminating in his getting the raspberry from the girl he loved.'

'What, again?'

'Yes. It's curious about Freddie,' said the Crumpet, sipping a thoughtful martini. 'He rarely fails to click, but he never seems able to go on clicking. A whale at the Boy Meets Girl stuff, he is unfortunately equally unerring at the Boy Loses Girl.'

'Which of the troupe was it who gave him the air this time?' asked an interested Pieface.

'Mavis Peasmarch. Lord Bodsham's daughter.'

'But, dash it,' protested the Pieface, 'that can't be right. She returned him to store ages ago. You told us about it yourself. That time in New York when he got mixed up with the female in the pink négligée picked out with ultramarine lovebirds.'

The Crumpet nodded.

'Quite true. He was, as you say, handed his portfolio on that occasion. But Freddie is a pretty gifted explainer, if you give him time to mould and shape his story, and on their return to England he appears to have squared himself somehow. She took him on again – on appro., as it were. The idea was that if he proved himself steady and serious, those wedding bells would ring out. If not, not a tinkle.

'Such was the position of affairs when he learned from this Peasmarch that she and her father were proposing to park themselves for the summer months at the Hotel Magnifique at Bramley-on-Sea.'

Freddie's instant reaction to this news was, of course (said the Crumpet), an urge to wangle a visit there himself, and he devoted the whole force of his intellect to trying to think how this could be done. He shrank from spending good money on a hotel, but on the other hand his proud soul scorned a boarding-house, and what they call an *impasse* might have resulted, had he not discovered that Bingo Little and Mrs Bingo had taken a shack at Bramley in order that the Bingo baby should get its whack of ozone. Bramley, as I dare say you have seen mentioned on the posters, is so bracing, and if you are a parent you have to think of these things. Brace the baby, and you are that much ahead of the game.

To cadge an invitation was with Freddie the work of a moment, and a few days later he arrived with suitcase and two-seater, deposited the former, garaged the latter, kissed the baby and settled in.

Many fellows might have objected to the presence on the premises of a bib-and-bottle juvenile, but Freddie has always been a good mixer, and he and this infant hit it off from the start like a couple of sailors on shore leave. It became a regular thing with him to take the half-portion down to the beach and stand by while it mucked about with its spade and bucket. And it was as he was acting as master of the revels one sunny day that there came ambling along a well-nourished girl with golden hair, who paused and scrutinized the Bingo issue with a genial smile.

'Is the baby building a sand castle?' she said.

'Well, yes and no,' replied Freddie civilly. 'It thinks it is, but if you ask me, little of a constructive nature will result.'

'Still, so long as it's happy.'

'Oh, quite.'

'Nice day.'

'Beautiful.'

'Could you tell me the correct time?'

'Precisely eleven.'

'Coo!' said the girl. 'I must hurry, or I shall be late. I'm meeting a gentleman friend of mine on the pier at half-past ten.'

And that was that. I mean, just one of those casual encounters which are so common at the seashore, with not a word spoken on either side that could bring the blush of shame to the cheek of modesty. I stress this, because this substantial blonde was to become entangled in Freddie's affairs and I want to make it clear at the outset that from start to finish he was as pure as the driven snow. Sir Galahad could have taken his correspondence course.

It was about a couple of days after this that a picture postcard, forwarded from his London address, informed him that Mavis and her father were already in residence at the Magnifique, and he dashed into the two-seater and drove round there with a beating heart. It was his intention to take the loved one for a spin, followed by a spot of tea at some wayside shoppe.

This project, however, was rendered null and void by the fact that she was out. Old Bodsham, receiving Freddie in the suite, told him that she had gone to take her little brother Wilfred back to his school.

'We had him for lunch,' said the Bod.

'No, did you?' said Freddie. 'A bit indigestible, what?' He laughed heartily for some moments at his ready wit; then, seeing that the gag had not got across, cheesed it. He remembered now that there had always been something a bit Wednesday-matinéeish about the fifth Earl of Bodsham. An austere man, known to his circle of acquaintances as The Curse of the Eastern Counties. 'He's at school here, is he?'

'At St. Asaph's. An establishment conducted by an old college friend of mine, the Rev. Aubrey Upjohn.'

'Good Lord!' said Freddie, feeling what a small world it was. 'I used to be at St. Asaph's.'

'Indeed?'

'Absolutely. I served a three years' sentence there before going on to Eton. Well, I'll be pushing along, then. Give Mavis my love, will you, and say I'll be round bright and early in the morning.'

He buzzed off and hopped into the car again, and for the space of half an hour or so drove about Bramley, feeling a bit at a loose end. And he was passing through a spot called Marina Crescent, a sort of jungle of boarding-houses, when he became aware that stirring things were happening in his immediate vicinity.

Along the road towards him there had been approaching a well-nourished girl with golden hair. I don't suppose he had noticed her – or, if he had, it was merely to say to himself 'Ah, the substantial blonde I met on the beach the other morning' and dismiss her from his thoughts. But at this moment she suddenly thrust herself on his attention by breaking into a rapid gallop, and at the same time a hoarse cry rent the air, not unlike that of the lion of the desert scenting its prey, and Freddie perceived charging out of a side street an elderly man with whiskers, who looked as if he might be a retired sea captain or a drysalter or something.

The spectacle perplexed him. He had always known that Bramley was bracing, but he had never supposed that it was as bracing as all this. And he had pulled up in order to get a better view, when the substantial blonde, putting on a burst of speed in the straight, reached the car and hurled herself into it.

'Quick!' she said.

'Quick?' said Freddie. He was puzzled. 'In what sense do you use the word "Quick"?' he asked, and was about to go further into the thing when the whiskered bird came dashing up and scooped the girl out of the car as if she had been a winkle and his hand a pin.

The girl grabbed hold of Freddie, and Freddie grabbed hold of the steering wheel, and the whiskered bird continued to freeze on to the girl, and for a while the human chain carried on along these lines. Then there was a rending sound, and the girl and Freddie came apart.

The whiskered bozo regarded him balefully.

'If we weren't in a public place,' he said, 'I would horsewhip you. If I had a horsewhip.'

And with these words he dragged the well-nourished girl from the scene, leaving Freddie, as you may well suppose, quite a bit perturbed and a long way from grasping the inner meaning.

The recent fracas had left him half in and half out of the car, and he completed the process by alighting. He had an idea that the whiskered ancient might have scratched his paint. But fortunately everything was all right, and he was leaning against the bonnet, smoking a soothing cigarette, when Mavis Peasmarch spoke behind him.

'Frederick!' she said.

Freddie tells me that at the sound of that loved voice he sprang six feet straight up in the air, but I imagine this to be an exaggeration. About eighteen inches, probably. Still, he sprang quite high enough to cause those leaning out of the windows of Marina Crescent to fall into the error of supposing him to be an adagio dancer practising a new step.

'Oh, hullo, darling!' he said.

He tried to speak in a gay and debonair manner, but he could not but recognize that he had missed his objective by a mile. Gazing at Mavis Peasmarch, he noted about her a sort of rigidity which he didn't like. Her eyes were stern and cold, and her lips tightly set. Mavis had inherited from her father that austere Puritanism which makes the old boy so avoided by the County, and this she was now exuding at every pore.

'So there you are!' he said, still having a stab at the gay and debonair.

'Yes,' said Mavis Peasmarch.

'I'm here, too,' said Freddie.

'So I see,' said Mavis Peasmarch.

'I'm staying with a pal. I thought I'd come here and surprise you.'

'You have,' said Mavis Peasmarch. She gave a sniff that sounded like a nor'-easter ripping the sails of a stricken vessel. 'Frederick, what does this mean?'

'Eh?'

'That girl.'

'Oh, that *girl?*' said Freddie. 'Yes, I see what you mean. You are speaking of that girl. Most extraordinary, wasn't it?'

'Most.'

'She jumped into my car, did you notice?'

'I did. An old friend?'

'No, no. A stranger, and practically total, at that.'

'Oh?' said Mavis Peasmarch, and let go another sniff that went echoing down the street. 'Who was the old man?'

'I don't know. Another stranger, even more total.'

'He said he wanted to horsewhip you.'

'Yes, I heard him. Dashed familiar.'

'Why did he want to horsewhip you?'

'Ah, there you've got me. The man's thought processes are a sealed book to me.'

'The impression I received was that he resented your having made his daughter the plaything of an idle hour.'

'But I didn't. As a matter of fact, I haven't had much spare time since I got here.'

'Oh?'

'The solution that suggests itself to me is that we have stumbled up against one of those E. Phillips Oppenheim situations. Yes, that would explain the whole thing. Here's how I figure it out. The girl is an international spy. She got hold of the plans of the fortifications and was taking them to an accomplice, when along came the whiskered bird, a secret service man. You could see those whiskers were a disguise. He thought I was the accomplice.'

'Oh?'

'How's your brother Wilfred?' asked Freddie, changing the subject.

'Will you please drive me to my hotel?' said Mavis, changing it again.

'Oh, right,' said Freddie. 'Right.'

That night, Freddie lay awake, ill at ease. There had been something in the adored object's manner, when he dropped her at the hotel, which made him speculate as to whether that explanation of his had got over quite so solidly as he had hoped. He had suggested coming in and having a cosy chat, and she had said No, please, I have a headache. He had said how well she was looking, and she had said Oh? And when he had asked her if she loved her little Freddie, she had made no audible response.

All in all, it looked to Freddie as if what is technically called a lover's tiff had set in with a good deal of severity, and as he lay tossing on his pillow he pondered quite a bit on how this could be adjusted.

What was needed here, he felt, was a gesture – some spectacular performance on his part which would prove that his heart was in the right place.

But what spectacular performance?

He toyed with the idea of saving Mavis from drowning, only to dismiss it when he remembered that on the rare occasions when she took a dip in the salty she never went in above the waist.

He thought of rescuing old Bodsham from a burning building. But how to procure that burning building? He couldn't just set a match to the Hotel Magnifique and expect it to go up in flames.

And then, working through the family, he came to little Wilfred, and immediately got a Grade-A inspiration. It was via Wilfred that he must oil back into Mavis's esteem. And it could be done, he saw, by going to St. Asaph's and asking the Rev. Aubrey Upjohn to give the school a half-holiday. This kindly act would put him right back in the money.

He could picture the scene. Wilfred would come bounding in to tea one afternoon. 'Coo!' Mavis would exclaim. 'What on earth are you doing here? Have you run away from school?' 'No,' Wilfred would reply, 'the school has run away from me. In other words, thanks to Freddie Widgeon, that prince of square-shooters, we have been given a half-holiday.' 'Well, I'm blowed!' Mavis would ejaculate. 'Heaven bless Freddie Widgeon! I had a feeling all along that I'd been misjudging that bird.'

At this point, Freddie fell asleep.

Often, when you come to important decisions overnight, you find after sleeping on them that they are a bit blue around the edges. But morning, when it came, found Freddie still resolved to go through with his day's good deed. If, however, I were to tell you that he liked the prospect, I should be deceiving you. It is not too much to say that he quailed at it. Years had passed since his knickerbocker days, but the Rev. Aubrey Upjohn was still green in his memory. A man spiritually akin to Simon Legree and the late Captain Bligh of the *Bounty*, with whose disciplinary methods his own had much in common, he had made a deep impression on Freddie's plastic mind, and the thought of breezing in and trying to sting him for a half-holiday was one that froze the blood more than a bit.

But two things bore him on: (a) his great love, and (b) the fact that it suddenly occurred to him that he could obtain a powerful talking point by borrowing Bingo's baby and taking it along with him.

Schoolmasters, he knew, are always anxious to build for the future. To them, the infant of today is the pupil at so much per term of tomorrow. It would strengthen his strategic position enormously if he dangled Bingo's baby before the man's eyes and said: 'Upjohn, I can swing a bit of custom your way. My influence with the parents of this child is stupendous. Treat me right, and down it goes on your waiting list.' It would make all the difference.

So, waiting till Bingo's back and Mrs Bingo's back were turned, he scooped up Junior and started out. And presently he was ringing the front door bell of St. Asaph's, the younger generation over his arm, concealed beneath a light overcoat. The parlourmaid showed him into the study, and he was left there to drink in the details of the well-remembered room which he had not seen for so many years.

Now, it so happened that he had hit the place at the moment when the Rev. Aubrey was taking the senior class in Bible history, and when a headmaster has got his teeth into a senior class he does not readily sheathe the sword. There was consequently a longish stage wait, and as the minutes passed Freddie began to find the atmosphere of the study distinctly oppressive.

The last time he had been in this room, you see, the set-up had been a bit embarrassing. He had been bending over a chair, while the Rev. Aubrey Upjohn, strongly posted in his rear, stood measuring the distance with half-closed eyes, preparatory to bringing the old malacca down on his upturned trousers seat. And memories like this bring with them a touch of sadness.

Outside the french window the sun was shining, and it seemed to Freddie that what was needed to dissipate the feeling of depression from which he had begun to suffer was a stroll in the garden with a cigarette. He sauntered out, accordingly, and had paced the length of the grounds and was gazing idly over the fence at the end of them, when he perceived that beyond this fence a certain liveliness was in progress.

He was looking into a small garden, at the back of which was a house. And at an upper window of this house was a girl. She was waving her arms at him.

It is never easy to convey every shade of your meaning by waving your arms at a distance of forty yards, and Freddie not unnaturally missed quite a good deal of the gist. Actually, what the girl was trying to tell him was that she had recently met at the bandstand on the pier a man called George Perkins, employed in a London firm of bookmakers doing business under the trade name of Joe Sprockett; that a mutual fondness for the Overture to *Zampa* had drawn them together; that she had become deeply enamoured of him; that her tender sentiments had been fully reciprocated; that her father, who belonged to a religious sect which disapproved of bookmakers, had refused to sanction the match or even to be introduced to the above Perkins; that he – her father – had intercepted a note from the devout lover, arranging for a meeting at the latter's boarding-house (10 Marina Crescent) and a quick wedding at the local registrar's; and that he – she was still alluding to her father – had now locked her in her room until, in his phrase, she should come to her senses. And what she wanted Freddie to do was let her out. Because good old George was waiting at 10 Marina Crescent with the licence, and if she could only link up with him they could put the thing through promptly.

Freddie, as I say, did not get quite all of this, but he got enough of it to show him that here was a damsel in distress, and he was stirred to his foundations. He had not thought that this sort of thing happened outside the thrillers, and even there he had supposed it to be confined to moated castles. And this wasn't a moated castle by any means. It was a two-storey desirable residence with a slate roof, standing in park-like grounds extending to upwards of a quarter of an acre. It looked the sort of place that might belong to a retired sea captain or possibly a drysalter.

Full of the old knight-errant spirit, for he has always been a pushover for damsels in distress, he leaped the fence with sparkling eyes. And it was only when he was standing beneath the window that he recognized in the girl who was goggling at him through the glass like some rare fish in an aquarium his old acquaintance, the substantial blonde.

The sight cooled him off considerably. He is rather a superstitious sort of chap, and he had begun to feel that this billowy curver wasn't lucky for him. He remembered now that a gipsy had once warned him to beware of a fair woman, and for a moment it was touch and go whether he wouldn't turn away and ignore the whole unpleasant affair. However, the old knight-errant spirit was doing its stuff, and he decided to carry on as planned. Gathering from a quick twist of her eyebrows that the key was in the outside of the door, he nipped in through the sitting-room window, raced upstairs and did the needful. And a moment later she was emerging like a cork out of a bottle and shooting down the stairs. She whizzed into the sitting-room and whizzed through the window, and he whizzed after her. And the first thing he saw as he came skimming over the sill was her galloping round the lawn, closely attended by the whiskered bloke who had scooped her out of the car in Marina Crescent. He had a three-pronged fork in his possession and was whacking at her with the handle, getting a bull's-eye at about every second shot.

It came as a great surprise to Freddie, for he had distinctly understood from the way the girl had twiddled her fingers that her father was at the croquet club, and for a moment he paused, uncertain what to do.

He decided to withdraw. No chivalrous man likes to see a woman in receipt of a series of juicy ones with a fork handle, but the thing seemed to him one of those purely family disputes which can only be threshed out between father and daughter. He had started to edge away, accordingly, when the whiskered bloke observed him and came charging in his direction, shouting the old drysalters' battle cry. One can follow his train of thought, of course. He supposed Freddie to be George Perkins, the lovelorn bookie, and wished to see the colour of his insides. With a good deal of emotion, Freddie saw that he was now holding the fork by the handle.

Exactly what the harvest would have been, had nothing occurred to interfere with the old gentleman's plans, it is hard to say. But by great good fortune he tripped over a flower-pot while he was still out of jabbing distance and came an impressive purler. And before he could get right side up again, Freddie had seized the girl, hurled her over the fence, leaped the fence himself and started lugging her across the grounds of St. Asaph's to his car, which he had left at the front door.

The going had been so good, and the substantial blonde was in such indifferent condition, that even when they were in the car and bowling off little came through in the way of conversation. The substantial blonde, having gasped out a request that he drive her to 10 Marina Crescent, lay back panting, and was still panting when they reached journey's end. He decanted her and drove off. And it was as he drove off that he became aware of something missing. Something he should have had on his person was not on his person.

He mused.

His cigarette case?

No, he had his cigarette case.

His hat?

No, he had his hat.

His small change? . . .

And then he remembered. Bingo's baby. He had left it chewing a bit of indiarubber in the Rev. Aubrey Upjohn's study.

Well, with his nervous system still all churned up by his recent experiences, an interview with his old preceptor was not a thing to which he looked forward with anything in the nature of ecstasy, but he's a pretty clear-thinking chap, and he realized that you can't go strewing babies all over the place and just leave them. So he went back to St. Asaph's and trotted round to the study window. And there inside was the Rev. Aubrey, pacing the floor in a manner which the most vapid and irreflective observer would have recognized as distraught.

I suppose practically the last thing an unmarried schoolmaster wants to find in his sanctum is an unexplained baby, apparently come for an extended visit; and the Rev. Aubrey Upjohn, on entering the study shortly after Freddie had left it and noting contents, had sustained a shock of no slight order. He viewed the situation with frank concern.

And he was turning to pace the floor again, when he got another shock. He had hoped to be alone, to think this thing over from every angle, and there was a young man watching him from the window. On this young man's face there was what seemed to him a sneering grin. It was really an ingratiating smile, of course, but you couldn't expect a man in the Rev. Aubrey's frame of mind to know that.

'Oh, hullo,' said Freddie. 'You remember me, don't you?'

'No, I do not remember you,' cried the Rev. Aubrey. 'Go away.'

Freddie broadened the ingratiating smile an inch or two.

'Former pupil. Name of Widgeon.'

The Rev. Aubrey passed a weary hand over his brow. One can understand how he must have felt. First this frightful blow, I mean to say, and on top of that the re-entry into his life of a chap he had hoped he'd seen the last of years and years ago.

'Yes,' he said, in a low, toneless voice. 'Yes, I remember you. Widgeon.'

'F.F.'

'F., as you say, F. What do you want?'

'I came back for my baby,' said Freddie, like an apologetic plumber.

The Rev. Aubrey started.

'Is this your baby?'

'Well, technically, no. On loan, merely. Some time ago, my pal Bingo Little married Rosie M. Banks, the well-known female novelist. This is what you might call the upshot.'

The Rev. Aubrey seemed to be struggling with some powerful emotion.

'Then it was you who left this baby in my study?'

'Yes. You see – '

'Ha!' said the Rev. Aubrey, and went off with a pop, as if suffering from spontaneous combustion.

Freddie tells me that few things have impressed him more than the address to which he now listened. He didn't like it, but it extorted a grudging admiration. Here was this man, he meant to say, unable as a clerk in Holy Orders to use any of the words which would have been at the disposal of a layman, and yet by sheer force of character rising triumphantly over the handicap. Without saying a thing that couldn't have been said in the strictest drawing-room, the Rev. Aubrey Upjohn contrived to produce in Freddie the illusion that he had had a falling out with the bucko mate of a tramp steamer. And every word he uttered made it more difficult to work the conversation round to the subject of half-holidays.

Long before he had reached his 'thirdly', Freddie was feeling as if he had been chewed up by powerful machinery, and when he was at length permitted to back out, he felt that he had had a merciful escape. For quite a while it had seemed more than likely that he was going to be requested to bend over that chair again. And such was the Rev. Aubrey's magnetic personality that he would have done it, he tells me, like a shot.

Much shaken, he drove back to the Bingo residence, and the first thing he saw on arriving there was Bingo standing on the steps, looking bereaved to the gills.

'Freddie,' yipped Bingo, 'have you seen Algernon?'

Freddie's mind was not at its clearest.

'No,' he said. 'I don't think I've run across him. Algernon who? Pal of yours? Nice chap?'

Bingo hopped like the high hills.

'My baby, you ass.'

'Oh, the good old baby? Yes, I've got him.'

'Six hundred and fifty-seven curses!' said Bingo. 'What the devil did you want to go dashing off with him for? Do you realize we've been hunting for him all the morning?'

'You wanted him for something special?'

'I was just going to notify the police and have dragnets spread.'

Freddie could see that an apology was in order.

'I'm sorry,' he said. 'Still, all's well that ends well. Here he is. Oh no, he isn't,' he added, having made a quick inspection of the interior of the car. 'I say, this is most unfortunate. I seem to have left him again.'

'Left him?'

'What with all the talk that was going on, he slipped my mind. But I can give you his address. Care of the Rev. Aubrey Upjohn, St. Asaph's, Mafeking Road, Bramley-on-Sea. All you have to do is step round at your leisure and collect him. I say, is lunch ready?'

'Lunch?' Bingo laughed a hideous, mirthless laugh. At least, that's what Freddie thinks it was. It sounded like a bursting tyre. 'A fat lot of lunch you're going to get. The cook's got hysterics, the kitchen-maid's got hysterics, and so have the parlourmaid and the housemaid. Rosie started having hysterics as early as eleven-thirty, and is now in bed with an ice pack. When she finds out about this, I wouldn't be in your shoes for a million quid. Two million,' added Bingo. 'Or, rather, three.'

This was an aspect of the matter which had not occurred to Freddie. He saw that there was a good deal in it.

'Do you know, Bingo,' he said, 'I believe I ought to be getting back to London today.'

'I would.'

'Several things I've got to do there, several most important things. I dare say, if I whipped back to town, you could send my luggage after me?'

'A pleasure.'

'Thanks,' said Freddie. 'You won't forget the address, will you? St. Asaph's, Mafeking Road. Mention my name, and say you've come for the baby I inadvertently left in the study. And now, I think, I ought to be getting round to see Mavis. She'll be wondering what has become of me.'

He tooled off, and a few minutes later was entering the lobby of the Hotel Magnifique. The first thing he saw was Mavis and her father standing by a potted palm.

'Hullo, hullo,' he said, toddling up.

'Ah, Frederick,' said old Bodsham.

I don't know if you remember, when I was telling you about that time in New York, my mentioning that at a rather sticky point in the proceedings Freddie had noticed that old Bodsham was looking like a codfish with something on its mind. The same conditions prevailed now.

'Frederick,' proceeded the Bod, 'Mavis has been telling me a most unpleasant story.'

Freddie hardly knew what to say to this. He was just throwing a few sentences together in his mind about the modern girl being sound at heart despite her freedom of speech, and how there isn't really any harm in it if she occasionally gets off one from the smoking-room – tolerant, broad-minded stuff, if you know what I mean – when old Bodsham resumed.

'She tells me you have become entangled with a young woman with golden hair.'

'A fat young woman with golden hair,' added Mavis, specifying more exactly.

Freddie waved his arms passionately, like a semaphore.

'Nothing in it,' he cried. 'Nothing whatever. The whole thing greatly exaggerated. Mavis,' he said, 'I am surprised and considerably pained. I should have thought that you would have had more trust in me. Kind hearts are more than coronets and simple faith than Norman blood,' he went on, for he had always remembered that gag after having to write it out two hundred times at school for loosing off a stink bomb in the form-room. 'I told you she was a total stranger.'

'Then how does it happen that you were driving her through the streets of Bramley in your car this morning?' said old Bodsham.

'Yes,' said Mavis. 'That is what I want to know.'

'It is a point,' said old Bodsham, 'upon which we would both be glad to receive information.'

Catch Freddie at a moment like this, and you catch him at his best. His heart, leaping from its moorings, had loosened one of his front teeth, but there was absolutely nothing in his manner to indicate it. His eyes, as he stared at them, were those of a spotless bimbo cruelly wronged by a monstrous accusation.

'Me?' he said incredulously.

'You,' said old Bodsham.

'I saw you myself,' said Mavis.

I doubt if there is another member of this club who could have uttered at this juncture the light, careless laugh that Freddie did.

'What an extraordinary thing,' he said. 'One can only suppose that there must be somebody in this resort who resembles me so closely in appearance that the keenest eye is deceived. I assure you, Bod – I mean, Lord Bodsham – and you, Mavis – that my morning has been far too full to permit of my giving joy rides to blondes, even if the mere thought of doing so wouldn't have sickened me to the very soul. The idea having crossed my mind that little Wilfred would appreciate it, I went to St. Asaph's to ask the Rev. Aubrey Upjohn to give the school a half-holiday. I want no thanks, of course. I merely mention the matter to show how ridiculous this idea of yours is that I was buzzing about with blondes in my two-seater. The Rev. Aubrey will tell you that I was in conference with him for the dickens of a time. After which, I was in conference with my friend, Bingo Little. And after that I came here.'

There was a silence.

'Odd,' said the Bod.

'Very odd,' said Mavis.

They were plainly rattled. And Freddie was just beginning to have that feeling, than which few are pleasanter, of having got away with it in the teeth of fearful odds, when the revolving door of the hotel moved as if impelled by some irresistible force, and through it came a bulging figure in mauve, surmounted by golden hair. Reading from left to right, the substantial blonde.

'Coo!' she exclaimed, sighting Freddie. 'There you are, ducky! Excuse me half a jiff,' she added to Mavis and the Bod, who had rocked back on their heels at the sight of her, and she linked her arm in Freddie's and drew him aside.

'I hadn't time to thank you before,' she said. 'Besides being too out of breath. Papa is very nippy on his feet, and it takes it out of a girl, trying to dodge a fork handle. What luck finding you here like this. My gentleman friend and I were married at the registrar's just after I left you, and we're having the wedding breakfast here. And if it hadn't been for you, there wouldn't have been a wedding breakfast. I can't tell you how grateful I am.'

And, as if feeling that actions speak louder than words, she flung her arms about Freddie and kissed him heartily. She then buzzed off to the ladies' room to powder her nose, leaving Freddie rooted to the spot.

He didn't, however, remain rooted long. After one quick glance at Mavis and old Bodsham, he was off like a streak to the nearest exit. That glance, quick though it had been, had shown him that this was the end. The Bod was looking at Mavis, and Mavis was looking at the Bod. And then they both turned and looked at him, and there was that in their eyes which told him, as I say, that it was the finish. Good explainer though he is, there were some things which he knew he could not explain, and this was one of them.

That is why, if our annual tournament had been held this year at Bramley-on-Sea, you would not have found Frederick Widgeon in the ranks, playing to his handicap of twenty-four. He makes no secret of the fact that he is permanently through with Bramley-on-Sea. If it wants to brace anybody, let it jolly well brace somebody else, about sums up what he feels.

EXTRACTS

THE MATING SEASON

The following extracts have all been taken from P.G. Wodehouse's novel The Mating Season. *Readers anxious to read between the lines are referred to the complete text!*

'I leave tomorrow for a place called Deverill Hall in Hampshire to help at the village concert. It seems that the vicar's niece insisted on having me in the troupe, and what's puzzling me is how this girl of God heard of me. One hadn't supposed one's reputation was so far flung.'

'You silly ass, she's Corky.'

'Corky?'

I was stunned. There are few better eggs in existence than Cora ('Corky') Pirbright, with whom I have been on the matiest of terms since the days when in our formative years we attended the same dancing class, but nothing in her deportment had ever given me the idea that she was related to the clergy.

'My Uncle Sidney is the vicar down there, and my aunt's away at Bournemouth. In her absence, Corky is keeping house for him.'

'My God! Poor old Sid! She tidies his study, no doubt?'

'Probably.'

'Straightens his tie?'

'I wouldn't be surprised.'

'And tells him he smokes too much, and every time he gets comfortably settled in an arm-chair boosts him out of it so that she can smooth the cushions. He must be feeling as if he were living in the Book of Revelations.'

It seemed to me, for I am pretty quick, that she had it in for this Dobbs. I said so, and she concurred, a quick frown marring the alabaster purity of her brow.

'I have. I'm devoted to my poor old Uncle Sidney, and this uncouth bluebottle is a thorn in his flesh. He's the village atheist.'

'Oh, really? An atheist, is he? I never went in for that sort of thing much myself. In fact, at my private school I once won a prize for Scripture Knowledge.'

'He annoys Uncle Sidney by popping out at him from side streets and making offensive cracks about Jonah and the Whale. This cross-talk act has been sent from heaven. In ordinary life, I mean, you get so few opportunities of socking cops with umbrellas, and if ever a cop needed the treatment, it is Ernest Dobbs. When he isn't smirching Jonah and the Whale with his low sneers, he's asking Uncle Sidney where Cain got his wife. You can't say that sort of thing is pleasant for a sensitive vicar, so hew to the line, my poppet, and let the chips fall where they may.'

*　　*　　*

When I was a piefaced lad of some twelve summers, doing my stretch at Malvern House, Bramley-on-Sea, the private school conducted by the Rev. Aubrey Upjohn, I remember hearing the Rev. Aubrey give the late Sir Philip Sidney a big build-up because, when wounded at the battle of somewhere and offered a quick one by a companion in arms, he told the chap who was setting them up to leave him out of that round and slip his spot to a nearby stretcher-case, whose need was greater than his. This spirit of selfless sacrifice, said the Rev. Aubrey, was what he would like to see in you boys – particularly you, Wooster, and how many times have I told you not to gape at me in that half-witted way? Close your mouth, boy, and sit up.

'And now, Bertie, I must leave you. I promised to play gin rummy with Queenie, and I am already late. She wants cheering up, poor child. You've heard about her tragedy? The severing of her engagement to the flatty Dobbs?'

'No, really? Is her engagement off? Then that's why she was looking like that, I suppose. I ran into her after lunch,' I explained, 'and I got the impression that the heart was heavy. What went wrong?'

'She didn't like him being an atheist, and he wouldn't stop being an atheist, and finally he said something about Jonah and the Whale which it was impossible for her to overlook. This morning she returned the ring, his letters and a china ornament with "A Present From Blackpool" on it, which he bought her last summer while visiting relatives in the north. It's hit her pretty hard, I'm afraid. She's passing through the furnace. She loves him madly and yearns to be his, but she can't take that stuff about Jonah and the Whale. One can only hope that gin rummy will do something to ease the pain.'

'What had you been doing?'

'Who, me?'

'Yes, you.'

'Oh,' said Gussie in an offhand way, as if it were only what might have been expected of an English gentleman, 'I had been strewing frogs.'

I goggled.

'Doing *what*?'

'Strewing frogs. In Constable Dobbs's boudoir. The vicar suggested it.'

'The vicar?'

'I mean it was he who gave Corky the idea. She had been brooding a lot, poor girl, on Dobbs's high-handed behaviour in connection with her dog, and last night the vicar happened to speak of Pharaoh and all those Plagues he got when he wouldn't let the Children of Israel go. You probably recall the incident? His words started a train of thought. It occurred to Corky that if Dobbs were visited by a Plague of Frogs, it might quite possibly change his heart and make him let Sam Goldwyn go. So she asked me to look in at his cottage and attend to the matter. She said it would please her and be good for Dobbs and would only take a few minutes of my time. She felt that the Plague of Lice might be even more effective, but she is a practical, clear-thinking girl and realized that lice are hard to come by, whereas you can find frogs in any hedgerow.'

I was gazing with considerable apprehension at a particularly dangerous specimen on my left, a pleasure-seeker with hair oil on his head and those mobile lips to which the raspberry springs automatically, when a mild spatter of applause from the two-bob seats showed that we were off. The vicar was opening the proceedings with a short address.

Apart from the fact that I was aware that he played chess and shared with Catsmeat's current fiancée a dislike for hearing policemen make cracks about Jonah and the Whale, the Rev. Sidney Pirbright had hitherto been a sealed book to me, and this was, of course, the first time I had seen him in action. A tall, drooping man, looking as if he had been stuffed in a hurry by an incompetent taxidermist, it became apparent immediately that he was not one of those boisterous vicars who, when opening a village concert, bound on the stage with a whoop and a holler, give the parishioners a huge Hullo, slam across a couple of travelling-salesman-and-farmer's-daughter stories and bound off, beaming. He seemed low-spirited, as I suppose he had every right to be. With Corky permanently on the premises, doing the Little Mother, and Gussie rolling up for practically every meal, and on top of that a gorilla like young Thos coming and parking himself in the spare bedroom, you could scarcely expect him to bubble over with *joie de vivre*. These things take their toll.

At any rate, he didn't. His theme was the Church Organ, in aid of which these grim doings had been set afoot, and it was in a vein of pessimism that he spoke of its prospects. The Church Organ, he told us frankly, was in a hell of a bad way. For years it had been going around with holes in its socks, doing the Brother-can-you-spare-a-dime stuff, and now it was about due to hand in its dinner pail. There had been a time when he had hoped that the pull-together spirit might have given it a shot in the arm, but the way it looked to him at the moment, things had gone too far and he was prepared to bet his shirt on the bally contrivance going down the drain and staying there.

The reaction of a gaggle of coffee and sandwich chewers in the drawing-room of an aristocratic home who, just as they are getting down to it, observe the local flatty muscling in through the door, vary according to what Jeeves calls the psychology of the individual. Thus, while Esmond Haddock welcomed the newcomer with a genial 'Loo-loo-loo', the aunts raised their eyebrows with a good deal of To-what-are-we-indebted-for-the-honour-of-this-visitness and the vicar drew himself up austerely, suggesting in his manner that one crack out of the zealous officer about Jonah and the Whale and he would know what to do about it. Gertrude Winkworth, who had been listless, continued listless, Silversmith preserved the detached air which butlers wear on all occasions, and the parlourmaid Queenie turned pale and uttered a stifled 'Oo-er!' giving the impression of a woman on the point of wailing for her demon lover. I, personally, put in a bit of quick gulping. The mood of *bien être* left me, and I was conscious of a coolness about the feet. When the run of events has precipitated, as Jeeves would say, a situation of such delicacy as existed at Deverill Hall, it jars you to find the place filling up with rozzers.

It was to Esmond Haddock that the constable directed his opening remark.

'I've come on an unpleasant errand, sir,' he said, and the chill in the Wooster feet became accentuated. 'But before I go into that there,' he proceeded, now addressing himself to the Rev. Sidney Pirbright, 'there's this here. I wonder if I might have a word with you, sir, on a spiritual subject?'

I saw the sainted Sidney stiffen, and knew that he was saying to himself 'Here it comes'.

'It's with ref to my having seen the light, sir.'

Somebody gave a choking gasp, like a Pekinese that has taken on a chump chop too large for its frail strength, and looking around I saw that it was Queenie. She was staring at Constable Dobbs wide-eyed and parted-lipped.

This choking gasp might have attracted more attention had it not dead-heated with another, equally choking, which proceeded from the thorax of the Rev. Sidney. He, too, was staring wide-eyed. He looked like a vicar who has just seen the outsider on whom he has placed his surplice nose its way through the throng of runners and flash in the lead past the judge's box.

'Dobbs! What did you say? You have seen the light?'

I could have told the officer he was a chump to nod so soon after taking that juicy one on the napper from the serviceable rubber instrument, but he did so, and the next thing he said was 'Ouch!' But the English policeman is made of splendid stuff, and after behaving for a moment like a man who has just swallowed one of Jeeves's morning specials he resumed his normal air, which was that of a stuffed gorilla.

'R,' he said. 'And I'll tell you how it come about, sir. On the evening of the twenty-third inst. . . . well, tonight, as a matter of fact . . . I was proceeding about my duties, chasing a marauder up a tree, when I was unexpectedly struck by a thunderbolt.'

This, as might have been expected, went big. The vicar said, 'A thunderbolt', two of the aunts said, 'A *thunderbolt*?' and Esmond Haddock said, 'Yoicks'.

'Yes, sir,' proceeded the officer, 'a thunderbolt. Caught me on the back of the head, it did, and hasn't half raised a lump.'

The vicar said, 'Most extraordinary', the other two aunts said, 'Tch, tch' and Esmond said, 'Tally ho'.

'Well, sir, I'm no fool,' continued Ernest Dobbs. 'I can take a hint. "Dobbs," I said to myself, "no use kidding yourself about what *this* is, Dobbs. It's a warning from above, Dobbs," I said to myself. "If it's got as far as thunderbolts, Dobbs," I said to myself, "it's time you made a drawstic revision of your spiritual outlook, Dobbs," I said to myself. So, if you follow my meaning, sir, I've seen the light, and what I wanted to ask you, sir, was, Do I have to join the Infants' Bible Class or can I start singing in the choir right away?'

I mentioned earlier in this narrative that I had never actually seen a shepherd welcoming a strayed lamb back into the fold, but watching Dame Daphne Winkworth on the occasion to which I allude I had picked up a pointer or two about the technique, so was able to recognize that this was what was going to happen now. You could see from his glowing eyes and benevolent smile, not to mention the hand raised as if about to bestow a blessing, that this totally unexpected reversal of form on the part of the local backslider had taken the Rev. Sidney's mind right off the church organ. I think that in about another couple of ticks he would have come across with something pretty impressive in the way of simple, manly words, but, as it so happened, he hadn't time to get set. Even as his lips parted, there was a noise like a rising pheasant from the outskirts and some solid object left the ranks and hurled itself on Constable Dobbs's chest.

Closer inspection showed this to be Queenie. She was clinging to the representative of the Law like a poultice, and from the fact that she was saying 'Oh, Ernie!' and bedewing his uniform with happy tears I deduced, being pretty shrewd, that what she was trying to convey was that all was forgiven and forgotten and that she was expecting the prompt return of the ring, the letters and the china ornament with 'A Present From Blackpool' on it. And as it did not escape my notice that he, on his side, was covering her upturned face with burning kisses and saying 'Oh, Queenie!' I gathered that Tortured Souls Preferred had taken another upward trend and that one could chalk up on the slate two more sundered hearts reunited in the springtime.

These tender scenes affect different people in different ways. I myself, realizing that Catsmeat's honourable obligations to this girl might now be considered cancelled, was definitely bucked by the spectacle. But the emotion aroused in Silversmith was plainly a shuddering horror that such goings-on should be going on in the drawing-room of Deverill Hall. Pulling a quick Stern Father, he waddled up to the happy pair and with a powerful jerk of the wrist detached his child and led her from the room.

Constable Dobbs, though still dazed, recovered himself sufficiently to apologize for his display of naked emotion, and the Rev. Sidney said he quite, quite understood.

'Come and see me tomorrow, Dobbs,' he said benevolently, 'and we will have a long talk.'

UNCLE DYNAMITE

Uncle Dynamite *is the second 'Uncle Fred' novel, featuring Frederick Altamont Cornwallis, fifth Earl of Ickenham. One strand of an exceedingly complex set of plots and stratagems is singled out in the following separate extracts: the attempts of the distraught Lady Bostock to find a suitable judge for the Bonny Babies competition at Ashenden Oakshott Village Fete, as a substitute for the curate who has been inconsiderate enough to catch measles; and the way Uncle Fred (in disguise as Major Brabazon-Plank) prevents the real Major Brabazon-Plank from denouncing him by threatening him with having to judge the competition himself. Major Plank wriggles on the hook, but cannot escape!*

From Lady Bostock's aspect only Sherlock Holmes, perhaps, would have been able to deduce that she had just heard from the vicar over the telephone that the curate was down with measles, but even Doctor Watson could have seen that her soul had in some way been badly jolted. So moved was she that, though a polished hostess, she paid no attention to Pongo, who was now standing on the other leg.

'Aylmer!'

'Well?'

'Aylmer . . . The vicar . . .'

'Well?'

'The vicar says Mr Brotherhood has got measles. He wants us to go and see him at once.'

'Who the devil's Mr Brotherhood?'

'The curate. You know Mr Brotherhood, the curate. That nice young man with the pimples. He has gone and got measles, and I was relying on him to judge the babies.'

'What babies?'

'The bonny babies, At the fete.'

A word about this fete. It was the high spot of Ashenden Oakshott's social year, when all that was bravest and fairest in the village assembled in the Manor grounds and made various kinds of whoopee. Races were run, country dances danced, bonny babies judged in order of merit in the big tent and tea and buns consumed in almost incredible quantities. Picture a blend of the Derby and a garden party at Buckingham Palace, add Belshazzar's Feast, and you have the Ashenden Oakshott Fete.

One can readily appreciate, therefore, Lady Bostock's concern at the disaster which had occurred. A lady of the manor, with an important fete coming along and the curate in bed with measles, is in the distressing position of an impresario whose star fails him a couple of days before the big production or a general whose crack regiment gets lumbago on the eve of battle.

'Hullo, Aunt Emily,' he said in sepulchral tones. 'Knitting a sock?'

'Yes, dear. A sock.'

'Oh?' said Bill, still speaking like a voice from the tomb. 'A sock? Fine.'

He stood there, staring before him with unseeing eyes, and she touched his hand gently.

'I wouldn't worry about it too much, dear.'

'I don't see how one could,' said Bill. 'How many of these frightful babies will there be?'

'There were forty-three last year.'

'Forty-three!'

'Be brave, William. If Mr Brotherhood could do it, you can.'

The flaw in this reasoning was so obvious that Bill was able to detect it at once.

'Curates are different. They train them specially to judge bonny babies. At the theological colleges. Start them off with ventriloquists' dummies, I shouldn't wonder. Forty-three, did you say? And probably dozens more this time. These blighters breed like rabbits. Gosh, I wish I was back in Brazil.'

'Why don't they get the curate to do it?' Major Brabazon-Plank cried, plainly struggling with a strong sense of grievance. 'When we had these damned baby competitions at Lower Shagley, it was always the curates who judged them. It's what curates are for.'

'The curate has got measles,' said Lord Ickenham.

'Silly ass.'

'An unsympathetic thing to say of a man who is lying on a bed of pain with pink spots all over him, but I can make allowances for your feelings, appreciating how bitter a moment this must be for you, my poor old Bimbo. I suppose there is nothing much more sickening than wanting to expose a fellow and not being able to, and I would love to help you out if I could. But I really don't know what to suggest. You might. . . . No, that's no good. Or. . . . No, I doubt if that would work, either. I'm afraid you will have to give up the idea. The only poor consolation I can offer you is that it will be all the same in another hundred years. Well, my dear chap, it's been delightful running into you again after all this time, and I wish I could stay and chat, but I fear I must be pushing along. You know how busy we Brabazon-Planks always are. Look me up some time at my residence, which is quite near here, and we will have a long talk about the old school days and Brazil and, of course,' said Lord Ickenham indulgently, 'any other subject you may wish to discuss. If you can raise it by then, bring the two bob with you.'

With another kindly pat on the shoulder he went out, and Major Plank, breathing heavily, reached for the tankard and finished its contents.

THE CODE OF THE WOOSTERS

The Code of the Woosters, *the third in the Bertie Wooster/Jeeves series of novels, concerns the romances of Gussie and Madeline, and of 'Stiffy' Byng and the large, clumsy, but well-meaning Reverend 'Stinker' Pinker, curate of Totleigh-in-the-Wold.*

Stiffy's map, as a rule, tends to be rather grave and dreamy, giving the impression that she is thinking deep, beautiful thoughts. Quite misleading, of course. I don't suppose she would recognize a deep, beautiful thought if you handed it to her on a skewer with tartare sauce. Like Jeeves, she doesn't often smile, but now her lips had parted – ecstatically, I think – I should have to check up with Jeeves – and her eyes were sparkling.

'What a man!' she said. 'We're engaged, you know.'

'Oh, are you?'

'Yes, but don't tell a soul. It's frightfully secret. Uncle Watkyn mustn't know about it till he has been well sweetened.'

'And who is this Harold?'

'The curate down in the village.' She turned to the dog Bartholomew. 'Is lovely kind curate going to pinch bad, ugly policeman's helmet for his muzzer, zen, and make her very, very happy?' she said.

Or words to that general trend. I can't do the dialect, of course.

I stared at the young pill, appalled at her moral code, if you could call it that. You know, the more I see of women, the more I think that there ought to be a law. Something has got to be done about this sex, or the whole fabric of Society will collapse, and then what silly asses we shall all look.

'Curate?' I said. 'But, Stiffy, you can't ask a curate to go about pinching policemen's helmets.'

'Why not?'

'Well, it's most unusual. You'll get the poor bird unfrocked.'

'Unfrocked?'

'It's something they do to parsons when they catch them bending. And this will inevitably be the outcome of the frightful task you have apportioned to the sainted Harold.'

'I don't see that it's a frightful task.'

'You aren't telling me that it's the sort of thing that comes naturally to curates?'

'Yes, I am. It ought to be right up Harold's street. When he was at Magdalen, before he saw the light, he was the dickens of a chap. Always doing things like that.'

Her mention of Magdalen interested me. It had been my own college.

'Magdalen man, is he? What year? Perhaps I know him.'

'Of course you do. He often speaks of you, and was delighted when I told him you were coming here. Harold Pinker.'

I was astounded.

'Harold Pinker? Old Stinker Pinker? Great Scott! One of my dearest pals. I've often wondered where he had got to. And all the while he had sneaked off and become a curate. It just shows you how true it is that one-half of the world doesn't know how the other three-quarters lives. Stinker Pinker, by Jove! You really mean that old Stinker now cures souls?'

'Certainly. And jolly well, too. The nibs think very highly of him. Any moment now, he may get a vicarage, and then watch his smoke. He'll be a bishop some day.'

The excitement of discovering a long-lost buddy waned. I found myself returning to the practical issues. I became grave.

And I'll tell you why I became grave. It was all very well for Stiffy to say that this thing would be right up old Stinker's street. She didn't know him as I did. I had watched Harold Pinker through the formative years of his life, and I knew him for what he was – a large, lumbering, Newfoundland puppy of a chap – full of zeal, yes – always doing his best, true; but never quite able to make the grade; a man, in short, who if there was a chance of bungling an enterprise and landing himself in the soup, would snatch at it. At the idea of him being turned on to perform the extraordinarily delicate task of swiping Constable Oates's helmet, the blood froze. He hadn't a chance of getting away with it.

I thought of Stinker, the youth. Built rather on the lines of Roderick Spode, he had played Rugby football not only for his University but also for England, and at the art of hurling an opponent into a mud puddle and jumping on his neck with cleated boots had had few, if any, superiors. If I had wanted someone to help me out with a mad bull, he would have been my first choice. If by some mischance I had found myself trapped in the underground den of the Secret Nine, there was nobody I would rather have seen coming down the chimney than the Rev. Harold Pinker.

But mere thews and sinews do not qualify a man to pinch policemen's helmets. You need finesse.

'He will, will he?' I said. 'A fat lot of bishing he's going to do, if he's caught sneaking helmets from members of his flock.'

'You can understand Uncle Watkyn's feelings. His daughter tells him she is going to get married. "Oh, yes?" he says. "Well, let's have a dekko at the chap." And along rolls Gussie. A nasty jar for a father.'

'Quite.'

'Well, you can't tell me that a time when he is reeling under the blow of having Gussie for a son-in-law is the moment for breaking it to him that I want to marry the curate.'

I saw her point. I recollected Freddie Threepwood telling me that there had been trouble at Blandings about a cousin of his wanting to marry a curate. In that case, I gathered, the strain had been eased by the discovery that the fellow was the heir of a well-to-do Liverpool shipping millionaire; but, as a broad, general rule, parents do not like their daughters marrying curates, and I take it that the same thing applies to uncles with their nieces.

'You've got to face it. Curates are not so hot. So before anything can be done in the way of removing the veil of secrecy, we have got to sell Harold to Uncle Watkyn. If we play our cards properly, I am hoping that he will give him a vicarage which he has in his gift. Then we shall begin to get somewhere.'

I didn't like her use of the word 'we', but I saw what she was driving at, and I was sorry to have to insert a spanner in her hopes and dreams.

'You wish me to put in a word for Stinker? You would like me to draw your uncle aside and tell him what a splendid fellow Stinker is? There is nothing I would enjoy more, my dear Stiffy, but unfortunately we are not on those terms.'

'No, no, nothing like that.'

'Well, I don't see what more I can do.'

'You will,' she said, and again I was conscious of that subtle feeling of uneasiness. I told myself that I must be firm. But I could not but remember Roberta Wickham and the hot-water bottle. A man thinks he is being chilled steel – or adamant, if you prefer the expression – and suddenly the mists clear away and he finds that he has allowed a girl to talk him into something frightful. Samson had the same experience with Delilah.

'Oh?' I said, guardedly.

She paused in order to tickle the dog Bartholomew under the left ear. Then she resumed.

'Just praising Harold to Uncle Watkyn isn't any use. You need something much cleverer than that. You want to engineer some terrifically brainy scheme that will put him over with a bang. I thought I had got it a few days ago. Do you ever read *Milady's Boudoir*?'

'I once contributed an article to it on "What The Well-Dressed Man Is Wearing", but I am not a regular reader. Why?'

'There was a story in it last week about a Duke who wouldn't let his daughter marry the young secretary, so the secretary got a friend of his to take the Duke out on the lake and upset the boat, and then he dived in and saved the Duke, and the Duke said "Right ho."'

I resolved that no time should be lost in quashing this idea.

'Any notion you may have entertained that I am going to take Sir W. Bassett out in a boat and upset him can be dismissed instanter. To start with, he wouldn't come out on a lake with me.'

'No. And we haven't a lake. And Harold said that if I was thinking of the pond in the village, I could forget it, as it was much too cold to dive into ponds at this time of year. Harold is funny in some ways.'

'I applaud his sturdy common sense.'

'Then I got an idea from another story. It was about a young lover who gets a friend of his to dress up as a tramp and attack the girl's father, and then he dashes in and rescues him.'

I patted her hand gently.

'The flaw in all these ideas of yours,' I pointed out, 'is that the hero always seems to have a half-witted friend who is eager to place himself in the foulest positions on his behalf. In Stinker's case, this is not so. I am fond of Stinker – you could even go so far as to say that I love him like a brother – but there are sharply defined limits to what I am prepared to do to further his interests.'

'Well, it doesn't matter, because he put the presidential veto on that one, too. Something about what the vicar would say if it all came out. But he loves my new one.'

'Oh, you've got a new one?'

'Yes, and it's terrific. The beauty of it is that Harold's part in it is above reproach. A thousand vicars couldn't get the goods on him. The only snag was that he has to have someone working with him, and until I heard you were coming down here I couldn't think who we were to get. But now that you have arrived, all is well.'

'It is, is it? I informed you before, young Byng, and I now inform you again that nothing will induce me to mix myself up with your loathsome schemes.'

'Oh, but, Bertie, you must! We're relying on you. And all you have to do is practically nothing. Just steal Uncle Watkyn's cow-creamer.'

I don't know what you would have done if a girl in heather-mixture tweeds had sprung this on you, scarcely eight hours after a mauve-faced aunt had sprung the same. It is possible that you would have reeled. Most chaps would, I imagine. Personally, I was more amused than aghast. Indeed, if memory serves me aright, I laughed. If so, it was just as well, for it was about the last chance I had.

'Oh, yes?' I said. 'Tell me more,' I said, feeling that it would be entertaining to allow the little blighter to run on. 'Steal his cow-creamer, eh?'

'Yes. It's a thing he brought back from London yesterday for his collection. A sort of silver cow with a kind of blotto look on its face. He thinks the world of it. He had it on the table in front of him at dinner last night, and was gassing away about it. And it was then that I got the idea. I thought that if Harold could pinch it, and then bring it back, Uncle Watkyn would be so grateful that he would start spouting vicarages like a geyser. And then I spotted the catch.'

'Oh, there was a catch?'

'Of course. Don't you see? How would Harold be supposed to have got the thing? If a silver cow is in somebody's collection, and it disappears, and next day a curate rolls round with it, that curate has got to do some good, quick explaining. Obviously, it must be made to look like an outside job.'

'I see. You want me to put on a black mask and break in through the window and snitch this *objet d'art* and hand it over to Stinker? I see. I see.'

I spoke with satirical bitterness, and I should have thought that anyone could have seen that satirical bitterness was what I was speaking with, but she merely looked at me with admiration and approval.

'You are clever, Bertie. That's exactly it. Of course, you needn't wear a mask.'

'You don't think it would help me throw myself into the part?' I said with s. b., as before.

'Well, it might. That's up to you. But the great thing is to get through the window. Wear gloves, of course, because of the fingerprints.'

'Of course.'

'Then Harold will be waiting outside, and he will take the thing from you.'

'And after that I go off and do my stretch at Dartmoor?'

'Oh, no. You escape in the struggle, of course.'

'What struggle?'

'And Harold rushes into the house, all over blood – '

'Whose blood?'

'Well, I said yours, and Harold thought his. There have got to be signs of a struggle, to make it more interesting, and my idea was that he should hit you on the nose. But he said the thing would carry greater weight if he was all covered with gore. So how we've left it is that you both hit each other on the nose. And then Harold rouses the house and comes in and shows Uncle Watkyn the cow-creamer and explains what happened, and everything's fine. Because, I mean, Uncle Watkyn couldn't just say "Oh, thanks" and leave it at that, could he? He would be compelled, if he had a spark of decency in him, to cough up that vicarage. Don't you think it's a wonderful scheme, Bertie?'

'I wasn't expecting you,' I said. 'I thought you had gone to the Working Men's Institute, to tickle the ivories in accompaniment to old Stinker's coloured lecture on the Holy Land.'

'I did.'

'Back early, aren't you?'

'Yes. The lecture was off. Harold broke the slides.'

'Oh?' I said, feeling that he was just the sort of chap who would break slides. 'How did that happen?'

She passed a listless hand over the brow of the dog Bartholomew, who had stepped up to fraternize.

'He dropped them.'

'What made him do that?'

'He had a shock, when I broke off our engagement.'

'What!'

'Yes.' A gleam came into her eyes, as if she were reliving unpleasant scenes, and her voice took on the sort of metallic sharpness which I have so often noticed in that of my Aunt Agatha during our get-togethers. Her listlessness disappeared, and for the first time she spoke with a girlish vehemence. 'I got to Harold's cottage, and I went in, and after we'd talked of this and that for a while, I said "When are you going to pinch Eustace Oates's helmet, darling?" And would you believe it, he looked at me in a horrible, sheepish, hang-dog way and said that he had been wrestling with his conscience in the hope of getting its OK, but that it simply wouldn't hear of him pinching Eustace Oates's helmet, so it was all off. "Oh?" I said, drawing myself up. "All off, is it? Well, so is our engagement," and he dropped a double handful of coloured slides of the Holy Land, and I came away.'

'You don't mean that?'

'Yes, I do. And I consider that I have had a very lucky escape. If he is the sort of man who is going to refuse me every little thing I ask, I'm glad I found it out in time. I'm delighted about the whole thing.'

Here, with a sniff like the tearing of a piece of calico, she buried the bean in the hands, and broke into what are called uncontrollable sobs.

Stiffy, after that moment of surprised inaction which was to be expected in a girl who hears tapping sounds at her window, had risen and gone to investigate. I couldn't see a thing from where I was sitting, but she was evidently more fortunately placed. As she drew back the curtain, I saw her clap a hand to her throat, like someone in a play, and a sharp cry escaped her, audible even above the ghastly row which was proceeding from the lips of the frothing terrier.

'Harold!' she yipped, and putting two and two together I gathered that the bird on the balcony must be old Stinker Pinker, my favourite curate.

It was with a sort of joyful yelp, like that of a woman getting together with her demon lover, that the little geezer had spoken his name, but it was evident that reflection now told her that after what had occurred between this man of God and herself this was not quite the tone. Her next words were uttered with a cold, hostile intonation. I was able to hear them, because she had stooped and picked up the bounder Bartholomew, clamping a hand over his mouth to still his cries – a thing I wouldn't have done for a goodish bit of money.

'What do you want?'

Owing to the lull in Bartholomew, the stuff was coming through well now. Stinker's voice was a bit muffled by the intervening sheet of glass, but I got it nicely.

'Stiffy!'

'Well?'

'Can I come in?'

'No, you can't.'

'But I've brought you something.'

A sudden yowl of ecstasy broke from the young pimple.

'Harold! You angel lamb! You haven't got it, after all?'

'Yes.'

'Oh, Harold, my dream of joy!'

She opened the window with eager fingers, and a cold draught came in and played about my ankles. It was not followed, as I had supposed it would be, by old Stinker. He continued to hang about on the outskirts, and a moment later his motive in doing so was made clear.

'I say, Stiffy, old girl, is that hound of yours under control?'

'Yes, rather. Wait a minute.'

She carried the animal to the cupboard and bunged him in, closing the door behind him. And from the fact that no further bulletins were received from him, I imagine he curled up and went to sleep. These Scotties are philosophers, well able to adapt themselves to changing conditions. They can take it as well as dish it out.

'All clear, angel,' she said, and returned to the window, arriving there just in time to be folded in the embrace of the incoming Stinker.

It was not easy for some moments to sort out the male from the female ingredients in the ensuing tangle, but eventually he disengaged himself and I was able to see him steadily and see him whole. And when I did so, I noticed that there was rather more of him than there had been when I had seen him last. Country butter and the easy life these curates lead had added a pound or two to an always impressive figure. To find the lean, finely trained Stinker of my nonage, I felt that one would have to catch him in Lent.

But the change in him, I soon perceived, was purely superficial. The manner in which he now tripped over a rug and cannoned into an occasional table, upsetting it with all the old thoroughness, showed me that at heart he still remained the same galumphing man with two left feet, who had always been constitutionally incapable of walking through the great Gobi desert without knocking something over.

Stinker's was a face which in the old College days had glowed with health and heartiness. The health was still there – he looked like a clerical beetroot – but of heartiness at this moment one noted rather a shortage. His features were drawn, as if Conscience were gnawing at his vitals. And no doubt it was, for in one hand he was carrying the helmet which I had last observed perched on the dome of Constable Eustace Oates. With a quick, impulsive movement, like that of a man trying to rid himself of a dead fish, he thrust it at Stiffy, who received it with a soft, tender squeal of ecstasy.

'I brought it,' he said dully.

'Oh, Harold!'

'I brought your gloves, too. You left them behind. At least, I've brought one of them. I couldn't find the other.'

'Thank you, darling. But never mind about gloves, my wonder man. Tell me everything that happened.'

He was about to do so, when he paused, and I saw that he was staring at me with a rather feverish look in his eyes. Then he turned and stared at Jeeves. One could read what was passing in his mind. He was debating within himself whether we were real, or whether the nervous strain to which he had been subjected was causing him to see things.

'Stiffy,' he said, lowering his voice, 'don't look now, but is there something on top of that chest of drawers?'

'Eh? Oh, yes, that's Bertie Wooster.'

'Oh, it is?' said Stinker, brightening visibly. 'I wasn't quite sure. Is that somebody on the cupboard, too?'

'That's Bertie's man Jeeves.'

'How do you do?' said Stinker.

'How do you do, sir?' said Jeeves.

We climbed down, and I came forward with outstretched hand, anxious to get the reunion going.

'What ho, Stinker.'

'Hullo, Bertie.'

'Long time since we met.'

'It is a bit, isn't it?'

'I hear you're a curate now.'

'Yes, that's right.'

'How are the souls?'

'Oh, fine, thanks.'

There was a pause, and I suppose I would have gone on to ask him if he had seen anything of old So-and-so lately or knew what had become of old What's-his-name, as one does when the conversation shows a tendency to drag on these occasions of ancient College chums meeting again after long separation, but before I could do so, Stiffy, who had been crooning over the helmet like a mother over the cot of her sleeping child, stuck it on her head with a merry chuckle, and the spectacle appeared to bring back to Stinker like a slosh in the waistcoat the realization of what he had done. You've probably heard the expression 'The wretched man seemed fully conscious of his position'. That was Harold Pinker at this juncture. He shied like a startled horse, knocked over another table, tottered to a chair, knocked that over, picked it up and sat down, burying his face in his hands.

'If the Infants' Bible Class should hear of this!' he said, shuddering strongly.

I saw what he meant. A man in his position has to watch his step. What people expect from a curate is a zealous performance of his parochial duties. They like to think of him as a chap who preaches about Hivites, Jebusites and what not, speaks the word in season to the backslider, conveys soup and blankets to the deserving bedridden, and all that sort of thing. When they find him de-helmeting policemen, they look at one another with the raised eyebrow of censure, and ask themselves if he is quite the right man for the job. That was what was bothering Stinker and preventing him being the old effervescent curate whose jolly laugh had made the last School Treat go with such a bang.

Stiffy endeavoured to hearten him.

'I'm sorry, darling. If it upsets you, I'll put it away.' She crossed to the chest of drawers, and did so. 'But why it should,' she said, returning, 'I can't imagine. I should have thought it would have made you so proud and happy. And now tell me everything that happened.'

'Yes,' I said. 'One would like the firsthand story.'

'Did you creep behind him like a leopard?' asked Stiffy.

'Of course he did,' I said, admonishing the silly young shrimp. 'You don't suppose he pranced up in full view of the fellow? No doubt you trailed him with unremitting snaki-ness, eh, Stinker, and did the deed when he was relaxing on a stile or somewhere over a quiet pipe?'

Stinker sat staring straight before him, that drawn look still on his face.

'He wasn't on the stile. He was leaning against it. After you left me, Stiffy, I went for a walk, to think things over, and I had just crossed Plunkett's meadow and was going to climb the stile into the next one, when I saw something dark in front of me, and there he was.'

I nodded. I could visualize the scene.

'I hope,' I said, 'that you remembered to give the forward shove before the upwards lift?'

'It wasn't necessary. The helmet was not on his head. He had taken it off and put it on the ground. And I just crept up and grabbed it.'

I started, pursing the lips a bit.

'Not quite playing the game, Stinker.'

'Yes, it was,' said Stiffy, with a good deal of warmth. 'I call it very clever of him.'

I could not recede from my position. At the Drones, we hold strong views on these things.

'There is a right way and a wrong way of pinching policemen's helmets,' I said firmly.

'You're talking absolute nonsense,' said Stiffy. 'I think you were wonderful, darling.'

I shrugged my shoulders.

'How do you feel about it, Jeeves?'

'I scarcely think that it would be fitting for me to offer an opinion, sir.'

'No,' said Stiffy. 'And it jolly well isn't fitting for you to offer an opinion, young piefaced Bertie Wooster. Who do you think you are,' she demanded, with renewed warmth, 'coming strolling into a girl's bedroom, sticking on dog about the right way and the wrong way of pinching helmets? It isn't as if you were such a wonder at it yourself, considering that you got collared and hauled up next morning at Bosher Street, where you had to grovel to Uncle Watkyn in the hope of getting off with a fine.'

I took this up promptly.

'I did not grovel to the old disease. My manner throughout was calm and dignified, like that of a Red Indian at the stake. And when you speak of me hoping to get off with a fine – '

Here Stiffy interrupted, to beg me to put a sock in it.

'Well, all I was about to say was that the sentence stunned me. I felt so strongly that it was a case for a mere reprimand. However, this is beside the point – which is that Stinker in the recent encounter did not play to the rules of the game. I consider his behaviour morally tantamount to shooting a sitting bird. I cannot alter my opinion.'

'And I can't alter my opinion that you have no business in my bedroom. What are you doing here?'

'Yes, I was wondering that,' said Stinker, touching on the point for the first time. And I could see, of course, how he might quite well be surprised at finding this mob scene in what he had supposed the exclusive sleeping apartment of the loved one.

I eyed her sternly.

'You know what I am doing here. I told you. I came – '

'Oh, yes. Bertie came to borrow a book, darling. But' – here her eyes lingered on mine in a cold and sinister manner – 'I'm afraid I can't let him have it just yet. I have not finished with it myself. By the way,' she continued, still holding me with that compelling stare, 'Bertie says he will be delighted to help us with that cow-creamer scheme.'

'Will you, old man?' said Stinker eagerly.

'Of course he will,' said Stiffy. 'He was saying only just now what a pleasure it would be.'

'You won't mind me hitting you on the nose?'

'Of course he won't.'

'You see, we must have blood. Blood is of the essence.'

'Of course, of course, of course,' said Stiffy. Her manner was impatient. She seemed in a hurry to terminate the scene. 'He quite understands that.'

'When would you feel like doing it, Bertie?'

'He feels like doing it tonight,' said Stiffy. 'No sense in putting things off. Be waiting outside at midnight, darling. Everybody will have gone to bed by then. Midnight will suit you, Bertie? Yes, Bertie says it will suit him splendidly. So that's all settled. And now you really must be going, precious. If somebody came in and found you here, they might think it odd. Good night, darling.'

'Good night, darling.'

'Good night, darling.'

'Good night, darling.'

'Wait!' I said, cutting in on these revolting exchanges, for I wished to make a last appeal to Stinker's finer feelings.

'He can't wait. He's got to go. Remember, angel. On the spot, ready to the last button, at twelve pip emma. Good night, darling.'

'Good night, darling.'

'Good night, darling.'

'Good night, darling.'

They passed on to the balcony, the nauseous endearments receding in the distance, and I turned to Jeeves, my face stern and hard.

'Faugh, Jeeves!'

'Sir?'

'I said "Faugh!" I am a pretty broadminded man, but this has shocked me – I may say to the core. It is not so much the behaviour of Stiffy that I find so revolting. She is a female, and the tendency of females to be unable to distinguish between right and wrong is notorious. But that Harold Pinker, a clerk in Holy Orders, a chap who buttons his collar at the back, should countenance this thing appals me. He knows she has got that book. He knows that she is holding me up with it. But does he insist on her returning it? No! He lends himself to the raw work with open enthusiasm. A nice look-out for the Totleigh-in-the-Wold flock, trying to keep on the straight and narrow path with a shepherd like that! A pretty example he sets to this Infants' Bible Class of which he speaks! A few years of sitting at the feet of Harold Pinker and imbibing his extraordinary views on morality and ethics, and every bally child on the list will be serving a long stretch at Wormwood Scrubs for blackmail.'

*   *   *

He took up a pen and leaned forward, tapping it against his left forefinger.

'Somebody stole Constable Oates's helmet tonight,' he said, changing the subject.

'Oh, yes.'

'Yes. Unfortunately he was not able to see the miscreant.'

'No?'

'No. At the moment when the outrage took place, his back was turned.'

'Dashed difficult, of course, to see miscreants, if your back's turned.'

'Yes.'

'Yes.'

There was a pause. And as, in spite of the fact that we seemed to be agreeing on every point, I continued to sense a strain in the atmosphere, I tried to lighten things with a gag which I remembered from the old *in statu pupillari* days.

'Sort of makes you say to yourself "*Quis custodiet ipsos custodes*", what?'

'I beg your pardon?'

'Latin joke,' I explained. '*Quis* – who – *custodiet* – shall guard – *ipsos custodes* – the guardians themselves? Rather funny, I mean to say,' I proceeded, making it clear to the meanest intelligence, 'a chap who's supposed to stop chaps pinching things from chaps having a chap come along and pinch something from him.'

'Ah, I see your point. Yes, I can conceive that a certain type of mind might detect a humorous side to the affair. But I can assure you, Mr Wooster, that that is not the side which presents itself to me as a Justice of the Peace. I take the very gravest view of the matter, and this, when once he is apprehended and placed in custody, I shall do my utmost to persuade the culprit to share.'

I didn't like the sound of this at all. A sudden alarm for old Stinker's well-being swept over me.

'I say, what do you think he would get?'

'I appreciate your zeal for knowledge, Mr Wooster, but at the moment I am not prepared to confide in you. In the words of the late Lord Asquith, I can only say "Wait and see". I think it is possible that your curiosity may be gratified before long.'

I didn't want to rake up old sores, always being a bit of a lad for letting the dead past bury its dead, but I thought it might be as well to give him a pointer.

'You fined me five quid,' I reminded him.

'So you informed me this afternoon,' he said, pince-nezing me coldly. 'But if I understood correctly what you were saying, the outrage for which you were brought before me at Bosher Street was perpetrated on the night of the annual boat race between the Universities of Oxford and Cambridge, when a certain licence is traditionally granted by the authorities. In the present case, there are no such extenuating circumstances. I should certainly not punish the wanton stealing of Government property from the person of Constable Oates with a mere fine.'

'You don't mean it would be chokey?'

'I said that I was not prepared to confide in you, but having gone so far I will. The answer to your question, Mr Wooster, is in the affirmative.'

There was a silence. He sat tapping his finger with the pen. I, if memory serves me correctly, straightened my tie. I was deeply concerned. The thought of poor old Stinker being bunged into the Bastille was enough to disturb anyone with a kindly interest in his career and prospects. Nothing retards a curate's advancement in his chosen profession more surely than a spell in the jug.

*   *   *

'No, Bertie, darling, it cannot be. You see, I love somebody else.'

Old Bassett started.

'Eh? Who?'

'The most wonderful man in the world.'

'He has a name, I presume?'

'Harold Pinker.'

'Harold Pinker? . . . Pinker . . . The only Pinker I know is – '

'The curate. That's right. He's the chap.'

'You love the curate?'

'Ah!' said Stiffy, rolling her eyes up and looking like Aunt Dahlia when she had spoken of the merits of blackmail. 'We've been secretly engaged for weeks.'

It was plain from old Bassett's manner that he was not prepared to classify this under the heading of tidings of great joy. His brows were knitted, like those of some diner in a restaurant who, sailing into his dozen oysters, finds that the first one to pass his lips is a wrong 'un. I saw that Stiffy had shown a shrewd knowledge of human nature, if you could call his that, when she had told me that this man would have to be heavily sweetened before the news could be broken. You could see that he shared the almost universal opinion of parents and uncles that curates were nothing to start strewing roses out of a hat about.

'You know that vicarage that you have in your gift, Uncle Watkyn. What Harold and I were thinking was that you might give him that, and then we could get married at once. You see, apart from the increased dough, it would start him off on the road to higher things. Up till now, Harold has been working under wraps. As a curate, he has had no scope. But slip him a vicarage, and watch him let himself out. There is literally no eminence to which that boy will not rise, once he spits on his hands and starts in.'

She wiggled from base to apex with girlish enthusiasm, but there was no girlish enthusiasm in old Bassett's demeanour. Well, there wouldn't be, of course, but what I mean is there wasn't.

'Ridiculous!'

'Why?'

'I could not dream – '

'Why not?'

'In the first place, you are far too young – '

'What nonsense. Three of the girls I was at school with were married last year. I'm senile compared with some of the infants you see toddling up the aisle nowadays.'

Old Bassett thumped the desk – coming down, I was glad to see, on an upturned paper fastener. The bodily anguish induced by this lent vehemence to his tone.

'The whole thing is quite absurd and utterly out of the question. I refuse to consider the idea for an instant.'

'But what have you got against Harold?'

'I have nothing, as you put it, against him. He seems zealous in his duties and popular in the parish – '

'He's a baa-lamb.'

'No doubt.'

'He played football for England.'

'Very possibly.'

'And he's marvellous at tennis.'

'I dare say he is. But that is not a reason why he should marry my niece. What means has he, if any, beyond his stipend?'

'About five hundred a year.'

'Tchah!'

'Well, I don't call that bad. Five hundred's pretty good sugar, if you ask me. Besides, money doesn't matter.'

'It matters a great deal.'

'You really feel that, do you?'

'Certainly. You must be practical.'

'Right ho, I will. If you'd rather I married for money, I'll marry for money. Bertie, it's on. Start getting measured for the wedding trousers.'

Her words created what is known as a genuine sensation. Old Bassett's 'What!' and my 'Here, I say, dash it!' popped out neck and neck and collided in mid air, my heart-cry having, perhaps, an even greater horse-power than his. I was frankly appalled. Experience has taught me that you never know with girls, and it might quite possibly happen, I felt, that she would go through with this frightful project as a gesture. Nobody could teach me anything about gestures. Brinkley Court in the preceding summer had crawled with them.

'Bertie is rolling in the stuff and, as you suggest, one might do worse than take a whack at the Wooster millions. Of course, Bertie dear, I am only marrying you to make you happy. I can never love you as I love Harold. But as Uncle Watkyn has taken this violent prejudice against him – '

Old Bassett hit the paper fastener again, but this time didn't seem to notice it.

'My dear child, don't talk such nonsense. You are quite mistaken. You must have completely misunderstood me. I have no prejudice against this young man Pinker. I like and respect him. If you really think your happiness lies in becoming his wife, I would be the last man to stand in your way. By all means, marry him. The alternative – '

He said no more, but gave me a long, shuddering look. Then, as if the sight of me were more than his frail strength could endure, he removed his gaze, only to bring it back again and give me a short, quick one. He then closed his eyes and leaned back in his chair, breathing stertorously. And as there didn't seem anything to keep me, I sidled out. The last I saw of him, he was submitting without any great animation to a niece's embrace.

I suppose that when you have an uncle like Sir Watkyn Bassett on the receiving end, a niece's embrace is a thing you tend to make pretty snappy. It wasn't more than about a minute before Stiffy came out and immediately went into her dance.

'What a man! What a man! What a man! What a man! What a man!' she said, waving her arms and giving other indications of *bien être*. 'Jeeves,' she explained, as if she supposed that I might imagine her to be alluding to the recent Bassett. 'Did he say it would work? He did. And was he right? He was. Bertie, could one kiss Jeeves?'

'Certainly not.'

'Shall I kiss you?'

'No, thank you. All I require from you, young Byng, is that notebook.'

'Well, I must kiss someone, and I'm dashed if I'm going to kiss Eustace Oates.'

She broke off. A graver look came into her dial.

'Eustace Oates!' she repeated meditatively. 'That reminds me. In the rush of recent events, I had forgotten him. I exchanged a few words with Eustace Oates just now, Bertie, while I was waiting on the stairs for the balloon to go up, and he was sinister to a degree.'

'Where's that notebook?'

'Never mind about the notebook. The subject under discussion is Eustace Oates and his sinisterness. He's on my trail about that helmet.'

'What!'

'Absolutely. I'm Suspect Number One. He told me that he reads a lot of detective stories, and he says that the first thing a detective makes a bee-line for is motive. After that, opportunity. And finally clues. Well, as he pointed out, with that high-handed behaviour of his about Bartholomew rankling in my bosom, I had a motive all right, and seeing that I was out and about at the time of the crime I had the opportunity, too. And as for clues, what do you think he had with him, when I saw him? One of my gloves! He had picked it up on the scene of the outrage – while measuring footprints or looking for cigar ash, I suppose. You remember when Harold brought me back my gloves, there was only one of them. The other he apparently dropped while scooping in the helmet.'

A sort of dull, bruised feeling weighed me down as I mused on this latest manifestation of Harold Pinker's goofiness as if a strong hand had whanged me over the cupola with a blackjack. There was such a sort of hideous ingenuity in the way he thought up new methods of inviting ruin.

'He would!'

'What do you mean, he would?'

'Well, he did, didn't he?'

'That's not the same as saying he would – in a beastly, sneering, supercilious tone, as if you were so frightfully hot yourself. I can't understand you, Bertie – the way you're always criticizing poor Harold. I though you were so fond of him.'

'I love him like a b. But that doesn't alter my opinion that of all the pumpkin-headed foozlers who ever preached about Hivites and Jebusites, he is the foremost.'

'He isn't half as pumpkin-headed as you.'

'He is, at a conservative estimate, about twenty-seven times as pumpkin-headed as me. He begins where I leave off. It may be a strong thing to say, but he's more pumpkin-headed than Gussie.'

With a visible effort, she swallowed the rising choler.

'Well, never mind about that. The point is that Eustace Oates is on my trail, and I've got to look slippy and find a better safe-deposit vault for that helmet than my chest of drawers. Before I know where I am, the Ogpu will be searching my room. Where would be a good place, do you think?'

I dismissed the thing wearily.

'Oh, dash it, use your own judgement. To return to the main issue, where is that notebook?'

'Oh, Bertie, you're a perfect bore about that notebook. Can't you talk of anything else?'

'No, I can't. Where is it?'

'You're going to laugh when I tell you.'

I gave her an austere look.

'It is possible that I may some day laugh again – when I have got well away from this house of terror, but there is a fat chance of my doing so at this early date. Where is that book?'

'Well, if you really must know, I hid it in the cow-creamer.'

Everyone, I imagine, has read stories in which things turned black and swam before people. As I heard these words, Stiffy turned black and swam before me.

*   *   *

'And you suppose that that will cause him to hold his hand?' I smiled one of those bitter, sardonic smiles. 'I think you are attributing to the old poison germ a niceness of feeling and a respect for the laws of hospitality which nothing in his record suggests that he possesses. You can take it from me that he definitely is going to search the room, and I imagine that the only reason he hasn't arrived already is that he is still scouring the house for Gussie.'

'Gussie?'

'He is at the moment chasing Gussie with a hunting-crop. But a man cannot go on doing that indefinitely. Sooner or later he will give it up, and then we shall have him here, complete with magnifying glass and bloodhounds.'

The gravity of the situash had at last impressed itself upon her. She uttered a squeak of dismay, and her eyes became a bit soup-platey.

'Oh, Bertie! Then I'm afraid I've put you in rather a spot.'

'That covers the facts like a dust-sheet.'

'I'm sorry now I ever asked Harold to pinch the thing. It was a mistake. I admit it. Still, after all, even if Uncle Watkyn does come here and find it, it doesn't matter much, does it?'

'Did you hear that, Jeeves?'

'Yes, sir.'

'So did I. I see. It doesn't matter, you feel?'

'Well, what I mean is your reputation won't really suffer much, will it? Everybody knows that you can't keep your hands off policemen's helmets. This'll be just another one.'

'Ha! And what leads you to suppose, young Stiffy, that when the Assyrian comes down like a wolf on the fold I shall meekly assume the guilt and not blazon the truth – what, Jeeves?'

'Forth to the world, sir.'

'Thank you, Jeeves. What makes you suppose that I shall meekly assume the guilt and not blazon the truth forth to the world?'

I wouldn't have supposed that her eyes could have widened any more, but they did perceptibly. Another dismayed squeak escaped her. Indeed, such was its volume that it might perhaps be better to call it a squeal.

'But, Bertie!'

'Well?'

'Bertie, listen!'

'I'm listening.'

'Surely you will take the rap? You can't let Harold get it in the neck. You were telling me this afternoon that he would be unfrocked. I won't have him unfrocked. Where is he going to get if they unfrock him? That sort of thing gives a curate a frightful black eye. Why can't you say you did it? All it would mean is that you would be kicked out of the house, and I don't suppose you're so anxious to stay on, are you?'

'Possibly you are not aware that your bally uncle is proposing to send the perpetrator of this outrage to chokey.'

'Oh, no. At the worst, just a fine.'

'Nothing of the kind. He specifically told me chokey.'

'He didn't mean it. I expect there was – '

'No, there was not a twinkle in his eye.'

'Then that settles it. I can't have my precious, angel Harold doing a stretch.'

'How about your precious, angel Bertram?'

'But Harold's sensitive.'

'So am I sensitive.'

'Not half so sensitive as Harold. Bertie, surely you aren't going to be difficult about this? You're much too good a sport. Didn't you tell me once that the Code of the Woosters was "Never let a pal down"?'

She had found the talking point. People who appeal to the Code of the Woosters rarely fail to touch a chord in Bertram. My iron front began to crumble.

'That's all very fine – '

'Bertie, darling!'

'Yes, I know, but, dash it all – '

'Bertie!'

'Oh, well!'

'You will take the rap?'

'I suppose so.'

She yodelled ecstatically, and I think that if I had not side-stepped she would have flung her arms about my neck. Certainly she came leaping forward with some such purpose apparently in view. Foiled by my agility, she began to tear off a few steps of that spring dance to which she was so addicted.

'Thank you, Bertie, darling. I knew you would be sweet about it. I can't tell you how grateful I am, and how much I admire you. You remind me of Carter Patterson . . . no, that's not it . . . Nick Carter . . . no, not Nick Carter. . . . Who does Mr Wooster remind me of, Jeeves?'

'Sidney Carton, miss.'

'That's right. Sidney Carton. But he was smalltime stuff compared with you, Bertie.'

SERVICE WITH A SMILE

*In the following extracts from this novel, Lord Ickenham, alias Uncle Fred, brings the Rever-
end Bill Bailey to Blandings Castle disguised as 'Cuthbert Meriwether'. From this point it is
only a small leap to the breaking of hearts and the stealing of pigs. . . .*

'Who is this fellow?'

'Bill Bailey.'

Lord Ickenham seemed surprised.

'He's back, is he?'

'Eh?'

'I was given to understand that he had left home. I seem to remember his wife being
rather concerned about it.'

Pongo saw that his uncle had got everything mixed up, as elderly gentlemen will.

'Oh, this chap isn't really Bill. I believe he was christened Cuthbert. But if a fellow's
name is Bailey, you've more or less got to call him Bill.'

'Of course, noblesse oblige. Friend of yours?'

'Bosom. Up at Oxford with him.'

'Tell him to join us here.'

'Can't be done. I've arranged to meet him in Milton Street.'

'Where's that?'

'In South Kensington.'

Lord Ickenham pursed his lips.

'South Kensington? Where sin stalks naked through the dark alleys and only might is
right. Give this man a miss. He'll lead you astray.'

'He won't jolly well lead me astray. And why? Because for one thing he's a curate and
for another he's getting married. The rendezvous is at the Milton Street Registry Office.'

'You are his witness?'

'That's right.'

'And who is the bride?'

'American girl.'

'Nice?'

'Bill speaks well of her.'

'What's her name?'

'Schoonmaker.'

Lord Ickenham leaped in his seat.

'Good heavens! Not little Myra Schoonmaker?'

'I don't know if she's little or not. I've never seen her. But her name's Myra all right.
Why – do you know her?'

A tender look had come into Lord Ickenham's handsome face. He twirled his moustache sentimentally.

'Do I know her! Many's the time I've given her her bath. Not recently, of course, but years ago when I was earning my living in New York. Jimmy Schoonmaker was my great buddy in those days. I don't get over to God's country much now, your aunt thinks it better otherwise, and I've often wondered how he was making out. He promised, when I knew him, to become a big shot in the financial world. Even then, though comparatively young, he was able to shoot a cigar across his face without touching it with his fingers, which we all know is the first step to establishing oneself as a tycoon. I expect by this time he's the Wolf of Wall Street, and is probably offended if he isn't investigated every other week by a Senate Commission. Well, it all seems very odd to me.'

'What's odd?'

'His daughter getting married at a registry office. I should have thought she would have had a big choral wedding with bridesmaids and bishops and all the fixings.'

'Ah, I see what you mean.' Pongo looked cautiously over his shoulder. No one appeared to be within earshot. 'Yes, you would think so, wouldn't you? But Bill's nuptials have got to be solemnized with more than a spot of secrecy and silence. The course of true love hasn't been running too smooth. Hell-hounds have been bunging spanners into it.'

'What hell-hounds would those be?'

'I should have said one hell-hound. You know her. Lady Constance Keeble.'

'What, dear old Connie? How that name brings back fragrant memories. I wonder if you recall the time when you and I went to Blandings Castle, I posing as Sir Roderick Glossop, the loony doctor, you as his nephew Basil?'

'I recall it,' said Pongo with a strong shudder. The visit alluded to had given him nightmares for months.

'Happy days, happy days! I enjoyed my stay enormously, and wish I could repeat it. The bracing air, the pleasant society, the occasional refreshing look at Emsworth's pig, it all combined to pep me up and brush away the cobwebs. But how does Connie come into it?'

'She forbade the banns.'

'I still don't follow the scenario. Why was she in a position to do so?'

'What happened was this. She and Schoonmaker are old pals – I got all this from Bill, so I assume we can take it as accurate – and he wanted his daughter to have a London season, so he brought her over here and left her in Lady C.'s charge.'

'All clear so far.'

'And plumb spang in the middle of their London season Lady C. discovered that the beazel was walking out with Bill. Ascertaining that he was a curate, she became as sore as a gumboil.'

'She does not like curates?'

'That's the idea one gets.'

'Odd. She doesn't like me, either. Very hard to please, that woman. What's wrong with curates?'

'Well, they're all pretty hard up. Bill hasn't a bean.'

'I begin to see. Humble suitor. Curious how prejudiced so many people are against humble suitors. My own case is one in point. When I was courting your Aunt Jane, her parents took the bleakest view of the situation, and weren't their faces red when one day I suddenly became that noblest of created beings, an Earl, a hell of a fellow with four christian names and a coronet hanging on a peg in the downstairs cupboard. Her father, scorning me because I was a soda-jerker at the time, frequently, I believe, alluded to me as "that bum", but it was very different when I presented myself at his Park Avenue residence with a coronet on the back of my head and a volume of Debrett under my arm. He gave me his blessing and a cigar. No chance of Bill Bailey becoming an earl, I suppose?'

'Not unless he murders about fifty-seven uncles and cousins.'

'Which a curate, of course, would hesitate to do. So what was Connie's procedure?'

'She lugged the poor wench off to Blandings, and she's been there ever since, practically in durance vile, her every movement watched. But this Myra seems to be a sensible, levelheaded girl, because, learning from her spies that Lady C. was to go to Shrewsbury for a hair-do and wouldn't be around till dinnertime, she 'phoned Bill that she would be free that day and would nip up to London and marry him. She told him to meet her at the Milton Street Registry Office, where the project could be put through speedily and at small expense.'

'I see. Very shrewd. I often think these runaway marriages are best. No fuss and feathers. After all, who wants a lot of bishops cluttering up the place? I often say, when you've seen one bishop, you've seen them all.' Lord Ickenham paused. 'Well,' he said, looking at his watch. 'I suppose it's about time we were getting along. Don't want to be late.'

Pongo started. To his sensitive ears this sounded extremely like the beginning of one of their pleasant and instructive afternoons. In just such a tone of voice had his relative a few years earlier suggested that they might look in at the dog races, for there was, he said, no better way of studying the soul of the people than to mingle with them in their simple pastimes.

'We? You aren't coming?'

'Of course I'm coming. Two witnesses are always better than one, and little Myra – '

'I can't guarantee that she's little.'

'And Myra, whatever her size, would never forgive me if I were not there to hold her hand when the firing squad assembles.'

Pongo chewed his lower lip, this way and that dividing the swift mind.

'Well, all right. But no larks.'

'My dear boy? As if I should dream of being frivolous on such a sacred occasion. Of course, if I find this Bill Bailey of yours unworthy of her, I shall put a stopper on the proceedings, as any man of sensibility would. What sort of a chap is he? Pale and fragile, I suppose, with a touch of consumption and a tendency to recite the collect for the day in a high tenor voice?'

'Pale and fragile, my foot. He boxed three years for Oxford.'

'He did?'

'And went through the opposition like a dose of salts.'

'Then all should be well. I expect I shall take the fellow to my bosom.'

His expectation was fulfilled. The Rev. Cuthbert Bailey met with his instant approval. He liked his curates substantial, and Bill proved to be definitely the large economy size, the sort of curate whom one could picture giving the local backslider the choice between seeing the light or getting plugged in the eye. Amplifying his earlier remarks, Pongo on the journey to Milton Street had told his uncle that in the parish of Bottleton East, where he had recently held a cure of souls, Bill Bailey had been universally respected, and Lord Ickenham could readily appreciate why. He himself would have treated with the utmost respect any young man so obviously capable of a sweet left hook followed by a snappy right to the button. A captious critic might have felt on seeing the Rev. Cuthbert that it would have been more suitable for one in Holy Orders to have looked a little less like the logical contender for the world's heavyweight championship, but it was impossible to regard his rugged features and bulging shoulders without an immediate feeling of awe.

Impossible, too, not to like his manifest honesty and simplicity. It seemed to Lord Ickenham that in probing beneath the forbidding exterior to the gentle soul it hid his little Myra had done the smart thing.

They fell into pleasant conversation, but after the first few exchanges it was plain to Lord Ickenham that the young man of God was becoming extremely nervous. Nor was the reason for this difficult to divine. Some twenty minutes had elapsed, and there were still no signs of the bride-to-be, and nothing so surely saps the morale of a bridegroom on his wedding day as the failure of the party of the second part to put in an appearance at the tryst.

One of the things that made Lord Emsworth such a fascinating travelling companion was the fact that shortly after the start of any journey he always fell into a restful sleep. The train bearing him and guests to Market Blandings had glided from the platform of Paddington Station, as promised by the railway authorities, whose word is their bond, at 11.45, and at 12.10 he was lying back in his seat with his eyes closed, making little whistling noises punctuated at intervals by an occasional snort. Lord Ickenham, accordingly, was able to talk to the junior member of the party without the risk, always to be avoided when there is plotting afoot, of being overheard.

'Nervous, Bill?' he said, regarding the Rev. Cuthbert sympathetically. He had seemed to notice during the early stages of the journey a tendency on the other's part to twitch like a galvanized frog and allow a sort of glaze to creep over his eyes.

Bill Bailey breathed deeply.

'I'm feeling as I did when I tottered up the pulpit steps to deliver my first sermon.'

'I quite understand. While there is no more admirably educational experience for a young fellow starting out in life than going to stay at a country house under a false name, it does tend to chill the feet to no little extent. Pongo, though he comes from a stout-hearted family, felt just as you do when I took him to Blandings Castle as Sir Roderick Glossop's nephew Basil. I remember telling him at the time that he reminded me of Hamlet. The same moodiness and irresolution, coupled with a strongly marked disposition to get out of the train and walk back to London. Having become accustomed to this kind of thing myself, so much so that now I don't think it quite sporting to go to stay with people under my own name, I have lost that cat-on-hot-bricks feeling which I must have had at one time, but I can readily imagine that for a novice an experience of this sort cannot fail to be quite testing. Your sermon was a success, I trust?'

'Well, they didn't rush the pulpit.'

'You are too modest, Bill Bailey. I'll bet you had them rolling in the aisles and carried out on stretchers. And this visit to Blandings Castle will, I know, prove equally triumphant.'

'He wanted Myra to have a London season.'

'Just the kindly sort of thing he would do. Did she enjoy it?'

Lady Constance frowned.

'I was unfortunately obliged to take her away from London after we had been there a few weeks. I found that she had become involved with a quite impossible young man.'

There was shocked horror in Lord Ickenham's 'Tut-tut!'

'She insisted that they were engaged. Absurd, of course.'

'Why absurd?'

'He is a curate.'

'I have known some quite respectable curates.'

'Have you ever known one who had any money?'

'Well, no. They don't often have much, do they? I suppose a curate who was quick with his fingers would make a certain amount out of the Sunday offertory bag, but nothing more than a small, steady income.'

'Bill was out taking a stroll just now, and she came along. He said, "Oh, hullo. Nice morning".'

'And she said "Quate"?'

'No, she said, "I should like a word with you, Mr Bailey".'

'Mr *Bailey*? She knew who he was?'

'She's known from the moment he got here. Apparently when she lived in London, she used to mess about in Bottleton East, doing good works among the poor and all that, so of course she saw him there and recognized him when he showed up at the Castle. Bill's is the sort of face one remembers.'

Lord Ickenham agreed that it did indeed stamp itself on the mental retina. He was looking grave. Expecting at the outset to be called on to deal with some trifling girlish malaise, probably imaginary, he saw that here was a major crisis. If defied, he realized, Lavender Briggs would at once take Lady Constance into her confidence, with the worst results. Hell has no fury like a woman scorned, and very few like a woman who finds that she has been tricked into entertaining at her home a curate at the thought of whom she has been shuddering for weeks. Unquestionably Lady Constance would take umbrage. There would be pique on her part, and even dudgeon, and Bill's visit to Blandings Castle would be abruptly curtailed. In a matter of minutes the unfortunate young pastor of souls would be slung out of this Paradise on his ear like Lucifer, son of the morning.

'And then?'

'She said he had got to steal the pig.'

'And what did he say?'

'He told her to go to hell.'

'Strange advice from a curate.'

'I'm just giving you the rough idea.'

'Quate.'

'Actually, he said Lord Emsworth was his host and had been very kind to him, and he was very fond of him and he'd be darned if he'd bring his grey hairs in sorrow to the grave by pinching his pig, and apart from that what would his bishop have to say, if the matter was drawn to his attention?'

Lord Ickenham nodded.

'One sees what he meant. Curates must watch their step. One false move, like being caught stealing pigs, and bang goes any chance they may have had of rising to become Princes of the Church. And she – ?'

'Told him to think it over, the – '

Lord Ickenham raised a hand.

'I know the word that is trembling on your lips, child, but don't utter it. Let us keep the conversation at as high a level as possible. Well, I agree with you that the crisis is one that calls for thought. I wonder if the simplest thing might not be for Bill just to fold his tent like the Arabs and silently steal away.'

'You mean leave the castle? Leave me?'

'It seems the wise move.'

'I won't have him steal away!'

'Surely it is better to steal away than a pig?'

'I'd die here without him. Can't you think of something better than that?'

'What we want is to gain time.'

'How can we? The – '

'Please!'

'The woman said she had to have his answer tomorrow.'

'As soon as that? Well, Bill will have to consent and tell her that she must give him a couple of days to nerve himself to the task.'

'What's the good of that?'

'We gain time.'

'Only two days.'

'But two days during which I shall be giving the full force of the Ickenham brain to the problem, and there are few problems capable of standing up to that treatment for long. They can't take it.'

'And when the two days are up and you haven't thought of anything?'

'Why, then,' admitted Lord Ickenham, 'the situation becomes a little sticky.'

'There are many things you do not know, Miss Briggs,' said Lord Ickenham gravely, 'including the fact that you have got a large smut on your nose.'

'Oh, have I?' said Lavender Briggs, opening her bag in a flutter and reaching hurriedly for her mirror. She plied the cleansing tissue. 'Is that better?'

'Practically perfect. I wish I could say as much for your general position.'

'I don't understand.'

'You will. You're in the soup, Miss Briggs. The gaff has been blown, and the jig is up. The pitiless light of day has been thrown on your pig-purloining plans. Bill Bailey has told all.'

'What!'

'Yes, he has squealed to the FBI. Where you made your mistake was in under-estimating his integrity. These curates have scruples. The Reverend Cuthbert Bailey's are the talk of Bottleton East. Your proposition revolted him, and only the fact that you didn't offer him any kept him from spurning your gold. He went straight to Lord Emsworth and came clean.'

Mr Schoonmaker, who had been pacing the floor in the manner popularized by tigers at a zoo, suddenly halted in mid-stride, and the animation died out of his face as though turned off with a switch. He looked like a man suddenly reminded of something unpleasant, as indeed he had been.

'Who's this guy Meriwether?' he demanded.

'Meriwether?' said Lord Ickenham, who had had an idea that the name would be coming up shortly. 'Didn't Connie tell you about him?'

'Only that you brought him here.'

Lord Ickenham could understand this reticence. He recalled that his hostess, going into the matter at their recent conference, had decided that silence was best. It would have been difficult, as she had said, were she to place the facts before her betrothed, to explain why she had allowed Bill to continue enjoying her hospitality.

'Yes, I brought him here. He's a young friend of mine. His name actually is Bailey, but he generally travels incognito. He's a curate. He brushes and polishes the souls of the parishioners of Bottleton East, a district of London, where he is greatly respected. I'll tell you something about Bill Bailey, Jimmy. I have an idea he's a good deal attracted by your daughter Myra. Not easy to tell for certain because he wears the mask, but I wouldn't be at all surprised if he wasn't in love with her. One or two little signs I've noticed. Poor lad, it must have been a sad shock for him when he learned that she's going to marry Archie Gilpin.'

Mr Schoonmaker snorted. This habit of his of behaving like a bursting paper bag was new to Lord Ickenham. Probably, he thought, a mannerism acquired since his rise to riches. No doubt there was some form of unwritten law that compelled millionaires to act that way.

'She isn't,' said Mr Schoonmaker.

'Isn't what?'

'Going to marry Archie Gilpin. She eloped with Meriwether this morning.'

'You astound me. Are you sure? Where did you hear that?'

'She left a note for Connie.'

'Well, this is wonderful news,' said Lord Ickenham, his face lighting up. 'I'm not surprised you're dancing about all over the place on the tips of your toes. He's a splendid young fellow. Boxed three years for Oxford and, so I learn from a usually reliable source, went through the opposition like a dose of salts. I congratulate you, Jimmy.'

Mr Schoonmaker seemed to be experiencing some difficulty in sharing his joyous enthusiasm.

'I call it a disaster. Connie thinks so, too – that's why she was in floods of tears. And she says you're responsible.'

'Who, me?' said Lord Ickenham, amazed, not knowing that the copyright in those words was held by George Cyril Wellbeloved. 'What had I got to do with it?'

'You brought him here.'

'Merely because I thought he looked a little peaked and needed a breath of country air. Honestly, Jimmy,' said Lord Ickenham, speaking rather severely, 'I don't see what you're beefing about. If I hadn't brought him here, he wouldn't have eloped with Myra, thus causing Connie to burst into floods of tears, thus causing you to lose your diffidence and take her hand gently in yours and say, "Connie, darling". If it hadn't been for these outside stimuli, you would still be calling her Lady Constance and wincing like a salted snail every time you saw her profile. You ought to be thanking me on bended knee, unless the passage of time has made you stiff in the joints. What's your objection to Bill Bailey?'

'Connie says he hasn't a cent to his name.'

'Well, you've enough for all. Haven't you ever heard of sharing the wealth?'

'I don't like Myra marrying a curate.'

'The very husband you should have wished her. The one thing a financier wants is a clergyman in the family. What happens next time the Senate Commission has you on the carpet and starts a probe? You say "As proof of my respectability, gentlemen, I may mention that my daughter is married to a curate. You don't find curates marrying into a man's family if there's anything fishy about him", and they look silly and apologize.'

STIFF UPPER LIP, JEEVES

The following extracts have all been taken from this novel, featuring Bertie Wooster, much of the plot of which concerns 'Stiffy' Byng's efforts to improve the career prospects of her curate fiancé, the Reverend 'Stinker' Pinker. Now read on. . . .

I was trying to tell myself that all this Totleigh Towers business was purely coincidental and meant nothing, when the smoking-room waiter slid up and informed me that a gentleman stood without, asking to have speech with me. A clerical gentleman named Pinker, he said, and I gave another of my visible starts, the presentiment stronger on the wing than ever.

It wasn't that I had any objection to the sainted Pinker. I loved him like a b. We were up at Oxford together, and our relations have always been on strictly David and Jonathan lines. But while technically not a resident of Totleigh Towers, he helped the vicar vet the souls of the local yokels in the adjoining village of Totleigh-in-the-Wold, and that was near enough to it to make this sudden popping up of his deepen the apprehension I was feeling. It seemed to me that it only needed Sir Watkyn Bassett, Madeline Bassett, Roderick Spode and the dog Bartholomew to saunter in arm in arm, and I would have a full hand. My respect for my guardian angel's astuteness hit a new high. A gloomy bird, with a marked disposition to take the dark view and make one's flesh creep, but there was no gainsaying that he knew his stuff.

'Bung him in,' I said dully, and in due season the Rev. H. P. Pinker lumbered across the threshold and advancing with outstretched hand tripped over his feet and upset a small table, his almost invariable practice when moving from spot to spot in any room where there's furniture.

Which was odd, when you came to think of it, because after representing his University for four years and his country for six on the football field, he still turns out for the Harlequins when he can get a Saturday off from saving souls, and when footballing is as steady on his pins as a hart or roe or whatever the animals are that don't trip over their feet and upset things. I've seen him a couple of times in the arena, and was profoundly impressed by his virtuosity. Rugby football is more or less a sealed book to me, I never having gone in for it, but even I could see that he was good. The lissomness with which he moved hither and thither was most impressive, as was his homicidal ardour when 'doing what I believe is called tackling. Like the Canadian Mounted Police he always got his man, and when he did so the air was vibrant with the excited cries of morticians in the audience making bids for the body.

He's engaged to be married to Stiffy Byng, and his long years of football should prove an excellent preparation for setting up house with her. The way I look at it is that when a fellow has had pluguglies in cleated boots doing a Shuffle-Off-To-Buffalo on his face Saturday after Saturday since he was a slip of a boy, he must get to fear nothing, not even marriage with a girl like Stiffy, who from early childhood has seldom let the sun go down without starting some loony enterprise calculated to bleach the hair of one and all.

There was plenty and to spare of the Rev. H. P. Pinker. Even as a boy, I imagine, he must have burst seams and broken try-your-weight machines, and grown to man's estate he might have been Roderick Spode's twin brother. Purely in the matter of thews, sinews and tonnage, I mean, of course, for whereas Roderick Spode went about seeking whom he might devour and was a consistent menace to pedestrians and traffic, Stinker, though no doubt a fiend in human shape when assisting the Harlequins Rugby football club to dismember some rival troupe of athletes, was in private life a gentle soul with whom a child could have played. In fact, I once saw a child doing so.

Usually when you meet this man of God, you find him beaming. I believe his merry smile is one of the sights of Totleigh-in-the-Wold, as it was of Magdalen College, Oxford, when we were up there together. But now I seemed to note in his aspect a certain gravity, as if he had just discovered schism in his flock or found a couple of choir boys smoking reefers in the churchyard. He gave me the impression of a two-hundred-pound curate with something on his mind beside his hair. Upsetting another table, he took a seat and said he was glad he had caught me.

'I thought I'd find you at the Drones.'

'You have,' I assured him. 'What brings you to the metrop?'

'I came up for a Harlequins committee meeting.'

'And how were they all?'

'Oh, fine.'

'That's good. I've been worrying myself sick about the Harlequins committee. Well, how have you been keeping, Stinker?'

'I've been all right.'

'Are you free for dinner?'

'Sorry, I've got to get back to Totleigh.'

'Too bad. Jeeves tells me Sir Watkyn and Madeline and Stiffy have been staying with my aunt at Brinkley.'

'Yes.'

'Have they returned?'

'Yes.'

'And how's Stiffy?'

'Oh, fine.'

'And Bartholomew?'

'Oh, fine.'

'And your parishioners? Going strong, I trust?'

'Oh yes, they're fine.'

I wonder if anything strikes you about the slice of give-and-take I've just recorded. No? Oh, surely. I mean, here were we, Stinker Pinker and Bertram Wooster, buddies who had known each other virtually from the egg, and we were talking like a couple of strangers making conversation on a train. At least, he was, and more and more I became convinced that his bosom was full of the perilous stuff that weighs upon the heart, as I remember Jeeves putting it once.

I persevered in my efforts to uncork him.

'Well, Stinker,' I said, 'what's new? Has Pop Bassett given you that vicarage yet?'

This caused him to open up a bit. His manner became more animated.

'No, not yet. He doesn't seem able to make up his mind. One day he says he will, the next day he says he's not so sure, he'll have to think it over.'

I frowned. I disapproved of this shilly-shallying. I could see how it must be throwing a spanner into Stinker's whole foreign policy, putting him in a spot and causing him alarm and despondency. He can't marry Stiffy on a curate's stipend, so they've got to wait till Pop Bassett gives him a vicarage which he has in his gift. And while I personally, though fond of the young gumboil, would run a mile in tight shoes to avoid marrying Stiffy, I knew him to be strongly in favour of signing her up.

'Something always happens to put him off. I think he was about ready to close the deal before he went to stay at Brinkley, but most unfortunately I bumped into a valuable vase of his and broke it. It seemed to rankle rather.'

I heaved a sigh. It's always what Jeeves would call most disturbing to hear that a chap with whom you have plucked the gowans fine, as the expression is, isn't making out as well as could be wished. I was all set to follow this Pinker's career with considerable interest, but the way things were shaping it began to look as if there wasn't going to be a career to follow.

'You move in a mysterious way your wonders to perform, Stinker. I believe you would bump into something if you were crossing the Gobi desert.'

'I've never been in the Gobi desert.'

'Well, don't go. It isn't safe.'

'You can't say Uncle Watkyn isn't a dirty dog.'

'I would never dream of saying he isn't – and always has been – the dirtiest of dogs. It bears out what I have frequently maintained, that there are no depths to which magistrates won't stoop. I don't wonder you look askance. Your Uncle Watkyn stands revealed as a chiseller of the lowest type. But nothing to be done about it, of course.'

'I don't know so much about that.'

'Why, have you tried doing anything?'

'In a sort of way. I arranged that Harold should preach a very strong sermon on Naboth's Vineyard. Not that I suppose you've ever heard of Naboth's Vineyard.'

I bridled. She had offended my *amour propre*.

'I doubt if there's a man in London and the home counties who has the facts relating to Naboth's Vineyard more thoroughly at his fingertips than me. The news may not have reached you, but when at school I once won a prize for Scripture Knowledge.'

'I bet you cheated.'

'Not at all. Sheer merit. Did Stinker co-operate?'

'Yes, he thought it was a splendid idea and went about sucking throat pastilles for a week, so as to be in good voice.'

I would have liked to put him abreast of this latest development, but, as I say, there are things we don't discuss, so I merely drank deep of the flowing bowl and told him that Gussie had just been a pleasant visitor.

'He tells me Stinker Pinker wants to see ʳᵉ about something.'

'No doubt with reference to the episode of Sir Watkyn and the hard-boiled egg, sir.'

'Don't tell me it was Stinker who threw it.'

'No, sir, the miscreant is believed to have been a lad in his early teens. But the young fellow's impulsive action has led to unfortunate consequences. It has caused Sir Watkyn to entertain doubts as to the wisdom of entrusting a vicarage to a curate incapable of maintaining order at a School Treat. Miss Byng, while confiding this information to me, appeared greatly distressed. She had supposed – I quote her verbatim – that the thing was in the bag, and she is naturally much disturbed.'

Gussie was saved the necessity of searching for words by the fact that he was being shaken like a cocktail in a manner that precluded speech, if precluded is the word I want. His spectacles fell off and came to rest near where I was standing. I picked them up with a view to returning them to him when he had need of them, which I could see would not be immediately.

As this Fink-Nottle was a boyhood friend, with whom, as I have said, I had frequently shared my last bar of milk chocolate, and as it was plain that if someone didn't intervene pretty soon he was in danger of having all his internal organs shaken into a sort of macédoine or hash, the thought of taking some steps to put an end to this distressing scene naturally crossed my mind. The problem presenting several points of interest was, of course, what steps to take. My tonnage was quite insufficient to enable me to engage Spode in hand to hand conflict, and I toyed with the idea of striking him on the back of the head with a log of wood. But this project was rendered null and void by the fact that there were no logs of wood present. These yew alleys or rhododendron walks provide twigs and fallen leaves, but nothing in the shape of logs capable of being used as clubs. And I had just decided that something might be accomplished by leaping on Spode's back and twining my arms around his neck, when I heard Stiffy cry 'Harold!'

One gathered what she was driving at. Gussie was no particular buddy of hers, but she was a tender-hearted young prune and one always likes to save a fellow creature's life, if possible. She was calling on Stinker to get into the act and save Gussie's. And a quick look at him showed me that he was at a loss to know how to proceed. He stood there passing a finger thoughtfully over his chin, like a cat in an adage.

I knew what was stopping him getting action. It was not . . . it's on the tip of my tongue . . . begins with a p . . . I've heard Jeeves use the word . . . pusillanimity, that's it, meaning broadly that a fellow is suffering from a pronounced case of cold feet . . . it was not, as I was saying when I interrupted myself, pusillanimity that held him back. Under normal conditions lions could have taken his correspondence course, and had he encountered Spode on the football field, he would have had no hesitation in springing at his neck and twisting it into a lover's knot. The trouble was that he was a curate, and the brass hats of the Church look askance at curates who swat the parishioners. Sock your flock, and you're sunk. So now he shrank from intervening, and when he did intervene, it was merely with the soft word that's supposed to turn away wrath.

'I say, you know, what?' he said.

I could have told him he was approaching the thing from the wrong angle. When a gorilla like Spode is letting his angry passions rise, there is little or no percentage in the mild remonstrance. Seeming to realize this, he advanced to where the blighter was now, or so it appeared, trying to strangle Gussie and laid a hand on his shoulder. Then, seeing that this, too, achieved no solid results, he pulled. There was a rending sound, and the clutching hand relaxed its grip.

I don't know if you've ever tried detaching a snow leopard of the Himalayas from its prey – probably not, as most people don't find themselves out that way much – but if you did, you would feel fairly safe in budgeting for a show of annoyance on the animal's part. It was the same with Spode. Incensed at what I suppose seemed to him this unwarrantable interference with his aims and objects, he hit Stinker on the nose, and all the doubts that had been bothering that man of God vanished in a flash.

I should imagine that if there's one thing that makes a fellow forget that he's in Holy Orders, it's a crisp punch on the beezer. A moment before, Stinker had been all concern about the disapproval of his superiors in the Cloth, but now, as I read his mind, he was saying to himself, 'To hell with my superiors in the Cloth', or however a curate would put it, 'Let them eat cake'.

It was a superb spectacle while it lasted, and I was able to understand what people meant when they spoke of the Church Militant. A good deal to my regret, it did not last long. Spode was full of the will to win, but Stinker had the science. It was not for nothing that he had added a boxing blue to his football blue when at the old Alma Mater. There was a brief mix-up, and the next thing one observed was Spode on the ground, looking like the corpse which had been in the water several days. His left eye was swelling visibly, and a referee could have counted a hundred over him without eliciting a response.

Stiffy, with a brief 'At-a-boy!', led Stinker off, no doubt to bathe his nose and staunch the vital flow, which was considerable, and I handed Gussie his glasses. He stood twiddling them in a sort of trance, and I made a suggestion which I felt was in his best interests.

'Not presuming to dictate, Gussie, but wouldn't it be wise to remove yourself before Spode comes to? From what I know of him, I think he's one of those fellows who wake up cross.'

I have seldom seen anyone move quicker. We were out of the yew alley, if it was a yew alley, or the rhododendron walk, if that's what it was, almost before the words had left my lips. We continued to set a good pace, but eventually we slowed up a bit, and he was able to comment on the recent scene.

'That was a ghastly experience, Bertie,' he said.

'Can't have been at all pleasant,' I agreed.

'My whole past life seemed to flash before me.'

'That's odd. You weren't drowning.'

'No, but the principle's the same. I can tell you I was thankful when Pinker made his presence felt. What a splendid chap he is.'

'One of the best.'

'That's what today's Church needs, more curates capable of hauling off and letting fellows like Spode have it where it does most good. One feels so safe when he's around.'

I put a point which seemed to have escaped his notice.

'But he won't always be around. He has Infants' Bible Classes and Mothers' Meetings and all that sort of thing to occupy his time. And don't forget that Spode, though crushed to earth, will rise again.'

His jaw sagged a bit.

'I never thought of that.'

'If you take my advice, you'll clear out and go underground for a while. Stiffy would lend you her car.'

'I believe you're right,' he said, adding something about out of the mouths of babes and sucklings which I thought a bit offensive. 'I'll leave this evening.'

'I'm glad to see you so cheerful, Uncle Watkyn. I was afraid my news might have upset you.'

'Upset me!' said Pop Bassett incredulously. 'Whatever put that idea in your head?'

'Well, you're short one son-in-law .'

'It is precisely that that has made this the happiest day of my life.'

'Then you can make it the happiest of mine,' said Stiffy, striking while the iron was h. 'By giving Harold that vicarage.'

Most of my attention, as you may well imagine, being concentrated on contemplating the soup in which I was immersed, I cannot say whether or not Pop Bassett hesitated, but if he did, it was only for an instant. No doubt for a second or two the vision of that hard-boiled egg rose before him and he was conscious again of the resentment he had been feeling at Stinker's failure to keep a firm hand on the junior members of his flock, but the thought that Augustus Fink-Nottle was not to be his son-in-law drove the young cleric's shortcomings from his mind. Filled with the milk of human kindness so nearly to the brim that you could almost hear it sloshing about inside him, ne was in no shape to deny anyone anything. I really believe that if at this point in the proceedings I had tried to touch him for a fiver, he would have parted without a cry.

'Of course, of course, of course, of course,' he said, carolling like one of Jeeves's larks on the wing. 'I am sure that Pinker will make an excellent vicar.'

'The best,' said Stiffy. 'He's wasted as a curate. No scope, running under wraps. Unleash him as a vicar, and he'll be the talk of the established church. He's as hot as a pistol.'

'I have always had the highest opinion of Harold Pinker.'

'I'm not surprised. All the nibs feel the same. They know he's got what it takes. Very sound on doctrine, and can preach like a streak.'

'Yes, I enjoy his sermons. Manly and straightforward.'

'That's because he's one of these healthy outdoor open air men. Muscular Christianity, that's his dish. He used to play football for England.'

'Indeed?'

'He was what's called a prop forward.'

'Really?'

At the words 'prop forward' I had, of course, started visibly. I hadn't known that that's what Stinker was, and I was thinking how ironical life could be. I mean to say, there was Plank searching high and low for a forward of this nature, saying to himself that he would pretty soon have to give up the hopeless quest, and there was I in a position to fill the bill for him, but owing to the strained condition of our relations unable to put him on to this good thing. Very sad, I felt, and the thought occurred to me, as it had often done before, that one ought to be kind even to the very humblest, because you never know when they may not come in useful.

'Then may I tell Harold that the balloon's going up?' said Stiffy.

'I beg your pardon?'

'I mean it's official about this vicarage?'

'Certainly, certainly, certainly.'

'Oh, Uncle Watkyn! How can I thank you?'

'Quite all right, my dear,' said Pop Bassett, more Dickensy than ever. 'And now,' he went on, parting from his moorings and making for the door, 'you will excuse me, Stephanie, and you, Mr Wooster. I must go to Madeline and – '

'Congratulate her?'

'I was about to say dry her tears.'

'If any.'

'You think she will not be in a state of dejection?'

'Would any girl be, who's been saved by a miracle from having to marry Gussie Fink-Nottle?'

'True. Very true,' said Pop Bassett, and he was out of the room like one of those wing threequarters who, even if they can't learn to give the reverse pass, are fast.

If there had been any uncertainty as to whether Sir Watkyn Bassett had done a buck-and-wing dance, there was none about Stiffy doing one now. She pirouetted freely, and the dullest eye could discern that it was only the fact that she hadn't one on that kept her from strewing roses from her hat. I had seldom seen a young shrimp so above herself. And I, having Stinker's best interests at heart, packed all my troubles in the old kitbag for the time being and rejoiced with her. If there's one thing Bertram Wooster is and always has been nippy at, it's forgetting his personal worries when a pal is celebrating some stroke of good fortune.

For some time Stiffy monopolized the conversation, not letting me get a word in edgeways. Women are singularly gifted in this respect. The frailest of them has the lung power of a gramophone record and the flow of speech of a Regimental Sergeant Major. I have known my Aunt Agatha to go on calling me names long after you would have supposed that both breath and inventiveness would have given out.

Her theme was the stupendous bit of good luck which was about to befall Stinker's new parishioners, for they would be getting not only the perfect vicar, a saintly character who would do the square thing by their souls, but in addition the sort of vicar's wife you dream about. It was only when she paused after drawing a picture of herself doling out soup to the deserving poor and asking in a gentle voice after their rheumatism that I was able to rise to a point of order. In the midst of all the joyfulness and back-slapping a sobering thought had occurred to me.

'I agree with you,' I said, 'that this would appear to be the happy ending, and I can quite see how you have arrived at the conclusion that it's the maddest merriest day of all the glad new year, but there's something you ought to give a thought to, and it seems to me you're overlooking it.'

'What's that? I didn't think I'd missed anything.'

'This promise of Pop Bassett's to give you the vicarage.'

'All in order, surely? What's your kick?'

'I was only thinking that, if I were you, I'd get it in writing.'

This stopped her as if she had bumped into a prop forward. The ecstatic animation faded from her face, to be replaced by the anxious look and the quick chewing of the lower lip. It was plain that I had given her food for thought.

'You don't think Uncle Watkyn would doublecross us?'

'There are no limits to what your foul Uncle Watkyn can do, if the mood takes him,' I responded gravely. 'I wouldn't trust him an inch. Where's Stinker?'

'Out on the lawn, I think.'

'Then get hold of him and bring him here and have Pop Bassett embody the thing in the form of a letter.'

'I suppose you know you're making my flesh creep?'

'Merely pointing out the road to safety.'

She mused awhile, and the lower lip got a bit more chewing done to it.

'All right,' she said at length. 'I'll fetch Harold.'

'And it wouldn't hurt to bring a couple of lawyers, too,' I said as she whizzed past me.

*   *   *

I was able to remain calm and nonchalant, or as calm and nonchalant as you can be when a fellow eight foot six in height with one eye bunged up and the other behaving like an oxyacetylene blowpipe is glaring at you.

'Yes, sir,' said Spode, 'it'll be chokey for you.'

And he was going on to say that he would derive great pleasure from coming on visiting days and making faces at me through the bars, when Pop Bassett returned.

But a very different Bassett from the fizzy rejoicer who had exited so short a while before. Then he had been all buck and beans, as any father would have been whose daughter was not going to marry Gussie Fink-Nottle. Now his face was drawn and his general demeanour that of an incautious luncher who discovers when there is no time to draw back that he has swallowed a rather too elderly oyster.

'Madeline tells me,' he began. Then he saw Spode's eye, and broke off. It was the sort of eye which, even if you have a lot on your mind, you can't help noticing. 'Good gracious, Roderick,' he said, 'did you have a fall?'

'Fall, my foot,' said Spode, 'I was socked by a curate.'

'Good heavens! What curate?'

'There's only one in these parts, isn't there?'

'You mean you were assaulted by Mr Pinker? You astound me, Roderick.'

Spode spoke with genuine feeling.

'Not half as much as he astounded *me*. He was more or less of a revelation to me, I don't mind telling you, because I didn't know curates had left hooks like that. He's got a knack of feinting you off balance and then coming in with a sort of corkscrew punch which it's impossible not to admire. I must get him to teach it to me some time.'

'You speak as though you bore him no animosity.'

'Of course I don't. A very pleasant little scrap with no ill feeling on either side. I've nothing against Pinker. The one I've got it in for is the cook. She beaned me with a china basin. From behind, of all unsporting things. If you'll excuse me, I'll go and have a word with that cook.'

He was so obviously looking forward to telling Emerald Stoker what he thought of her that it gave me quite a pang to have to break it to him that his errand would be bootless.

'You can't,' I pointed out. 'She is no longer with us.'

'Don't be an ass. She's in the kitchen, isn't she?'

'I'm sorry, no. She's eloped with Gussie Fink-Nottle. A wedding has been arranged and will take place as soon as the Archbish of Canterbury lets him have a special licence.'

Stinker's nose, as was only to be expected, had swollen a good deal since last heard from, but he seemed in excellent spirits, and Stiffy couldn't have been merrier and brighter. Both were obviously thinking in terms of the happy ending, and my heart bled freely for the unfortunate young slobs. I had observed Pop Bassett closely while Spode was telling him about Stinker's left hook, and what I had read on his countenance had not been encouraging.

These patrons of livings with vicarages to bestow always hold rather rigid views as regards the qualifications they demand from the curates they are thinking of promoting to fields of higher activity, and left hooks, however adroit, are not among them. If Pop Bassett had been a fight promoter on the look-out for talent and Stinker a promising novice anxious to be put on his next programme for a six-round preliminary bout, he would no doubt have gazed on him with a kindly eye. As it was, the eye he was now directing at him was as cold and bleak as if an old crony had been standing before him in the dock, charged with having moved pigs without a permit or failed to abate a smoky chimney. I could see trouble looming, and I wouldn't have risked a bet on the happy e. even at the most liberal odds.

The stickiness of the atmosphere, so patent to my keener sense, had not communicated itself to Stiffy. No voice was whispering in her ear that she was about to be let down with a thud which would jar her to the back teeth. She was all smiles and viv-whatever-the-word-is, plainly convinced that the signing on the dotted line was now a mere formality.

'Here we are, Uncle Watkyn,' she said, beaming freely.

'So I see.'

'I've brought Harold.'

'So I perceive.'

'We've talked it over, and we think we ought to have the thing embodied in the form of a letter.'

Pop Bassett's eye grew colder and bleaker, and the feeling I had that we were all back in Bosher Street Police Court deepened. Nothing, it seemed to me, was needed to complete the illusion except a magistrate's clerk with a cold in the head, a fug you could cut with a knife and a few young barristers hanging about hoping for dock briefs.

'I fear I do not understand you,' he said.

'Oh, come, Uncle Watkyn, you know you're brighter than that. I'm talking about Harold's vicarage.'

'I was not aware that Mr Pinker had a vicarage.'

'The one you're going to give him, I mean.'

'Oh?' said Pop Bassett, and I have seldom heard an 'Oh?' that had a nastier sound. 'I have just seen Roderick,' he added, getting down to the *res*.

At the mention of Spode's name Stiffy giggled, and I could have told her it was a mistake. There is a time for girlish frivolity, and a time when it is misplaced. It had not escaped my notice that Pop Bassett had begun to swell like one of those curious circular fish you catch down in Florida, and in addition to this he was rumbling as I imagine volcanoes do before starting in on the neighbouring householders and making them wish they had settled elsewhere.

But even now Stiffy seemed to have no sense of impending doom. She uttered another silvery laugh. I've noticed this slowness in getting hep to atmospheric conditions in other girls. The young of the gentler sex never appear to realize that there are moments when the last thing required by their audience is the silvery laugh.

'I'll bet he had a shiner.'

'I beg your pardon?'

'Was his eye black?'

'It was.'

'I thought it would be. Harold's strength is as the strength of ten, because his heart is pure. Well, how about that embodying letter? I have a fountain pen. Let's get the show on the road.'

I was expecting Pop Bassett to give an impersonation of a bomb falling on an ammunition dump, but he didn't. Instead, he continued to exhibit that sort of chilly stiffness which you see in magistrates when they're fining people five quid for boyish peccadilloes.

'You appear to be under a misapprehension, Stephanie,' he said in the metallic voice he had once used when addressing the prisoner Wooster. 'I have no intention of entrusting Mr Pinker with a vicarage.'

Stiffy took it big. She shook from wind-swept hair-do to shoe-sole, and if she hadn't clutched at Stinker's arm might have taken a toss. One could understand her emotion. She had been coasting along, confident that she had it made, and suddenly out of a blue and smiling sky these words of doom. No doubt it was the suddenness and unexpectedness of the wallop that unmanned her, if you can call it unmanning when it happens to a girl. I suppose she was feeling very much as Spode had felt when Emerald Stoker's basin had connected with his occiput. Her eyes bulged, and her voice came out in a passionate squeak.

'But, Uncle Watkyn! You promised!'

I could have told her she was wasting her breath trying to appeal to the old buzzard's better feelings, because magistrates, even when ex, don't have any. The tremolo in her voice might have been expected to melt what is usually called a heart of stone, but it had no more effect on Pop Bassett than the chirping of the household canary.

'Provisionally only,' he said. 'I was not aware, when I did so, that Mr Pinker had brutally assaulted Roderick.'

At these words Stinker, who had been listening to the exchanges in a rigid sort of way, creating the illusion that he had been stuffed by a good taxidermist, came suddenly to life, though as all he did was make a sound like the last drops of water going out of a bath tub, it was hardly worth the trouble and expense. He succeeded, however, in attracting Pop Bassett's attention, and the latter gave him the eye.

'Yes, Mr Pinker?'

It was a moment or two before Stinker followed up the gurgling noise with speech. And even then it wasn't much in the way of speech. He said:

'I – er – He – er –'

'Proceed, Mr Pinker.'

'It was – I mean it wasn't –'

'If you could make yourself a little plainer, Mr Pinker, it would be of great assistance to our investigations into the matter under discussion. I must confess to finding you far from lucid.'

It was the type of crack he had been accustomed in the old Bosher Street days to seeing in print with 'laughter' after it in brackets, but on this occasion it fell flatter than a Dover sole. It didn't get a snicker out of me, nor out of Stinker, who merely knocked over a small china ornament and turned a deeper vermilion, while Stiffy came back at him in great shape.

'There's no need to talk like a magistrate, Uncle Watkyn.'

'I beg your pardon?'

'In fact, it would be better if you stopped talking at all and let me explain. What Harold's trying to tell you is that he didn't brutally assault Roderick, Roderick brutally assaulted him.'

'Indeed? That was not the way I heard the story.'

'Well, it's the way it happened.'

'I am perfectly willing to hear your version of the deplorable incident.'

'All right, then. Here it comes. Harold was cooing to Roderick like a turtle dove, and Roderick suddenly hauled off and plugged him squarely on the beezer. If you don't believe me, take a look at it. The poor angel spouted blood like a Versailles fountain. Well, what would you have expected Harold to do? Turn the other nose?'

'I would have expected him to remember his position as a clerk in Holy Orders. He should have complained to me, and I would have seen to it that Roderick made ample apology.'

A sound like the shot heard round the world rang through the room. It was Stiffy snorting.

'Apology!' she cried, having got the snort out of her system. 'What's the good of apologies? Harold took the only possible course. He sailed in and laid Roderick out cold, as anyone would have done in his place.'

'Anyone who had not his cloth to think of.'

'For goodness' sake, Uncle Watkyn, a fellow can't be thinking of cloth all the time. It was an emergency. Roderick was murdering Gussie Fink-Nottle.'

'And Mr Pinker *stopped* him? Great heavens!'

.There was a pause while Pop Bassett struggled with his feelings. Then Stiffy, as Stinker had done with Spode, had a shot at the honeyed word. She had spoken of Stinker cooing to Spode like a turtle dove, and if memory served me aright that was just how he had cooed, and it was of a cooing turtle dove that she now reminded me. Like most girls, she can always get a melting note into her voice if she thinks there's any percentage to be derived from it.

'It's not like you, Uncle Watkyn, to go back on your solemn promise.'

I could have corrected her there. I would have thought it was just like him.

'I can't believe it's really you who's doing this cruel thing to me. It's so unlike you. You have always been so kind to me. You have made me love and respect you. I have come to look on you as a second father. Don't louse the whole thing up now.'

A powerful plea, which with any other man would undoubtedly have brought home the bacon. With Pop Bassett it didn't get to first base. He had been looking like a man with no bowels – of compassion, I mean, of course – and he went on looking like one.

'If by that peculiar expression you intend to imply that you are expecting me to change my mind and give Mr Pinker this vicarage, I must disappoint you. I shall do no such thing. I consider that he has shown himself unfit to be a vicar, and I am surprised that after what has occurred he can reconcile it with his conscience to continue his duties as a curate.'

Strong stuff, of course, and it drew from Stinker what may have been a hollow groan or may have been a hiccough. I myself looked coldly at the old egg and I rather think I curled my lip, though I should say it was very doubtful if he noticed.

'Do you happen to know where I can find a chap called Pinker?'

'My name's Pinker.'

'Are you sure? I thought Bassett said it was Wooster.'

'No, Wooster's the one who's going to marry Sir Watkyn's daughter.'

'So he is. It all comes back to me now. I wonder if you can be the fellow I want. The Pinker I'm after is a curate.'

'I'm a curate.'

'You are? Yes, by Jove, you're perfectly right. I see your collar buttons at the back. You're not H. P. Pinker by any chance?'

'Yes.'

'Prop forward for Oxford and England a few years ago?'

'Yes.'

'Well, would you be interested in becoming a vicar?'

There was a crashing sound, and I knew that Stinker in his emotion must have upset his customary table. After a while he said in a husky voice that the one thing he wanted was to get his hooks on a vicarge or words to that effect, and Plank said he was glad to hear it.

'My chap at Hockley-cum-Meston is downing tools now that his ninetieth birthday is approaching, and I've been scouring the countryside for a spare. Extraordinarily difficult the quest has been, because what I wanted was a vicar who was a good prop forward, and it isn't often you find a parson who knows one end of a football from the other. I've never seen you play, I'm sorry to say, because I've been abroad so much, but with your record you must obviously be outstanding. So you can take up your duties as soon as old Bellamy goes into storage. When I get home, I'll embody the thing in the form of a letter.'

Stinker said he didn't know how to thank him, and Plank said that was all right, no need of any thanks.

'I'm the one who ought to be grateful. We're all right at half-back and three-quarters, but we lost to Upper Bleaching last year simply because our prop forward proved a broken reed. This year we'll show 'em. Amazing bit of luck finding you, and I could never have done it if it hadn't been for a friend of mine, a Chief Inspector Witherspoon of Scotland Yard. He 'phoned me just now and told me you were to be found at Totleigh-in-the-Wold. He said if I called at Totleigh Towers, they would give me your address. Extraordinary how these Scotland Yard fellows nose things out.'

'Good evening, sir,' he said. 'Would you care for an appetizer? I was obliging Mr Butterfield by bringing them. He is engaged at the moment in listening at the door of the room where Sir Watkyn is in conference with Miss Bassett. He tells me he is compiling his Memoirs, never misses an opportunity of gathering suitable material.'

I gave the man one of my looks. My face was cold and hard, like a School Treat egg. I can't remember a time when I've been fuller of righteous indignation.

'What I want, Jeeves, is not a slab of wet bread with a dead sardine on it – '

'Anchovy, sir.'

'Or anchovy. I am in no mood to split straws. I require an explanation, and a categorical one, at that.'

'Sir?'

'You can't evade the issue by saying "Sir?" Answer me this, Jeeves, with a simple Yes or No. Why did you tell Plank to come to Totleigh Towers?'

I thought the query would crumple him up like a damp sock, but he didn't so much as shuffle a foot.

'My heart was melted by Miss Byng's tale of her misfortunes, sir. I chanced to encounter the young lady and found her in a state of considerable despondency as the result of Sir Watkyn's refusal to bestow a vicarage on Mr Pinker. I perceived immediately that it was within my power to alleviate her distress. I had learned at the post office at Hockley-cum-Meston that the incumbent there was retiring shortly, and being cognizant of Major Plank's desire to strengthen the Hockley-cum-Meston forward line, I felt that it would be an excellent idea to place him in communication with Mr Pinker. In order to be in a position to marry Miss Byng, Mr Pinker requires a vicarage, and in order to compete successfully with rival villages in the football arena Major Plank is in need of a vicar with Mr Pinker's wide experience as a prop forward. Their interests appeared to me to be identical.'

'Well, it worked all right. Stinker has clicked.'

'He is to succeed Mr Bellamy as incumbent at Hockley-cum-Meston?'

'As soon as Bellamy calls it a day.'

'I am very happy to hear it, sir.'

I didn't reply for a while, being obliged to attend to a sudden touch of cramp.

This ironed out, I said, still icy:

'You may be happy, but I haven't been for the last quarter of an hour or so, nestling behind the sofa and expecting Plank at any moment to unmask me. It didn't occur to you to envisage what would happen if he met me?'

'I was sure that your keen intelligence would enable you to find a means of avoiding him, sir, as indeed it did. You concealed yourself behind the sofa?'

'On all fours.'

'A very shrewd manoeuvre on your part, if I may say so, sir. It showed a resource and swiftness of thought which it would be difficult to overpraise.'

My iciness melted. It is not too much to say that I was mollified. It's not often that I'm given the old oil in this fashion, most of my circle, notably my Aunt Agatha, being more prone to the slam than the rave. And it was only after I had been savouring that 'keen intelligence' gag, if savouring is the word I want, for some moments that I suddenly remembered that marriage with Madeline Bassett loomed ahead, and I gave a start so visible that he asked me if I was feeling unwell.

I shook the loaf.

'Physically, no, Jeeves. Spiritually, yes.'

'I do not quite understand you, sir.'

'Well, here is the news, and this is Bertram Wooster reading it. I'm going to be married.'

'Indeed, sir?'

'Yes, Jeeves, married. The banns are as good as up.'

'Would it be taking a liberty if I were to ask – '

'Who to? You don't need to ask. Gussie Fink-Nottle has eloped with Emerald Stoker, thus creating a . . . what is it?'

'Would vacuum be the word you are seeking, sir?'

'That's right. A vacuum which I shall have to fill. Unless you can think of some way of getting me out of it.'

'I will devote considerable thought to the matter, sir.'

'Thank you, Jeeves,' I said, and would have spoken further, but at this moment I saw the door opening and speechlessness supervened. But it wasn't, as I had feared, Plank, it was only Stiffy.

'Hullo, you two,' she said. 'I'm looking for Harold.'

I could see at a g. that Jeeves had been right in describing her demeanour as despondent. The brow was clouded and the general appearance that of an overwrought soul. I was glad to be in a position to inject a little sunshine into her life. Pigeon-holing my own troubles for future reference, I said:

'He's looking for you. He has a strange story to relate. You know Plank?'

'What about him?'

'I'll tell you what about him. Plank to you hitherto has been merely a shadowy figure who hangs out at Hockley-cum-Meston and sells black amber statuettes to people, but he has another side to him.'

She betrayed a certain impatience.

'If you think I'm interested in Plank – '

'Aren't you?'

'No, I'm not.'

'You will be. He has, as I was saying, another side to him. He is a landed proprietor with vicarages in his gift, and to cut a long story down to a short-short, as one always likes to do when possible, he has just given one to Stinker.'

I had been right in supposing that the information would have a marked effect on her dark mood. I have never actually seen a corpse spring from its bier and start being the life and soul of the party, but I should imagine that its deportment would closely resemble that of this young Byng as the impact of my words came home to her. A sudden light shot into her eyes, which, as Plank had correctly said, were large and blue, and an ecstatic 'Well, Lord love a duck!' escaped her. Then the doubts seemed to creep in, for the eyes clouded over again.

'Is this true?'

'Absolutely official.'

'You aren't pulling my leg?'

I drew myself up rather haughtily.

'I wouldn't dream of pulling your leg. Do you think Bertram Wooster is the sort of chap who thinks it funny to raise people's hopes, only to . . . what, Jeeves?'

'Dash them to the ground, sir.'

'Thank you, Jeeves.'

'Not at all, sir.'

'You may take this information as coming straight from the mouth of the stable cat. I was present when the deal went through. Behind the sofa, but present.'

She still seemed at a loss.

'But I don't understand. Plank has never met Harold.'

'Jeeves brought them together.'

'Did you, Jeeves?'

'Yes, miss.'

'At-a-boy!'

'Thank you, miss.'

'And he's really given Harold a vicarage?'

'The vicarage of Hockley-cum-Meston. He's embodying it in the form of a letter tonight. At the moment there's a vicar still vicking, but he's infirm and old and wants to turn it up as soon as they can put on an understudy. The way things look, I should imagine that we shall be able to unleash Stinker on the Hockley-cum-Meston souls in the course of the next few days.'

My simple words and earnest manner had resolved the last of her doubts. The misgivings she may have had as to whether this was the real ginger vanished. Her eyes shone more like twin stars than anything, and she uttered animal cries and danced a few dance steps. Presently she paused, and put a question.

'What's Plank like?'

'How do you mean, what's he like?'

'He hasn't a beard, has he?'

'No, no beard.'

'That's good, because I want to kiss him, and if he had a beard, it would give me pause.'

'Dismiss the notion,' I urged, for Plank's psychology was an open book to me. The whole trend of that confirmed bachelor's conversation had left me with the impression that he would find it infinitely preferable to be spiked in the leg with a native dagger than to have popsies covering his upturned face with kisses. 'He'd have a fit.'

'Well, I must kiss somebody. Shall I kiss you, Jeeves?'

'No, thank you, miss.'

'You, Bertie?'

'I'd rather you didn't.'

'Then I've a good mind to go and kiss Uncle Watkyn, louse of the first water though he has recently shown himself.'

'How do you mean, recently?'

'And having kissed him I shall tell him the news and taunt him vigorously with having let a good thing get away from him. I shall tell him that when he declined to avail himself of Harold's services he was like the Indian.'

I did not get her drift.

'What Indian?'

'The base one my governesses used to make me read about, the poor simp whose hand . . How does it go, Jeeves?'

'Threw a pearl away richer than all his tribe, miss.'

'That's right. And I shall tell him I hope the vicar he does get will be a weed of a man who has a chronic cold in the head and bleats. Oh, by the way, talking of Uncle Watkyn reminds me. I shan't have any use for this now.'

And so speaking she produced the black amber eyesore from the recesses of her costume like a conjuror taking a rabbit out of a hat.

NUGGETS

I remember old Stinker Pinker, who towards the end of his career at Oxford used to go in for social service in London's tougher districts, describing to me once in some detail the sensations he had experienced one afternoon, while spreading the light in Bethnal Green, on being unexpectedly kicked in the stomach by a costermonger. It gave him, he told me, a strange, dreamy feeling, together with an odd illusion of having walked into a thick fog.

The Code of the Woosters, 1938

The Rev. 'Stinker' Pinker was dripping with high principles. . . .

The Code of the Woosters, 1938

Uncle Sidney looked a little taken aback for a moment, and seemed as if he were on the point of saying some of the things he gave up saying when he took Orders, but everything has turned out for the best.

The Mating Season, 1949

Three minutes later the revellers on the lawn were interested to observe a sight rare at the better class of English garden party. Out of a clump of laurel bushes that bordered the smoothly mown turf there came charging a stout, pink gentleman of middle age who hopped from side to side as he ran. He was wearing a loin-cloth, and seemed in a hurry. They had just time to recognize in this newcomer their hostess's brother, Colonel Sir Francis Pashley-Drake, when he snatched a cloth from the nearest table, draped it round him, and with a quick leap took refuge behind the portly form of the Bishop of Stortford, who was talking to the local Master of Hounds about the difficulty he had in keeping his vicars off the incense.

Charlotte and Aubrey had paused in the shelter of the laurels. Aubrey, peering through this zareba, clicked his tongue regretfully.

'He's taken cover again,' he said. 'I'm afraid we shall find it difficult to dig him out of there. He's gone to earth behind a bishop.'

'Unpleasantness at Bludleigh Court', *Mr Mulliner Speaking*, 1929

The cook burst into tears and said something about the Wrath of the Lord and the Cities of the Plain – she being a bit on the Biblical side.

'Ukridge and the Home from Home', *Lord Emsworth and Others*, 1937

A curate pal of mine in Limehouse had sprained his ankle while trying to teach the choir boys to dance the carioca.

Service with a Smile, 1962

On her face was the look of a mother whose daughter has seen the light and will shortly be marrying a deserving young clergyman with a bachelor uncle high up in the shipping business.

'The Go-Getter', *Blandings Castle and Elsewhere*, 1935

Anne Benedick had been waiting in the hall of Lord Uffenham's club some ten minutes before his lordship finally appeared, descending the broad staircase with one hand glued to the arm of a worried-looking bishop, with whom he was discussing Supra-lapsarianism. At the sight of Anne, he relaxed his grip, and the bishop shot gratefully off in the direction of the Silence Room.

Money in the Bank, 1946

'Not only were we scooped in and shanghaied to church twice on the Sunday, regardless of age or sex, but on the Monday morning at eight o'clock – eight, mark you – there were family prayers in the dining-room.'

'Fate', *Young Men in Spats*, 1936

'She is very far from being one of the boys. You needn't let it get about, of course, but that girl, to my certain knowledge, plays the organ in the local church and may often be seen taking soup to the deserving villagers with many a gracious word.'

'Fate', *Young Men in Spats*, 1936

It was one of those aloof smiles that the Honorary Secretary of a Bible Class might have given the elderly aunt of a promising pupil.

'Fate', *Young Men in Spats*, 1936

His trust in Bodmin the hatter is like the unspotted faith of a young curate in his bishop.

'The Amazing Hat Mystery', *Young Men in Spats*, 1936

'So that was that. A stunning blow, you will agree. Many fellows would have fallen crushed beneath it. But not me, Corky. Who was it said: "You can't keep a good man down"?'

'Jonah, taunting the whale.'

'Well, that was what I said to myself.'

'Success Story', *Nothing Serious*, 1950

'Certainly not, sir,' he said with cold rebuke, staring at me like an archdeacon who has found a choirboy sucking acid drops during divine service. 'Would you have me betray a position of trust?'

'Success Story', *Nothing Serious*, 1950

'And they plan to get married?'

'As soon as Gussie can get a special licence. You have to apply to the Archbishop of Canterbury, and I'm told he stings you for quite a bit.'

Stiff Upper Lip, Jeeves, 1963

At two minutes past five one Tuesday afternoon the venerable Bishop of Stortford, entering the room where his daughter Kathleen sat, found her engrossed in what he presumed to be a work of devotion but which proved on closer inspection to be a novel entitled *Cocktail Time*. Peeping over her shoulder, he was able to read a paragraph or two. She had got, it should be mentioned, to the middle of Chapter 13. At 5.05 sharp he was wrenching the volume from her grasp, at 5.06 tottering from the room, at 5.10 in his study scrutinizing Chapter 13 to see if he had really seen what he had thought he had seen.

He had.

At 12.15 on the following Sunday he was in the pulpit of the church of St Jude the Resilient, Eaton Square, delivering a sermon on the text 'He that touches pitch shall be defiled' (Ecclesiasticus xiii.1) which had the fashionable congregation rolling in the aisles and tearing up the pews. The burden of his address was a denunciation of the novel *Cocktail Time* in the course of which he described it as obscene, immoral, shocking, impure, corrupt, shameless, graceless and depraved, and all over the sacred edifice you could see eager men jotting the name down on their shirt cuffs, scarcely able to wait to add it to their library list.

Cocktail Time, 1958

Except for an occasional lecture by the vicar on his holiday in the Holy Land, illustrated with lantern slides, there was not a great deal of night life in Dovetail Hammer.

Cocktail Time, 1958

'Except for the time when the curate tripped over a loose shoelace and fell down the pulpit steps, I don't think I have ever had a more wonderful moment than when good old Bottle suddenly started ticking Tom off from the platform.'

Right Ho, Jeeves, 1934

And the Reverend Briscoe ambled in, his purpose, as it appeared immediately, to purchase half a pound of the pink sweets and half a pound of the yellow as a present for the more deserving of his choirboys.

Aunts Aren't Gentlemen, 1974

'I won't believe you're married until I see the bishop and assistant clergy mopping their foreheads and saying, "Well, that's that. We really got the young blighter off at last".'

Aunts Aren't Gentlemen, 1974

'Sir Roderick Glossop, as I see it, was one of two brothers and, as so often happens, the younger brother did not equal the elder's success in life. He became a curate, dreaming away the years in a country parish, and when he died, leaving only a copy of *Hymns Ancient and Modern* and a son called Basil, Sir Roderick found himself stuck with the latter. So with the idea of saving something out of the wreck he made him his secretary. That's what I call a nice, well-rounded story.'

Uncle Fred in the Springtime, 1939

He found the key. He opened the cellar door. And there before him were bottles and bottles nestling in their bins, each one more than capable of restoring his mental outlook to its customary form. And he was in the very act of reaching out for the one nearest to hand when Linda's face seemed to rise before his eyes and he remembered his promise to her. 'Lay off the lotion,' she had said to him, or words of that general import, and he had replied that he would. Even if the Archbishop of Canterbury were to come and beg him to join him in a few for the tonsils, he had said, no business would result.

Frozen Assets, 1964

At this moment his eye fell on the table at the top of the room, along which, on either side of the President, were seated some twenty of the elect: and it now flashed upon him that of these at least eight must almost certainly be intending to make speeches. And right in the middle of them, with a nasty, vicious look in his eye, sat a bishop.

Anybody who has ever attended Old Boys' dinners knows that bishops are tough stuff. They take their time, these prelates. They mouth their words and shape their periods. They roam with frightful deliberation from the grave to the gay, from the manly straightforward to the whimsically jocular. Not one of them but is good for at least twenty-five minutes.

Big Money, 1931

She gave a sort of despairing gesture, like a vicar's daughter who has discovered Erastianism in the village.

Laughing Gas, 1936

She looked like a vicar's daughter who plays hockey and ticks off the villagers when they want to marry their deceased wives' sisters.

Laughing Gas, 1936